THE FALLEN and THE ELECT

By

Jerry J. K. Rogers

Annie
I truly hope
you enjoy
the stories

Jerry J K Rogers

Copyright

The Fallen and the Elect

Copyright © 2014 Jerry Rogers

All Rights Reserved.

First Print Edition

http://www.jjkr-writings.info

ISBN 978-0-692-24111-0

Dedication

With all my heart, I dedicate this book to Mark, Annie, Mark II, Cameron, Emilie, Alex and Luke. The encouragement all of you provided, as well as providing a fun and relaxing place to collect my thoughts and work on this project, mean more than all of you will ever realize.

Table of Contents

I. The Eulogy of Angels: Abriel's Song

The Fallen and The Elect

Chapter 1

Alder Dennison was pissed. His family should have been ready to go half an hour ago. His wife Maria said the kids were ready; she just needed to finish her makeup. Now she was changing their nine-month old son Matthew's diaper again.

"Come on, let's go," Alder blasted from the doorway to the garage in his tenor voice, "I don't wanna be late." He glanced at his watch, one thirty. Maria finally worked her way downstairs, Matthew in her arms. Michelle, his older sister by almost three and a half years, patiently took each step with the surety and confidence of a much older child. Once on the landing, she darted to the doorway, grabbed her favorite Winnie the Pooh doll from the floor, and was helped by her dad into her car seat of the Toyota Sienna minivan. Maria followed walking gingerly so as not to disturb Matthew, who was drifting to sleep.

"You know, if you helped out more with the kids I would've been ready. I had to change your son," Maria said, gently resting Matthew in his baby carrier and securing it to the passenger-side rear seat. "You could have easily taken care of his diaper before coming down. I know you smelled something was wrong when you were playing with him."

"Hell, all he seems to do is eat, crap and sleep," Alder replied, securing the driver side-sliding door.

"Takes after daddy, doesn't he boo bear?" Maria whispered to Matthew in the "goo goo gaga" voice most adults use when talking to a baby, loud enough for Alder to hear. "You pack the kids' diaper and travel bags?" Maria asked directing her question to Alder tinted with disdain. Still frustrated with him for not helping with getting the children ready earlier, she became more infuriated as she added the current incident to his recent string of not supporting her more with the kids. He only seemed concerned with playing with the children.

"They should be back there." Alder made sure they were in the minivan. He didn't want to have any reason to return home and miss the ceremony. He and Maria were both excited about attending after finding out they won a spot on the primary guests' list and not on the alternates list of raffled seats. Yet from her present bout of being frustrated at him, Alder would not have known of her supposed excitement.

Driving onto the freeway, traffic turned out to be lighter than expected for a Saturday afternoon. Alder knew that if he sped they could still arrive early enough to find a decent parking spot. Yet with the entire family in the vehicle, hovering around the posted speed limit was his only option; they might still arrive before the closing and locking of the funeral home doors.

* * * *

The seafood focused hors d'oeuvres table was a place of temporary reprieve for Stephen Williams. He wanted to avoid the crowd for as long as possible, most who were mulling around their seats in the main chapel of the funeral home waiting for the service to begin. The buffet table, one of seven, bore smoked salmon, mini-crab cakes topped with a dollop of roasted red pepper aioli, prosciutto-wrapped shrimp, a small tower of seasoned shrimp, miniature fruit cups, and multiple wafers and crackers. Traditionally, many would find an overindulgent buffet out of the ordinary for a funeral. These days, when a family could afford it, opulent displays were a status symbol as if to impress in case there were a heavenly visitation.

Grabbing a small gold-trimmed porcelain plate, Stephen added several pieces of the hor d'oeuvres fair with eager anticipation to savor the delicacies. Glancing back at the main congregation of attendees, the senior director for marketing William Sumner noticed him, smiled, and dashed in his direction extending his hand. "Stephen, how's it going?"

Stephen reciprocated the handshake after moving the plate to his other hand. "I'm doing fine. How 'bout you?"

"Better than that dead little shit laid out stiff in the box," William answered. Stephen knew William didn't like Jeffrey Bradfield. William felt Jeffrey's father had brooded over him incessantly to the detriment of the company. Even though he'd worked in a different division, Jeffrey's constant management fiascos caused problems that William felt would need correction for a catalog of accounting errors and misrepresentations.

"Where's your buddy Alder?" William continued.

"Don't know; he should've been here by now," Stephen answered, returning to stockpiling his plate.

"So, you think we'll have a visitor today?"

"Depends on Jeffrey's life I guess. No one knows why they show up, if they do," Stephen noted.

"So how well did you know Jeffrey Bradfield?"

"Not too well. We dealt with him on a few accruals that didn't get posted to the proper month. Other than that, didn't have to deal with him too much," Stephen lied. Stephen and Alder did work quite a bit with Jeffrey Bradfield. They continually corrected Bradfield's budget updates, redid the assignment of expense codes and reworked the other numerous accounting errors for his department, some seriously putting his department in the red. Stephen knew that if Jeffrey Bradfield hadn't been the son of the senior vice president for production, the company wouldn't have tolerated the incompetence and would've fired him. A car accident netted the same effect.

William pressed on with the questions, "So have you seen one before?"

"Nope." Stephen finished loading his plate.

"Well I'm hoping something will happen this time. I keep dragging my kids to these hoping something would happen. We even got a new digital camera with enough megapixels to grab the tiniest detail, with one of the fastest shutter speeds around."

"Will it work? I heard everyone who's tried to take a picture, it comes out either completely black or just a splotch in a blurred background."

"Hey, this was special ordered. I paid a few g's for this one," William boasted as he pulled a Nikon digital SLR camera from a camera bag hanging on his shoulder and placing the strap around his neck.

Stephen hadn't noticed the camera bag. He found himself focused on the plates of food in his hand and wanted to raze the succulent appetizers until another thought hit him. "Can you have that in here?"

"Don't forget my position in the company. I managed to allow for any personal camera devices in case of a visitor," William bragged.

Stephen felt disappointed because he didn't get the word about the waiver for camera related devices. He left his cell phone in his car.

"Hey, do you smell that?" William queried looking around the foyer attempting to find the source of the aroma. "It smells like a damn flower shop in here."

You suspect a heavenly visit will take place when you begin to smell the scent of fresh flowers like a bouquet of roses, hibiscus, or tulips. Some even said there's a hint of a fragrant scent similar to sweet cinnamon or clove and that a simple waft would calm an agitated soul. That was the closest anyone came to accurately describing the aroma in earlier news reports and newspaper articles. Not everyone could smell the arrival, however. Stephen was one who couldn't. His sense of smell had been deteriorating over the last couple of years, and if there were to be a visitation, he would miss this part of the experience.

Several attendees made a final grab for food from the buffets tables in the foyer area before the homily and pastoral memoriam would begin. William was already making his way back into the main sanctuary of the chapel to join his family. As the other attendees rushed to claim open seats, Stephen made one final glance past the foyer waiting area to see if Alder and his family had arrived. No sign of him. The ushers urged him back to the chapel area while letting in a husband, wife, and their toddler son from the standby line. *There's three lucky bastards,* Stephen thought.

* * * *

"Ah shit," Alder broadcasted, looking down range on the highway to see four lanes of brake lights.

"What's wrong?" Maria asked while entertaining Matthew not having to worry about Michelle, who had fallen asleep as soon as the minivan began to move.

"Traffic. And damn it, we just missed the exit to get off and try to detour this crap."

"Are we going to be late?"

Alder glanced at the clock on the dash of the minivan. "We may now."

Finally managing to exit the highway in hopes of bypassing the congested swarm of cars, Alder found himself driving in an unfamiliar area of Los Angeles. His attempt to navigate in a parallel course to the highway became unsuccessful when two-lane streets became one way and took tangent angles mimicking the nearby river. Alder became upset with himself that he hadn't replaced the faulty GPS device sooner. "Damn, we're lost," he thought.

"Great, now we'll definitely be late," Maria jabbed.

Alder wasn't too happy with the disparaging tone of her comment. "Is something wrong?"

"If you don't know, I don't have to tell you."

"What type of sense does that make?"

Maria decided not to answer and remained quiet the remainder of the trip.

To forget about how annoyed he was with his wife, Alder thought about trying to contact his co-worker and friend Stephen to let him know they would be late. Then he remembered that Stephen probably wouldn't be able to answer his cell phone since there were restrictions on bringing personal devices capable of taking pictures. Alder wasn't aware of the lifted restrictions.

* * * *

Large crowds consistently attended funerals for the famous, prestigious, wealthy, or well known. These days so many individuals wanted to go, raffles or other sponsored events were held to see who could attend. Everyone assumed there would be more of a chance for a visitation during such a funeral when the events first began more than ten years before. Soon, aggregated information determined there were hundreds of visitations each year all over the world regardless of the socioeconomic status of those who passed away. Irrespective of the religion or belief, reports abounded of strange angelic visitors. Even the funerals of avowed atheists or nonreligious individuals would present manifestations, which led some to believe in the universality of God and his angels. Over the years, there were fewer nonbelievers. Many however, who, despite what they saw, remained nonbelievers, assuming some sort of special effects trick or mass hallucination. Even though special effects couldn't explain how the angelic visitors knew so much about the deceased only the nonbeliever themselves could know, they still chose not to believe. Religious leaders, churches and spiritual organizations all tried to explain the phenomena. No one could produce any direct physical evidence other than the subliminal echoes of aromas, abstract footprints in places where the carpet held them, and the euphoria of those observing something so magnanimous.

Initial reports classified witnesses as having the same category of delusion as those who allegedly observed aliens and UFOs. Then when some of the skeptics-- priests, pastors, rabbis, imams, and memorial officiators during successive funerals--began to perceive the same visions as their peers, their veracity solidified the arrival of heavenly visitors. All of this occurring shortly after the disappearance of millions, the world being unnerved feared the funeral appearances. Over time as the populace acclimated to the visitation, the angelic presences demonstrated benevolence; the visitations became the cement for the religious systems across the world, helping to meld a common belief in a single god for all mankind. The faiths of the world incrementally built a new cooperative relationship by looking for common threads between their beliefs.

Stephen noticed the crowd was moderate sized while again scanning the sanctuary and foyer for his friend and his family. He wasn't sure if all the attendees knew Jeffrey or were only there hoping to witness a potential paranormal event. Stephen saw attendees' heads craning and taking deep sniffs of the air, hoping that reports similar to other visits, a deluge of aromas would embrace their noses. And even though Jeffrey's family had requested for a device-free service, occasionally someone would attempt to snap a clandestine picture or record a video with a phone or digital camera.

Traditional melancholy music whispering from the PA system in the background of the chapel seemed opposite the effervescent sense of anticipation and wonderment. Stephen noticed Jeffrey's few family members didn't display an overt sense of mourning or loss. Everyone was confident something was going to happen.

The reverend began the eulogium according to the family's arranged program, though he seemed distracted by the fragrant air. Stephen thought it odd the clergyman didn't use a bible or any other religious guidance for the ceremony.

"Jeffrey Bradfield was a beloved father and son," the reverend started, "He was considered by all who knew him to be magnanimous and helping. Jeffrey was dedicated to his family and his job. He served the community and, like his family, was very much a philanthropist. Why Jeffrey was taken away from us? We will never know." The reverend continued speaking for the next fifteen minutes, and then with nothing more to say, many in the assembly of supposed mourners seemed disappointed. It was during the reverend's benediction before the removal of the casket for the departure for the cemetery, something above caught his attention. Stephen followed his gaze and saw that the ceiling of the chapel glowed with an eerie translucence.

Instantly, in the twinkling of an eye, a personage, clothed in flowing robes appearing to be made of the purest and finest white linen, its visible skin without blemish, mark, or discoloration, stood in the front of the audience within the chapel. There was no slow dramatic descent, no spectacular entrance riding on a rainbow, just an instantaneous arrival of radiant light emanating from the entire presence of the heavenly figure. Stephen thought witnesses from reports in the newspaper must have embellished preceding arrivals.

The aura of silver-white light shimmered and made it impossible to tell whether he, or she, possessed wings. The visitor's brilliance didn't overpower the audience's ability to see. The spectators whispered among themselves about their view of the angel. William remembered his Nikon and reached to snap a picture. He would swear the camera shocked him. Others attempting to use their cameras, or camera on their phones or tablets experienced the same sensation, some even dropping their devices on the floor.

The form stood motionless for several minutes. The pronounced humanity of the muscular structured body became more majestic. Immersed in an ethereal aura, the distinguishable outline of grandiose wings took greater form. Piercing eyes with pupils black as coal scanned the onlookers. Stephen felt as if the angel were looking directly into each attendee's souls. Time seemed to stop. The outside ambient light coming through the windows of the chapel dimmed. Muffled silence enclosed the chapel. An uneasy quiet settled among the spectators. Stephen couldn't hear his own heavy breathing as if someone had turned on a noise-cancellation system. The air now still and no longer filled with the scent of flowers, began to the smell as if the stirring of dust and dew were preceding a rainstorm.

It was now that Stephen saw the semblance of a scroll as the angel pulled it from what appeared to be a large pouch attached to a golden rope fashioned as a belt. The spool was unrolled. Expecting to see some form of paper or vellum was a wafer-thin, brass-like foil material. The heavenly creature turned a bit to its left; Stephen could see letters slowly emblazon on the surface of the metallic parchment. According to reports, this had never happened before. The angel would arrive, present the eulogy, and then depart. *I don't like the looks of this*, Stephen thought to himself. A queasy uncomfortable feeling began to settle in; he decided to leave. Working his way to the center aisle, people in his row glared at him for the distraction

The angel spoke, its voice melodic and harmonic as if it were singing upon one first hearing. Its voice quickly became stern and jarring once comprehended. "The speaker has given a wonderful extolment on the life of Jeffrey Bradfield. I tell you there is a true life story of Jeffrey Anders Bradfield, a deceitful, narcissistic and abusive life of one not worthy to be written in the boo-"

Members of the audience gasped loudly as the angel continued. Stephen didn't want to hear any more. The unsettling atmosphere magnified further unnerving him. He finally navigated himself out of his pew and darted down the aisle to depart the chapel. The ushers gave no opposition to his desire to leave. They stood motionless by the entryway with their eyes widened and transfixed on the supernatural event. Nearing the exit, the light behind him brightened enveloping the sanctuary and into the expanse of the foyer. It became hard to see. Stephen felt he couldn't escape fast enough and whatever was happening to his rear would overtake him. It was as if he were in a bad dream running down a long hallway, never reaching the end.

As Stephen approached the doorway leading outside, he caught a final burst of words from the angel, "...so as those whose names are written here upon this page are to be judg.." The last human related sounds inside Stephen thought he heard were moans and shrieks before all went silent just as he rushed out through the funeral home entrance. A voice echoed in his head, "Remember my name, Abriel."

Guests on the standby list waiting outside in line realized that something extraordinary was taking place; many waited with excitement for those inside to come out and present a firsthand report. Some urgently attempted to enter the chapel but found the doors locked. Others more astute after seeing Stephen's panicked face, and confident that they heard disturbing and haunting sounds from inside, retreated to their vehicles in the parking lot. Stephen stumbled across the concrete sidewalk to a small patch of grass and sat down on the ground. His vision faded. The crowd gathering around, the funeral home, cars in the parking lot, trees, and lampposts all went black. Stephen realized he was now blind.

Those who didn't scurry away in fear attempted to ask him a barrage of questions, "What happened? Was there an angel? Did he talk? What was it like?"

Through the bombardment of questions, Stephen recognized the voice of one of the interrogators. "Stephen what happened."

"Alder, is that you? Where are you?"

"What do you mean where am I? I'm right here in front of you," Alder answered, kneeling down in front of his friend.

"Alder, I can't see."

Those remaining hearing this and the disturbing sounds from the chapel, gathered their friends and family and scattered to their cars. A couple of men who tried earlier to enter the chapel now found the doors unlocked and rushed into the building.

"What do you mean you can't see?" Alder responded. Maria caught up to her husband, who had run ahead to his friend when he saw him rush out of the building as they were driving up in the parking lot.

Stephen's eyes watered. "I can't see. Where were you?"

"Dude, we were running late. What happened?"

A man in his late forties who had gone in through the unlocked doors came running back out. "They're all dead, everyone inside is dead."

Chapter 2

Detectives Green and Matthews flashed their badges as they worked their way through the crowd of news reporters, photojournalists, and spectators outside of the funeral home. A frenzy of camera flashes enhanced the light from the street lamps of the parking lot each time the medical examiners' technicians couriered gurneys with covered bodies outside to waiting county vehicles. Working their way inside, the detectives passed through the foyer area where samples of food were being collected by crime scene investigators. Several bodies lay sprawled near the back exits of the chapel area leading into the foyer. Entering the chapel, they observed more bodies scattered throughout the sanctuary tended to by the coroners, medical examiners, and technicians both detectives knew were from the main Los Angeles offices as well as the Santa Clarita and High Desert facilities.

Policemen and crime scene investigators scurried about to collect physical evidence, take photos of body positions and the buffet tables, and gather anything else that may be relevant to the investigation. Other workers were placing bodies on gurneys, searching and tagging personal effects, spilled food, plates, purses, and camera bags. Looking for the lead city medical examiner, Dr. McKay, the two detectives found him near the front pews.

"Doc, how's it goin? What can you tell us?"

Dr. McKay finished examining the body of a young man considered 18 or 19 years of age, dressed sharply in a custom-made suit with silk maroon tie, sprawled on the floor in front of a bench pew. After scrounging through the suit jacket and pants pockets, determined that the deceased man carried no identification, only a Starbucks card and a set of car keys, the auto key emblazed with an Audi logo. The examiner glanced up at Detectives Matthews and Green and smirked, "I'd say they're all dead."

"Very funny," Detective Green responded.

"What are you two doing here? I didn't know you were assigned to this crime scene."

"Our lucky butts got assigned to investigate the witness to this mess here. He turned out to be useless. According to the doctor, he was still in severe shock, so we ended up with some free time. We wanted to head over to see if we could find out some background on what happened for when we talk to him again. Any ideas? What about the time of death?"

"Well, according to all the other technicians' examinations so far for the bodies we checked, the time of death seems to be between 2:00 and 3:00, best estimation closer to 2:30 based on liver temps."

"That's about the time the witnesses outside said Stephen Williams came out," Detective Matthews commented.

"Who's Stephen Williams?" the doctor inquired.

"The witness to what happened in here," Detective Green answered. "You're already taking out the bodies? Don't you usually wait until a full forensics is worked up on the scene? Something like this should take at least a day or two to process."

"Our boss told us this is special, and not to spend a lot of time working it in the field. They don't want to panic the public if it was something supernatural. Rumor has it some higher-up religious leaders pulled some serious strings, even up at the federal level."

"No shit?"

"Well, we still need to run tox screens, body exams, and crap. With nearly a hundred bodies, we should do that back in the morgue. Plus it'll be awhile before we get anything definitive."

"What do you have un-definitive?" Detective Green asked.

"What do you think happened?" Detective Matthews asked, interjecting himself into the conversation and expelling a cough less raspy and congestive than the previous ones.

"Look around, could have been the food. Yet you notice that none of the bodies show any signs of distress from food poisoning? Not one of them regurgitated or expelled anything. Besides, with this many fatalities, they all wouldn't have necessarily consumed the same thing. And some of them probably didn't eat anything for that matter. So I'd rule out food poisoning at least right now. Maybe it was a gas leak. Who knows? It could have even been some sort of terrorist chemical attack. Your buddies in blue and the fire department didn't let us in until the building was cleared by hazmat."

Detective Matthews studied the scene to see if anything of importance stood out while the doctor carried on with his explanation. Noticing the remaining bodies, he realized that all of their eyes were open and had a distinct fogging of the pupils and irises.

"Doc?" Detective Matthews asked. "Is it normal for all of their eyes to be open like that?"

"Hmmm," Dr. McKay looked carefully into the eyes of the corpse of the young man. Not only were they fixed open, the natural color of the iris and pupils appeared cloudy, a distinct shade of gray he'd never seen before. Afterward he scuttled over to a couple of the remaining bodies, a middle-aged woman extravagantly dressed next to an older man in a nicely tailored suit with hair graying and a Nikon SLR camera, tagged with a "police evidence," around his neck. The eyes of both bodies were rigidly open, the natural color of the iris and pupils foggy. The doctor looked about for other bodies to examine finding many already removed. Index card markers next to the doctor's location identified the two offspring of the deceased he was currently examining. Other index marker cards were scattered about the pews. Hurrying over to the other side of the chapel to view another body as it was placed on a gurney, the same result; the eyes were open and cloudy. Dr. McKay knew he would need to review the photos and video to determine if the corpses already removed were the same. He returned to work on his original body still pondering the discovery the detectives had made.

"Ok Doc, I just got to ask, what's going on here?" Detective Matthews asked, disturbed.

"Well first off," the doctor replied, "I don't believe that crap about an angel doing this. Why, if they do exist and were here to give eulogies, would this one get a wild hair up its ass and decide to become a mass murderer?"

19

"You don't believe in angels?" Detective Matthews asked.

"No one to date has been able to produce a photo, video, or anything else to say otherwise. It's just been someone spouting off, 'Ohh, I saw an angel.' Come on, get real."

"Then back to our earlier question, what happened here?" Detective Green asked again.

"Get back to me in the morning. Then I'll tell you what didn't happen."

Chapter 3

Who could be knocking at this time of the night? Father Hernandez angrily thought. One of his parishioners could be in emotional or spiritual distress. It might be Jerome Bellows. The priest had counseled him during the last several months for his recently deceased wife. Then Agatha Pannetti came to mind. Recently diagnosed with advanced lung cancer, she had requested special prayers and rosaries for healing health, asking the Father to research a patron saint for intercessions.

The Father's anger subsided. He was upset at himself for having entertained indignant thoughts. Still, he questioned whether it couldn't have waited until daylight. Glancing at the wall clock, he noted 3:10 a.m. Tying off the belt of his robe, he approached the front door, turned on the porch light, and moved the curtain on the door window to view his visitor. It was Bishop Andrew Grielle, his mentor and the Diocese superintendent.

"Your Excellency?" Father Hernandez exclaimed while opening the door. "What can I do for you?"

"Sorry to disturb you so early in the morning Father Hernandez," Bishop Grielle responded as he worked his way into the parsonage and sat on the ample rust-colored leather armchair in the living room before he was invited into the house. "We have a situation. I'm not sure if you heard about what transpired at the funeral home yesterday afternoon?"

"Yes, evidently there was a visitation with tragic consequences."

"We're still sorting out the details with nothing yet officially released."

"You know your Excellency, if this is true, it could have some very serious ramifications for the Church."

"I'm well aware of the ramifications. The same as I was when the millions disappeared, including much of the clergy and church leadership."

"What's the Church's stance on what's happened?"

"That's why I'm here. There's no official position at this time until we investigate this more."

"I don't understand?"

Bishop Grielle gave a heavy sigh while looking around the living room, unsure of his next statement. He focused his attention back to Father Hernandez. "I'll get straight to the point. How much do you know about angels?"

"I wrote several dissertations while in seminary and a few essays several years ago when the eulogy supposedly began."

"Yes, his Eminence noted he read some of your work and found them quite intriguing. A couple quite controversial if I remember right."

"Many did find them controversial. I attempted to bring up alternative points of view to my own as well as those of traditional church teachings, everything from when they were created to their purported roles and functions. I even began an initial examination as to the importance and possible meaning of their names. By questioning our beliefs, I truly believe we solidify and ratify them."

"Hmmm, and from my understanding, you never partook of a visitation during any funeral services you presided over since this whole angel affair started?"

"No."

"Good, because of that, I believe that'll work well in keeping you objective. I need you to investigate what may have happened on behalf of the Church."

"Shouldn't this be done formally with the ..."

Bishop Grielle interrupted, crossing his leg and taking the unyielding position of sitting back in the chair with his hands behind his head. "We need to keep this as informal as possible. We don't need to bring attention to what you'll be doing."

"I'm sorry. I still don't understand your Excellency."

"You must attempt to find out if there was a visitation, and why this evil has befallen those poor souls."

"I'm not sure if I have that level of expertise. I've been here for years at Our Lady of the Light serving as a modest pastor. Wouldn't this be better suited for someone in the Diocese hierarchy instead of me?"

"While communicating with his Eminence, we decided we didn't want to involve those with preconceived religious political viewpoints on what is happening," Bishop Grielle answered. "Besides, we'll be assigning someone to work with you who's a bit more experienced. She'll be meeting you later today."

"She?" Father Hernandez asked, unconsciously raising an eyebrow.

"Sister Justine Dawson. You'll find her background to be extremely beneficial to your investigation. I'm going to ask you to humble yourself and follow her lead if need be."

Father Hernandez was a little agitated by the bishop's comments. "You presume I'm going to undertake this investigation."

"Understand I would like for you to take this on voluntarily. If need be, take this as you being strongly induced and persuaded by his Eminence and myself."

"Not to be obstinate, I still believe I'm not," Father Hernandez said, emphasizing the word *not,* "the best person for this. There's just too much that I don't know."

"That's why you're well suited for this. Your objectivity will help guide you to discover a true clarification of what did happen. Realize this, there are things you may learn that I cannot pass on to you at this time. During your investigation, Cardinal Millhouse noted you'd find out things that you'll need to keep to yourself. You must not question what you do find but report back to us immediately."

"I don't know if I can agree to that your Excellency."

"There is one thing I will tell you. It appears several members of the congregation from your sister parish passed away in the incident. Two were prominent long-term deacons."

Father Hernandez's eyes widened from the shock. "Holy Mother of God. How many from St. Augustine's perished?"

"From initial news reports, 98 souls in all were lost. We estimate 20 to 25 from St. Augustine. However, the deacons are of most concern."

"What were their names?" Father Hernandez asked.

"Morgan Bradfield and William Sumner; they were active in the parish. More important, they and the company they worked for were instrumental in working on significant endeavors for the Church."

"What company?"

"Everest International Bio-Medical Group." Bishop Grielle saw Father Hernandez didn't understand the significance. "They were working on ways to produce inexpensive vaccines for underdeveloped countries and lower income families here in the United States. And they sponsored and funded several free clinics here in the city."

"And what of Father Gates? Was he officiating the funeral?"

Bishop Grielle scratched his balding head and sunk deep in the chair. "Jeffrey Bradfield, the decedent, was a Protestant. He was never confirmed in the Church. His own pastor officiated the ceremony. Father Gates wanted to attend in support of his parishioners."

"So then he's fine?"

The bishop rubbed his forehead with the fingertips of his hand as if giving himself a massage. "On the way to funeral home, he came across an accident and stopped to render help. A pickup truck traveling in the opposite direction was carrying a tire that wasn't properly tied down in the back. The truck hit a bump, which hurled the tire from the rear of the truck, and then it rolled, bounced down the shoulder, jumped the median, and struck Father Gates, who was assisting one of the accident victims. He was killed instantly."

Chapter 4

Detective Green struggled to open the door of the office he shared with Detective Matthews with his arms full of 9x12 manila envelopes and file folders routed from the forensics labs and labeled with the case numbers assigned for the funeral home incident. He dumped the load on his desk. Because of the scope of the event, information was already flowing from other investigators, which was something he hadn't anticipated.

Opening an envelope labeled "Camera Contents (Copies) – Turin Raines," he pulled out several unassuming photographs of potential attendees standing in line in what appeared to be outside front of the funeral home. Other photos displayed the food set up in the foyer. The most interesting photographs were those of family members taken by the camera's owner in the chapel. He opened another envelope, this one titled "Camera Contents (Copies – William Sumner)." His review of the photos revealed the same image compositions of several attendees standing in line, probably friends or family of the photographer. With this set of photos imprinted with time stamps and metadata, Detective Green realized he could build a time line up to the fatal incident. The latest photo in the set noted the time 2:27. It showed quite a few attendees in the pews gazing up towards the ceiling. Several photos showed

Stephen off in the background by one of the buffet tables and a couple with him randomly interspersed with the gathering of attendees.

Walking into the office, Detective Matthews found his partner sitting at his desk looking through the case files. "What you got there?" He asked.

Detective Green glanced up. Detective Matthews passed through the doorway with a cup of Dunkin' Donuts coffee. "Did you get me some?"

"Didn't know you'd be here already. I came in early hoping I could look through some of the other evidence before we go back and talk to Stephen Williams," Detective Matthews responded.

"Yeah, I had the same idea. Just going through some of it now."

"Anything interesting?"

"Not yet."

Detective Matthews sat down at his desk and grabbed several of the envelopes and folders from the stack on his partner's desk. Both of them, engrossed in viewing and analyzing the information, were a little startled when the phone rang. Detective Green answered, "Detective Green."

A quick pause and he continued, "We're both here now." After another lull, "We'll be right down." He hung up the phone.

"What's up?" Detective Matthews asked.

"Lieutenant is calling everyone in for a special meeting downstairs. In 30 minutes in the briefing room."

Both organized their desktops before heading down.

*   *   *   *

The briefing room was full with all 25 seats taken by other detectives and patrolmen. The overflow of other officers occupied the sidewalls. At the podium in front stood Lieutenant Scott Wilson younger than most of the force in attendance and was considered by many an astute political strategist. Despite his age, most of the station house liked him because he was charismatic, he socialized well with his subordinates, and he didn't step on his coworkers during his advancement through the ranks of the division. Detective Green, one of the few, found it hard to work with him, especially since he felt he had amassed more experience being a field detective almost three times as long as Scott Wilson had been on the force. Detective Matthews, on the other hand, didn't care.

Four men in suits entered the briefing room and stood with erect stances behind Lieutenant Wilson next to the white board. One-on-one chatter ended abruptly as most of the officers and detectives each speculated who the men were.

"Detectives, officers," the lieutenant began. "First off, just a reminder of something I'm quite sure you are all well aware, don't release any information to the public. The department is having public affairs withhold all information until something more definitive is determined. The coroner won't have anything for us for at least a couple of days, so those hoping to have more information will have to wait." He sorted through and scanned several of the papers on top the podium before continuing. "Some of you working key points of this investigation may have already received some of the evidence from the crime scene. We received permission from the Feds to release what we do have. They will be taking the lead until it's determined that it was not a terrorist-related act. They've already used a considerable amount of resources on this investigation." Many in the room grumbled at the comment.

Detective Matthews attempted to suppress his continual coughing; sometimes he was successful, other times the vibration of phlegm in his throat would amplify the sound. The lieutenant continued despite Detective Matthews's unintentional interruptions. "They think one possible motive is revenge for not being invited as a primary attendee or getting standby tickets to the funeral. Detectives Salinski, Johnson, Eidelbacher, and Juarez will work with Special Agent Normans as lead, reviewing and interviewing the list of all potential attendees. I know some of you already interviewed witnesses and those waiting outside in the standby line yesterday afternoon; do it again."

As the lieutenant continued discussing other assignments, both Detectives Green and Matthews found their attention wandering until their names were mentioned. "Detectives Green and Matthews will work with Special Agent Underwood talking to the only known witness. I'll need to talk to this team right after we're done here. Plus there was a new development since last night. Three more bodies were found that weren't in the chapel: an attendant working in the basement, a shift manager working in the back office, and a receptionist. Folks, now is no time for speculation; we need to gather solid evidence and work to determine what went down at the crime scene. We'll meet back here today at 1700 to discuss any new findings and pass it on to the command center for this investigation. Dismiss."

The officers assigned to the cases spilled out into the hallway to meet with their agent counterparts while the others headed back to their offices or small cubicles. Detectives Green and Matthews caught up with Agent Underwood and made the obligatory introductions. The agent's grip was solid and firm. As they finished up, Lieutenant Wilson walked up to the three men. "I see you've met. What do you plan to do today?"

Agent Underwood was about to answer when Detective Green interjected, "We're going back to the hospital to finish interviewing Stephen Williams. Hopefully he's more coherent today."

"Detective Green, that's one of the things I wanted to talk to you both abou ...," the lieutenant began. Agent Underwood interrupted, "We already interviewed Mr. Williams this morning. There's nothing new he can tell us at this time. If need be, we'll head back to talk to him later."

Detective Matthews's eyebrow arched. Detective Green reacted with an angry outburst. This was another reason Detective Green didn't like the lieutenant; he easily could've led off with this information. "What the hell?" Detective Green blurted out, focusing on the lieutenant. "Why weren't we involved with this? This is bullshit."

Conversations in the hallway went silent. Everyone focused on Detective Green. They resumed their conversations realizing his outburst was incidental.

"Did you get a chance to review the photos and videos from the crime scene?" Agent Underwood answered for the lieutenant, maintaining a calm, collected voice.

"Yeah? So what?"

"We jumped on this, and our video forensics team downloaded and scoured the images and video overnight. Several showed Mr. Williams in the background until just before the estimated time of the event. He's not relevant at this time."

Lieutenant Wilson broke into the conversation. "Detectives, special agent, there's one other thing. An outside investigation team from the Church may be joining up with you later at the crime scene or visiting Stephen Williams at the hospital."

All three men focused a look of disbelief at the lieutenant. Detective Green turned toward the special agent and presented him with a sarcastic grin, "Sucks doesn't it?"

"Who authorized that?" Special Agent Underwood asked.

"It was cleared through your SAIC in the command center."

Agent Underwood pulled out a tattered and scratched smartphone device, scrolled through a contacts list, and stepped away from the group to the other side of the hallway with the phone to his ear.

"Detectives, look, between you and me, I don't think the FBI will be around during this investigation too long. They're just going through the motions right now. You know there's no way in hell they would've allowed anyone from outside our department to enter the crime scene this early in the game."

"Then why in hell are we, especially the Church?" Detective Green asked, still faintly upset.

Lieutenant Wilson moved in a little closer to the men, reducing the volume of his voice. "From my understanding, Cardinal Millhouse asked a personal favor from the chief. At first the chief denied his request, but when Millhouse somehow managed to get the Feds to allow it to happen, they called the mayor, and next thing you know, they were allowed to investigate. Look, just babysit them and make sure they don't get in the way of our guys? OK."

"Why would they even want to get involved?" Detective Matthews asked, finally chiming in.

"They want to rule out anything supernatural. Imagine what it does to the Church if angels are going around killing people."

"Sure, if you believe in that crap. How many are we supposed to babysit?"

"Not sure yet, but the other inside chatter is that some are already trying to call this an accident or inconsequential mishap, maybe a gas leak or fumes from improper ventilation from the adjacent crematorium."

"We just need to do our job lieutenant. Let us find out what happened," Detective Matthews injected along with a congested cough.

"Look, you both just need to deal with it. Agent Underwood is lead until determined otherwise. End of story."

Detective Green found it difficult to accept the lieutenant's edict. But he decided to back down, knowing there are battles you fall on your sword over, others where you withdraw. Detective Matthews tended to be more laissez-faire in these situations. Sometimes this would upset Detective Green even more because he'd think Detective Matthews didn't care. Detective Matthews's view was that if something is going to happen, it's going to happen, you can't change fate. Whenever the two of them would discuss worldviews, religion, or politics, one saw life in terms of decision determining destiny and the other as destiny without influence on decisions. Both retreated to their office and left Agent Underwood talking on his cell phone in the hallway.

At their desks, they both resumed looking through the photos from several other of the victims' cameras. They were a bit peeved when Agent Underwood entered into the office without knocking. Detective Matthews could see Detective Green getting upset, his partner's face was turning several shades of red. He thought he should diffuse the situation and said, "Agent Underwood, we're reviewing some of the photos from the incident. Want to go over some of them with us?"

"No thanks. Our analysts already reviewed quite a few of them last night. I dropped the ones we cleared on your desks this morning. They didn't find much of anything."

Detective Green, barely managing to keep his control, reacted harshly, "Why in hell would you give them to us?"

"We believe in sharing information," the agent responded.

"Then why work behind our backs instead of bringing us in right away, and why not tell us about talking with Stephen Williams instead of us being coldcocked after the brief?"

Agent Underwood maintained his stone-faced expression but clearly sensed the antagonism in Detective Green's comments. "It wasn't my decision. I can tell you why we think Stephen Williams isn't a person of interest at this time."

Detective Green was stunned. Detective Matthews accepted the comment and, instead of getting ready to sign on to the online case file system, he pushed his keyboard to the side to focus his attention directly on the conversation.

Agent Underwood continued, "I don't know if you've noticed that a lot of the photos on your desk have time stamps, and they run up to the time right before the incident. Any images after that were either deleted or simply disappeared from the memory. Even cameras using film were the same; frames up until about 2:29 p.m. held images. Successive frames were blank. There were some who were using their phones' or camera video recorder. We came across the same results; the video went blank at that same time. So we immediately thought maybe some sort of electromagnetic device."

"What did the video show before then?" Detective Matthews asked.

"Pretty much the same thing as the stills, just a bunch of activity inside and outside of the chapel at the funeral home. We saw attendees coming in, taking seats, eating food, and then the service beginning up until it appeared it was ending. After that, everything went blank."

"So what about Stephen Williams?" Detective Green asked.

"Investigators searching the crime scene found a security system with several cameras and a DVR. Our forensic digital specialists are still reviewing the video. Initially, it looks like no one tampered with it. What we've seen so far is an overhead view of the chapel with funeral in progress. Just before the incident, a lot of the victims looked to be sniffing the air and looking up, and some of them were looking in the direction of the altar.

"You can see Stephen Williams in his pew after getting some food. A little less than a minute before the incident, the video went bright white and blank for almost 90 seconds. When the image reappears, everyone in the chapel is dead with no visible trauma and Stephen Williams isn't in the chapel. That's when he went outside to the parking lot. One minute they're alive then, wham, they're dead."

"Couldn't he have been working with someone else?" Detective Matthews inquired.

"That's why we're still working this. When we see people smelling the air and looking around, we're thinking maybe there was a release of some sort of noxious gas. Yet we couldn't find any type of device or any tampering with the ducting or anything else in the ventilation system, nothing illicit. Discounting the other three victims being found in different parts of the facility, it's beginning to seem like some sort of weird, unexplainable accident."

"When you talked to Stephen Williams, did he spout off some weird crap about angels?" Detective Green asked, calmer than before.

"The reality is no angels were seen on any of the cameras, or video, or anywhere else. With all the hypothetical angel visits over the years, there's never been a report of one going rogue and killing a room full of people. Our only witness mentioned a lot of stuff, that's another reason we're thinking some sort of gas or chemical leak causing delirium or hallucinations."

"Aren't you making a lot of assumptions?" Detective Matthews noted rhetorically.

"No, we're making an analysis based on evidence presented. This was not a supernatural event. None of the peripheral signs of this being a terrorist or orchestrated event are there either, and no one's claimed responsibility, so we just don't know."

Chapter 5

The air was hot. The air was still. The air was muggy. Michael Saunders hated the air here this time of day. He attempted to distract himself while jogging. He missed the clear skies and cool breezes earlier in the year, the way the sun reflected across the ocean as it receded behind the horizon, light dancing off wind-agitated ripples in a sheet of sparkling crystals. During these days, a muddied splotch of gold and amber crudely pasted in the sky took the sun's place looking murky, dingy, and diffused through the haze. If not for the undulations of the water, it sometimes looked as if the water and sky were blended into the same palette. Michael pondered people who said God was an awesome creator and his creation awe inspiring, but not this image painted on the canvas of encroaching twilight. While engrossed in the sunset, Michael nearly ran into a young couple setting up a blanket by the jogging path next to the sandy beach. He observed a small cooler, long-stemmed wine glasses, and Tupperware selection of cheeses. How can anyone enjoy having a picnic out here on this miserable, sweltering day? He asked himself.

Breaking away from the stream of other joggers, cyclists, and walkers, Michael spotted his normal landmarks. The neighbors were engaged in their customary activities: working in their yards, working out on their patios, or sitting on lawn chairs in the small garages of the town houses and condos and watching passersby. As he approached his own small front porch, Michael witnessed a male and female walking up the small set of steps and getting ready to knock on the door. The female he recognized. Her name was Justine Dawson. His heart skipped a beat. Even with ten years having passed, she was still breathtakingly beautiful. Dressed conservatively in a gray skirt suit, black blouse, and black pumps and wearing a silver necklace with a cross, what he initially mistook for her black hair was a modest habit. He realized she had taken her vows and become a nun. Next to her was a man he didn't recognize with a light taupe skin complexion, wrinkled and baggy eyes, and Hispanic features, wearing blue jeans and a medium-gray shirt. By his Romanesque collar, he knew his male guest's occupation--priest.

"It's been quite a few years. So you went and made the jump? Guess I should call you sister?" Michael commented to Sister Justine as he wiped the sweat from his head and flicked the excess toward the ground. "Who's this?" he asked as he glanced over to the unknown man. "Your new boy toy?"

Father Hernandez was taken aback by the comment from the lean man with golden-brown skin and mildly curly dark brown hair, his right hazel eye looking more muted in color than the left one, and who appeared to be in his early thirties. He surmised that Michael had interracial parents.

Michael detected a hint of anger in Sister Justine's expression while she attempted to present a look of indifference.

"Look, I followed through on what was best, that was serving in the Church," she retorted.

"Yeah, some church."

"You can't expect the answers to be smack in your face all the time. You have to..."

Michael interrupted by reaching out his sweaty right hand to shake the unknown man's hand. "I'm Michael Saunders. And you, boy toy, would be?"

Father Hernandez reluctantly reached out to shake Michael's hand, wiping Michael's sweat off his hand on his trousers when they finished. "I'm Father Jose Avis Hernandez, senior priest at Our Lady of Light parish. I'm not sure what's going on here..."

Michael interrupted again, "What do you both want?"

Father Hernandez responded, "We're here because we're told you were an expert with..."

Sister Justine interrupted this time, "I believe Abriel is back."

Father Hernandez turned sharply toward Sister Justine, amazed at her comment. Michael's attitude of mild anger and sarcasm changed to stoicism. "Are you sure?"

"Bishop Grielle sent us."

"Why do you think Abriel is back?"

"Because of what happened at the funeral home."

Michael's eyes widened, "What happened at what funeral home?"

"Still don't follow the news? Even after all these years?"

"Not all the time. I don't need to hear about the stupid things stupid people do. What happened?"

"One of the funeral homes here in town, 101 dead."

"So?"

"There's one possible witness, who immediately went blind after the event."

Father's Hernandez's head volleyed back and forth during the discussion between Sister Justine and Michael, whirling with the surprise of a history between the two that Bishop Grielle didn't pass on to him during his late-night visit. Michael reached in the pocket of his jogging shorts, pulled out a key, and unlocked the door to his house.

"Let's go inside," Michael directed to his guests.

Father Hernandez and Sister Justine entered the small Spartan-like decorated home. A simple beige cloth couch and plain oak coffee table occupied the living room. There were no pieces of artwork, paintings, or photos anywhere on the off-white walls. It wasn't clear whether their hue was intended or the result of fading over the years. An unadorned analog clock hung on the accent wall; it was an hour slow. In the dining area, the only furniture was a simple country-style dinner table with four wooden chairs standing sentry to a traditional Shaker-style China cabinet in the room. The walls were bare and the same off-white color as the living room. Next to the dining room was a bedroom converted into a library and office area. It contained a desk cluttered with papers, file folders, magazines and a couple of religious journals. Two of the walls in the room staged several bookcases filled with an assortment of disorganized books. Outside the door of the study, a laundry basket rested on the floor filled with crumpled clothing. It wasn't clear whether the clothes were clean or dirty. A couple of the articles appeared to be female blouses. Sister Justine ignored the oddity; Father Hernandez didn't notice.

"I'm going to take a shower. Make yourselves comfortable in the study," Michael commented going into his bedroom. Looking into the mirror on his bureau, he thought, *What the hell is she doing here?* She was no longer in his life. He wanted it that way after hearing from her those years ago, "Michael, we can never be together. My plan is to serve God. We can only be friends." She made her decision by rejecting his marriage proposal. Just being friends would've been too hard. He assumed she was using the church as an excuse because she was afraid of how serious they had become and possibly being pregnant. Instead of bogging himself down in reflecting on the past Michael forced himself to undress and proceed with his shower.

Entering Michael's study, Father Hernandez and Sister Justine had to sidestep an open 2-foot by 2-foot square cardboard box half filled with unread newspapers, some bound with string, some rubber bands, others still inside plastic bags, resting just inside the doorway. Looking around Michael's office-library, Sister Justine scanned book titles covering angelology, religion and society, Spiritism, church history, a Greek and Hebrew lexicon, a couple of different types of concordances, bible dictionary, and several other religious titles. Father Hernandez found himself more interested in the questions he ruminated over concerning Michael and Sister Justine. On the wall, another analog clock displayed the incorrect time, again an hour slow. Sister Justine leisurely walked to the bookshelf nearest the door and scanned the numerous titles. Father Hernandez glanced at the desk, observing a couple of stacks of papers with grades.

Several minutes of quiet passed when Father Hernandez decided to ask one of his questions. "Sister Justine, just what is the nature of your background with Michael Saunders? Is there some sort of history between you two that I should be aware of?"

Sister Justine paused for a few minutes to thumb through a medieval history textbook, noting that Michael was one of the contributing editors. Finally she spoke, "We grew up together, since we were kids all the way through high school and college. Early on in college, I felt the call to serve God as an educator. That's why I joined my particular order. Michael followed along and wanted to become a priest. I was dedicated to my pursuit and would challenge him on his devotion from time to time." Sister Justine held back that she and Michael were in a serious relationship years ago before her decision and commitment to become a nun. In ways, Michael never admitted to himself, she knew they could never be together.

"Is that why he's so aloof with you, because you challenged him in his beliefs?"

"That, and after the disappearance, many of his friends and family went missing. He felt in every way possible that God had left him, at least what he thought he believed to be God. That crushed his faith, which I don't think was that strong to begin with."

Father Hernandez moved some books over to the side of a black-cushioned futon in the corner and sat down. "So, then, why come to him to find information concerning our investigation. Surely there's someone who has more of a belief in this disturbing incident?"

"I believe you'll find Michael to be well qualified for this."

"Would that have something to do with someone you referred to earlier called Abriel?"

Sister Justine was silent. Father Hernandez pressed on, "Who is this Abriel? And what does he or she have to do with the funeral home incident?"

"I'm sorry Father, I can't tell you yet."

"Why not?"

"Probably because that snake Monsignor Grielle told her not to say anything," Michael chimed in, standing in the doorway in a T-shirt, faded jeans, and no socks with hair still damp from his shower.

"He's a full bishop now Michael," Sister Justine commented. "One of the last ones promoted in years."

Michael reached into the laundry basket and pulled out a red and yellow flowered Hawaiian shirt. He took a quick sniff and put it on. "Bishop Grielle huh? I'm surprised he's not a cardinal, or hell even the Pope."

"God and the Church promote when they deem fit," Father Hernandez interjected.

"Hey, the boy toy chimes in," Michael quipped.

"Mr. Saunders, I would appreciate it if you referred to me as Father," Father Hernandez said sternly while standing up.

Michael, surprised by the genuine forcefulness in the father's voice, perceived he was attempting to establish himself as the dominant male. He had considered the priest's sense of humility to be a cover for being reserved and introverted.

Michael raised an eyebrow and displayed a small grin. "Awright, I guess I can do that Father boy toy," he said.

"Michael!" Sister Justine exclaimed angrily.

"Don't worry about it Sister, he's just being driven by his human nature," Father Hernandez said patiently.

"You know, neither of you even corrected me about the bishop being a snake," Michael commented as he moved over to his desk and sat in a faded blue swivel chair.

"Look, he's not a snake and we're not here about Bishop Grielle," Father Hernandez countered. "We're here to get some background about what happened at the funeral home and the possibility of an angel causing the death of over a hundred poor souls."

Michael slouched in his chair and stretched out his legs. Father Hernandez noticed he was still barefoot. "What do you wanna know?" Michael asked.

Father Hernandez sat back down on the futon and in a calm, focused voice directed his question to both Michael and Sister Justine, given that she had remained quiet during the trip over to the house not answering any of his questions. "First off, what do you both know about angels?"

Michael answered first, "I know that I studied them quite extensively before I left seminary. Lots of people say they've seen angels, especially over the last ten years during all these presumed visitations at funerals. I don't know if I believe in them. I've learned the use of angels is a basis for a common mythos to validate a belief in an afterlife," Michael noted, with a look of dawning understanding on his face. "I really should develop that more."

Father Hernandez was visibly surprised. He hadn't fully comprehended Sister Justine's earlier comment. "You were in seminary? Studying to be a priest?"

"Yep, almost all the way through. Just about ready to execute the rite of ordination. I quit right after the disappearance."

"What happened?

"Because a lot of Catholic, Evangelical, Fundamental, Mormon, and other churches with different kinds of Christian belief systems were still populated with large numbers of good-hearted religious believers here on this mud ball, a lot of people, like myself, believed there definitely was no rapture. Then you have portions of the population of Muslim nations, Jews, and Hindus, along with other religions who were never the true converts or believers in their native religion, all also disappearing. Maybe the New Agers were right that the missing were whisked away to be reeducated and then to be returned with a renewed sense of global awareness, or some crap like that."

"So you didn't think anything religious happened with all of those disappearing?"

"To summarize Justin Chamberlain, I've come to see religion as a social construct, building common norms and standards as a means to establish a moral and social foundation that binds cultures and societies together. I never saw any proof of a God."

"You were influenced by Justin Chamberlain's, *Myth, and It's Power in Culture.*"

Michael responded to Father Hernandez with another large grin, "The reference of the metaphor in religious traditions is to something transcendent, which is literally not anything."

Sister Justine, although finding the conversation somewhat interesting, felt these two could go on talking for some time and lose focus on the assignment. But at least they weren't badgering each other. She put back an old physics textbook she had taken from a shelf and said sharply, "I'm glad you both found some common interest between the two of you. Now it would be great if you could remember why we're here and get back on track."

Sister Justine's directness amazed both men.

"Well my dear, aren't we more of a straight shooter these days?" Michael quipped. "If you were more like that ten years ago, you could've prevented a lot…"

"Let it go Michael," she interrupted.

"You don't understand what……"

"Michael stop. We're not going to have that discussion now or ever. The past is the past. It's either a guidepost or hitching post. Move on and let it be."

Father Hernandez recognized it was his turn to steer the conversation back onto the original topic. "Mr. Saunders?" Father Hernandez interjected.

Michael raised an eyebrow at the father's formal address.

Father Hernandez continued, "We'd like to discuss with you some of your opinions as to the funeral home incident yesterday."

"And what did Sister Justine tell you so far padre?"

46

"She hasn't revealed much at this time."

"Really, because I don't know how I can help. The research notes I had from last time were stolen by the Sister's slime bag of a bishop."

Sister Justine ignored the sharpness of Michael's comment, feeling the need of a new tactic to counter Michael's antagonism. "We don't know if that's what happened to our notes, Michael." She calmly replied.

"Research notes on what?" Father Hernandez questioned.

Michael gave Father Hernandez a small smirk. The Father was not sure why Michael was being so smug. Michael focused his attention on Sister Justine, who was entertaining herself with perusing the books on his smaller, unfinished, oak bookshelf.

"Research on the previous trip down to, wait a minute, you never told him about Aguascalientes?" Michael asked Sister Justine.

"No." She answered timidly.

"Hmmm, well I gotta teach a class in about an hour, and you know what? I'm hungry," Michael remarked while grabbing a stack of graded papers from his desk and shoving them disheveled in a faded brown, soft-case leather attaché. Closing the locking tabs, he clutched it and departed from the room without saying another word. His two guests were astonished to be alone.

"Sister, why are we here? He's not going to help us. We have God's work to do," Father Hernandez noted.

"Father, just wait," she pleaded.

Michael popped his head in the doorway. "You two coming? We can talk while we eat at my favorite deli."

He flashed a playful grin towards Father Hernandez. "Lunch is on you boy toy."

* * * *

"I'd like to order the free-range chicken salad with organic tomatoes and lettuce," Sister Justine requested of the server at the counter.

"Organic?" Michael snickered. "It kills me when someone says 'organic'. Aren't tomatoes and lettuce organic by their very nature? It's not like you're eating inorganic tomatoes or lettuce made out of Styrofoam or cardboard."

"You know Michael, you can be a real...patootie sometimes." Sister Justine's scolding of Michael caught Father Hernandez off guard.

"Patootie?" Michael responded while chuckling.

"I've dedicated myself not to curse."

"Just say that I can be a real ass. I don't think God is going come and strike you down just because of a word. Just say what you're thinking. Just because it sounds sterile doesn't mean the words you use are going to change your intent or meaning. Different word, it's still the same meaning. Better yet, butthole would've been better or, hey, even asshole. But patootie, might as well say rear end or gluteus maximus. Maybe patootie is more colorful though for a nun."

"Michael, just shut up already." Sister Justine snapped, focusing her attention back on the deli clerk, who showed approval of her comment to Michael, astounded someone would talk to a nun in a mocking manner. Completing her order, Sister Justine grabbed her orange plastic tray with a diet Pepsi and bag of kettle chips, and found an empty table outside on the patio. After placing their orders, Michael and Father Hernandez followed.

"So you gotta tell me, is this one of the best delis you've ever been to?" Michael asked, quizzing his two religious companions. Both were halfway through consuming their lunch platter. All three had pretty much kept quiet during the meal.

"I must admit it's not bad at all," Sister Justine forced herself to answer, forgiving Michael for the earlier incident.

Father Hernandez nodded in agreement, his mouth still full.

As soon as Michael was ready to take another bite, a squeaky voice caught the attention of the three. "Excuse me professor."

Standing by the table was a petite, sandy-blonde hair college student carrying several books. Numerous flower tattoos covered her right arm. Her hair was tied in a loose bun stabbed with several pens and pencils. "Will there be a quiz this Friday?" she asked, her eyes darting rapidly between the other occupants at the table. Sister Justine sensed a brief piercing gaze when she was the focus.

"Which class are you in hun?"

"Introduction to World Religions," the student replied, centering her attention back to Michael.

"Oh, and did I mention that there was going to be a quiz this Friday?"

"No, but it was on the syllabus."

"And have I been following the syllabus up to this point in the class?"

"Well, yes."

"What's your name?"

"Alicia."

"Then there's a good chance, Alicia, that there'll be a quiz this Friday," Michael noted in a caustic tone.

"Thank you professor," Alicia responded, somewhat perturbed.

"By the way Alicia, what's that about anyway?" Michael asked pointing and waving his finger in a haphazard pattern at Alicia's hair bun.

"I don't understand professor?"

"Your hair? Utility or fashion statement?"

Alicia reacted to Michael's question with a quizzical look.

"The pens and pencils in your hair. Are they there as a fashion statement or are you using your hair as a pen holder?"

"Oh." Alicia smiled. "Both."

"Well it looks silly."

Her smile converted to a tiny frown. Alicia turned and walked away appearing hurt. Father Hernandez thought to himself that he might not be the only target of Michael's abrasiveness. It seemed to be one of his attributes. Sister Justine didn't remember Michael being this sardonic. She dismissed the exchange and continued eating.

"OK Mr. Saunders," Father Hernandez began to comment before being interrupted by Michael.

"Michael, just call me Michael."

"So Michael, let's talk about this angel situation," Father Hernandez continued.

"Yes, let's talk about angels. Ever wonder about angels, I mean if they got wings, do you think they fly around up above spiritually pissing on us?" He questioned with a wry smile.

Father Hernandez and Sister Justine both gave Michael a piercing look. Michael knew his comments were on target. He already knew of Sister Justine's background and her sincerity and wanted to know the seriousness of Father Hernandez.

"Look Michael, we'd like to discuss this. It could help us out quite a bit."

"You know, if that snake boss of yours hadn't stolen my notes and research documentation, I could give you quite a bit."

"Michael," Sister Justine interjected, "he didn't steal your notes and information."

"So says his cheering section. Anyway, what do you want to know about these alleged visits?"

Father Hernandez began, "I do know that they started about ten years ago. According to the sighting information collected by the Vatican, the first one was in France. If I remember correctly, it was right after the worldwide disappearance."

"Yeah right," Michael responded somewhat snidely.

"Why do I have the feeling you're gonna tell me that's not the case?"

"You'd be correct. The first supposed event was almost a week prior to the mass disappearance. It was in a small church located outside of Aguascalientes, Mexico."

"What? Why didn't any of the Church leadership mention this?"

"The church sent two individuals down to examine what happened but decided to keep it quiet."

"What did happen?" Father Hernandez asked, noticing that Sister Justine continued to eat as if oblivious to the conversation.

"How many died the other day at the funeral home?" Michael continued.

"They think 98."

"Let's just say that almost half that many died down in Mexico."

"You mean this happened before?"

"Yep."

"Wait a minute, who were the two who investigated what happened down in Mexico?"

Michael smirked. Sister Justine stopped eating to give the Father a look that was both stoic and sympathetic.

"You two?" Father Hernandez continued. "Why didn't you mention this before Sister? Or the Church?"

"You're probably going to find out there's a lot she hasn't mentioned yet, and probably because our friend the bishop told her not to until the right time."

"Sister?" Father Hernandez asked.

Sister Justine remained quiet for a minute before responding. "We thought it'd be best to wait and introduce things incrementally, to help you absorb the magnitude of what's happening."

"Incrementally? I don't see why the Bishop couldn't have mentioned this when he came to visit me."

"I never try to understand why he does things the way he does," Sister Justine commented.

"Well, what else don't I know? What exactly happened down in Mexico?"

Michael sat back in his chair with his arms folded and a large grin on his face. "Go ahead Justine, tell him. Hell, I can't remember since my notes are gone."

Sister Justine capitulated. "Well, at the parish outside of Aguascalientes, 46 were found dead inside the church after a funeral service. We went down to investigate for Rome. They didn't want anyone with too high a profile in the Church going down and making it seem like something out of the ordinary happened. We got there a couple of days after the event. The Federales wouldn't let us in the church though. We came to find out that the locals felt God put a curse on the place. They hadn't even removed the bodies. Many of the local doctors and clinics in the area had quarantined the church and town fearing a virus outbreak of some sort. Of course, no one has ever heard of anything killing that many that fast. Those who found the bodies weren't infected. Didn't seem like there was any sort of biological event. Even stranger was that they mentioned they couldn't even smell the rotting bodies. It was as if everything in the church was masked by an extremely sweet smell. When an international team arrived and conducted their first investigation, they believed there was a viral outbreak. They felt the immediate quarantine had helped contain any further infections."

"Was there a virus?"

"No one knows. If there was, medical staff and responders at the time were surprised at how fast and lethal it was. Through all of that, there was only one survivor who reportedly been in the church at the time of the event."

"A survivor?"

"Yeah. He was quarantined in one of the local clinics with those who went into the church and discovered the bodies. He was even isolated and kept under watch by the local gendarme. Those in town who talked to him said he mentioned he'd seen an angel before passing out and going blind. And guess what he said the angel's name was?"

"Abriel?"

"Everyone thought he'd gone mad since he started talking about angels."

"And he went blind? What happened?"

"Once again, no one knows. Doctors couldn't find anything wrong, the same as to the only witness to what's happened here in town, Stephen Williams."

"Did you get a chance to talk to him?"

"We did, but our time with him was limited. He told us everything he could recall. We even got a chance to see the church where the incident occurred. Afterward, we were called back to the States and arrangements were to be made for him to come up and talk to us and others in the Church."

"Well, what happened?"

"He was one of the ones who went missing during the worldwide mass disappearance."

Michael got up to empty his tray into the trash can and returned to his seat as Sister Justine continued to explain the events in Mexico. He was amazed at how much she remembered. Much of it he'd tried to put out of his mind.

"And when did all of this happen again?" Father Hernandez continued with his querying.

"Over ten years ago a week before the mass disappearance."

A thought flashed into Father Hernandez's mind. "And Bishop Grielle doesn't think it was a biological event then or now does he Sister? He thinks there's some sort of connection doesn't he?"

"We don't know. Back then, we never came to a definitive conclusion as to what happened. That's why, when Michael is done with his class today, we're going to come back and pick him up and we're going to head over and talk to the survivor. Then sometime over the next couple of days we're gonna head over to the funeral home."

"What?" both men responded.

Chapter 6

To say that Detective Green was a little upset at having to escort Michael Saunders, Sister Justine, and Father Hernandez while they investigated the incident scene would be an understatement. He was thoroughly livid. He was confident he was wasting his time while not out investigating with his peers and their FBI counterparts. It didn't help that their FBI liaison had been called back to the station's incident control center to be assigned to another active investigation team. And having to provide key crime scene information and portions of their investigation to the Church's team didn't help to improve his attitude.

Detective Matthews, whose hacking cough disrupted the eerie silence, took the assignment in stride taking time to play a word puzzle game on his smart phone. The three others perused the empty chapel annex deep in thought and attempted to rationalize the cause of all the deaths. In the foyer, they inspected the platters, buffet trays now devoid of food with plastic number markers and chits placed in their stead. Fanciful wicker baskets fortressing elaborate patterned silverware, stacks of unused gold-trimmed porcelain plates both large and small, folded cloth napkins, and several artistic centerpieces sat undisturbed upon seven white-cloth-covered service tables. Sister Justine and Father

Hernandez glanced at a couple of the photos and the floor plan they received from the police. Nothing appeared moved out of place. Whereas most of the fatalities had been in the sanctuary, only a couple of body markers rested on the floor by the doorway from the foyer to the main sanctuary and near the buffet tables.

An hour passed; both detectives kept to themselves believing they wouldn't find anything new since the site was thoroughly scoured over the previous couple of days. If there were an alleged visitation, the remnants turned out to be elusive. They deliberated whether they would ever find anything else.

Father Hernandez gingerly walked the outer perimeter of the pews, careful not to disturb the number markers where the bodies laid three days prior. He browsed the marker positions and then surveyed a copy of the floor plan to ensure their placement still matched. Michael and Sister Justine pondered the front of the sanctuary near the altar. According to what Stephen had said during their earlier interview with him, it was where the angel was to have made his appearance. The dark maroon carpet on the two steps and adjoining dais appeared completely new, without a blemish of dirt. Where the casket would've rested during the ceremony, the softened sunlight shining through the Picasso-esque patterned stained glass windows and downward-directed diffused ceiling lighting gave an otherworld impression. A wisp of air circulated through the chapel. Michael was now intrigued by his sense of smell. Sniffing with an inquisitive look on his face, Sister Justine watched a rapid change to Michael's expression, and before she could

57

phrase and ask a question, he dropped to all fours and smelled the carpet.

"Michael, what are you..."

Before she could finish, Michael stood up and put his hands on Sister Justine's shoulders to coax her down. He told her to take a whiff. Eyes widening, they both stared at each other with amazement. By this time, the other three men had raced to the altar where the Michael and Sister Justine were still on all fours.

"What's so interesting?" Father Hernandez asked first.

"Get down here and smell boy toy," Michael answered.

An irritated scowl formed on the Father's face. When assailed with the puppy-dog look of "please" on Sister Justine's face, he complied. His eyes widened after taking a sniff. The two police detectives followed seeing the priest's reaction.

"So, it smells nice," Detective Green, noted thinking he was going to smell something out of the ordinary. "They use carpet freshener, big deal."

"You don't understand detective," Father Hernandez said. "Remember what Stephen Williams said, and according to reports of other angelic events, they mentioned a distinct smell of flowers, almonds, and an indescribable sweet scent. That's exactly what this smells like."

"You know how some smells invoke memories?" Michael asked Sister Justine.

"Yeah, I was just thinking the same thing," she replied.

"What's going on?" Father Hernandez asked.

"Ever smell something so delightful you can't describe it, yet it brings back earlier memories? Well, this smell reminds us of exactly the same smell we experienced down in Mexico years ago. If I didn't know better, I would call this the same smell."

Detective Green stood up and worked his way to the end of the dais by the wall next to a brightly polished brass, three-legged flowerpot stand. "Well then, let's check something out." Reaching the wall, he got back down on all fours again to take another whiff of the carpet: carpet shampoo, glue compounds, and a synthetic plastic-like smell, nothing resembling what he just experienced by the altar.

"Well, what do you smell?" Detective Matthews asked standing up.

"Just carpet."

The remaining three stood up. The action of Father Hernandez putting the floor plan atop the altar caught Detective Matthews's attention. Staring attentively for a few seconds and tilting his head to the left, he shifted himself around to view the map to where the wall he was facing was toward the top of the page.

"What's up Dion?" Detective Green asked, noticing his partner's actions.

Detective Matthews remained quiet. Staring intently at the page, he focused on the evidence marker number positions identifying where the deceased bodies had lain. Patterns began to appear.

"Dion, what's going on?" his partner questioned again.

"Hold on," Detective Matthews responded. No one noticed the rasp in his voice was now completely cleared.

Detective Matthews gazed for several minutes at the 11x17-inch sheet containing the chapel floor plan. Dismissing each actual number, he viewed each grid square as if a distinct spot and was confident a pattern did exist. Even though the shapes of the pews, walls, doorway, and other objects drawn on the blueprint were outlined, they didn't distract Detective Matthews from seeing the pattern of dots form two words. "Do you guys see that?"

Everybody else stared at the floor plan. Each in their own perspective could only make out a random pattern of numbers overlaying the layout of the furniture. Father Hernandez and Sister Justine thought possibly there was an image of a face or religious symbol. They dismissed it as superfluous after viewing a few more minutes. Detective Matthews was confident of the pattern his mind formed. Grabbing a pencil from his pocket, he started to connect the dots. Although each letter he connected was not the same size or orientation, he continued forming the words. They became more pronounced to the others watching: "two hearts."

No one could utter a word, each bemused for different reasons. Detective Green divorced the words from any significance with the incident, thinking this was just a mere coincidence. Both Father Hernandez and Sister Justine began thinking of the significance of the words in relation to their understanding and knowledge of the Bible: no immediate correlation. Michael thought of himself and his past relationship with Sister Justine. Associating nothing else with the words, his mind went blank. Detective Matthews felt this was way above him and made sure he wrote the words into his notepad and recorded the date and time.

"Well? What does it mean? You're the religious experts," Detective Green asked.

"We'll need to take this back and do some research. We'll probably cross-reference with church history, Biblical references, who knows?" Father Hernandez answered.

"So what you're saying," Michael jumped in, "is you don't have the slightest idea what any of this means?"

"You do? Aren't you supposed to be the real expert?"

"No, it's probably just a coincidence those words were formed from the pattern of the bodies."

"My thought exactly," Detective Green commented. "Does this mean anything?"

"Let's see if we can find anything else. You never know what it could mean," Sister Justine said.

"So how come no one saw this before now?" Detective Matthews asked.

There was silence. No one could think of an immediate response. Father Hernandez decided to answer. "Maybe because no one was looking for it."

All five felt energized by the revelation and continued to look for any clues as to what might have happened in the chapel. Two hours passed. Michael now felt this might not have been too much of a waste after all. Coming out to placate Sister Justine was his main purpose, and if he didn't find anything useful, he would call it quits and head out on his own way, abandoning the investigation. They broke away from the altar to search the sanctuary of the chapel, the other viewing rooms, the office and administration areas, and the waiting rooms. They decided not to check the body holding area, preparation area, or other areas downstairs, feeling they were of no relevance. In the rooms they did check, every time something appeared somewhat out of place, out of the ordinary, or distinctive in some way, they would spend extra time surveying the area.

Father Hernandez examined one of the offices where one victim died outside the sanctuary while working at his desk trying to see if the number marker and floor plan held any hidden secrets or patterns. Studying the sheet for 15 minutes, nothing jumped out, just a simple number. Sister Justine analyzed the multi-tiered candelabra on the dais, even going as far as trying to see if there was any significance in the different heights of each burned-down candle. Michael decided not to be as thorough. This was partly because he felt that if the words they'd found were important, in the obtrusive nature of how they were discovered, anything else found probably wouldn't be as obscure.

Another hour passed. Detective Green recommended that it would be a good time to finish up. Finding that the map of the bodies on the floor plan spelled out two words was peculiar, but if they did find anything else, it wouldn't be as dramatic. The soft marimba ringtone of Detective Green's cell phone echoed in the chapel. It was Dr. McKay's number displayed on the caller ID.

"Hey Doc, what is it?" Detective Green asked. "We'll be right there," he said, ending the call after a minute of silence. "We gotta go," he directed to his companions. "Doc is saying there's something strange going on concerning the bodies from what happened here."

Neither detective nor Father Hernandez noticed Michael and Sister Justine pass a glance of concern to one another.

* * * *

The detectives rushed into the coroner's work area and into a flurry of activity. The entire medical examiner staff was on duty; many they knew from different shifts while working on previous homicide cases.

"What's going on Doc?" Detective Green asked after finding Dr. McKay.

"We're gonna isolate all the bodies from the funeral home incident."

"What do you mean you're isolating the bodies?"

"We're debating if we should call the FBI back in here or the CDC. We have no idea what's going on."

"What is going on?" Detective Matthews asked, disturbed by the activity they'd seen since arriving at the hospital.

"We don't think anything communicable is at play; we think it may be a toxin or chemical agent of some sort."

Dr. McKay saw that both men were confused. "Follow me," he directed. The detectives followed the doctor through a partially lit hallway into a small viewing room with a large window but no furniture. Through the open curtains, they could see a section of the examiner's work area with a body covered in a sheet on a gurney-sized metallic table. Inside the examination area, a couple of orderlies and assistants were active in doing what appeared to be sanitizing the work areas in extensive protective gear, full face shields including goggles, full protective suits, and extended length gloves that were duct taped to the suits.

"Doc, what's going on?" Detective Matthews queried again.

Dr. McKay activated the intercom into the exam room. "Rusty, bring the body over here by the window and remove the sheet from the face."

A large, overweight, redheaded and freckled technician on the other side of the window put his cleaning gear to the side to comply with Dr. McKay's request. Detective Green and Detective Matthews both recoiled when they saw dark, empty sockets where eyes should've been on a middle-aged woman's face.

"What the fuck?" Detective Green blurted out. Detective Matthews, equally upset, internalized his reactions.

"Rusty, open the mouth," the doctor commanded to the technician through the intercom.

Opening the mouth, the tongue was black and withered like a sunbaked wrinkled worm. Rusty closed the mouth and recovered the body to minimize his contact.

"They weren't like this earlier," Detective Matthews noted, his voice broadcasting his apprehension. "All the corpses from the incident are like that. From what we can tell, it started a couple of hours ago. Here's the messed-up part; even the original decedent, Jeffrey

Bradfield, we brought back his embalmed body and it now exhibits the same signs."

"How's that possible? If I remember correctly, he was killed in a car accident."

"That's pretty much why we don't think it's a virus. Viruses themselves can sometimes survive in the bodily fluids for quite a few days after they've passed away, but to continue and propagate physiological changes is just impossible. Since the body of Jeffery Bradfield had been through the embalming process, the chances of having infected bodily fluids would be minuscule, if even possible. I've never seen any type of decomposition like this before. This is just too weird."

"Then what the hell do you think it is?" Detective Green asked.

"It's got to be some sort of bacterial pathogen or chemical agent. That's the only explanation. We're definitely not taking any chances. Head down and give a blood sample just in case, and get in touch with anyone you may have been in contact with recently. We may have to initiate quarantine procedures."

Detective Matthews darted out of the viewing room.

"Where the hell is he going?"

"Going to get the three folks from the Church we've been babysitting. They're outside in their car waiting for us. We came straight here after you called."

"Good, get them in here."

After several minutes of waiting, Detective Matthews returned with Michael and the two clergy members, each one worried.

"What's going on?" Father Hernandez was the first to ask.

"We may have to place you under quarantine," Dr. McKay answered. "The bodies from the funeral home are exhibiting strange effects. We don't know what it is, but we wanna be safe."

"What type of effects?" both Michael and Sister Justine asked in unison.

"The eyes seem to have withered or dissolved and the tongue..."

The doctor attempted to finish his answer and was interrupted by Michael. "The tongue looks grotesquely shriveled up?"

"You know something about this?" Father Hernandez blurted out, glaring at Michael, holding himself back. The Father was irate to discover there was even more background information they hadn't revealed to him. Dr. McKay and the detectives, mortified and curious, gave Michael a sharp look as well.

"Who the hell are you? And what do you know about this?" Dr. McKay demanded.

Sister Justine felt the need to intervene: "We've seen this same thing before, down in Mexico. After an investigation by the World Health Organization and other medical teams, nothing could be found to explain the change to the deceased bodies."

"You mean this happened before?"

Michael and Sister Justine stared at each other for a couple of minutes to determine the lucky person to give the doctor an answer.

With Michael's expression, Sister Justine knew he would remain steadfast in not responding, so she did. "In a church in a region outside of Aguascalientes, Mexico, quite a few years ago, there were some who died in similar circumstances to the ones here. A couple of days after their death, the bodies showed exactly the same signs. WHO ruled out a virus or other communicable disease because those who came across the bodies exhibited no signs of sickness whatsoever."

"Well I don't give a damn about WHO or Mexico, all I can do is go by what I see going on here right now. Something is going on here and you all are just going to have to stay and wait here until you're quarantined and cleared."

"I think you'll find that won't be necessary," Sister Justine declared.

"Why's that, and who the hell are you to tell me what's necessary or not?" Dr. Mckay asked, rebuking the Sister with his tone.

"I'm Sister Justine Dawson and this is Father Jose Hernandez. That's Michael Saunders," she said pointing to her two companions. "We're investigating the event at Thomson and Thomson on behalf of the Holy Church."

Dr. McKay had been oblivious to Sister Justine's outfit because it resembled contemporary business attire. Her jacket was a conservative shade of mauve and the skirt was dark maroon with a grey blouse. Nor had he noticed the crucifix on the gold chain around her neck or the Roman collar around Father Hernandez's neck. The priest's jeans had distracted the doctor. The activity from the outbreak had prevented any peripheral attention to the details of what anyone was wearing. His outburst came to mind.

"Sorry Father, Sister. I didn't realize. Please excuse my language," the doctor said adjusting his tone. "But you still can't leave; we're going to have to quarantine you."

"How long?" Detective Matthews asked.

"As long as it takes to figure what's going on. Hell, sorry, heck, with so much going on the last couple of days, and all the those who came in contact with these bodies, especially with the support we got from neighboring cities, this is going to be a mess." Dr. McKay headed out of the waiting area to continue working on the emergency at hand.

Michael plopped down on one of the waiting area couches segmented into separate chair sections. Father Hernandez sat down on the set of chairs opposite Michael, resting his head in his hands, awaiting the boredom he was about to endure. The two cops placed calls to family and coworkers letting them know they wouldn't be available for a while. Sister Justine started typing on her smartphone.

"So boy toy, what do you think is going on? You think angels are responsible for all of this?" Michael asked, trying to get a feel for the background and knowledge of his fellow researcher.

"If they are, they've got to be agents of the evil one."

"Why do you say that? God's been known to sanction his fair share of killing. Hell, just think about when God sent the two angels to destroy the clichéd city of Sodom in Genesis 19, everyone was killed--men, women, children, everyone."

"Yeah, but not for well over 2000 years in the scope you're referencing. And he rained down fire and brimstone."

"Same God though isn't it he? He just executes his providence differently."

"So you think God could have allowed this."

"I don't know. Doesn't God allow all things to happen for his purpose and will?" Michael asked. "Why use proxies when he can just will whatever he wants?"

"And who are we to question God?" Father Hernandez asked. "Isn't He free to do whatever He wants by whatever means possible?"

"So then you're saying God could have done all this?" Michael questioned, with evident sarcasm.

"No. I still think a great evil is at work here. There were families, even children killed. There's no other explanation except for something evil."

Dr. McKay returned to the waiting area wearing a smile. "Consulting with some of my counterparts who've been talking to the CDC and WHO, it looks like you're only gonna have to stay for about another 12 to 24 hours just as a precaution. Follow me upstairs, we've made some arrangements for you."

* * * *

Bishop Grielle was relieved to receive an email from his contact out in the field. It read,

Similar signs of visitation and bodies demonstrating same effects as those in Mexico. Will be in quarantine for approx 24 hours as a precaution. Request our original notes provided to you ten years ago to cross-reference and aid in our research.

Bishop Grielle replied, *Earlier documentation that was collected concerning previous events were destroyed at request of Rome. Please continue and provide updates when possible.*

Bishop Grielle opened an unread email from his boss titled "Investigation to be Called Off." Opening it he read, *It appears our patron and partner was successful in finding out the FBI will be closing out the investigation earlier than we anticipated. My suspicion is that certain discussions were successful. The official cause to be announced is that off gassing from the feed line to the crematorium had a leak. Rome and other key offices feel unofficially that these circumstances are extremely similar to Mexico. The Holy Father believes with full veracity that an angel was involved with the event.*

* * * *

Alder was mentally exhausted answering another round of questions from two police detectives and accompanying FBI agent visiting his home. The same questions were repeatedly being bombarded towards him, only asked slightly different. He could sense their frustration just as much as he was frustrated covering the same ground with no relevant information exposed.

"Well we're getting ready to try and visit my friend Stephen in the hospital. So can we move this along?" Alder interjected hoping to end the interrogation.

Detective Salinski responded, his high pitch voice annoying Alder. "I don't know if you realize, they're still not allowing anyone to talk to him at this time, apart from law enforcement, of course."

"We'd still like to try," Alder answered.

"Well then, just a couple of more questions," Detective Salinski continued.

"I don't think so. We've definitely answered enough questions the last couple of days. I don't know what more we could answer."

"Alright then, thank you for your time Mr. Dennison," Agent Normans interposed, firmly directing the signal for departure to both detectives.

As soon as the three investigators left the house, Alder wanted another drink. He pulled out a fresh diamond-cut crystal tumbler and filled it half-full with bourbon. He saw a look of disapproval in his wife's light brown eyes.

"You want some?" Alder quipped, reacting to her stare and offering her his glass.

She remained quiet.

"Fine, more for me."

Alder's comment made Maria more upset. He just stood by the bar watching as his wife reorient a couple of knick knacks on the shelf unit, grab one of Michelle's dolls from the steps on the staircase and storm upstairs. "We're going to leave in 'bout half an hour," he commented.

"We're not going with you if you keep drinking like that. Besides, he's your friend anyway," Maria sharply answered, reaching the top step, realizing she hollered loud enough to wake both children from their nap.

Alder glanced at his glass half filled with bourbon. The thought of pouring out the liquor crossed his mind, but he decided to finish off the drink.

Thinking about what Detective Salinski warned him concerning Stephen, he pulled out his phone and called the medical center to find out Stephen was still being sequestered from seeing any visitors. Alder prepared another drink and caught up on a couple of TV shows, using the quiet time to unwind before having to return to work in the morning after several days off.

Chapter 7

Alder sensed the overcast of mourning when he arrived at work. The loss of coworkers and family recently passed away emotionally weighted down many of the employees in the headquarters of Everest International Bio-Medical Group. The two security guards who monitored the front entrance of the R & D administration facility were normally jovial when greeting the employees in the morning. Today, they could barely force a smile or hand wave and were robotic in their responses after checking employees' company ID cards. In the elevator, the atmosphere was dense, the air oddly still. No one uttered a word. No one dared to look anyone else in the eye getting on or off, afraid they'd have to discuss what had happened several days earlier. The mirror like surface of the elevator walls made the cubed and confined spaces seem larger adding to the passengers' anxiety. Alder couldn't wait to get off.

The accounting bullpen was more quiet than normal. As Alder passed each cubicle, he saw in the ones that weren't empty, two or three clerks, accountants, or bookkeepers whispered amongst themselves appearing to console one another. The ones who missed the opportunity to attend the funeral were now considering themselves fortunate. Not winning the raffle for spare seats to Jeffrey's funeral, and the possibility of witnessing an angel, now seemed like luck. Several of the workers stopped their conversations when they saw Alder pass by; a couple of them thought they caught an odor of alcohol mixed with cologne follow in his wake. Their noses were accurate.

The kitchenette and break room, where there were normally three or four workers chatting about the previous evening's television shows, family escapades, or office gossip, was barren. The coffee pot was still full, the area neat and orderly. Usually the evidence of the cleaning service's work the previous evening had vanished several minutes after employees began to arrive in the morning. By this time of the morning, the kitchenette would be ravaged with napkins wadded and strewn about the countertop, misses from the small discard container next to the condiments and stirrer container, and granules of sugar sometimes blanketing coffee rings on the countertop.

Alder's work area had the status of a hard walled office, his cubicle having side panels higher than many of those in the bullpen and an actual door. He and Stephen shared the office space, Stephen's desk still empty after these troubling days. Some papers, file folders, and documents on colored paper rested in the inbox, far fewer than Alder anticipated. With his mild headache, he appreciated the minimal work that appeared to be before him. Looking through the paperwork, signing onto his computer, and reviewing his action plan for the day, the work schedule was unchanged since leaving the previous Friday. The work of crunching numbers, reviewing the general ledger, and validating the short backlog of departmental charge backs didn't seem so daunting until it hit Alder that he'd have to absorb Stephen's workload, and no one was sure how long he would be out. He would need to distribute the work to the other team members in the accounting bullpen. Bill payment authorizations, capital project reviews, and other major undertakings normally managed by his former director who worked directly for Jeffrey Bradfield would be in limbo now. If Alder did begin handling the paperwork held in abeyance, like any administrative machinations, it would need to be acted upon and initialed or digitally signed showing it had been coordinated at every level of the approval process. Now there was a bureaucratic void. Thinking about the anticipated workload intensified Alder's headache. It was time for a cup of coffee.

The kitchenette was still empty. Someone had grabbed a cup since Alder walked by a few minutes earlier as he saw less coffee in the glass pot. He pulled his favorite mug from the cabinet and poured in a little creamer and sugar, followed by dark roasted coffee. Alder caught sight of someone out of the corner of his eye, a tall, well-defined man in his fifties with silver hair dressed in a conservative dark blue suit. His pockmarked face was etched with age and stress. He stood confident and erect like the Cyclops Polyphemus obstructing and guarding the exit of the cave on the Isle of Sicily. It was Gary Applethorpe, a senior vice president for Everest in charge of the research and development group of companies and subsidiaries.

"Hello Mr. Applethorpe, like a cup of coffee?" Alder asked.

"No thanks. Just go ahead and finish up what you're doing there and meet me in your office," Gary said and moved away from the doorway.

Alder rummaged through his mind as to why Gary Applethorpe wanted to talk to him? He had taken several days off to mourn the loss of his coworkers. Work definitely was beginning to back up and not processed as fast as the company would like. Alder wasn't sure if three days off was too much time. Had Gary come down to reprimand him? That was his specialty. Even though the company had authorized the memorial leave, it was somewhat implied that one shouldn't take too much time, especially if those lost weren't direct reports or close working associates. When Alder got back to his office, Gary was sitting in Stephen's chair, waiting until Alder situated himself before beginning the conversation.

"So how are you doing through all of this?" Gary asked, smelling a mild odor of alcohol, already formulating an answer in his mind regardless of how Alder answered.

Alder decided to bypass the question. "What can I do for you sir?"

"It's a shame there's such a loss in the company. You know we lost several executives and key researchers from the genetic engineering side of the house."

"Well, Jeffrey is going to be missed," Alder commented, not sure if Gary was aware of Jeffrey's postings, ledger entries, capital expenditure justification tallies that he and Stephen continually corrected.

"Come on, call it like it was, Jeffrey's accounting documentation was generally screwed up. We all knew that. He's one of the ones we're not gonna miss. You and Stephen correcting his mistakes kept us out of trouble more times than I can even recall. That's why I'm down here." Pausing and scanning the cubicle office for a couple of minutes, Gary continued. "I'll get straight to the point, would you consider yourself trustworthy?"

Alder responded with a quizzical look, unsure if he knew the point of the question or if it was presented to him as some sort of test. Alder decided he would just go ahead an answer he felt comfortable with that was straightforward.

"Yeah, I'd like to think I'm trustworthy," Alder answered.

"We in Everest think so too." Gary followed, marginally lowering his voice. "I have another question for you. How well do you and Stephen get along?"

"We get along very well. We sometimes spend a lot of time together after work, going to get a few drinks, sports bar, stuff like that. Sometimes he comes over and has dinner with my family."

"Hmm, you think you'd have any problems working with Stephen if you weren't his peer anymore?"

"I'm not sure I understand," Alder responded.

"With what happened in the company, there's a management vacuum. Jeffrey is gone as well as several other members of the accounting staff. Plus we're not sure of the long-term effect of Stephen' blindness. What we'd like to do is make you a junior director over the R & D accounting department. Think you can handle it?"

Alder was stunned. He couldn't answer.

"Look, I know it's quite a bit to take in, but come by my office in an hour and we can talk more about it," Gary added.

Alder was still in shock and couldn't think of anything to say. The promotion would be a serious increase in responsibility. From being a manager supervising several lead accountants, he would skip over being a senior manager all the way to being director, a junior executive position. Not only that, Alder would be in charge of the accounting for the R & D division internal to the company. This was one of the most respected divisions in all of Everest's business units and subsidiaries. Just from the postings and muck-ups by Jeffrey, Alder knew the company performed clandestine research for new high profile products and inventions across the entire globe in countries like Canada, Mexico, Brazil, England, Finland, Italy, Japan, Northern Africa, and Egypt.

Alder was finally able to muster up something to say. It wasn't much, "I don't know what to say. Why me?"

Gary responded with an indistinct but pleasant smile. "We think you show a lot of potential. You've shown you can be trusted. You kept a lot of what Jeffrey accidentally revealed between you and Stephen. Those projects are extremely sensitive and could have a substantial financial impact if competitors or market news got wind of them. Moreover, your folks down here seem to work extremely well together as a team."

"What about Stephen?"

"What about him? We're not sure how long he's going to be out, or if he's returning at all. Nonetheless, we as a company have to move on. I'll see you in an hour in my office?"

This time, Alder didn't hesitate in responding, "I'll be there."

"Good, and don't tell anyone down here in the bull pen yet. We want to include this in a formal announcement with some of the other changes caused by these unfortunate events."

"Not a problem," Alder responded, wanting to make sure he sounded confident.

A couple of minutes later Sherry, a direct report of his and a front line supervisor for a small team of accountants working charge backs for capital projects, peaked into Alder's office waiting for Gary to leave the area.

"Well, what did he want?" she questioned.

Alder glanced up to see a short African American woman with ebony dark skin, a bit overweight, in her late thirties. The floral print dress she wore hugged her shapely form.

"He didn't want anything special. Just wondering how we're all doing here considering all that's happened," he replied.

"Bullshit. You know Gary doesn't stop in down here unless it's something important."

Alder appreciated that Sherry could be forward and direct. She had even demonstrated the tenacity to stand up to Jeffrey Bradfield, when both Alder and Stephen were out of town and he tried to accuse her section of incorrect entries on the end-of-quarter postings she authorized. The entries were incorrect after Jeffrey had provided Sherry's team the incorrect information. He tried to shift the blame and she scolded him thoroughly for even attempting to try and place the responsibility on the accountants in her bull pen. After that incident, Jeffrey never looked her in the eye again and tried to avoid her in the aisles of the cubicle farm and hallways. She didn't care either way. She also didn't hold grudges-- another quality he liked. If he had the opportunity to promote someone as a manager once he moved into his new position, it would be her.

"No seriously, it wasn't that important," Alder insisted, attempting to maintain a firm expression of don't ask again.

"Mm hmm," Sherry countered, standing in the doorway for nearly a minute staring at him; Alder remained unwavering.

"Look, I'm sure if it was important, we'd all hear about it," Alder said hoping she would get the hint. "I need to get started on some of this paperwork. Anything else?"

"You know something," Sherry acknowledged, presenting a small grin. She decided to leave.

* * * *

For the remainder of the day, forgetting the circumstances leading up to the promotion, Alder was giddy from excitement and confident he could do the job after talking with Gary. But he wasn't sure if he could contain his nonverbal signals. Although Sherry asked directly, the others only speculated why Gary Applethorpe had gone in to see Alder and then invited Alder back to his office. Many thought it could be that Stephen wasn't coming back to work. Others were thinking maybe some transitory changes in the reporting structure for supervisors. Alder was amazed that the usually stunningly accurate "grapevine" was wrong in this situation. Many in the company knew there would be an immediate need to fill the recent vacancies. For his new position, none foresaw the selection of Alder. Most of the accountants, who worked for him, or their peers, thought Alder had pinnacled to his full potential. He was an excellent accountant but only a mediocre manager.

As the end of the workday was upon him, Alder wished he could finally hurry home to tell his wife the news. No official announcement had made its way yet from the executive offices; maybe it would take a couple of days. Nevertheless, he began to flirt with the idea that the executive board had reconsidered the offer of the position. Alder thought that Maria was mildly obsessive-compulsive and, after recent events, highly emotional. Mentioning it to his wife and having to recant his news later would only add to her short temper and recent mood swings, which Alder attributed to the stress of change. The co-workers who were gone had become more than simple family acquaintances; they had come over for dinner or family game night or all gone out for drinks from time to time to get away from their kids. They wouldn't be coming over anymore. Alder wasn't sure she could effectively cope with the loss of new friends. In reality, it was his drinking that had frustrated her more.

Gary stuck his head in Alder's office. "You know what, let's go for a drink. It'll be a good chance to meet up with a couple of your peers from other departments we're going to promote."

Alder shut down his computer, pulled his chip-encoded common access card from its slot, and neatly stacked the papers on his desk. He didn't need convincing; he was ready to go.

* * * *

Maria was irritated. It was almost midnight and Alder was just walking in the front door. It had been 16 hours since he left for work. Smelling alcohol on him just upset her even more. At first, she was angry for him not calling to tell her that he would be late getting home and missing dinner. Now she was furious that he was out drinking again. "Where the hell have you been?" she shrieked.

Alder grabbed Maria's hand, put his other hand on the small of her back, and attempted to dance with her on the polished solid wood of the foyer.

She rebuffed his attempts. "Will you stop?" Maria saw a smile on Alder's face and found it hard to stay civil enough not wake up the children. "Why are you smiling like that? You should have been home hours ago."

"I just got done having dinner and drinks with Gary Applethorpe, Branson, and a couple of other guys from work."

"So? You should have at least called and let me know where you were. Not only that, weren't you going to go see Stephen today after work?"

The smile drained from Alder's face. "Why've you been so worried about him?"

"I don't know. Am I? He's your friend."

Alder, now upset with Maria, stood for several seconds attempting to determine how to process his wife's reaction to him being late, now shifted to him not visiting Stephen. Maybe he subconsciously didn't want to visit him and found excuses to keep from doing so.

Although Alder's thought processes were somewhat diminished from the evening of drinking, he recalled his original cause for elation. It didn't fully express itself in the jovial manner he anticipated when he mentioned it to Maria. "Well, then I suppose you wouldn't be happy that I got promoted today?" his comment coming off sounding infantile and derisive. "I was made an accounting director for one of the largest sections in the Everest R & D Group," he grumbled.

"I didn't know you could be like this!" Maria responded turning away and heading into the living room.

Alder was extremely confused. "Like what?"

"Not even a week passed by, and you're already working your way up the corporate ladder by crapping on your friends."

"Where the hell is this coming from?"

"Were you just waiting for an opportunity to pop up?" Maria angrily commented sitting on the couch.

"Wait a minute missy. I didn't ask for Jeffrey or the others to die or for Stephen to go blind."

"What about Stephen, the way you've been avoiding going to visit him?"

"I'm not trying to avoid going to see him. I just don't think now's the right time. Being in the hospital, going through therapy, trying to get situated, what can I do? I'd probably be more in the way than anything else."

"Oh I see, you have time for work but not your friends?" Maria snapped.

"Look, this could be a big opportunity for us."

"Like you coming home late? Yeah that's real opportunity all right."

"Where the hell is this coming from?" Alder queried again, somewhat bewildered.

"And I suppose if … oh never mind, if you can't figure it out," Maria complained as she got off the couch and made way for the stairway. Alder intercepted her at the landing.

"Figure out what?" he asked, still confused.

Maria knew she should answer. She promised herself she wouldn't leave in the middle of an argument or serious discussion, at least not attempting to work out a resolution, or at a bare minimum, a compromise. She had broken that promise to herself many times before but this time she didn't want to leave the situation at hand unresolved. She'd fought with her first husband the evening prior to the mass disappearance. An argument unsettled, Maria going off to bed upset and angry then waking up the next morning and he was gone, one of the countless faces never to be seen again. She was overwhelmed with a terrible feeling of remorse. It was a sense of abandonment not overcome until a couple of years later when she met Alder in a survivors support group. Then, he was funny, compassionate, and levelheaded. Now he seemed aloof and distant most every day.

"What if something were to happen to me or the kids? Would you just forget about us and move on as if we weren't important in your life?"

Alder could hear the distress in her voice. Maybe it would be best to comfort her. He reached his arms out and embraced his wife. "Of course I wouldn't forget about you or the kids. The three of you are everything to me."

"Really?" Maria rested her head on Alder's shoulder.

"Yes, really," he answered. "Look, you know what? I'll make sure to go and visit Stephen tomorrow. OK?"

Maria gazed up into Alder's coffee-colored eyes with her large deep dark brown eyes glistening from the tears she held back. "OK," she responded, squeezing tighter. Alder genuinely reciprocated.

Alder recognized this was the first time in a long while that he had sincerely embraced her, the first time in a long time she felt secure in his arms. She had lost so much: Although she considered her previous husband, friends, and family members extreme religious churchgoing nuts, she still loved and cared for them. Her life was now with Alder, the only foundation of their history was the bond of supporting one another during meetings for disappearance survivors. Alder had empathy for Maria's feelings; he had been attracted to her vulnerability. However, shortly after they got married, he discovered the support group was the only thing they had in common. He enjoyed drinking, she didn't. He enjoyed going out from time to time; she was more of an introvert and homebody. None of that mattered now; he only knew he needed to provide comfort to her during this period of her insecurity.

* * * *

There was no media frenzy at the hospital. *Thank God*, Alder thought. The staff attending to Stephen had mentioned he was transferred to the rehab center during the night to avoid the chaos of cameras, news reporters, and gawkers. Driving to the disability rehab center in Long Beach wasn't as hard to get to as Alder had envisioned. The new GPS helped immensely. He was pleased to find one of only two available parking spots three slots away from the main entrance.

The outside of the two-story alabaster white facility was ornate and structured more like a museum with a pair of Doric columns supporting the portico. The majestic fascia relieved Alder's apprehension. He had been expecting to see a facility reflecting the way he envisioned his friend: dilapidated. Even though Stephen was only blind, Alder magnified his coworker's sight infirmity into a full scale incapacitating disability.

Through the glass double doors and past the reception area, was a small lobby with faded earth-tone furniture from the mid-1970s. Across the lobby and waiting area, opposite the main entrance, were another set of doors leading out to an open-air courtyard surrounded by the building. In both the lobby and courtyard among numerous elderly patients sitting motionless in wheelchairs, were several patients in their later twenties or early thirties possessing long white canes with red tips or Seeing Eye dogs with occupational therapists scattered about. Alder might think he was visiting a par standard nursing home, if not for the younger patients. His apprehension returned. He was afraid to visit Stephen. He would need to overcome the urge to head back out of the building, to his car, and drive away.

After presenting ID to the receptionist and inquiring as to Stephen's room, Alder made his way to the second floor, to the opposite end of the building where the walls were dingy, aged, and yellowed like old eggshells. Scuffmarks scattered across the surface confirmed the neglect. The white tiled floor with gray speckles looked like it hadn't been waxed for weeks. Arriving at Stephen's room, he found himself standing rigidly outside the doorway. Several minutes passed, he was hesitant to open the door. Stephen wouldn't know if he never went in. He could tell Maria he did visit the rehab center. Alder knew it would be a lie--well, a partial lie because he did at least go into the facility. Alder doubted the one drink this morning was enough to get through this. Debating on whether to stay, he didn't sense a big-framed nurse come up behind. She had been watching him from the nurses' station for a couple of minutes, noticing he appeared apprehensive.

"May I help you?" she asked.

Alder jumped, not expecting to hear a shrilly, high-pitched, mouse like voice to his rear. When he turned around, he was surprised to see that the shrill voice had come from a large and moderately overweight nurse.

"I'm fine thank you," Alder answered. "Just building up the courage to visit my coworker." Alder didn't know why he didn't call Stephen his friend.

The nurse grinned as she navigated around him into the doorway of Stephen's room. She set the rubber stopper down to prop open the door and then proceeded to Stephen's bedside. "Hello Mr. Williams. How are you? Do you need any water or anything special before your therapist arrives?"

"No I'm good," Alder heard from a disheartened, baritone voice mumble from inside the hospital room.

"Well if you do, just remember to hit the button and someone will be right in. By the way, you have a guest out in the hallway."

Alder was appalled. Now that he knew he couldn't stand out in the hallway any longer; he began to get nervous. Walking in, the nurse returned Alder's piercing stare with a simple grin unaffected by his anger. She was accustomed to friends and family being afraid to engage the patient when first visiting the recently disabled. With his hazel eyes now staring in the direction of the door, Stephen sat in a simple chair next to the hospital bed.

"Hello Stephen."

Stephen's eyes somewhat widened. "Alder?"

"Yeah, it's me." Alder didn't have an idea of what to say next.

Stephen bridged the pregnant pause, "How's Maria and the kids?"

"They're fine considering."

"Considering?" Stephen responded, confused by Alder's answer.

"Well it's just that, considering...well-being here...I mean look at what happened at Jeffrey's funeral. What if we'd been there? Would we be alive? Would we be blind? I don't even know what to think."

"Well I don't know either, but I tell you what, it sucks to be blind."

"I wouldn't kno..." Alder caught himself missing Stephen's attempt at lightening the mood. He decided to try and change the direction of the conversation. "How are things for you? Are they taking good care of you?"

Stephen could sense Alder was still standing in the doorway. "You know you can sit down if you want?"

Alder obliged by scouting out the space, not finding a chair, grabbed one from the hallway. When Alder returned, Stephen answered his question. "Things here are fine I guess. Food sucks though."

"So what happens now?"

"I start my self-sufficiency training later today. My sister came down to help. She's staying over at my place right now."

"Is there anything you need?"

"No thanks. And now that I'm not considered a suspect, I can go through rehab and training and then get released from this place."

"Really, I heard on the news they were still considering you someone of interest because you got out and survived. At one point, they thought Maria and I were somehow involved because we had tickets to attend yet miraculously we didn't make it. We got questioned several times by the Feds and the police."

"I did to, way too many times. There were even some investigators from the Catholic Church who stopped by to talk to me about what happened. I'll just be glad to get out of here, not sure about work."

Alder hadn't been sure how he would broach the subject of their jobs, but now there was an opening.

"They're talking about possibly a disability buy out for you. The company isn't quite set up to redo our accounting processes in Braille. Nice-size package though from what I've been hearing."

Stephen ruminated on Alder's comment for a couple minutes. "So you'll have to put up with someone else managing the team?"

"Wel-l-l-l, Gary Applethorpe stopped by Thursday because of the recent openings." Alder paused, and instead of drawing out his response, decided to be straightforward and blunt. "I'm getting promoted to junior director. I'll be in charge of the accounting departments for the R & D sections of the company."

"All of R & D?"

"No, just a couple of subsidiaries on the bio side, bio-med, genetic engineering, things like that."

Stephen wasn't sure how to respond. The impact hadn't set in since he was focused on coping with being blind instead of his career. Now it moved to a lower priority in his life. He had hoped that one day he would be promoted and rise further in the company. The immense number of divisions and subsidiaries in Everest such as bio-medical research, pharmaceuticals, bionics, and genetic engineering would have provided plenty of opportunities. Now it was all gone, yet hearing about Alder's promotion to a director's level position over an entire division was devastating to Stephen. He concealed it very well.

"I guess I should congratulate you, and not worry since I can't see anyway. Hell, I guess if I could come back to work, I'd have to correct all your blunder-head guidance on project postings like we did Jeffrey's," Stephen quipped, not sure if Alder caught on to his attempt at a joke.

Alder laughed nervously. "Ah, I wouldn't worry about that. I'm quite sure there's other bonehead things I can screw up though. I start on Monday."

Stephen was a bit overwhelmed. "Kinda quick isn't it?"

"Because of last week there've been a lot of openings and they want to move forward."

"Damn, the seats are barely cold and already they're filling them up," Stephen said sardonically.

"Gary said a lot of their projects are at a critical point where leadership across all departments is vital."

"Sounds like it's more your problem than mine. I guess I don't have too much to worry about anyway, except dealing with my blindness."

Alder recalled many of the rumors in the company that the medical staff at the hospital couldn't find out what caused Stephen's blindness. The doctors at first thought it might have been psychosomatic primarily because of the traumatic event. Then evidence of physical trauma would present itself but when they tried to treat the cause, the symptoms disappeared. Stephen's medical team needed to rule out numerous possible causes for his blindness before Stephen could be released from the hospital.

"So, they don't know why you're blind yet I take it?" Alder asked.

"No, and already my attention-grabbing sister booked me on a talk show tomorrow morning."

"No shit. Which one?"

"*Carson's Sunday Report.*"

"He can be a bit of an asshole, can't he?"

"Yeah, but my sister doesn't know that."

"So where's the rest of the media hounds? I didn't think it would be as quiet as it was when I got here."

"I've been told the mayor put out a press release not to descend on the rehab center and disturb the patients. From what the nurses told me, he pretty much told them he'd put them in jail if any showed up here."

Alder was amazed. "And they listened?"

"From what I heard, a lot did show up."

"So where are they?"

"The mayor started having them arrested. And when they heard the Feds were involved, things started snowballing and they were afraid to come around. Listening to the nurses, I heard the newspapers got some serious phone calls from the city and Feds."

"Well hell, how did they know I wasn't a reporter?" Alder queried.

"You check in at the reception desk?" Stephen replied.

"Yeah."

"I gave them a list of people. So when you checked in and headed up here, they probably called the nurses' station to let them know you were on the list. Anyone showing up without a call to the nurses' station is turned away."

"Well it's definitely quiet around here." Alder was at a loss for words again. The urge to ask one key question was repeatedly being sequestered by the conversation. Now with a break in the discussion, his curiosity defeated his reluctance. "Stephen, what really happened?"

Stephen focused his head directly toward Alder's voice. "I don't know," he paused. "I was there before anything happened, then next thing I know I'm out in the parking lot, you come up to me and I can't see anything."

"Did you see an angel?" Alder asked in a heavy whisper.

Stephen attempted to recall the entire event from when he arrived at the funeral home to those he talked to there while trying to accept the thought he would never be able to talk to those people again. Holding back tears, he went through the mental exercises of remembering each of the faces of his colleagues, their families, Jeffrey's family, and the raffle winners who were able to attend. No one attending the funeral expected that day would be their last. The eulogy service replayed in his mind up to the time the angel appeared.

Stephen finally answered after a prolonged silence. "I just don't know; I saw something."

II. The Eulogy of Angels: The Golden Fire of
   Gishmael

Chapter 8

The shining and flickering aura surrounding the robed body appeared fluid and translucent. He or she, no one could tell the gender, stood sternly in front of the casket and looked like a sentry with the semblance of a sword across its chest. The blade, barely distinguishable from the angel's body, danced with golden flames. Then there were the eyes, and for those who witnessed the previous visitations, this one's eyes shone as if they were the deepest black onyx. Ever since the radiant figure appeared, some of those present at the funeral had glanced at their watches and saw that 15 minutes elapsed. No one spoke a word. Many were afraid, as time continued to pass, of a repeat of the previous week with only one survivor. For others, their fears subsided to boredom as they waited for something interesting to happen. Some tried to reach for their cameras only to feel the numbing sting of an electrostatic shock. Others tried to make phone calls but had no signal or dial tone. The angel met anyone who tried to leave his or her seat or go to an exit with an intense stare, its face presenting an unyielding, commanding look, its aura intensifying, which forced people to stay in their original places.

The angel stared directly at a 31-year-old black woman, professionally dressed, sitting toward the front of the congregation and spoke to her. "Rhonda, make your calls. Return. I will be waiting." The rest of the people in the chapel only heard vague vocalizations composed of harmonic tonal sounds. Rhonda, frozen with fear for a few moments, methodically got up out of her seat and worked her way to the exit of the sanctuary. No one even attempted to follow.

The angel refocused its attention toward an older, distinguished-looking man, graying on the temples, smartly dressed in a custom-tailored suit, who then began to sweat. The longer the angel stared, the more perspiration blanketed the man's forehead, the sheen reflecting the ambient room lights and radiance of the angel. The man developed the sensation of a fullness in his chest and knew he didn't want to be there anymore.

* * * *

"Ready on the set!" The director roared. "Two minutes to air."

A stagehand led Stephen from the green room and then seated in a comfortable lounge chair perpendicular to the host, who was already sitting in his chair. The host's name was Carson Stewart. Both men were submitting to the final hustle of tie straightening, hair adjusting, and makeup application. Stephen only heard hurried stagehand activity around himself, working hard not to get startled each time someone touched him to prep him. Through all the activity, Carson attempted to discuss last-minute notes, comments, and instructions with Stephen on how to act during the interview. Stephen listened as best he could through all the distractions. He hoped he wouldn't make too many mistakes.

"One minute!" he director hollered. "One minute to air."

Carson quieted. Stephen sensed the bustle of activity ebbing. The noise abated with an occasional command or instruction being softly woofed out with the obligatory acknowledgment between stagehands, crewmembers and production staff. The show was about to begin. Stephen suddenly smelled a strong odor of roses and almonds. Since going blind, he'd been acutely aware of the heightening of his other senses. He couldn't believe how intense they'd become, much stronger than the stories he'd heard about what happens when people go blind. There were times he thought he could understand people who were talking in different languages but he dismissed it as auditory anomalies.

"I think one of your crew members is wearing too much perfume," Stephen commented to anyone who might have been listening.

"What? What are you talking about?" Carson answered. He was annoyed that airtime was approaching and Stephen had started to talk indiscriminately.

"Your stagehands, someone is wearing a lot of perfume."

"Don't worry about it," Carson quipped while giving Stephen a quizzical look and realizing that the only crewmembers working the last couple of minutes were male.

"Five, four," the director whispered and then transitioned to the finger motions of three, two, one, signaling Carson to begin.

"Hello San Gorgonio Valley cities, we welcome you live this Sunday morning with me, your host, Carson

Stewart. Today we're here with Stephen Jamison, the only survivor of the Thomson and Thomson funeral home event from a week ago. Welcome Stephen."

Stephen found himself being distracted. It wasn't because Carson had stated his last name incorrectly; that was done in an attempt to hide his identity to keep fanatics from showing up on his doorstep, as if he were some sort of religious icon. It was because not being able to smell so acutely most of his life, suddenly the aroma of roses and almonds became pronounced. "I'm sorry," Stephen, answered to end the pregnant pause following Carson's introduction. "Thank you for having me," Stephen continued as he recalled the instructions given to him just before the start of the show.

"So Stephen, a lot of our viewers have questions regarding what happened that day at Thomson and Thomson. Why don't we begin there? Tell us," Carson paused for added effect, "what did happen?" Carson was proud knowing he had trumped the national news interview shows. His was the only news talk show to get an exclusive interview with Stephen after the initial investigation was over and Stephen could now talk to the press. Amazed by the clarity of his memories, Stephen recounted the event.

Carson continued. "So why do you think everyone died that fateful morning, or do you think they were killed?

"I don't know."

"Well, do you think the angel killed everybody in the funeral home?"

"I don't know."

"Well, you described very vividly what you thought you saw and what you heard as you were leaving; the angel mentioned that all those in attendance were being, I think you said you thought the word was, 'judged'? Why do you think you were spared, or do you think you were being jud ..."

Stephen interrupted. "Like I said, I don't know..."

"Ummm hmm," Carson noted with a tone of substantial skepticism. "So Stephen, tell us about your blindness and the fact that the doctors can't find anything physically wrong with you? How do you explain that?"

"Look, all I know is that I could see but now I'm blind. Yes, they told me it might be psychological due to the trauma of witnessing what happened. I just know that I don't have an answer for you."

"OK, and now what about the speculation that it could have been something natural like carbon monoxide or some other noxious gas in the building. I mean, come on; the initial police report said there was no trauma found on any of the bodies, nothing unusual, and nothing supernatural."

"What about the angel? That looked quite weird to me," Stephen chimed in.

"So there was an angel?"

"Yes. You think I'm making that up?"

"Come on, isn't it possible that nothing religious, nothing supernatural, nothing extraordinary happened? I mean we know that yes, many have been claiming to see angels at funerals, but there aren't any pictures that we know of, and many others rule out the religious aspect. I mean, remember after the disappearance of millions ten years ago? According to the remaining religious leaders and the Bible," Carson flashed air quotes in sync with the word *Bible*, "we were going to enter into seven years of hell on earth. It's been ten years. Isn't that something other than what most were led to believe? And if these are angelic visits, isn't it in contradiction to what supposed believers think in reference to their religion?"

"I don't have an answer for you. I'm sorry, I don't know too much about religion."

* * * *

While the interview was taking place at the television studio, Rhonda fumbled through her purse and found her phone. She made her first call. She was glad Aaron was quick to answer. "Aaron, get back over and pick me up now! And bring the crew. We need to set up a feed."

"We're all still eating," the stuffed mouth on the other end of the call responded.

"Well stop stuffing your face and get your fat ass back over here now! We're going live with a story. I'll explain when you get here."

Hanging up the phone, Rhonda made her second call.

* * * *

"So are you a religious man Stephen?" Carson quizzed.

"I never considered myself to be one. I used to go to church with my wife from time to time. I never really believed all of it the same way she did."

"So, you're still married?"

The sweet aroma of flowers and almond with a hint of cinnamon was now overpowering to Stephen. Little flashes of blue flickered in the blackness of his sight. They blended into a solid spot of pure white at the dead center of the darkness. Then, as if looking through a tube, in an instant, the distinct shape of a robed radiant being near a couple of stagehands by a camera setup came into startling focus to Stephen. He jumped up and then backed into his chair, causing it to flip backward. Deep uneasiness volcanoed within the cameraman, his stomach going queasy, and the hair on his arms stood up as if charged static electricity filled the air. The weighted feeling of someone standing directly behind him melded with a feeling of dread and fear causing him to wildly swing his camera around. No one was there.

"Camera 3, back on set now," a voice commanded in the cameraman's headset.

Carson observed the director signaling a station break. Carson then moved over and attempted to grab Stephen to keep him from falling backwards. "We'll be right back ladies and gentlemen, right after this short break."

"We're out for three minutes," the director called out.

"Thank God!" Carson yelled out frustrated. "What the hell's going on? Why in the hell did you jump like that?" he asked Stephen, who was looking back over the fallen chair in the direction of the cameras while a couple of stagehands ran onto the set to help him.

"Don't you see the... it? Standing by camera," Stephen answered in the direction of cameraman 3.

101

"What are you talking about?" Carson remarked. "I thought you were blind."

"The light from it is illuminating everything around it! Don't you see it?"

Carson, the stagehands, and the crewmembers hastily scanned the set. Nothing appeared out of the ordinary.

"Trish, thanks for that soft break," Carson commented to the director who was coming onto the set and assuming his guest had gone nutty.

"I wasn't calling a break because of what happened out here. The control room wanted to break in on the broadcast."

"Why? What the hell is going on?"

"Carson," a voice reverberated over the public address system. "When we come back, we're going to broadcast live audio from Rhonda on remote. When the remote camera is set up, then we're going to switch to video."

"Rhonda? I thought she was taking a long breakfast break for her grandmother's funeral?"

"That's where she is," Trish answered.

Damn, she's coldhearted, Carson thought. *She didn't even take the entire Sunday off to go to her grandmother's funeral and wake. Now she's ready to pop right to work.*

The crew stood up Stephen's overturned chair and adjusted the table between his chair and the host. Then they attempted to guide him back into his seat but he refused to move.

"What's so interesting that you have to cut into my interview?" Carson, a little perturbed, asked Trish.

"An angel," Stephen interjected. The set became quiet after his response.

"She's saying there's an angel there now and it looks like we got the chance to film it," Trish responded unhurriedly, a little shocked at Stephen's response. "Get ready to go to air."

"One minute to live audio feed," the voice boomed over the speakers. Silence continued to rest over the set. Stephen remained standing, facing the direction of the cameras. Only with excessive coaxing did he return to his seat. The angel stood fast. It was apparent to Carson and a stagehand that Stephen was flush and staring blankly into the distance. Carson began to confirm his doubt about Stephen claiming to be blind.

"Carson, when we go back live, we're going to zoom straight to you and patch the feed directly to Rhonda," Trish directed.

Carson straightened his red, diagonal-patterned tie, gathered his note cards, and focused his attention toward the camera. "Keep it together," he said, directing his comments to Stephen.

"Three seconds to air," the director bellowed.

* * * *

The experienced remote sound engineer had established the audio feed within minutes of arriving at the funeral home. He couldn't explain why the cell phone wouldn't reconnect after Rhonda's first seven attempts even though the signal strength showed full bars. She took that time to primp herself until the camera was ready. She was thankful she'd adorned herself for the funeral and would be set when the camera went live. The sound engineer prompted that it was only seconds to going on air. With her earpiece in, she could hear the studio cue to begin.

"This is Rhonda Peterson live from Crestview Funeral Home, where just a few minutes ago I was inside and witnessed the arrival of a bright, radiant being. For all intents and purposes, there's an actual angel here, and in a just a minute or two we hope to bring you a live view of this visitation as we prepare to go back inside. Many are worried about a possible repeat from a week ago at the infamous Thomson and Thomson funeral home incident. Even today, police and church leaders are at a loss as to what happened that tragic day. There are many rumors that the investigation has gone cold. Today, however, while attending the funeral of my grandmother, we are witnessing what I have seen to be a beautiful angel. Yet, as of now, there has been no eulogy presented. So why is the angel here? What does it have to tell us?" After pausing while the camera finished filming a quick B roll of the venue, she continued. "And now I'm being told that we are about ready to go live with the picture."

Rhonda listened in her ear piece to a question asked by Carson. She responded, "Carson, the angel did mention one thing, it directed me to make this call. It almost seems like it wants to be filmed. As we make our way inside, we're reaching the outer doors. Yet, unlike at Thomson and Thomson, they appear to have remained unlocked for us. We are now making our way into the main chapel. Ladies and gentlemen, I believe we are about to make history and film for the first time ever, an actual angel."

* * * *

Everyone in the studio, paralyzed with awe and anticipation, focused on the television monitors throughout the station; the images were coming through and showing the rear of Rhonda's head as she moved through the foyer of the funeral home. The control room director commanded the cameraman via the wireless communications link to adjust the focus of camera view. The news team moved down a small hallway and entered through the side of two large doors leading into the memorial room while filming an aura of indescribable incandescence. Moving closer to the doorway, the white levels on the image transmitted by the camera began to wash out other objects in the video. The control room director instructed the control room team to adjust the contrast levels, black levels, gain, or other necessary settings to fine-tune the feed in order to attempt and transmit a sharper picture. Every time they modified the color balance level or contrast setting, the intensity of the aura on received video image counteracted the adjustment. As the camera crew moved within inches of the chapel entrance, the radiance from the angel magnified. Simultaneously, the angel in the studio that Stephen had stayed focused on incrementally brightened. He felt the need to stand again. Carson got upset when he saw him.

"Sit down," Carson angrily whispered.

Stephen ignored him.

The news crew rounded the doorway. On the studio monitors, everyone observed at the end of the center aisle of the chapel was the image of an indistinct figure, bathed in white light, which washed out most of the screen. Mourners in the sanctuary of the memorial chapel were barely discernible from the background. Golden flames in the shape of a sword were visible in front of the upper torso of the angelic figure. The crew in the control room worked feverishly to clear the picture. They had some success when the image became visible for a little less than two seconds. A well-dressed older man walked backwards down the center aisle with his attention focused on the divine presence at the front of the chapel. No one noticed him holding his chest. During that same time, the angelic being spoke, its voice consisting of tonal harmonics, audibly ethereal and vague.

The video feed to the studio ceased. The studio shook with a small earthquake.

Stephen, still observing his angel, heard the exchange over the studio sound system. He heard others mumbling among themselves about the actual words spoken by the angel. In the next instant, his angel lurched toward Stephen, coming face–to-face, causing Stephen to duck down reflexively. The angelic figure faded, a voice echoed in Stephen's ears saying, "Aurora." His vision blackened as the sound like a massive rush of wind reverberated throughout the entire studio. Lights, cameras, computers, control boards, all illuminated devices dimmed; some of the electronic gear shut off completely. Another tremor rumbled through the studio. The production crewmembers who saw Stephen ducking for no reason were further startled by the menagerie of events. After a few moments of paralysis, Stephen's studio aide worked his way over to help him, ashen, back up and into his chair..

"Prepare to go to air. Carson, be ready to go live back to the feed," the director's voice bellowed.

"How do we know they're all still alive? What's if it's Thomson and Thomson all over again?" a lighting specialist blurted out, forgetting his place within the hierarchy of the studio personnel. No one responded.

Stagehands, makeup specialists, and other crew members all hustled to their respective locations off set after several seconds of stunned silence.

Carson again straightened his tie while viewing his live guest, skeptical of his blindness. *What if it's another tragic event? This could be good for ratings*, he thought. "Trish, do we still have a feed with Rhonda?" he asked.

"I need to go," Stephen commented, his voice shaky.

"What the hell," Carson retorted. "We still have an interview to finish."

Stephen stood up. "I need to go, where's my aide?"

"Damn it Trish, what the fuck?"

"Don't worry about him; we have a bigger story with the angel. Just prepare to go live and discuss what happened when we give you playback of the event."

"Shouldn't we keep him as the reputed expert witness of last week's event?" Carson asked angrily.

Trish ignored him. Carson promptly thought she was an idiot.

The studio intern worked his way onto the set and helped Stephen off the raised interview platform and back to the green room where his sister was waiting.

"Guys in the control room ready with the playback? Set is clear; we're ready to go live," Trish commanded.

A nervous, stuttering voice responded, "Uh, Trish... we got a problem... all the recording devices are empty."

"Were we sending this to our local affiliates? They should have it."

The nervous voice responded again. "Uhhh, we tried, we're coming up blank everywhere. I was just told viewers at home are calling the studio asking what we did to zap their digital recorders. Even someone with an old VCR claimed the video before and up till after the sighting is gone."

"Bullshit," Trish bellowed. "You better get a recording of what just happened or you're all fired!"

Crewmembers in the control room, grips, and stagehands on the studio floor, and anyone on the set who felt this circumstance might be a chance to set themselves apart from their colleagues worked frantically, vying to be able to claim they were responsible for restoring services. Personnel checked camera equipment, power lines, cables, circuit breakers, display units, sound boards, mixers, speaker cables, lighting assemblies, microphone boom setups--any electrical equipment or systems--everyone made sure nothing was overlooked that could have caused the brownout. Although most knew that whatever wiped out the recording must have been external to the studio. Looking busy was also a way to keep Trish from shouting at them for just standing around. With no one able to find a concrete cause of what happened, she digressed to the point of belittling nearly the entire crew on the set with the exception of Carson.

"Rhonda's on the phone," a voice bellowed over the PA system on the set.

The activity, most of it feigned by then, halted. After a couple of minutes, the voice continued. "She says they all appear to be alive."

The studio erupted into applause.

"Hold on; she says that almost everyone looks sunburned and like they're in shock; police and ambulances on the way." The diminishing cheers accentuated the expletive "oh shit" from the voice over the PA system.

Chapter 9

"You haven't spoken a word since we left the studio," Brenda commented to her brother, who sat withdrawn in the passenger seat of her car, his flesh tones pallor and pasty white. "Did you see something back there?"

Stephen remained quiet.

"Look, I didn't drive down here over 12 hours to help you out if you're gonna just ignore me. I can always go back to Bill and the kids. Lord knows I already miss them."

Still no response.

"Or have you even thought about what you're gonna do long term now?"

Stephen still remained silent.

"You know you're starting to scare me keeping quiet over there."

Stephen turned in the direction from which he heard his sister's soft-spoken voice. "Sorry sis, I'm still thinking about what happened back at the studio."

"What did happen back there?"

Stephen turned his head straight ahead. "I can't explain it. I saw an angel and no else could."

Brenda, troubled by her brother's comment, said "I thought you were blind?"

"I am. It's just for that quick instant the angel showed up and came at me, staring face-to-face. I swear I was going to piss in my pants."

"You know that doesn't sound sane. Especially since no one else could see anything."

"Yeah, but I thought they were all watching the other angel on TV. Didn't you see it?"

"I was reading a book until that little earthquake. You know I don't go for all this religious b. s. When one of the stagehands came in saying something was happening, that's when I started watching the monitors in the green room. By that time, everything was pretty much over."

"It's what the angel said that scared me. I don't know why."

Brenda glanced over in disbelief at her brother. "You're starting to worry me. You're seeing angels again? And what do you mean what the angel said?"

"I don't know. It said a word that I've heard or seen somewhere before, I just can't remember where."

"Well what did it say?"

"Aurora."

"Aurora? Who's Aurora? Is that the angel's name?"

All Stephen could do was stay quiet. The name made him anxious, he didn't know why. At this point, he was confused because the first time he thought the angel called itself Abriel. Now the name Aurora stirred a memory, one he couldn't place.

"You know you can stay with me and Bill. We have enough room. I'm starting to get worried about you. How will you take care of yourself now? Your insurance won't keep paying for therapy or an aide or long-term training."

Stephen remained quiet. Brenda found herself becoming frustrated with her little brother.

Chapter 10

Detectives Green and Matthews suspected they'd be called in when the televised event ended abruptly. Their instincts were correct; they received the call to head to Crestview and investigate. Follow-up reports mentioned there was only one death, the circumstances reversed from their previous investigation with multiple deaths and one witness. They were relieved not to have to deal with a mass death situation again. Regardless, when they arrived, Detective Green, even more than Detective Matthews, hoped there were additional detectives dispatched. Chaos and disorder fueled the intensity of activity. The crime scene investigators already arrived and were trying to calm down the funeral attendees still excited about the event. Dr. McKay, arriving shortly before the two policemen, had already started to examine the remains. Other detectives were busy questioning witnesses. Many of them pointed to a rip in the carpet extending the entire length of the center aisle of the chapel. It began where the angel allegedly stood up to where the decedent lay covered in a white cloth. The carpet tear exposed a symmetrical crack in the underlying concrete floor matching the same ripped pattern.

Once they arrived, Detective Green briefed all the detectives that he would take lead in the investigation. Detective Green decided he and Detective Matthews would work with the doctor, who was writing notes while kneeling next to the body, instead of questioning witnesses to the death.

"Here we are again Doc. What's going on?" Detective Green asked.

"No church snoops leashed to your sides?" Dr. McKay responded.

"Naw, at least not yet."

"Well, for all intents, this appears to be just a heart attack. Nothing weird is sticking out like last week, regardless of the stories," Dr. McKay noted.

"Regardless of what stories?" Detective Matthews probed.

"Listening to some of the stories these witnesses are telling your partners, they're mentioning some bizarre stuff. They're saying the angel stared down our dead friend, who looked like he got scared, decided to go, and was getting ready to leave when the angel supposedly struck its sword on the floor and the ground shook, a gold fire raced down the aisle, and the shaking knocked our buddy here to the ground."

"So that's how they explain that rip in the carpet down the aisle and the crack underneath?" Detective Matthews questioned not initially realizing the carpet and floor anomaly entering into the chapel.

"What do you think it was?" Detective Green inquired.

"Look, whatever was going on in here, our dead friend here probably decided to leave. He was already agitated from the funeral and felt the small earthquake and the foundation of the building shifting and cracking the floor, all of this scared him to death, literally. Simple heart attack," Dr. McKay surmised, noticing Detective

Matthews leisurely step away from him and Detective Green and stroll up to the front of the chapel area. Detective Green noticed his partner's actions. When he arrived where the angel was said to have appeared, Detective Matthews got down on his hands and knees and began sniffing. The bustling noise of police investigators and witnesses talking muted, whereas everyone was mystified watching the detective sweep across multiple areas of the floor on all fours. A handful thought he had gone insane. Detective Green was the only one not confused by his partner's actions.

"Don't worry, he does that from time to time," Detective Green reassured to Dr. McKay without revealing the intentions or mental state of his partner. Detective Matthews returned to them and hesitantly nodded, not sure he could be certain with all the fresh flowers in place perfuming the air. He did think a sweet aroma might've saturated the carpet.

"Do we know who he is?" Detective Matthews asked, directing his question toward the victim.

"From what we found out, some sort of researcher at a local biomedical company, Waterfall Medical Research, a subsidiary of Everest."

"Everest? Didn't a lot of victims at the Thomson and Thomson event work at Everest?"

Dr. McKay mulled over Detective Matthews' question before answering. "Just a coincidence. Those do happen you know."

Detective Matthews contemplated Dr. McKay's answer more than Detective Green did. He considered that there was more in common between the two events, an alleged angel and resulting fatalities. There was the one striking difference, here, the one fatality died of a purported heart attack versus the multitude a week ago dying under mysterious circumstances yet to be determined.

"And what about the ones who allegedly got sunburned? How'd that happen?" Detective Matthews continued.

Dr. McKay smirked. "Come on, if you think an angel did that, get real. They probably all did a spray-on before coming to the funeral."

"So you don't believe what you saw on TV?" Detective Green asked.

"That explains it right there. TV. Hell, reality shows are prompted and manipulated to increase ratings. Think about the things over the years that the news stations did to improve viewership. Same thing here, this is just a simple heart attack. Anyway, I didn't get a chance to watch it. Someone else told me about it."

The cadre of detectives spent several hours interviewing the people who'd been present at the funeral home. Some witnessed the doctor grab his chest during the final minutes of the manifestation. Detective Green deduced the decedent suffered a heart attack, with fright the most reasonable cause. Others mentioned they were too interested in the alleged heavenly creature to see the doctor. They described it as immensely beautiful yet intensely terrifying at the same time. The only unique information was from the children who said the angel told them its name, Gishmael. The teens and adults attending the service claimed they only heard haunting, unintelligible sounds. Detective Matthews was one of the only detectives writing the details from the children down on his notepad. The other investigators discounted their observations. Receiving the preliminary results from the CSIs, Detective Green decided he would release the initial official report citing the cause of death as a heart attack pending further results from the autopsy. No other detectives challenged the findings, especially as nothing evidentiary pointed to the contrary.

Detective Green's cell phone rang. The caller ID showed it was Lieutenant Wilson. The first thought in Detective Green's mind was that, due to the strange circumstances surrounding the current death, the FBI would be called back in. Answering the call, and after a few minutes discussing the circumstances of the case with his superior, Detective Green was informed that he and his partner would file their report with the intention that the police department would no longer investigate the case. Natural causes would be the explanation unless something blatantly showed premeditation or maliciousness. Detective Green concurred. He was then told the Church would be executing an independent investigation from this point on.

Chapter 11

The thunder from each lightning bolt rumbled as if giant horses were galloping through the skies in a race into the horizon. The formations of dark misty clouds drifting eastward were all flirting with activity until blue-tinged light danced to life within each. Every so often, a bolt of electricity revealed itself, piercing the sky to find its target on the ocean off in the distance. Michael thought it was strange for a storm to be coming in this time of year and possibly somewhat ominous. Rather than finishing his normal jogging route, he darted between a couple of the smaller homes bordering the beach near a rock jetty. Closing windows, shutting garage doors, securing patio umbrellas, residents in the area prepared for the unannounced tempest. The approaching squall contradicted the weather forecast in the newspaper, which was sunny skies and temperatures in the seventies.

As he approached his small front porch, he saw Father Hernandez and Sister Justine standing and waiting. *What are these two doing here on a Sunday; you would think they would be in mass.* He helped the best he could, based on the information they found. Michael was also solaced; his latent feelings for Sister Justine hadn't reemerged.

"You two again? What brings the progeny of Grielle here?" Michael asked, breathing somewhat heavily. A crackling thunderbolt ripped through the sky, startling all three.

"Should we get inside?" Father Hernandez asked, noticing the winds becoming more aggressive.

"We're fine out here, or are you afraid your creator is going to strike you down?" Michael mocked.

"Michael, we want you to come down to Mexico with us," Sister Justine asked.

"And what have you been smokin'? I'm not leaving mid-semester on some sort of angel hunt. I have classes to teach. And why the hell all the way down to Mexico?"

Father Hernandez answered this time. "Detective Matthews took the words back to the FBI to see if they made any sense. They tried something we could have tried ourselves. It's an anagram."

"An anagram? An anagram for what? I'm sure there's tens of words if you were to put the phrase in an anagram solver."

"Yes, and when they gave us the list, one phrase stood out, 'Hot Waters.'"

"And what the hell does that have to do wi-...wait... that's awfully thin."

"Maybe, but the Church feels we should go back down there, especially with what happened this morning. Bishop Grielle has even been authorized to offer you a stipend."

Michael grinned. "A stipend, now you're talk-...wait a minute, what happened this morning?"

119

Chapter 12

The first day in his new position came upon Alder faster than he anticipated. He started that next Monday a little over a week after the deaths. He spent the morning signing updated personnel records, nondisclosure agreements, ethical agreements for executives, and other pay-related documents. The more he considered the HR discussions and voluminous amount of paperwork to sign, the more he surmised he should have requested a review by a lawyer. Apart from the monolithic amounts of papers to sign when he and Maria bought their home, this was the first time he reviewed and analyzed any type of extensive legal documents. He barely remembered what half of the sheets contained. Alder just knew from the overall impression of the content that he was restricted to confidentiality on anything in the research and development branch. Since he would be overseeing the accounting for four R & D divisions and their associated projects, much of his work would be shrouded in secrecy.

After lunch Alder made sure he kept his scheduled appointment with his boss. In fact, looking at his watch, he saw he was a few moments early and the receptionist hadn't returned yet. He could wait to see if she'd return soon and announce him, and risk being considered late, or just knock and enter. Alder heard rumors that Gary's assistant could be territorial with her responsibilities, even those as mundane as announcing visitors. He made his decision and after knocking on the solid door, he waited for a response.

"Yes Sheila, what is it?" a commanding voice from behind the door said.

Alder turned the freshly polished brass door handle and entered. Gary was surprised to see it was Alder.

"Oh, come on in Alder. Go ahead and take a seat," Gary offered, pointing to a large leather seat opposite his desk.

Accepting the invitation, Alder entered the spacious retro-modern decorated office. Walking past a steel-framed, glass-top conference table, surrounded by several post-modern styled steel-framed chairs with woven mesh for the seat sections and back rests, Alder took an extended glance down and read the tabs for a couple of large file folders. One file folder was labeled "Capital Project: Citrus Frost." the other "Project Titan (Phase 3)." He recalled this was one of several project names inadvertently exposed by Jeffrey during his monthly ledger postings and accruals. Instead of using the generic ledger codes and project names, he'd sent update information with the raw information accidentally revealed, and then screamed and yelled at personnel in the accounting bullpens as if it were their fault. Alder felt angry again as he remembered receiving several of the belligerent tongue-lashings.

"So how'd everything go this morning?" Gary asked.

"Paperwork went fine."

"Good, I wanted to just spend a couple of minutes with you to expand on the importance of the nondisclosure information you signed. We know it's quite heavy-handed. We find there's a lot at stake in keeping trade secrets from our competitors. We're in the works establishing, maintaining, and protecting many genetic-engineering-related patents." Alder didn't have a comment to make, since he hadn't understood a majority of the documents he signed.

Gary continued. "I know you've been with Everest for quite a few years, as a matter of fact starting out in accounts payable as a clerk if I recall correctly. Do you fully understand what we do as a company?"

"Genetic engineering, biotech."

"Good, you wouldn't believe how many employees who work for us don't even know what we do or even read our corporate mission statement". Ultimately, our mission is to strive to make the world a better place through science. And you're right; we're involved in genetic engineering and biotechnologies to make improvements in medical and agriculture research. Here in the R & D accounting division, you're part of the team that manages the budgetary process for our parent company and subsidiaries across the world."

Alder felt he already knew a lot of the information Gary was giving him.

"Some of the projects go back for years and some cross disciplines, especially if we find other possible uses, though that's not as important. But some of our genetic engineering successes in biomedical, for example, have been helpful in developing techniques and processes for other sections such as agriculture."

"Any way in particular I should manage those capital investments?"

"You may not have to worry about too many of those major ones. You'll need to keep some projects close to your chest. Make sure they remain confidential. We're expecting nothing less from you and the other two new directors. Likewise, I'll be keeping some projects close to my chest. Even if there were a CFO in place, I'd still be the primary one actively assisting with managing the financials for the projects. Don't look at it as if I'm restricting your authority. It's just that I'm more intimate with some of these after working them for years. We're still going to need some coordination on your part though, for legal purposes."

Alder thought Gary was definitely limiting his authority to sign, yet capitulated. "Not a problem sir," he responded, thinking this might not be quite ethical. But he didn't want to pursue the legal ramifications.

"Good. Well, any questions for me before I send you back into the fire?"

"No, I'm good," Alder, responded. He lied. He didn't want to look like he needed help in the new position and have Gary question his selection in the first place.

"Well, if you have any questions, just ask. When Sheila gets back, I'll have her drop off some of the projects that need the most attention."

Chapter 13

The next day, returning from his run, Michael felt his internal clock had been incorrectly set; it was early in the morning and he enjoyed running in the late afternoon or early evening. Michael grabbed the paper from the front porch and poured himself a glass of orange juice mixed with apple juice. He sat down at the simple wooden table in the kitchen and started scanning the newspaper but was flabbergasted at the amount of trivial content. Michael was aware that most of his acquaintances were in the habit of reading their news on the world, the country, their community online but that wasn't his preference. He enjoyed the tactile sensation of reading physical media. After recent events, it might be a good idea to glance through the paper to see if there was anything that might lead to further research. He had to admit that he was still interested in the subject of angels but hadn't been able to figure out how to incorporate the theme into his class curriculum.

Newspapers now held less news and more entertainment drivel, community events, a smattering of local sports, and coupons and specials. The biggest focus for many who did read the newspaper was the obituaries. When first reported, angel sightings made headlines. News stories covering each event generally conveyed the same theme - why did they show up, what did they say, what did they look like. Two of the local newspapers interviewed Michael as a religious expert for a couple of news stories. Yet with all the events over the years, no one could capture a single picture or video. Over time, the stories moved to page two, then further in, ultimately ending up in the same section as the obituaries for gawkers, followers, and others who would view past events and attempt to forecast future visits. Funerals had become the new entertainment social activity. Families got into arguments about who would attend. Radio and television talk shows got into the hysteria, giving away attendance vouchers in contests held over the air. Companies held raffles. The un-ceremonial interment of bodies by counties for John and Jane Does became popular well-attended events with anticipation that an angel might show up.

Before the popularity of these visitations, people were often hesitant to attend funerals, forced to think of their own mortality. People now felt the possibility that an afterlife of eternal bliss for all mankind might exist. Michael remembered reading one article in which a witness stated the angel foretold of the beauty before us as we pass from this life to the next.

Just then, a short, sandy-haired young women, hair halfway down her back, wearing a campus T-shirt and red-and-blue-checked pajama bottoms entered the kitchen. She went straight to the refrigerator and pulled out a container of orange juice.

"I'd thought you'd left already," Michael questioned, still reading the paper.

"Why, you wanna get rid of me?" she responded.

"No, it's just that I need to finish getting ready for the trip to Mexico. Father Hernandez and Sister Justine will be here soon to go to the airport."

"And you don't want to be seen with me? Just like at the deli when you acted like you didn't know who I was. You know, that really pissed me off."

Michael put the paper down on the tabletop and eyed Alicia. *Now she brings this up.* "Look, I'm sorry. You have to remember that it's considered unprofessional for me to be seeing you anyway. And those two being religious and all, well you know? Plus it was as much your idea as mine to keep this somewhat discreet, especially with your boyfriend away in England. Remember it was you who said we should act like you were just one of my students."

"Well, did you mean what you said about my hair?"

Michael rummaged through his thoughts trying to recollect what she could be talking about in regards to her hair. He didn't recall making any specific comments over the last several days. "Now what the hell are you talking about?"

"Same time back at the deli when I had the pens and pencils in my hair?"

And she brings this up too? Michael thought. "You mean that it looked like a skewered bun was on the top of your head?" He recalled.

"Yeah."

"Sure as shit did."

"You can really be an asshole sometimes, you know that?" Alicia remarked.

"Your point is?" Michael countered.

Alicia remained quiet and returned to pouring a glass of orange juice.

"So, how long are you gonna be gone?" Alicia asked, trying to mask a hint of loneliness.

"A week or two, don't know. I guess it depends on what we find out," Michael answered.

Soft knocking at the door drew both away from their conversation. Michael glanced at the clock on the microwave. He was running about 30 minutes late. *Damn,* he thought. He tried to figure out how he fell behind in getting ready. Then he recalled Alicia had wanted to spend extra time cuddling and talking when they woke up. Michael thought, "*What the hell?*" since he wouldn't see her for a while. He got up to answer the door.

Father Hernandez and Sister Justine entered the kitchen behind Michael to see Alicia leaning against the countertop sipping a glass of orange juice. Both guests did not expect to see a young college aged female in the room. She possessed a familiar face but one the two visitors couldn't place in context. Michael was astounded that Alicia hadn't gone back into the bedroom.

"Father, Sister, this is Alicia. She's going to be housesitting for me. Alicia, this is Father Hernandez and Sister Justine. They're the ones I've told you that I'm working with, to try to figure out what happened at the funeral home where everyone died."

Father Hernandez was the first to reach out to shake her hand. "Nice to meet you."

Sister Justine mirrored the priest in her response.

Making sure there would be no awkward moments or comments, Michael spoke up. "I'm packed, I just gotta take a shower and get dressed. Then I'll be ready to go."

"You know what Mr. Saunders?" Father Hernandez said, trying to obscure his disapproval. "We still need to get gas for the car. We'll leave and come back in about 15 minutes. We'll still have plenty of time to get to the airport."

"Fine, I'll be ready when you get back."

Both Father Hernandez and Sister Justine tried to get a definitive final glance at Alicia before being escorted out by Michael. It was then that Sister Justine recalled where she'd seen Alicia.

"Michael, the girl at the deli? Come on? You should be ashamed," she remarked, whispering to make sure Michael's guest in the kitchen couldn't hear.

"What're you talking about? She's just house-sitting."

"Dressed like that?"

"She slept on the futon."

Sister Justine smirked, she didn't believe him. She followed Father Hernandez out the door. When Michael returned to the kitchen, Alicia stared at him with a quizzical expression he didn't recognize.

"If I didn't know better, I could swear you like her," Alicia noted. "You do, don't you?"

"What the hell are you talking about?" Michael said adamantly, trying to cover up emotions he assumed he successfully suppressed.

"I could see it. I wasn't sure at the deli, but just now, definitely."

Michael dismissed her comment. "She's a nun for god's sake. You know what, I'm gonna take a shower. I'll see you when I get out. And by the way, you don't have to worry about leaving; I told them you were house-sitting."

"I know, I was there when you said it," she quipped.

Securing the locks on his luggage, Michael imagined he would never see Justine again. Now he was getting ready to go with her on a research trip to Mexico. Yes, Alicia was in his life, but he couldn't say that he loved her. He did not have the feelings for her that he felt for Justine years ago. Michael was never sure he could get close to anyone again. Maybe it was his feeling betrayed by the Church, the disappearance of his family and his close friends, or Justine ending their relationship. For her, it was a committed relationship with God; a relationship that did not include him. Michael questioned why he initially started his quest to become a priest more than ten years ago. It was a question he couldn't answer. If he'd completed his studies and became ordained, realistically there would be no way he or Justine could ever be together. Maybe it was just the thought of being close to her that fueled his earlier motivation to attend seminary. Pushing his emotions aside, his curiosity was fueled by wanting to see if he could determine if what happened at the church in Mexico ten years ago and the recent tragedies were connected. He was back in the game doing something he immensely enjoyed, the research and investigation of the veracity of angels and related religious matters.

III. The Eulogy of Angels: Aguascalientes

Chapter 14

The sun-beaten-green taxi pulled up to the weatherworn Spanish-colonial-style church. Two new, 12-feet-tall, elaborately engraved wooden doors, in contrast to the rustic appearance of the edifice, stood majestically atop 12 aged concrete steps. The cab driver emptied the luggage and gear onto the sidewalk. A tanned, thin Hispanic man, no older than 26 or 27, came out to greet his American guests. His priestly collar, almost too large for his neck, did not fit snuggly or comfortably. If Father Hernandez, Michael, and Sister Justine had anticipated someone older, they were forced to remember that since the disappearance, many parishes had been emptied except for a few remaining members of the congregation, clergy and staff. In other churches, nearly all the congregation remained, yet the clergy and staff disappeared. Many of the remaining priests abandoned the Church, as had Michael. Many of the open positions at local parishes were first filled by clergy from other countries with an excess. Positions in the upper echelons went unfilled for years until replacements for vacant junior positions were recruited and trained. As the new pope had noted during a formal announcement from the succeeding "Council of Paris: Elected Survivors", their mission was to ensure that both the elected and the remaining faithful sheep continued to be shepherded.

The young priest came down the stairs reaching out to shake each of their hands and greeted his guests with what each took to be a genuine smile, with a firm handshake. "Welcome my friends. I'm Father Victorio Manuel Esteban Dominguez. I received the email from Cardinal Millhouse and Bishop Grielle informing us of your visit. Bishop Listanos and I just want to say we're available for anything you need."

Father Hernandez reciprocated the greeting. "We appreciate your hospitality Father. We promise not to be a burden."

"The Cardinal and Bishop weren't quite clear as to why exactly you're here. The email said you're doing some historical research on one of the previous supernatural eulogy events."

The three reached to grab their luggage, but Father Dominguez stopped them before they could lift any of the pieces. "Don't worry about your luggage, one of the church volunteers will be out in a moment to take it to the visitors' parsonage. Will you need transportation or anything else for tomorrow?"

"Yes, we'd like to head out to Our Lady of Hope in the El Refugio region."

Father Dominguez's jovial expression became stone-faced. "You're here to investigate the tragic event of ten years ago? There are those here in the city who still talk about it, especially since what happened in your country recently."

"Well, we're not sure if we're gonna find anything," Sister Justine commented.

"Wasn't there a team here ten years ago? I remember a couple of our older parishioners talking about it. They said the team acted more like an old married couple than clergy or church representatives."

Michael felt he needed to comment. "Myself and Sister Justine were that team, padre."

Father Dominguez was not sure how to react. "Oh. Sorry. Maybe you can tell me more of what happened, and what's going on, over dinner. Let's go ahead and get the three of you settled in."

* * * *

Michael enjoyed the authentic taste of the meal. The lime-and chili-flavored grilled chicken was more flavorful than overly spicy hot as cooked in Southern California, something he appreciated even though he did sometimes enjoy spicy foods. The accompanying black beans were tender and seasoned to perfection with onions, cumin, chili, garlic, and a hint of sorghum molasses.

"So Michael, how is it you're part of this investigation since you're no longer with the Church?" Father Dominguez asked, breaking the silence at the table. He had only received limited background information in the arrival-notification email.

"I was intrigued by angels and studied them intensely while in seminary. I wrote several papers on the subject on their nature, character, and history as well as their influence in Church and human history. For some reason, the powers that be thought I would be of benefit on this little jaunt."

"You mentioned that you and Sister Justine worked together when you came down?"

"So, Father Dominguez, have you ever officiated a funeral with an unexpected angelic guest showing up to present a eulogy?" Father Hernandez asked to change the subject.

"Well no, I've only been down here about a year now. It was pretty quiet here until I came on board. Priests from other churches would come to celebrate mass and accept confessions. The church was becoming run down. We're lucky because we receive a large and consistent donation from a major benefactor so we're able to remain open. Many of our associated churches have either already or are about to close their doors. Ironically, because of the large corporate donations to our parish, we were able to recently replace the primary doors to the sanctuary here and remain open. Plus, we're fortunate to be able to sponsor a couple of the local clinics here in the area."

"Did I understand correctly that you've only been down here for a year?" Father Hernandez asked.

"I grew up in Phoenix."

"So, then, with the task at hand, would you happen to know anyone we could talk to in El Refugio who may have been around ten years ago?"

"I couldn't be sure. We can ask around in the congregation."

"We'd like to visit the church," Sister Justine noted.

"Shouldn't be too much of a problem. You just have to be careful. It's been closed since the fatal event ten years ago and is considered condemned."

"Condemned? Really? Why?"

"The townspeople never gathered up the nerve to go back into the cathedral. They consider it cursed by God."

"Do you know if anyone else has been here to investigate anything further since we were here last time?" Michael questioned.

"I couldn't tell you," Father Dominguez responded. "Being here only a short time, I haven't had a chance to learn much more than the general lay of the land, spiritually speaking that is. I've never been out to El Refugio. But we found old records and journals, administrative notes, from the local churches in the area dating back years. Since the church was one of our sister parishes, there may be some information that could be of help, especially if it was transferred as part of the close down. When Lucinda comes in, she can help you navigate through some of the material and show you what's been cataloged to date."

Father Dominguez's three guests exchanged a glance; each struck with the same thought, there could well be information relating to their research. Michael initially thought the trip would end up being a waste of time. Now he was beginning to believe there could be a benefit to coming down.

"Sister, Michael, would you like to visit the church later? I think we should attempt to review and examine some of the documents that were found here first," said Father Hernandez.

Father Dominguez interjected before either could answer. "Father, I'm not quite sure you understand. We're still in the process of sorting and cataloging everything that's been found. This church has been the staging area for many of the records for the other churches that have been closing down throughout much of this area."

"Well, how soon do you think the Sisters on your staff would be able to find old records from Our Lady of Hope?"

Father Dominguez answered, giving his peer a bewildered expression. "Father, once again, I believe you don't understand; we currently don't have any nuns on our staff."

"You're right, I don't understand. What do you mean?"

"After all these years, the church is finally coming back to life. Bishop Listanos has been working feverishly with all of the parishes to attempt to staff properly. We are not all as lucky to have large congregations where attention is focused, such as in Los Angeles. With the papacy continually working to realign the orders of nuns to traditional spiritual roles, we're all pretty much relying on volunteers, deacons, and the like to take care of the duties here."

"Realign to 'traditional spiritual roles'?" Sister Justine chimed in. The men at the table sensed that she was irked but she contained a larger outburst. "Don't you mean more like subtle inquisition? Ever since many of the orders, especially those in the States, moved away from traditional roles, the wearing of traditional garb and habits, Rome has consistently tried to underhandedly or covertly influence how we live and work in serving God. We set out to expand the Church's influence in the world as we're called to do in accomplishing our good works. It could be by teaching in nontraditional ways in schools other than traditional Catholic schools. It could be serving in the field in mission outreach hospitals or clinics instead of being relegated only to Church hospitals. Take myself, for example, I work in a neighborhood center in a spiritual capacity."

"Wouldn't you agree that tradition provides the foundation of what we believe?"

"Now, I don't agree with all the changes attempted by all orders, for example, priests being able to marry. We still need to maintain a sense of humility and subservience, which is why I still wear the modest vestures from time to time. Many have shied away from the traditional attire as much as possible. After so many Sisters ended up disappearing, Rome backed off so as not to force more to leave. Only during the last couple of years, as the ranks have begun to grow again, was there an attempt to reign in the orders."

"I think it's an unfair characterization to call what Rome is doing an "inquisition." Since the branching out of the orders, the basic administration and operation of the local churches, schools, and hospitals has been dangerously eroded."

"If not for the freedoms of my order, I wouldn't have been able to work and teach in the inner city, which has brought many to the Church."

Michael chuckled and the other three turned to see him grinning.

"What's so funny Mr. Saunders?" Father Dominguez inquired, still wound up from his verbal sparring with Sister Justine.

"You three. The church has been debating issues like this for years and will debate them years from now. And you know what, you still probably won't solve shit."

"It's because of these debates that the Church is capable of remaining relevant in serving our Lord," Father Hernandez reacted.

"So you say. Many times in its history, the Church has been rigid in many of its traditions and beliefs. Hell, look at apostolic succession."

"You know Mr. Saunders, I'm not sure you're quite qualified to question a basic tenet of the Holy Church," Father Dominguez retorted.

"I think someone as young as you may not be as well versed to fully understand the intricacies and history of the Church," Michael countered.

"Not being that young and serving in the Church make him more qualified to speak on internal matters of the Church than someone who never finished seminary," Father Hernandez intervened, giving Michael a sharp stare that was returned in kind.

Michael and Father Hernandez locked their gaze. No one spoke for a couple of minutes. After watching the tag-team debate against Michael, Sister Justine felt she needed to break the uncomfortable face-off and attempt to end the confrontation. "Maybe we should work out our game plan for the next couple of days?"

The three men reluctantly agreed and grudgingly worked out their strategy for heading out to the church in El Refugio. Michael decided to call it an evening after finishing his meal and excused himself from the table. Father Dominguez waited until Michael had departed the dining area and was out of earshot before asking, "So why is Mr. Saunders a part of your investigation team? I understand he was involved during the first investigation at Our Lady of Hope. What could he offer now, especially not being involved with the Church anymore?"

"Bishop Grielle perhaps thought there might be something we missed last time or that he could provide a unique insight. Plus, he did come across alleged remnants of an angel," Sister Justine commented, defending Michael.

"It just seems that he's somewhat obstinate," Father Dominguez commented.

Justine continued. "Do you have an available computer, Father? I'd like to pull up a couple of documents I think you both may be interested in."

Father Dominguez offered the computer in his office. Sister Justine and Father Hernandez found Father Dominguez's office somewhat modest even though it had a couple of small warehouse-style metal bookshelves, a faded painting of the Madonna and child spanning from ceiling to floor, and a chipped and dinged credenza topped with a couple of small religious statues. The Father's desk was an old government-issue-type relic resembling something you would expect to see in a military museum. In front of the desk were two large and comfortable, brown leather chairs, the only furniture that didn't appear to be aged, used, or acquired from a surplus store. The adobe-bricked wall behind the desk displayed several certificates and diplomas. Atop the gray desk lay a Bible, notepad, computer monitor, keyboard, and mouse. The computer itself rested on the floor. Sister Justine went over to the keyboard, turned on the monitor, and typed and navigated at an extremely fast pace. After a few minutes she called for her two associates to join her.

"Bishop Grielle authorized access to several of the archives for us in case you wanted to review some of the work Michael accomplished while in seminary," she stated.

The two priests joined the Sister at the monitor, each scanning through the documents as she scrolled. Some of the fragments of writing they both found to be of interest:

Outside of the Bible, angels have made many appearances in the establishment of movements and major religions. These angelic visitations have influenced those who had direct contact, many times building the foundation for many of the mainstream religions that exist today...

One of the first examples is the Latter-Day Saints religion of Mormonism founded in the 1820s. In historical context, the Angel Moroni visited Joseph Smith and provided alleged tablets that present a revelation divergent from the upbringing of the founder. This follows an alleged visitation where God the Father and Jesus appeared to Joseph and told him that all the creeds of Christianity were an abomination in their sight and he was to join none of them.

Theologians of distinct evangelical beliefs and other religions point out contradictions between the message given by Moroni and those in the Bible, especially in relation to the area of Israel...

Thus even from the viewpoint of the Mormon Church, to join with other churches would be completely contrary to the early teachings of their founders...

140

Many speculate that the message given by these angels is in direct contradiction to the Bible itself. If the Church is to hold the Bible as the authoritative foundation for its belief, how are angels presented so as not to conflict or present inconsistencies to the book's veracity when held up against sister beliefs? All these and other monotheistic Judeo-Christian and Islam-based religions contained communion with angels as part of their extra biblical books or are given new revelations for a new interpretation on the Bible. Can the same angels who seemingly serve the same God say two different things on the same subject and both be true? The Koran is believed to have been communicated by the angel Gabriel based on eternal tablets in heaven. We know it is Gabriel who is the one to have made the announcement of the Christ to Holy Mother Mary. Conversely, it's described that Gabriel, the same angel, told Mohammed that God has no son and is unable to become incarnate man.

Ellen G. White, of the Seventh Day Adventist movement, was in touch with an 'accompanying angel' (Present Truth, *pp. 21-22, 1849), who revealed to her the hidden truths of the Bible. On June 27, 1850, her accompanying angel said, the "time is almost finished ... that the last seven plagues were going to be poured out before the rapture" (*Early Writings, *p. 64*). Many of her followers believed in the imminence of these events during their lifetime. They did not...*

As the Church attempts to move forward with an ecumenical collaboration between many of these religions, and if these religions are based upon the revelation of angels, we must question the authenticity of such manifestations in religious history in establishing the tenants of faith. Either one of two answers exist. First, one religion is correct in their revelation by the angelic messenger and the other religions are incorrect; or, they--that is, all religions--are incorrect...

.

.

.

so in summation, a proposed angelic visit and declaration don't warrant the accuracy of a subsequent message. They could be deceiving recipients from a greater truth.

Father Hernandez was the first to react. "I bet some of this is considered somewhat controversial in the Church and to some of its doctrines."

"His research and writings were why he was selected to determine the truth of the event down here ten years ago. What you read is just a small fragment of his works."

"Really," Father Dominguez commented.

Sister Justine continued. "He wrote a detailed treatise on the order of angels, their existence as seen in other religions, and their influence on those who experienced them. Michael at one point was highly interested in angels and somewhat prolific with the subject in his writings. When a seminary student showed such a high level of devotion to a subject, the Church took notice."

"Are most of his works similar to this?" Father Dominguez asked. Father Hernandez already knew some of Michael's background based on what Bishop Grielle had told him but not to the level of detail Sister Justine had just introduced in the fragments of his writing.

Rolling back in the steel-framed chair to address both men, she continued. "Many are similar, some even more or less controversial. There's a couple Bishop Grielle wouldn't even allow me to read. Many in the Church leadership, especially after reading his writings, felt it best if we came down here to see if there was anything to the angel story. Even though he hadn't completed seminary, the Church hierarchy felt he was far advanced on the subject and could come back with a plausible explanation."

"What did he determine?"

"We attempted to interview to the primary witness but only got a quick chance to talk to him once we got to the clinic. We were going back to follow up the next day but we were recalled to the States. Then there were the mass disappearances; there was panic all over the world. After that, Michael lost his faith, with the vanishing of his family."

"So he didn't fall into the rapture theory either?" Father Hernandez queried.

"No."

"So how did you end up going with him the first time down here?" Father Dominguez asked curiously.

"He requested that I assist."

"You have a background in angelology?"

"Not really, though I became more interested after we began the investigation. Then when the angelic eulogies started, I became more involved."

"So then why'd he request you to begin with?" Father Hernandez continued with intensity after sensing the Sister was still holding back.

Sister Justine changed the subject to the investigation at hand. "So what time should we plan to head out to the El Refugio area? Someone will need to let Michael know."

"I can do that," Father Dominguez responded, noticing her deliberate maneuvering around Father Hernandez's question. "I'm going to finish up a homily series I've been working on. Then I'm gonna call it a night. You both get some rest."

* * * *

Settling in for the evening, Father Hernandez recognized right away he would need to pray and confess the antagonism effervescing in his soul toward Michael. Michael's presumed arrogance and knowledge of church doctrine irritated the priest immensely. Coupled with the decent condition of the room, which far exceeded the guest quarters in his parish, he couldn't help feel a bit envious. The quarters were reminiscent of a well-kept, inexpensive motel room. The alabaster sheets were crisp and folded with hospital corners; two pillows appeared like clouds resting at the headboard, the light-brown-and-green paisley bedding set nicely rolled back. A polished wooden desk sat squarely in the corner. After closer inspection of the desk, what the Father thought might have been laminate-covered particleboard was actually solid wood, possibly even mahogany. Matching single-drawer nightstands, with open shelf space below, soldiered at each side of the bed. Atop each nightstand were small brass-based reading lamps with stained-glass lamp shades. *How could this church afford such furnishings?* Father Hernandez thought.

Perhaps the review of several verses in the Bible for his evening devotionals would help distract him from his mental transgressions. He opened his Bible to a random page, which was something he tried to do once a week to gather unique insights he might have never considered or might've forgotten over time. The Father opened the book to Genesis, chapter 12, the story of Abraham and the announcement of the blessings and cursing toward the nation Israel. It was strange that in the last couple of weeks, each time he did this providential exercise, whether in the Old or New Testament, the verses pointed to that nation and God's purported protection of its people. It reminded him how his mentor's boss, Cardinal Millhouse, maintained unsympathetic, if not hostile, views toward Israel, sometimes inferring God was finished with the nation in his grand plan for Jews in human history, a viewpoint that neither he personally nor his mentor Bishop Grielle agreed with. Father Hernandez considered this could have been one of the reasons Bishop Grielle frequently wasn't made aware of many of the activities within the Diocese. Cardinal Millhouse's subtle ostracizing of Bishop Grielle was well observed by many of the other priests under the Bishop's tutelage. They were reserved in their true feelings, having no respect for the Bishop, believing he was one easily compromised on his ideals. Father Hernandez knew that with limited promotion possibilities, he would remain dedicated to his parish and the Church. The politics of the hierarchy or advancement wasn't his concern. After an hour of reading and prayers, Father Hernandez called it an early night.

Chapter 15

Michael wondered how he'd ended up in the backseat with Father Hernandez. Maybe it was modern day chivalry. Sister Justine did have a smaller frame, and both men had relinquished the front passenger seat of the small VW Pointer to give her more room. Protocol for the day could easily call for the Sister to be acquiescent to the Father, given that he was theoretically one level closer to the Holy Father. As Michael couldn't care less about who was higher on the spiritual totem pole anymore, and hadn't thought about it for nearly ten years, he thought to himself that there were other reasons for being accommodating to Sister Justine, primarily to show that he still possessed a semblance of manners. However, Sister Justine didn't care about Michael's standoffish attitude and dismissed it as a reflection of him being ten years consumed by the world.

Every jarring bump refocused Michael on the rough car trip to Our Lady of Hope. The road was in considerable disrepair with uneven pavement, potholes, and other roadway imperfections transmitted in each jolt by what was a lack of any working shock absorbers in the shuddering, worn-out car. The driver, Jose, was the only one not concerned with the discomfort of the ride. Michael didn't recall the trip being this rough during their previous visit. Sister Justine mentioned that it had been considerably smoother. Father Hernandez silently wanted the hour-long trip to end. The unchanging view of the empty land, semi-dry grass, and mountains protruding far in the background of the horizon didn't take away his indifference about the uncomfortable ride. Silent praying would help to pass the time.

Driving through town, there were a few scattered trees, their foliage sparse. The towered parapets of the church were the only visible structures larger than all the single-story homes, small shops, and two-story dwellings and apartments. These beige-toned, weathered, adobe-and-brick structures blended with the earth; it was as if many of the buildings grew from planted seeds and had sprouted straight up from the ground. The streets were deteriorating and crumbling along the edges. They were however, in somewhat better condition than the highway road.

As they arrived at the church, children played across the street in the small semblance of a park consisting of a few aged trees, patches of grass and shrubbery, a few wooden benches, a slide, and a swing set with two of the three swing seats broken. On one of the benches, set within an alcove of overgrown hedges, a burgeoning overweight elderly man was feeding scraps of meat to a three-legged beagle who hobbled to the pieces tossed on the ground.

The church structure now had plywood planks where once there were windows. The cracks in the small set of stairs leading to the main doors sprouted grass and weeds, the building itself was structurally sound. Jose drove around the rear of the edifice to where a wooden fence bordered what once had been the gardens, outside terrace, and patio that formed a mini-fortress around access to the rear door. They exited the car and worked their way through knee-high dry grass and brush. The rear door, like the front entrance, was the only other opening not boarded over.

Jose pulled a clump of different-sized keys from his pocket, some brass in color, some silver, a couple copper; one of the copper keys unlocked the door. Inside was a short hallway and an odor of moldy and stagnant air. The four viewed a doorway into a kitchen area just to the right of the entrance. Sister Justine noted a small stack of dusty plates on one side of the sink. She could have sworn they were in the same position as when she and Michael had last come through.

"Father, Sister, what you looking for?" Jose asked in hesitant English, ignoring Michael.

"We don't quite know yet," Father Hernandez answered.

Penetrating deeper into the building, the three began searching for anything unique, out of the ordinary, or relevant to their investigation. Michael and Sister Justine, now having more time than in their first visit, both considered that they still might not find anything relevant. The rear areas of the kitchen, two small office areas, a storage room, and a small meeting room all showed the same signs of abandonment already encountered throughout the church. A couple of the rooms displayed evidence of someone who had been bold enough to attempt and straighten up furniture, books, and knickknacks after the site was thought cursed by God. As expected, the sanctuary pews and dusty rows of dark-stained benches displayed being unused during the last decade. They found nothing of interest. Father Hernandez was becoming frustrated in his hope of finding anything to substantiate the indicators that had led to Our Lady of Hope. At first he reasoned he was tasked just to follow up, knowing nothing else would be found of spiritual significance. This would be so that the Church hierarchy could say they did their due diligence looking into the affair. However, the strange pattern from the layout of the deceased bodies and the reported televised visitation was more interesting than he once considered. The elation of finding the two distinct earlier clues in Los Angeles had encouraged him to think something more could be found.

The church visit turned out to be a letdown; Michael progressed to considering the trip more of a free vacation, although he did enjoy spending time again with Justine. It was Sister Justine, the most pragmatic of the three, dedicating full effort to the investigation. Pulling random hymnals and Bibles from the holders placed neatly behind the pews, blowing off dust and sneezing occasionally, she flipped through numerous pages for the doodles, scribbling, and notes written in Spanish, periodically asking Father Hernandez to ensure she translated correctly. Nothing showed any indications of an angel visit or of the fatal event in the church.

Father Hernandez observed her skimming through a hymnal and then returning its holder. "You think there may actually be something of importance in the hymnals or Bibles, Sister?"

Sister Justine took thought it likely that no one else had analyzed the books. "It's possible, then again, who knows if they were scrutinized when they straightened up in here."

"Are you saying it's not the same as when you both were down here last?"

Michael and Sister Justine glanced at each other. Michael commented first. "Come to think of it, we didn't get a chance to fully look at everything the first time. I do remember that when they did allow us in, it wasn't as organized as we see it now. A lot more dust now though. Personal effects are gone and, you know what, some of the hymnals were out. Probably used for the funeral service that was going on at the time."

All three attacked the hymnals and Bibles, skimming the pages, hoping to find something relevant. After an hour, nothing; both Father Hernandez and Sister Justine were disappointed, the Father feeling like he'd been punched in the stomach. Michael couldn't care less.

"So where do we go from here?" Father Hernandez asked disheartened, as he and Sister Justine huddled in one of the middle pews.

All three heard a small thudding knock at the main entrance of the sanctuary.

"Could that be Jose outside?" Sister Justine asked, quizzing her two companions.

Jose, walking in from the rear offices into the sanctuary asked, "Could be Jose, how?" After spending a couple of hours just sitting around in the back bored, he hoped the three were ready to leave.

Another small thud came from the front door. All four rushed to the front entrance of the church with Jose fumbling to grab the keys in his pocket. When he swung the door open, a small rubber ball bounced through the opening, almost hitting Jose in the chest. Outside the opened door, two small boys looking to be 8 or 9 years old, stood frozen with their mouths wide open. Startled to see the door open as they were bouncing a ball against it, they were horrified to see four figures emerging from the darkened doorway. Running away from the church down the street, the boys frantically yelled *"espíritus malignos, espíritus malignos"* in soprano voices.

"What the hell are they yelling about?" Michael asked wanting to verify he fully comprehended what the boys were saying.

"I think 'evil spirits,'" Father Hernandez answered.

"Sí, that's what they say," Jose added.

"Great," Michael commented. "This ought to be fun. I thought that's what they were saying."

It was Sister Justine who gathered the attention of the three men and focused on a middle-aged Hispanic woman who was now sitting on the bench previously occupied by the man and his pet beagle. The woman adjusted the shawl on her silver-streaked coal-colored hair and waved for the four to come over.

"Jose, go ahead and lock up the church. I think we've done enough looking today. And please bring the car around," Father Hernandez politely directed, keeping his eyes on the woman in the park.

"Sí, Padre," Jose responded.

Michael, as he walked across the street, wasn't sure why the woman appeared out of place. She was dressed in clothing similar to other residents in the town but the dress and shawl appeared to have been intentionally "distressed" to look shabby and weatherworn. Getting a closer look at her features, she appeared middle aged with a tanned olive complexion, and a small mole residing her right eye.

"Podemos ayudarle señora?" Father Hernandez asked, wondering if the woman needed help.

She responded in near-flawless English sprinkled with a mild accent: "As usual, my father was right. It's been ten years and he knew those who came before to investigate what happened in the church would return."

"Excuse me, but do we know you?" Sister Justine asked.

"My name is Ashere, and no, you do not know me; nevertheless, my father knows you. He watched the two of you when you were last down here."

"Well, may we meet your father?" Father Hernandez asked.

"Oh, my father left here quite a while ago. He did want me to pass on to you that, even though you won't find what you're looking for here in town, you should not give up. You'll find what you're looking for not long from now."

"And just what in the hell are we looking for?" Michael asked.

Ashere smiled, "Why, the angels and why what has happened here also happened in Los Angeles."

"What do you know about the angels?" Father Hernandez asked with a firm force the other two hadn't noticed from him except during previous tauntings by Michael.

"Only what my father has told me."

"And who is your father?"

"The most religious are the most blind," Ashere responded, then snapped her head to the right. Michael,

Sister Justine, and Father Hernandez reflexively followed suit, turning to see the two boys who were earlier playing and scared away from the church now at the far edge of the park dragging two adult males by their hands. Both men appeared reluctant to be towed along. The three could hear the boys, still frantic, speaking fast, and pointing to Father Hernandez, Sister Justine, and Michael saying repeatedly in essence: See, there they are! The evil spirits, they're over there!

Sister Justine focused her attention away from the boys back to the park bench but it was empty. "Where'd she go?"

The other two turned back, astonished to see the empty bench.

"Where the hell is she?" Michael asked.

They scanned the fractured, cracked, and pitted sidewalks of the park but Ashere was nowhere in view.

Father Hernandez went to engage the two men dragged by the boys. After seeing the Father's Roman collar, listening to his explanation for being in the deserted church, and then gently scolding the children, both men seemed satisfied. Father Hernandez took the opportunity to ask if they'd seen or knew of a woman with Ashere's description. One of the men said he didn't recall a woman with that name or even such a female living in the town. He then explained, seeming excited that he had someone new to talk to, that the little community was close. In the past, social life centered on the church, but since the deaths over ten years ago, many of the town's residents moved away. During the last five to six years, the small town was coming back to life, due in part to the reopening of a reputed clinic and small research lab in the nearby badlands. The church remained closed, still considered cursed.

The men returned to their previous endeavors, and it was at this time the three observed Jose's deteriorating vehicle pulling up next to the park. They decided to head back to Aguascalientes.

* * * *

As he removed his garments and collar upon return to his office after accomplishing his daily duties, including the receiving of confessions, Father Dominguez received his three visitors who sat down tired from their excursion. Somewhat sweaty, dusty, and confused, they kept their composure relatively intact. Father Hernandez and Sister Justine sat in the two large leather chairs in front of the desk. Father Hernandez pondered the stark contrast of the adornments and furnishings in Father Dominguez's office compared with those in the guest quarters. He imagined Michael's and Sister Justine's rooms were also well furnished.

Michael sat on a simple wood chair in the back of the room, rocking it back and forth on the two rear legs, his back propping his body weight against the adjacent wall. Knowing the chair to be somewhat aged and not well made, Father Dominguez wasn't sure if it might lose its integrity and cause Michael to fall to the floor. Instead of warning Michael, he thought the fall might humble him a bit.

"Sorry it took me so long. Today's confessions took a little longer than I anticipated. How'd your trip go?" Father Dominguez asked.

"The church itself didn't yield anything. There was one interesting thing though," Father Hernandez replied.

"What's that?" Father Dominguez responded while sitting down in his chair.

"We came across a strange character today. Her name was Ashere."

"Who?"

"Ashere."

"What happened?"

"We met her in the park across from the church. She mentioned something about her father knowing about our visit. She also knew we were there investigating the presence of angels."

Michael jumped into the conversation. "Ever think that she could have been a manifestation of an angel? I mean come on, one minute she's there, and then she's not."

The other three turned to face Michael, who was still rocking on the two rear legs of the chair. He rested the front legs of the chair on the ground, leaned forward, and placed his forearms on his legs. "Whether it's biblical history or in other religious mythos, angels, gods, demigods many times manifest themselves as human in brief encounters, usually resulting in those experiencing what we experienced."

"Then what do you think the purpose of the visit was?" Father Hernandez inquired skeptically.

"I think the answer is simple. She told us we would find what we're looking for, although not here in town."

"And what about her father, she mentioned her father knew us. What would that be about?"

Michael paused a minute before answering. "Haven't figured that one out yet. I don't remember meeting anybody interesting last time we were down here."

"I don't either," Sister Justine added.

"Well, I have some information for you," Father Dominguez commented. "Lucinda began working with a couple of volunteers and started sorting the boxes of paperwork from the archives of Our Lady of Hope. We're having them begin with what they could find from ten years ago. They came across the church records, journals, baptismal and confirmation logs, and other administrative documents generated during the tenure of Father Ynez."

"Father Ynez?" Father Hernandez probed.

"He was the senior Father both here and for our sister church, Our Lady of Hope."

Father Dominguez guided the three to an office area that had varying sized filing boxes stacked along the wall. In the center stood a large, rectangular, light-colored wood table with four chairs, one on each side. "We haven't done a full sort yet. Everything near the time frame you're looking for is already on the table."

"Much of the information is still here? It wasn't sent to Los Angeles or Rome after the initial events?" Sister Justine quizzed.

"Many of them were packed and ready to be shipped, and remember, shortly after you left the first time, the worldwide missing event happened. With the follow-on panic and chaos in the world, the Church probably forgot all about them. Lucky for you."

157

Father Hernandez, Sister Justine, and Michael skimmed the notepads, papers, and parchments. Michael approached reviewing the information apathetically, thinking they wouldn't find anything pertinent thinking much of the research process was turning out to be a waste of time. Father Hernandez and Sister Justine on the other hand, attacked examining the paperwork with intensity and vigor. All three worked late into the night and didn't find anything confirming Michael's supposition about an angelic visit. They decided to call it an evening with the heaviness of sleep encroaching.

* * * *

After an early breakfast, it was during the examination of the documents the next morning that Father Hernandez came upon the private journals of Father Ynez. "I can't believe it," he said, "these journal entries written by Father Ynez are invaluable. Oh my gosh, these equate to a mini-timeline concerning what happened during the first supposed visitation. How did these get past the Church?"

Michael eagerly studied the same journal. He was in his element, researching information. "I remember some of these events noted here. They probably didn't think these were important at the time, since most of the information didn't cover the major event, just daily administration b.s. There's a hell of a lot of paperwork here. They probably didn't collect everything and then never got back to it after what happened a week later with the disappearances and the confusion--planes dropping out of the sky, cars crashing into each other."

Father Hernandez continued with his train of thought. "It must have been missed altogether when someone just skimmed through the beginning pages of the ledgers and thought they didn't contain anything interesting. Listen to this," Father Hernandez read in Spanish from the pages, sometimes having to slow down for the benefit of Michael and Sister Justine, though knowledgeable, but not fluent.

After Brother Simon came out to assist with several confirmations, a baptismal, and a christening, due to the quarantine established in the area, he called to brief the situation. He was then directed to return to Our Lady of Hope.

Hearing about the death of his mentor Father Lopez has shaken Brother Simon very much. He is devastated, just as much also for those attending the funeral of Victorio Garza. Brother Simon mentioned that there is one survivor of what had happened in the sanctuary. An email has been forwarded to Cardinal Jimenez in Mexico City and Cardinal Millhouse in Los Angeles.

Father Hernandez skipped over several of the administrative entries and continued:

Brother Simon has called to pass on extraordinary information. The one witness and survivor inside the church claimed he was there for confession to relieve his soul of the guilt concerning something he had been working on. Upon waiting, he claimed the sweetest aroma embraced his nose and it was then an angel did appear. The name of this possible entity was said to be called Abriel, being the same one prompting him to leave

159

some sort of compound before an appointed time. He claims the angel was the source responsible for the deaths of all the souls within the church. May God have mercy on their souls.

"So is this where you encountered the name Abriel before?" Father Hernandez asked, directing his question to Michael and Sister Justine.

"Yes, during the brief time we spent with the survivor, I can't remember his name, he was the one who mentioned the angel's name," Sister Justine answered.

Father Hernandez continued reading.

To my surprise, the Holy Church, by means of Monsignor Grielle, who has been assigned to oversee the events at Our Lady of Hope, did communicate they would send one or more clergymen to come and investigate said angel. After telling His Excellence to dispatch a team would not be necessary, as it is believed the deaths were natural in cause due to a virus outbreak. Aversol Industries, our loving patron supporting our program to feed and immunize the less fortunate, has it upon themselves to open up their local clinic in El Refugio for the treatment of others who may become infected and maintain the quarantine on the one survivor in the church when all others expired.

"Ok, here's another entry."

The two investigators, sent on behalf of the Holy Church, are willing to accept the legitimacy of the one survivor. For reasons untold, they were instructed not to reveal to anyone, except unto Monsignor Grielle, what they have found to date. According to Brother Simon, it is said that the condition of the deceased was one of the reasons for the acceptance of the veracity of the survivor.

"Here's the final entry before the disappearance of Brother Simon and Father Ynez."

I was briefed by Monsignor G. that the Church recalled our brother and sister in the Lord for circumstances unknown. We're extremely puzzled by Brother Simon's report that the World Health Organization team is unable to find anyone else infected or casualties of a virus to have killed the leadership, congregation, and church visitors at Our Lady of Hope. It is believed that whatever did happen here is natural in occurrence and warrants no further investigation, regardless of what was thought by the team that was recalled. I find I must disagree with the findings of the two sent to investigate the reported angel sighting."

There was silence for several minutes. Michael commented first, "A lot of this we already knew. As a matter of fact, if I had my notes..." Michael stopped midsentence and gave Sister Justine and Father Hernandez an angry stare before continuing, "we could compare them to see if anything stands out that we may have missed."

"Michael, grow up. Your notes weren't stolen and I'm quite sure there's enough here to help us figure out what's going on."

"So why did you two think there was something supernatural?" Father Hernandez chimed in.

"A couple of days after the deaths, the state of decomposition was abnormal, the eyes and tongue appeared dissolved or rotted out, just like those who died in L.A.," Sister Justine answered.

"Hence the entry by Father Ynez about the deceased bodies," Michael added.

"So how come there's no name for the alleged witness?" Father Hernandez asked.

"He didn't have a passport, no identification or anything to determine who he was. During the course of the next week, well, he disappeared with the others," Sister Justine responded.

Michael, now a bit more interested, jumped in and started reviewing the journal pages with greater attention. Father Hernandez continued going through paperwork. Sister Justine searched some of the other boxes to determine the order they were arranged in and focus her search. Many of the boxes were initially organized by year, then month. She zeroed in on the apparent one for the month of the decade-old episode. She came across many of the journals and logs for officiated christenings, baptismals, confirmations, and funerals. Then she remembered to focus in on the funeral of the first incident. During their first visit, with the rush of activity from the medical teams, security forces, and news media, they weren't able to logically sit and consider the variables surrounding the situation. Scanning the pages, she found the dated entry for the funeral at Our Lady of Hope. It matched the other related entries on other documents that the angelic episode centered on the decedent Victorio Garza. Sister Justine perused new information on his membership in the church, and the date and cause of his death. Father Hernandez glanced in her direction and observed the expression on her face. He wasn't sure if she was perplexed or intrigued. Through the long days since the investigation began, he thought he might be further along in understanding her mannerisms.

"What's so interesting?" he asked curiously.

"Nothing, it's just kind of strange. Looking at some of the information here, it seems Victorio Garza was a deacon for the congregation and worked for a clinic sponsored by the Church in the area, volunteering time. On top of that, it mentions he was some sort of medical researcher," Sister Justine noted as she rustled through several more papers. "Yeah, here it mentions the company he worked for was called Aversol."

"Hmm, that is interesting. I think I recall going through Ynez's journal about the company being a sponsor organization of the local church. It was some sort of biomedical company," Father Hernandez added, searching through the papers. He stopped midway through after thinking about the first event in Los Angeles. "What's really a strange coincidence is that in the States, a lot of those who died either worked, or were family members of the ones who worked, for a biomedical company."

"Wasn't it a different company name though?" Sister Justine asked.

"Yeah, Waterfall Medical Research, a subsidiary of Everest Groups International, if I recall correctly."

"And what company did the survivor, Stephen Williams work for?" she continued.

Father Hernandez responded, "I think it was Everest as well."

"OK, aside from two different medical research companies both here and in the States, are there any other similar connections?" Michael jumped in. Both his associates remained quiet.

Reviewing the documentation before them, they couldn't come up with a response. "It's probably all just a coincidence anyway. We shouldn't waste our time," Michael continued.

Perusing more baptismal logs, funeral logs, confirmation logs, and other church administration documents for Our Lady of Hope, both Father Hernandez and Sister Justine could not find anything they considered of importance. Michael, unphased, had moved from his previous mild euphoria of finding the earlier journal entries.

"Are we really going to find anything else?" Michael asked skeptically.

"I don't know. Besides, it's getting late and I'm getting tired," Father Hernandez answered.

"Well good, because I want to go for a run," Michael said, making an untidy attempt to stack the papers, journal books, and other documents into logical stacks on the tabletop. "Plus, I'm getting hungry."

Michael partly told the truth. As much as he enjoyed researching, and was feeling the onset of jet lag, he did intend to go for a run. Yet he also wanted to try to recall as much as possible of what he read and add it to his personal journal clandestinely to avoid losing his notes again. He trusted Sister Justine but considered Father Hernandez an appendage to the serpent Bishop Grielle.

"We'll get with Father Dominguez and get something to eat when you get back from your jog," said Father Hernandez.

Michael took that as implied consent and didn't waste any time in departing. Father Hernandez thought Michael was weary and losing focus. Sister Justine was becoming frustrated there were no logical pathways to concrete answers. She continued perusing the documents with the feeling that something would jump out and tie it all together. After firm encouragement from Father Hernandez, she decided to call it an evening and accomplish her evening prayers and devotional study.

* * * *

Michael considered the day a complete waste. Going through the journals, logs, and other church records revealed nothing more than a scattering of previously seen information.

As he headed out into the streets, the late fall air bathed somber warmth upon his face. The cloudless sky was lifeless, quiet and the air stagnant and dense with unseasonable humidity, which made running strenuous. This added to the frustration he was beginning to feel again questioning why he had agreed to work on this investigation. Maybe he really did want to spend time with Sister Justine again. He had challenged her to leave the Church after the mass disappearance of family, friends, and even some professional antagonists who was against him while in seminary that held a more rigid evangelical fundamental view of their beliefs. But Justine, after coming to grips with the situation, took it as another test of faith. When she had to decide between God and Michael, her decision was to take a pledge to the Church and commit to her vows. To see her after nearly ten years, Michael thought any emotional attachments had been chased out by other distractions in his life, so the intensity of the current relationship took him by surprise.

As he ran through the distinct and unfamiliar neighborhoods, the setting sun barely reflected in the dirty windows of homes and small stores. The aromas of evening meals being prepared, tortillas warming, corn roasting, a fragrance resembling black beans in molasses based sauce simmering with the pungent spices of peppers, cilantro, and onions, all pierced his concentration forcing him to focus on his own growing hunger. When Michael did force himself to concentrate on the information he and the team had come across, memories of his visit here with Sister Justine ten years earlier came up in force. He also reflected on the odd visit of the mysterious woman on the bench, bewildering and vague with her comments before disappearing from their view.

Michael was coming up to the turnaround point in his run, and the more he debated whether remaining in Mexico would be of benefit, the more he felt it was a useless trip. The church in El Refugio revealed nothing. He dismissed the issue with Ashere as a red herring. The notes, journals, logs, and other paperwork the three looked at refreshed memories of his earlier notes and information long missing. However, there was nothing new revealed to help identify what had happened down in Mexico or up in Los Angeles. The only commonality coming to mind was the single survivor and witness in both cases. Thinking more about it, the first time they talked to Stephen in Los Angeles, the more Michael determined that the interrogation had been superficial.

All Stephen told them was exactly what the newspapers had reported.

Just as surprising to Michael, was how well the change of the postmortem condition of all the deceased in the incidents in Los Angeles had been kept from the media. Still not sure if he wanted to continue with Father Hernandez and Sister Justine once they returned to Los Angeles, Michael did feel an urge to determine if angels do exist as spiritual beings to be accepted with one's own belief. After coming down the first time, and then being recalled before he could conclude about what happened, he felt as if the truth of what happened had been stolen along with his notes from the visit. If he did continue with the research and investigation, to get a sense of closure they would need to talk to Stephen again. A bonus would be the rich gravy of information to augment his religious studies program at the college.

At his turnaround point, Michael decided to take a different route back to the church. Activity on the streets was becoming sparse. He navigated down a street of rustic homes that looked like a good shortcut back to his temporary residence. Michael noticed an eerie silence blanketing the neighborhood. No children were playing, no bicyclists riding, no cars moving, no small food carts and vendors like in other streets. The noise of his feet pounding the crumbling pavement was the only sound echoing in his ears. At times Michael thought he heard another set of footsteps as if someone were running in unison behind him. Turning his head around while still jogging, no one was there. After several more yards, the reflective sound of feet pounding the ground behind him recurred. He turned around again; no one was there.

The receding sun created a multitude of shadows from the homes, parked cars, trees, bushes, and trashcans, which Michael thought were playing tricks on his eyes. Movement at the end of the street took shape as a large, murky mass with multiple legs. Slowing down, Michael looked intently and comprehended the obscure form transforming into a pack of dogs moving in his direction. Then a large brown and black German Shepherd, a smaller grey German Shepherd, two Rottweilers, one black, one black and brown, and two black mid-sized Doberman Pinschers started to emerge from the ambiguous cluster. Michael stopped to grab a couple of rocks, not sure they would be of any benefit, and calculated different escape scenarios. Should he run up to a door hoping to find it unlocked or, if locked, would knocking allow time for someone to come to his aid? The vehicles parked along the road were small and scarce and if he climbed on top, the menacing dogs could jump. The trees were only adolescent saplings that wouldn't allow him to climb, let alone support his 185 pounds. Only two full-grown trees looked as if like they could provide adequate support for climbing, but of course, they were between him and the dogs.

With no provocation, the dogs saw Michael, snarled, and broke into an immediate charge. *This is not good*, he thought, his previous planning useless as his instincts overwhelmed him. Michael turned and tried to run but tripped over his own feet and fell to the ground. Trying to stand back up and run, his legs frozen from fear, he looked down the street to see the distance between the barking dogs and himself shrinking. The dog leading the pack by nearly ten feet, a Doberman, pounced and leaped.

Michael shut his eyes and turned, instinctively putting his arms over his head to protect himself. Instead of feeling his flesh torn by the attacker's teeth, he felt a blast of air followed by a whooshing sound above him as if someone had swung a huge racket or bat. It was then, after hearing a massive thud followed by a dog's yelp, that Michael looked up to see the Doberman rolling down the street toward the pack. Astounded, Michael saw the remaining dogs turn their heads away from him. Their charging stopped. Their barking stopped. They laid down panting only 12 feet from him. The dogs looked to be obeying a command to halt and stay.

Michael turned around; for an instant, he thought he saw a tall robed figure silhouetted in the piercing brilliance of the descending sun, yet its radiance obscured his sight. In an instant, his eyesight adjusted to the flood of light; no one was there. He turned back to check the dogs; all were static, breathing heavily, except the Doberman, who was crawling back to the pack in submission. Michael slowly raised himself to his feet and took a step back. The dogs remained motionless. Once he added another 20 feet to the distance between him and the dogs, they finally stood up. With the black Rottweiler snarling, the pack turned and ran away from Michael down the road. Backtracking and detouring over a couple of blocks, Michael resumed his original route to complete his jog.

* * * *

During Michael's absence Father Hernandez found himself assisting in the evening service with Father Dominguez. This was one way he felt he could contribute and repay the Church for being an excellent host to him and his companions. He was amazed at how well Father Dominguez officiated the service, displaying maturity greater than many of the priests in his own Diocese. The service and communion progressed flawlessly. He was a little envious of the sizable congregation. At his parish in Los Angeles, he was lucky if 15 or 20 parishioners attended the midweek services; here, on a Thursday night, the cathedral was nearly full. He would need to confess his jealousy and covetousness when he returned the next day.

After securing his borrowed garments, the Father retired for the night by heading back to the visitors' parsonage. He decided to close out the evening with a cup of tea. In the kitchen, Michael sat at the table, still in his gym clothes, drying sweat stains under his arms and blotched on the chest area of his dark blue T-shirt.

Not expecting to see his episodic harasser sitting at the table, Father Hernandez decided to make an offer of peace. "I'm going to make myself a cup of tea, want one?"

"No thanks, padre," Michael gently answered.

"You've been sitting here awhile? Could've sworn you left to go jogging before this evening's mass," Father Hernandez replied.

"I did," Michael noted softly, surprising Father Hernandez with his muted demeanor.

The Father continued with his intended cup of tea, filling a teakettle with water and placing it on the front eye of the electric stove.

"So boy toy, what do you like to do in your spare time?" Michael asked.

The Father paused a few seconds, flabbergasted by Michael's attempt to initiate a conversation. "Well, if I get the chance, I like to play the piano. I learned when I was a kid and enjoyed it quite a bit, even though I didn't let my parents know. Every chance I got, I would play. What about you?"

"I like to run. You can run into a lot of interesting people and places. What's your favorite type of music to play?"

"I'd say it would be …"

"Do you still do any type of angel research?" Michael interrupted.

The Father overlooked the interruption while grabbing sugar from the cupboard. "I haven't done any in a while. I've …"

Michael interrupted again, "Do you think, if they do exist, they get involved with us in supernatural ways?"

"I'd say…everything all right Mr. Saunders?" Father Hernandez inquired, noticing that Michael appeared out of sorts.

"Ever have anything weird…" Michael started, looking at Father Hernandez intently for a few seconds, then continued, "Ah, to hell with it."

Michael got out of his seat and went to his room. Father Hernandez watched him, puzzled, knowing something was bothering him. He decided not to pursue the inquiry but finished gingerly placing tea in a metal tea strainer. He put Michael out of his mind.

* * * *

In front of the airport terminal, the incessant honking of a horn caught the attention of Michael, Sister Justine, and Father Hernandez as they were getting out of a taxi and gathering their luggage from the trunk. It was Jose's VW Pointer horn blaring. His Pointer weaved through the maze of taxis and cars in the roadway, navigating his way a car length away from the three and then jamming into an open spot just as a taxi pulled out. Jose jumped out of the car, left it running, and grabbed the three's luggage, carelessly throwing the pieces into his trunk.

"Father, Sister, come with me right away," he said in his native tongue in an agitated and excited tone.

"Jose, what are you doing here? What's going on?" Father Hernandez asked.

"We must go now. There is someone you must talk to, someone who has talked to your witness during the first visit," Jose stated, forcing the final piece of luggage into the car trunk.

The three stared at each other, amazed and puzzled. Not one of them could think of a reason not to go with Jose. They hurried into Jose's car. Before the doors were fully closed, Jose darted into the airport traffic without looking back or into his mirrors, which caused a taxi to swerve and nearly hit another vehicle as well as an ensuing chorus of honking.

"Jose, be careful!" Father Hernandez barked.

"Sorry Father. I go to church to see if you still there, and Father Dominguez tell me you decide to take earlier flight. I need bring you back into town as soon as I can," Jose responded.

"So what's this you said about someone talking to the witness of the first event?" Sister Justine asked from the rear seat, leaning forward to make sure Jose heard her question.

"Si' Sister. I go over my brother's house to visit him and his wife because one her family members passed away. We plan on going to the funeral later. Of course, we all talk if angel show up. We not want one to come, especially what happen in Los Angeles. Well, we talk and I mention I help escort you three around to see into the event…the one ten years ago…many don't believe an angel do such a thing."

As Jose continued to talk, his driving became more erratic, with him concentrating more on attempting to recall the course of his conversation with his family than on skillfully driving through the chaotic array of cars. The queasiness of motion sickness came upon Father Hernandez with the swerving from lane to lane on the divided road. All three cried out in unison for Jose to watch out. He wasn't paying attention to the small rusting pickup truck cutting in front of him and then hit the brakes because of the immediate slowdown of traffic. Jose was able to slow the vehicle enough to miss the truck's dangling rear bumper.

"So Jose, what's so important for us to miss our flight?" Michael asked, wondering why he was driving so recklessly. "Are you sure someone talked to the El Refugio witness ten years ago?"

"Si'," Jose answered. "He was an, what you call, orderly for clinic."

"And how would he remember what happened anyway?" Father Hernandez added.

"He may be old, his mind still young. He recently was very sick. He use to tell me and his grandchildren the most enjoyable stories. His grandson was *mi mejor amigo*." The three knew it meant his best friend.

A question occurred to Sister Justine. "So how come he didn't tell anyone anything about what happened before now?"

Jose focused on his driving for several more minutes before answering Sister Justine. She was patient, watching him navigate through the increased activity of cars, bicyclists, and scooters on the streets ahead of them. He'd reduced his speed from time to time to keep from hitting another vehicle. The two male passengers clenched their hands tightly, one on the dashboard, the other on the seat in front of him; all three passengers nervously watched their driver. When Jose had safely piloted his VW Pointer through the market section of town, and picked up speed unencumbered by traffic on the major thoroughfare, he felt comfortable answering the Sister's question. "Sister, he not want anyone think he cursed with virus. Just before quarantine, hear they to keep restricted everybody. He get worried not see his family and left right away. Knew he need work to support his family. Stay bad for him and family. They move to Mexico City hoping not being found. Even after disappearances, he still scared they come for him, he stay hidden. Only year ago he return back because of cancer and like to die in town he grew up."

Michael thought it interesting that, during the trip, Jose would attempt to speak in English with the team when he was nervous and revert to his native tongue during normal conversations. Michael butted in. "So you're saying that he talked to the same one we talked to when we were here the first time?"

"Si'," Jose answered.

The three were no longer interested in Jose's driving now as much as wanting to arrive at their destination. While they had all thought they would be heading back with barely any new information, suddenly the possibility of new revelations awaited them. After several more minutes, they arrived at a set of newly renovated two-story apartments that contrasted with the weatherworn flats in the rest of the quiet street. The front entranceway had a brown-and-white-striped fabric awning, clean compared with the others on the street flaunting dirt, pigeon droppings, and tree sap. Jose led the three into a well-lit hallway and up the staircase in the rear. At the top of the landing, Jose knocked on the first door then opened it and announced his entrance.

"Melinda?" Jose whispered, walking into the apartment at a slow steady pace, attempting not to make any extraneous noise.

A short and thin, 38-year-old, Hispanic woman with a pale-complexion appeared from around the corner in the nicely furnished domicile. She came over and kissed Jose gently on the cheek. After he explained to her who the three were, she led the four down a short hallway to a bedroom with a television on but the volume turned low. Once in the bedroom, they saw a frail, elderly man lying in bed with a simple sheet and blanket, staring distantly at

175

the television. Next to him on the floor lay an empty plastic bucket and bedpan. An odorous hint of vomit and urine lingered in the air.

"Papa, it's me, Jose," he softly called out in his native tongue. The old man turned his head to the doorway and watched the four enter.

"You bring the angel hunters with you?" the old man responded in Spanish. The three researchers, though well enough versed in Spanish, were a bit confused by the question.

Father Hernandez responded first in English, "Angel hunters?"

"Si'," Jose said, "when I tell him who you were and why you here, he called you that."

The old man interrupted, weakly pointing to Michael and Sister Justine. "I remember you two from the first time you came down," he noted in Spanish.

"I'm sorry but we don't remember you," she responded.

"Of course you wouldn't remember me. You were more interested in trying to talk to your witness of the angel visit at Our Lady of Hope, Dr. Vargas. I'm Jose, I was the janitor and orderly for the clinic."

Michael advanced toward the bed. "I don't recall him being a doctor," Michael said, intrigued by Jose's comment.

"We never got a chance to thoroughly talk to him. Unbelievably, he was still in a state of shock when we finally made it down, and before we could finish talking to him, we were sent home," Sister Justine added.

"Yes, you both left and it was at the same time they thought there was a virus outbreak. It was about that time the doctor was more clear."

"Doctor? Was he one of the clinic's doctors?"

"No...he said he was a...research doctor, working... studies viruses...for same company working with the Church," the old man expelled with labored breath.

"You all must leave now. He needs his rest," Melinda said forcefully.

"No," the old man interrupted, "they must stay."

Melinda, beholden to her grandfather-in-law, capitulated.

The old man continued, straining with labored breaths. "The doctor felt he had to...confess a heavy burden on his soul. He went to...the church to look for... a priest...found a funeral was...in progress. He decided to wait and it was then when he said they all smelled something so sweet and flowerlike, no one could explain it. Then he told me he witnessed the angel...all of a sudden...appear during the middle of the funeral service. It then began to talk about...the life... of the man who died. The doctor said they were...all in amazement. Next, in the middle of the service...everybody already shocked by what's going on, giving rosaries, Hail Maries...some even praying...crying...another angel shows up, interrupting the first. The two have a staring contest. He then said it was almost as if they had an argument...the second almost like it was commanding the first...to leave, ...most no one there understanding anything said, but he thought it said 'the Lord rebuke you and depart'... the first leaving, the second remaining...and mention his name is..."

"Abriel?" Michael interrupted. "He mentioned the name when we could to talk to him before we were recalled. He never mentioned anything about another angel. We took it for granted the first angel was this Abriel."

"He could have been in shock," Sister Justine injected.

"So how come he didn't mention any of this to anyone else at the time?" Father Hernandez asked, jumping in a questioning.

The old man answered, "When it was mentioned a possible virus...they thought the doctor's story was... because he was going loco from the virus ... the doctor mentioned the second angel ... appeared before."

"What?" the three investigators all said nearly in unison.

"The doctor didn't...say where...the angel...appeared before...death would follow."

"Appeared where?" Michael asked.

"He wouldn't say...just that he wanted to confess to a priest."

"You mentioned something about the doctor wanting to confess, did he give you any idea what he wanted to confess to?" Father Hernandez questioned.

"He felt ashamed...of research he...was working on...in a nearby lab. He felt he...he needed to confess...to clear his conscience."

"He didn't mention what type of research?" Michael asked.

"No...he said Aurora."

"Aurora? Who's Aurora? Is that the name of the other angel?" Michael asked.

"He never said."

"How did he come to tell you all of this?" Father Hernandez asked.

"I don't know. Maybe…because I was nearest at the time when he...decided to talk. Anyway...that's all I know."

Melinda, listening in the doorway, made herself known to the visitors, making sure they understood the intention of the old man. The three felt satisfied they had all the information they needed from Jose and yielded to her request for them to leave. When they arrived at the car, Sister Justine pulled out her smartphone and began typing.

"What the hell are you doing?" Michael interrogated.

"I'm reporting back what transpired upstairs just now," she answered.

"Why would you do that?"

Father Hernandez felt he needed to jump in, "You can't be that naïve, Mr. Saunders..."

"Stay out of this, boy toy," Michael sharply returned.

"Michael, he's right," Sister Justine exclaimed, "Remember who's paying for your trip down here. The Bishop has every right to know."

Michael didn't have a retort to the Sister's comment, at least one he felt comfortable saying without offending her greatly. Sister Justine continued typing on her smartphone.

Chapter 16

Bishop Grielle handed a cup of tea to his guest, Cardinal Millhouse, who was sitting in the chair opposite his desk. The Cardinal graciously accepted the hot beverage, stirring two teaspoons of sugar into the white porcelain teacup with paisley patterns in gold inlay. The Bishop returned to his seat behind his desk. After spending nearly half an hour discussing general church administration issues, Cardinal Millhouse decided to change the subject.

"So, what is the situation with the three you sanctioned to visit Mexico?" the Cardinal asked. "Many of us had our doubts."

The Cardinal's question caught Bishop Grielle somewhat off guard as he expected it earlier in their conversation. "We do need to find out what happened. With so many implications for the Church, too many unresolved. There are members of the fold in the congregations, throughout the Diocese, going to their priests asking lots of questions about why all this is happening and we don't have answers for them. The latest emails and text messages, from both Sister Justine and Father Hernandez, didn't reveal any real explanation about what happened here in the city or down in El Refugio. And from some of the preliminary messages, they haven't found anything apart from what was known already. They're heading home tomorrow," the Bishop explained.

"And what's this you mentioned in your email earlier, that they found some written information regarding the first visitation?" Cardinal Millhouse asked.

"Yes, they came across some archival journals and logs in storage."

"I thought Sister Justine acquired and turned in all the notes, research work, and information found on site from their first visit." Cardinal Millhouse queried, faintly arching his right eyebrow. Bishop Grielle maintained his composure.

"She did, your Eminence. To the best of our knowledge, the new information may have been an oversight, especially with the hectic nature of everything at that time down there."

"I see, just as well. We weren't sure if we would need to recall them."

"Well, considering you realized who the witness was the first time they went down, I know you wanted ensure that certain issues never got exposed. Of course, I was never told of the full implications of who that witness was," Bishop Grielle responded, sequestering his frustration with the constant surreptitious maneuverings by his mentor, especially during times like this, when he was not provided with a full understanding of why he was being directed to accomplish certain things. The Cardinal told him just enough to be successful in whatever endeavor was at hand.

"Then was it a good idea to send them down again?" Cardinal Millhouse asked.

"I'm sure that's not a problem this time around. What's been reported to date is that they're just rehashing a lot of the same territory, even with the new information they found."

Cardinal Millhouse's expression changed back to moderate concern. "Do we know why angels began giving eulogies? More important, why the tragedies occurred in El Refugio and here in the city? Has Michael Saunders really been helpful?"

"Remember, you agreed that the past research and knowledge of angelology that Michael Saunders possesses could help immensely with what's going on."

"Yes, and I remember that many of his writings were very controversial. Yet he, by far, he was one of the best persons suited for attempting to find out what did transpired. Can we trust him?"

"Sister Justine has been very faithful. She'll make sure he can be trusted."

Cardinal Millhouse wrinkled his nose and scratched his forehead; he was vexed.

"Yes, but you know as well as I that her Order has been giving the Diocese and Rome a great many problems with their liberal concepts, moving away from conventional orthodoxy," Cardinal Millhouse countered.

"Well yes--nonetheless, both she and Father Hernandez have been excellent at keeping us informed on what's going on. As soon as I receive a message, you and our patron friend will both receive copies."

The pop-up notification on the computer monitor caught Bishop Grielle's attention signaling he received a new email message. The email notification header was configured to display dark maroon for messages from the two in Mexico; the new email was flagged by the email rule set, so he knew the message was from either one. The sender line showed Sister Justine.

"Well," Bishop Grielle commented to his superior, while double-clicking on the email message, "It seems Sister Justine is maintaining her faithfulness. Here we are just discussing her and we receive a message."

"What does it say?"

"It says..." the bishop began and paused to read the message silently:

Delayed returning to Los Angeles. By chance, we were able to talk to a clinic worker who talked to original witness prior to his disappearance. Additional information about the initial angel visit obtained a bit more complex than anticipated. Second angel believed to be involved with El Refugio event. Found out witness made reference to a name, "Aurora." No additional information provided. Will discuss upon returning.

Bishop Grielle sat back in his chair. Cardinal Millhouse noticed a concerned look on his face and said, "Andrew, you look uneasy. What's wrong?"

"You might want to read this," the Bishop indicated, pointing at his screen.

"Go ahead and read the message."

Bishop Grielle read the message to his spiritual mentor and observed a distressed expression on his face.

"Recall the three immediately," the Cardinal said.

"Your Eminence, I believe we should let them finish what they've started," Bishop Grielle petitioned.

Cardinal Millhouse glared at the bishop, "I know you don't know the full extent of what is going on, but I can tell you just by that message, the ramifications are immense. Do you know the impact of what happened the first time down in Mexico?"

"I've heard rumors here and there."

"Well, the losses to the Church were more devastating than you can imagine. And we're still grappling with the impact of the most recent event."

"Wouldn't any information they come across help us find out what's going on? We didn't send them down there just for the show, did we? We owe it to the Church."

"What we owe," Cardinal Millhouse said, exacting in his response, "is for you to follow my will and bring the three back here immediately."

IV. The Shadow of Angels: Aurora

Chapter 17

Alder was beginning to feel the pressure of his new position. He admitted to himself that he was feeling overwhelmed. Even Gary, Alder's boss, was aware of his new director's stress. Alder had never fully comprehended the number and scope of projects Everest was involved with until after he started reviewing the overall budget and accounting numbers for his division. A bombardment of transactions to be approved--capital projects in building new labs, modifying testing facilities, and other major undertakings requiring budgetary documentation review, filled his inbox. His calendar was packed with constant budget meetings, discussing the progress of existing projects, funding for new projects, or the close-out of completed or unsuccessful projects. What didn't help was that some of the projects had spanned years. He wasn't sure how all the charge backs, capitalized costs, and expenditures were intended to be identified on the ledgers. Should they be under capital project names and budgets, R & D project names and their unique tertiary budgets, or another budgetary system that floated around based on Jeffrey's paperwork, just not well documented?

Alder pulled the bottom project folder from his inbox with the label: "Capital Project: Excalibur" on line one. Line two read "Department: Pharmaceuticals." Opening the folder, he read a summary sheet showing the capital project to modify one of the company's laboratories in Canada to develop and test new biotechnologies. The number of labs and projects Everest operated outside of the United States stunned Alder. He continued to review the summary sheet, which showed the business unit overseeing the proposal was requesting validation of major line item expenditures to ensure the project originators were on target with their forecasts. *Great, another meeting with another business unit to discuss another project*, he thought. He was now up to five major meetings next week, with different section leads wanting to discuss budget requests, forecasts, and overruns. Reviewing the rest of the sheet, he saw that an analysis would be needed to ensure the amount requested would fall in line with the overall amount budgeted to the R & D division. A post-it note adhered to the sheet with the request: "Please review and edit capital exec summary and justification." Alder put the folder to the side on his "to do" stack, now four folders high.

He pulled a folder from the bottom of another small stack covering agricultural genetic engineering projects on his desk. He opened the multipart folder to find the same format with the first page as a summary and routing sheet. This review would require minimal effort and consisted of follow-up information from previous routings. After examining the planned expenditure postings and modifications, Alder signed and put the folder on his completed stack. Now there were three.

Alder witnessed a tall, olive-skinned, young woman with Mediterranean features and long black hair enter his office without announcement. It was Sheila, Gary Applethorpe's assistant. She carried a multipart folder three to four inches thick, dwarfing the size of the other folders on his desk. Sheila was making it a habit to come in freely despite Alder's request that she knock or gesture from the door before coming in. His talking to Gary about it only emboldened her to continue.

"What do you want Sheila?" Alder inquired, attempting to preemptively gather the upper hand and feign ignorance of the documents she held.

Sheila stopped in front of Alder's desk and scanned his desktop like a predator surveying for a weakness in its prey. She smirked, opened the folder in her arms, pulled a sheet of paper out, and slung it purposefully in front of him.

"We need for you to initial this," she commanded.

"We?" Alder responded.

She raised a somewhat thick eyebrow on her beautiful face. "I don't think I stuttered, we. Gary is working this project and I need to get this paperwork signed off so that I can send it forward for action."

Alder glanced at the sheet. It was a standard journal voucher request form for a project with the primary name blacked out. Most of the subheadings on entries of funding transfers between spawned subprojects were also redacted. Looking at the numbers, they balanced out properly. The block for Alder's initials and the one for Gary's signature were they only areas that were blank. The other business unit coordinators had scribbled their initials and signatures in the appropriate blocks.

"And what exactly am I signing? Can I take a look at the supporting documentation to make sure these numbers line up within the budget forecast and outflow tracking?" Alder asked. Even though the numbers on the sheet were accurate, he wanted to ensure that the ledger entry transfers being requested were in line with the assigned project vouchers.

A heavy, angry sigh emanated from Sheila: "Look, just go ahead and initial," she demanded, rolling her eyes. "Everyone else did."

"So, what the hell am I signing? Technically all I have here is just a sheet with numbers. Look here, there's a reference to a subsidiary called Aversol. I don't have any information on them, no business unit code, no assigned ledger codes, nothing I can easily cross-reference against the original funding documents," Alder countered, pushing the paper back across his desk toward Sheila.

"You're not gonna sign it?"

"Not until I talk to Gary because I can't review the information I need."

"Fine," Sheila responded, snapping up the sheet of paper and putting it back in the folder as she left Alder's office.

Several minutes later, Alder received the intercom call he anticipated. Gary requested him in his office. Alder thought he heard a bit of glee in Sheila's voice as she talked to him.

Arriving at Gary's office, Alder walked directly by Sheila's desk and knocked on the door before he could be intercepted.

"Excuse me, Mr. Dennison," she blurted out angrily. Alder ignored her and knocked again.

"Yes Sheila?" Gary's voice echoed from the other side of the door. Alder opened the door.

"Oh, come on in Alder." Alder grinned at Sheila while closing the door behind him. He went and sat comfortably in one of the large seats next to the coffee table where they had had their earlier discussions. Gary joined him. Alder identified a couple of project folders and a collection of papers on the table resembling those Sheila had brought into his office earlier.

"You and Sheila still seem to be at odds with one another," Gary commented.

"We'll work it out."

"Good, I'm sure you'll both see eye to eye. I don't want to have to keep getting involved. These types of petty issues tend to muddy up the works."

"Hell, I'm just looking at it as a form of initiation from her since I'm the new kid on the block."

The comment garnered a small smile from Gary. "Well, your first week here is pretty much finished. How's it going so far?"

"OK, I guess."

"Well, I know there was a lot on your plate when you started this position. Don't forget you can delegate some of the projects and coordination to your direct reports."

Alder had delegated several of the minor accounting assignments to his three managers but had held onto the larger ventures. "Thanks Gary, but I just want to get a feel right now for the lay of the land."

"Fair enough. So what's this about not wanting to sign off on the journal voucher transfer approval sheet?" Gary asked.

"I don't feel too comfortable just blindly signing a sheet of paper associated with a project I know nothing

190

about," Alder responded assertively but not sternly so as not to upset his boss.

"Remember Alder, there were some projects I told you that I wanted to keep close to the vest? Well, that's one of them. What I will tell you is this; remember when we discussed the mission statement of Everest? This project in some ways is a culmination of that mission statement."

Alder's curiosity was ignited. *What did this project consist of*? He thought. He decided not to press the issue. "So then, you do need my signature?"

Gary continued. "I've been associated with this project through the years in one form or another, and now it's become a high-priority goal for me to see it through. We have some highly valued and respected investors sponsoring this research. There have been some serious roadblocks along the way but we're able to move forward now. And for a while, Jeffrey had managed that part of the funding administration. I'm quite sure you're already aware of some of the fuckups he caused. If it wasn't because of his father's influence and incessant intervening, we would've been able to deal with Jeffrey and not have to work hard to correct a hell of a lot of his inadvertent disclosures."

"Well, I definitely don't want to be a roadblock either," Alder, said. He wasn't sure why, but he was extremely troubled. He knew that by signing he could authorize essentially unauthorized budget transfers, payments, or expense charges against a non-associated capital project account. Not good. Alder knew to remain firm in his unwillingness to sign his name on the paperwork. He continued, "Gary, you know what, the reality is that I don't want to sign anything without an understanding of the transactions, expenses, and assigned codings."

Gary sat back into the couch. Was Gary offended, was he irate, or was he perhaps impressed by the fortitude Alder thought he was displaying? Alder could tell his boss was contemplating his response, analyzing him and his body language.

Gary went stone faced. Only a few seconds passed but to Alder they were like eons with Gary's austere expression. Gary reached down and pushed the file folder, abloom with papers and sticky pad notes, in front of Alder, and pulled out the same sheet Sheila presented earlier. It made Alder realize, since the mass disappearance, how the digital revolution severely curtailed the managing of day-to-day business; accessing computer systems, file servers, data files, and financial accounts had become very cumbersome for those remaining, if not impossible. There were reports of entire company IT departments left empty, with the network administrators able to access and reset passwords themselves gone. As he looked at the large folder, Alder sneaked a glance at the label: "Project: Aurora, Bio-Medical; Genetic Engineering–Prototype 4." It was another project with sensitive data that Jeffrey had carelessly exposed prior to his death. Alder thought that perhaps Gary was keeping a tighter rein with his managerial response to prevent any future unintended disclosures.

"Look, here's what we could do. We'll assign unique budget code identifiers for distinct items. Let's say pens, pencils, paper, whatever--those types of

192

expense items will be given a code identifying office supplies. Then let's say major expense items or capital items would each have a unique identifier. Only thing is you wouldn't know the actual item. There would be a preapproved cross-reference table we can keep secure. This way we can keep many of our secret expenses secret so our competitors won't get a good picture of what we're doing from the accounting side," Gary referenced.

"I don't know, still sounds kinda odd."

"That's one way of administering sensitive and secret skunk works projects. You have to think we want to protect the investments and intellectual property of the company."

"But there's still a chance ..."

"All I can say is just trust that when it comes to signing off these closed projects," Gary started interjecting to prevent Alder from continuing. Sheila entered into the office interrupting Gary.

"Mr. Applethorpe, they called back about the progress on the one project you had asked about earlier. They wanted to let you know they were successful in moving into the third phase."

Gary's face brightened. "Excellent, tell them I'll drive over right way." He focused his attention back to Alder, his giddiness from the phone call morphed back into a stern manifestation of authority. "Alder, sign," Gary commanded.

Back in his office, after the confrontation with Sheila, talk with Gary, and ever-growing stack of project folders on his desk, Alder glanced at this watch. It was already four in the afternoon and thought to himself, *I need a drink*. Hell, he might have just signed a sheet of paper that would result with him going straight to jail years later.

The next morning Alder returned to his office to see a battalion of varied file folders resting on his desktop. He knew they wouldn't have been worked on since last night. Feeling a bit dehydrated from his drinking endeavors the previous evening, Alder decided to head to the campus commissary to grab a cup of coffee. Once there, after filling a large Styrofoam cup nearly three-fourths full and adding a packet of hot chocolate, he joined Branson Wynn, a peer from Marketing promoted at the same time, having replace William Sumner. He was sitting by himself at a small table for two by a large, wall-sized window that overlooked the fountain adorning the main entrance of the campus complex. Longing face, sullen gaze, dejected expression, he externally exhibited Alder's internal frustrations. He also noticed new gray hairs assaulting Branson's low-cut Afro since their initial director's meeting.

"Thank God it's Friday," Alder said.

"What do you have planned for tomorrow?"

"Supposed to go shopping with the wife. Oh, joy. And then off to a birthday party for a friend of my daughter." Branson caught the sarcasm in Alder's voice. Alder continued, "Plus I promised the wife I'd go visit Stephen again."

"Shit, forgot all about him. It's been so damn busy. How's he doing anyway?"

"Last time I went to visit him he was doing fine. Still not adjusted to going blind though."

"Yeah, that's some weird shit that happened. Not to be rude, but all of that is the least of my worries. With all this crap going on, and trying to catch up with so much paperwork that's backed up, I don't know why I accepted this new position. There's a hell of a lot of cloak-and-dagger shit they're working on in R & D."

"For the government?" Alder speculated aloud. Branson made a point to know quite a few details of the business unit operations. Alder never knew as much, except what may have come through the grapevine, about the projects being worked in R & D. He thought that even after working in the division for a number of years, he was ignorant as to the company's mission objectives and revenue-generating accomplishments. Being promoted, he fooled Gary pretty well.

"Believe it or not, I don't think so," Branson answered. "I just know that they've been keeping so much shit secret lately because of all the deaths, they don't want to reveal too much to all the new faces in the new positions. Hell, business as usual right?"

Alder leaned into his coworker and dropped his voice. "Do you think we made the right choice accepting our new positions?"

"Can you say 'career suicide' if we hadn't?"

"Yeah, I suppose. Hell, with the stuff we're working on."

"Did you know we're trying to market a genetic engineering process to agribusiness? Without getting into the some of the consequences, we have to make sure we don't reveal some of the negative conseque...hell, I just better shut up about that," Branson said. Although he'd gotten to know Alder more during the last week in several of the meetings they held as peers, he still felt uncomfortable opening up freely to him.

195

Alder understood completely, and Branson sensed Alder's empathy in his revealing nod.

Branson continued, "I mean some things they'll pass on to us to help get the job done. Sometimes they just hold back key data, don't let us know everything we need to know about a project. How do they expect us to come up with an effective strategy?"

"I know where you're coming from. They want me to sign shit, but I have no idea what it's for."

"Try having your teams build a market strategy without any of the raw data you need to be successful."

"I don't follow," Alder noted, now wishing he knew more details about the business units instead of spending many years in the company focused on being a xenophobic accountant.

"On some of the projects that move from R&D to testing, we're to see if a market exists, maybe open up new ones, blah, blah, blah. Well, some of the projects go back for years through the transitions of various subsidiaries. We're told to look at where these may have failed before and find out why. In some cases, the products were flawed, like genetically modified food plants kicking off undesired results. Hell, in many cases they don't give us all the information we need to know about what was marketed. I have one team working on a project pulling data from up to three or four years ago. They find out the lab was renamed and then couldn't find out anything else relating to the previous company. One of the bigger pains in the ass is from an old string of medical clinics the company sponsored called Aversol, but something happened and they renamed them under the Waterfall trade name. Sometimes we go through this if there's fuckups or even perceived fuckups, when the product may not even be the cause of what ever happened, especially if it's a product that appears will have long-term legs. We have to go through rebranding, marketing blitzes, and in worst-case scenarios sometimes renaming companies to remove any association of defective or flawed commodities. Of course, we need to rebrand to keep from having a negative impact on future projects development based on the same technologies, otherwise key investors may up and pull their money. Hell, one we're working through goes as far back as over ten years ago. They won't give up any data. They just say deal with it and move on. Build a marketing strategy. Pisses me off."

"You mean projects like the one named Aurora?"

"You're not supposed to know that name," Branson shot back.

Clarity hit Alder. "Damn, I think that explains some of the long-term issues, like pension calculations under payroll, unsubstantiated payouts, crap like that. But you know what, even with the weird accounting, in the end somehow, it added up, at least for now. That's all, everything isn't necessarily revealed on our side either."

"Sounds like you're able to navigate through this mess better than my teams. Hell, I should stop complaining," Branson said, taking a drink from the Styrofoam cup sitting in front of him and scowling, his coffee having become lukewarm. "Shit, I sat here longer than I should. I should get back to work." Leaving the table, Branson reached out his hand and shook Alder's.

Alder remained rooted in his seat, not wanting to return to his office and confront the stack of folders he needed to review and sign. After a couple more swallows of his coffee-chocolate mixture, he worked up the confidence to face the paperwork. He felt he could use a drink.

Sherry, one of the newer managers he personally had been able to promote from among the pool of accountants and budget specialists in the bullpen, was waiting outside Alder's office with a nervous and tense look, holding a couple of project folders. *Great, more work*, he thought. It was both directly and indirectly because of her diligence and attention to detail, that many of the project folders were on his desk. She was skilled at finding the subtlest of erroneous postings and incorrect computations; and being skilled and knowledgeable and able to work issues between her peers, was a reason she was promoted to supervisor several years back. Her experience made it easy to select her as the newest manager for her section. Alder now tried to conjecture why she would be here waiting. After he invited her in, she stood opposite his desk politely turning down his request to take a seat while he sat down.

"What've you got there Sherry?" he asked.

"So I started doing some research and a lot of these numbers aren't making any sense. Some of the issues go back not just a few months, but years."

"Years?"

"Yeah, years. Here look," Sherry urged, stepping around next to Alder and flipping a folder open to a page with yellow stickies to point out where she had come across the discrepancies. The wafting smell of her overbearing perfume saturated his nostrils.

Reading through the pages, Alder smiled, amused at the coincidence that some of the issues he'd been speaking with Branson about several minutes earlier would manifest themselves again so soon. Sherry was puzzled by her boss's reaction.

"I think I see what's going on. Some of these issues look like they go back several years. They were charged under a project code associated with a different subsidiary name on the division's general ledger. You'll just have to do a little background to cross-reference some of this info and I think it should clear up."

"Yeah I thought so too, but I don't have access to those files on the network, and the hard copies of the records are in the archival staging area. Not being at director level, I can't request them to be pulled and scanned. Only you or someone higher can do that."

Alder became dispirited, not wanting to deal with any additional projects. Yet he knew he would have to work this issue out for Sherry so that she could continue her work. Keeping her engaged with many of the issues helped reduce the mounds of folders on his desk. "I'll take care of it and get back with you."

While Sherry walked out of the office, Alder glanced through the numbers on the summary sheets she'd generated. Everest was burning through quite a bit of money in the genetic engineering R & D division. Although the tally of the numbers looked as if legitimate, it almost appeared as if they were trying to conceal sources of their funding along with the actual amounts associated with key projects.

Chapter 18

The flight was tumultuous. At one point, the pilot said that the atmospheric conditions and severity of turbulence were extremely unusual for the type of weather they were flying through in the jet-route air corridor. The skies were clear, no reported wind direction changes. With no reports of disturbance from any aircraft in the area, ground control stations were worried about the sanity of the crew.

On autopilot, the aircraft lurched and jerked unpredictably. When the pilot manually handled the controls, when he adjusted the yoke or rudder in one direction, it jolted out of his hands or opposed his foot actions on the rudder petals as if someone were attempting to wrestle control of the plane from him. The resistance to the controls seemed internal to the cockpit. The pilot thought the plane was possessed. His copilot anxiously worked the navigation systems to ensure they stayed on the proper course setting in relation to the navigation aids while also working the radio communications to find a different altitude or route with less turbulence.

"God damn it," the pilot muttered, forcibly fighting the controls. "Are you sure no one else is experiencing anything at this altitude?" he queried of his copilot.

"No one is reporting any type of turbulence at all. I almost think ATC is thinking we're making this shit up," the copilot responded while the plane continued to be buffeted.

"Damn, is God pissed at someone on this flight?"

"Or maybe just the opposite, I saw a nun and priest boarding. Maybe something or someone is pissed at them."

"Well whatever it is, it feels like someone or something is trying to push us out of the sky. Try to request a new altitude."

Descending to the newly directed altitude, the plane unexpectedly dropped twice and the negative-g sensation overwhelmed most passengers with motion sickness. Michael thought he would throw up, only being able to drift into sleep during the last hour of the flight. Father Hernandez slept through most of the long flight. Sister Justine read a devotional. She was unencumbered by the violent turbulence. With the rough landing, Michael was jarred awake from his semi deep sleep. As the plane bounced a couple times once it hit the runway, he thought the pilot could easily receive credit for two landings.

Disembarking from the plane and awaiting their luggage at the carousel, the three remained quiet among the throngs of voices of other passengers, family and friends, and airport personnel throughout the baggage claim area. The three were all tired. Father Hernandez focused on returning to his parish, wondering if the deacons maintained proper order during his absence. Michael forced himself to at least think of what had happened over the last couple of days, especially the incident with the dogs. Rummaging through some of his thoughts while jogging the prior evening, Stephen Williams had come to mind; there was still an excellent opportunity to talk to an actual witness to an event. Everything they had gotten out of the earlier discussion with Stephen was superficial. Michael's craving to find the truth was ignited.

"We need to talk to Stephen again," Michael noted to his two companions.

The demeanor of the two showed they both thought Michael was kidding. Father Hernandez decided to respond first. "Very funny Mr. Saunders. We just need to get back, freshen up, and report back to Bishop Grielle first."

A wave of annoyance surged through Michael's soul. Bishop Grielle was one man he didn't want to meet throughout the entire investigation. "I'd rather take a wire brush and scrape my skin raw than talk to that snake," Michael remarked.

"Is that necessary?" Sister Justine injected.

Michael's luggage floated by in his peripheral vision. "Damn it," he said jumping between a little girl and her mother, not excusing himself. Grabbing the baggage and putting it down by Sister Justine and Father Hernandez, he continued, "Look, I don't know why, but something is really telling me we need to talk to Stephen again. Maybe he forgot something and we can jog his memory."

"Well I just want to get back to my residence, freshen up, and brief what we experienced. Then I want to get back to my sheep," Father Hernandez appealed.

"Your sheep?" Michael noted sarcastically, rolling his eyes. "I thought you two wanted to find out the truth of what happened?"

"The reality from what we've already found out is that we don't know why it's happening. We just need to accept that. We're no closer now than the first time you two started this investigation," Father Hernandez responded.

"Yeah, but I don't think we're done yet either," Michael noted, rolling his luggage away from the crowd toward the automatic doors leading outside.

Father Hernandez and Sister Justine captured their luggage from the conveyor system and departed to the curbside, catching up with Michael, who was attempting to hail a cab.

"Michael, what are you doing?" Sister Justine asked, confusion evident on her face.

"Catching a cab."

"Why? The car is in short-term parking."

"I know where the car is. I'm not going with you guys."

Father Hernandez interposed, "Look, we're not going to talk to Stephen Williams."

"You're right. We're not, but I am."

"We need to return and discuss what we came across so far with the Bishop."

Michael cringed, the ire evident on his face. "I'm not going to talk to that weasel, at least not now."

Sister Justine attempted to pacify the situation. "Look, we don't even know where he is."

A taxi pulled up to the curb with Michael opening the door showing his two companions the seriousness of his intentions.

Sister Justine gave up any further attempts to convince him to see the underwriter of their trip. "Fine,

203

we'll try to find Stephen Williams and talk to him. Then we'll go see the Bishop," she qualified.

Ready to step into the taxi after throwing his luggage in the rear seat, Michael replaced the irate expression on his face flashing a quick grin towards Sister Justine. He dismissed the taxi after pulling out his garment bag and small suitcase and heard cursing from the driver, who had to go around the terminal again to wait at the end of the long livery line at the airport entrance.

"So, how do we locate Stephen Williams?" Father Hernandez asked, irritated that their plans changed.

"I know who'd probably know," Sister Justine answered. She pulled out her smartphone, typed in a text message, and returned the phone to her coat pocket. She snatched her luggage, urging her companions to head out to the car. "I hope they're not busy."

"Who?" Michael asked.

"The cops who were with us when this all started."

"You think they'll know?"

"Why not? I'm sure they would want to keep tabs on him since he's still probably, if not their prime witness, their prime suspect depending on what they found out while we were gone."

Michael and Father Hernandez both thought it was a resourceful way to find Stephen. As they arrived at the car, her Gregorian Chant ringtone announced an incoming text message. Reading it, Sister Justine smiled. "I got the address. But they want to talk to us about the incident that occurred just before we left for Mexico."

After getting in the car and on the way to Stephen's residence, with Father Hernandez driving, Sister Justine promptly called the office of Detectives Green and

Matthews. Detective Matthews answered. Both men in the car listened patiently to one side of the conversation, unable to ascertain any intelligible information from Sister Justine's comments. When she was finished, she explained: "Well I don't know if you both remember the televised incident at the Crestview Funeral Home," she started. "Detective Matthews mentioned that the deceased individual was thought to have died because of a heart attack after they completed the autopsy. However, the next day as they were prepping the body for delivery to a mortician, the eyes were dissolved and the tongue withered and blackened."

"You gotta be kidding me, from a heart attack?" Michael stated rhetorically.

"And he was the only victim?" Father Hernandez asked, making sure he kept his eyes on the road.

"In reference to dying, yes, but quite a few of the attendees suffered from severe sunburn. At first they thought it was just mild cases but later it became second- or third-degree burns for quite a few of them."

"Ouch. Hell, anything else?" Michael wondered aloud.

"Michael, your language," Sister Justine responded, thinking Father Hernandez may not have appreciated the mild expletive. "In response to your answer, yes, the detectives said that a couple of children claimed the angel called itself Gishmael."

They all remained quiet for several minutes as they drove, pondering the name.

"Gishmael?" Father Hernandez commented first, "We'll have to research that name to see if it shows up in any of the catalogs of angels."

"I don't think you'll find it in any of the traditional religious journals or guides covering angels, boy toy," Michael interposed.

"And why not?"

"Remember, more than half of the reference guides are fictional or have no rational basis because they're based on mythology, lore, or other religions without any basis of veracity. During my time researching angels, I came across historical accounts that were fictionalized like the apocryphal Enochian book," Michael explained.

"I still think it's worth researching to see if anything might be found out from the name of the angels."

"Well, do what you need to do, boy toy, it's just that another important question to ask is how come only the children heard the angel's name?" Michael speculated. Father Hernandez sensed the question was rhetorical.

"Sounds like you already know the answer," Father Hernandez responded.

"No, but it's interesting. Makes me think of the book of Daniel, I believe Chapter 10, where only Daniel could see and communicate with the mysterious visitor. No one else around saw him. Of course, his traveling companions did run away. It shows a pattern that these angels may sometimes single out a person who to communicate with."

"I didn't realize you'd still remember so much from your days at seminary Mr. Saunders."

"Uhhh, I do teach religious studies, which includes the Bible padre," Michael noted derisively. "I still do my research."

"Did the detectives mention anything else about Crestview?" Father Hernandez asked Sister Justine, refocusing the discussion.

"No, but they did mention they're no longer actively working the case. They thought somehow I would've known."

"Why?"

"They found out someone high up in the Church was making a strong plea to limit the official police investigation and declare it an unexplained supernatural event."

"You think the Cardinal could've done that? I mean, does he have that much clout in the police department?" Father Hernandez ventured. "How can someone call off an entire police investigation?"

"You'd be surprised what the Cardinal is capable of doing, especially if the police chief or members of his staff are extremely devout Catholics," Michael jibed.

Sister Justine could sense the formation of another verbal head-butting competition. As she thought about their planned visit, she realized they would be arriving unannounced, which offered the opportunity to change the direction of the conversation. "Maybe we should call Stephen Williams to let him know we're on our way over."

"And give him a chance to refuse us? I don't think so," Michael responded.

"Sister Justine is right; we should at least show some courtesy and call ahead," Father Hernandez pressed, adding his two cents.

"There's a better chance he'll talk to us if we just show up. If we call ahead, he just may say no. Then we're screwed."

"Sister, please call the police detectives and get the number for Mr. Williams. We'll call and announce our request to talk him," Father Hernandez said sternly and politely.

On the way to his house, Sister Justine was unable to turn on her smartphone; the battery died. She thought it strange because she was able to charge it at the airport just before the final leg of their flight back, turning off the phone for most of the trip. Father Hernandez gave her his phone to use, but his device displayed zero bars until they drove up in front of Stephen's home.

Chapter 19

Cardinal Millhouse was hoping to have already received information to pass on to Rome from his protégé as soon he had gotten off the phone, especially after hearing that the church's sponsored key project at Everest was making excellent progress. It was the exposure of the project name Aurora flabbergasting him. Turning some of his attention to Church administration, and taking his mind off the angel investigation, he had before him several documents expounding on the dire financial conditions of several parishes. Even with the sporadic angelic eulogy accounts reported by dioceses, church attendance in several congregations continued to fall off, but in others, there was record attendance, which was especially true after the mass disappearance. During the last ten years, he made some challenging decisions to close several minsters. Many congregations were naught, more so those with nontraditional, Protestant-leaning stances.

Spending the remaining portion of his Saturday morning reviewing e-mails, the Cardinal was confident he would see something from Bishop Grielle to keep him abreast of the situation with the three investigators and any possible new information. Here, he was disappointed again. Glancing at his watch, it was approaching noon, and hunger pangs began to materialize, announcing lunch.

Leaving his office to head down to the dining area, Cardinal Millhouse was unexpectedly met by Bishop Grielle approaching in the hallway. "Andrew?"

"Your Eminence," Bishop Grielle acknowledged, making the customary greeting, culminating with the kissing of the ring.

"I didn't expect to see you here," Cardinal Millhouse responded. "I'm heading down to lunch. Join me?"

"Thank you, I'd be delighted."

"So what time do you expect your three dispatches to arrive?" the Cardinal asked of his protégé, the two walking down the icon-and picture-adorned hallway of the large cathedral, with warm sunlight breaching the large partially stained-glass windows aligned on one side and immersing the pieces of art hanging on the opposite walls.

"I imagine, with God's grace, they will be here this evening around 5 or 6 o'clock. Being delayed an extra day and missing their connecting flight out of Mexico City was unfortunate. Their plane landed a short while ago and they wanted some time to freshen up before coming in to brief us. They did say they've reason to believe they need to talk to Stephen Williams again to ask him about some of the new information they found in Mexico."

The Cardinal turned toward the bishop and furled his lip. "I feel you're starting to lose control of your team Andrew," the Cardinal noted and, sensing Bishop Grielle felt offended, continued with his comments. "You know, it's disturbing that they found out information concerning

Aurora. Our benefactor patron does feel like they're making great progress yet feels their efforts are not quite ready to be released. If your investigative research team finds out too much, they might not know how to interpret what they find."

"Your Eminence, the team is finding out what they were charged to. Plus, I'm not sure if I fully understand the relationship with our patron concerning Aurora," Bishop Grielle commented.

"Nothing much to say about it. Let's just say that what's to be revealed in due time will help establish the goal of an ecumenical church."

"How's that to be?" Bishop Grielle asked, somewhat confused.

"There's more commonality today than there was ten years ago. Rome is poised to take center stage in combining all faiths together."

"How?"

"My, my, my. My apprentice is full of questions today. I hate to use the cliché, but I may have said too much already. I do agree that the information they may have found will answer some troubling questions."

"Troubling questions your Eminence?" Bishop Grielle asked, halting and interrupting their stroll down the ornate hallway.

"Yes, I find it troubling that there seem to be so many coincidences. I find it strange that Father Gates is killed on the way to the funeral where a senior vice president and junior vice president of Everest International, and deacons of Father Gates's Diocese, themselves die. Also some of Everest's research staff are killed. Then you have events in Mexico ten years ago to the recent one here in Los Angeles where each has a single survivor and witness, both ending up blind. I don't know?"

"You think they're all tied together?"

"Did you know that Father Gates was the primary administrator, acting as facilitator between the Church and the local free clinics for our parishioners here in Southern California and Mexico?"

"Yes I did." Bishop Grielle was well aware of Father Gates' responsibilities, sometimes envious as he believed he himself should have been the coordinator in charge of outreach programs. Bishop Grielle knew that, if not for a promotions moratorium, the Cardinal would have found a way to elevate the Father's position in the Diocese. The Father's untimely demise halted the Cardinal's petitioning for a special waiver for promotion from Rome.

"God's work in helping the indigent will be impacted. Yet God does work in ways we do not understand. It is imperative to ensure Father Hernandez and Sister Justine return from finding out what is going on. They must show that there are forces working against us. We do not want any delays with our greater plans."

Of course, Bishop Grielle was still puzzled by the Cardinal's comments. "Then why bring them back in such a short amount of time, if we want to find out what truly happened?"

"It's in case they're successful."

"I'm confused, your Eminence."

Cardinal Millhouse continued walking. "When your three researchers or investigators, I'm not sure what

Jerry J. K. Rogers

you're calling them, when they arrive and brief us on
everything, I'll tell you more. Now let's go and eat."

Bishop Grielle was again suppressing frustration,
irritated by his mentor's ambiguity. Here he was seeing
his superior as being duplicitous in how he verbalized his
position versus how he carried out managing certain
events. Sending the three researchers to Mexico was a
perfect example. Cardinal Millhouse would espouse the
strong need to determine the cause of the tragic
supernatural event. But he then worked to restrict their
access to background information or subtly
micromanaged control of the team, ensuring they
wouldn't find out anything. As the Cardinal claimed
once before, nothing should be revealed that could
embarrass the Church, have the appearance of sacrilege,
or dissent from Church theology and doctrine. The
Bishop would never directly challenge his superior, and
he maintained his loyalty even when he might experience
apprehension about the Cardinal's overarching control.
After years of loyal service, he hoped he had established
a high level of trust. He thought the Cardinal would at
least disclose, even incrementally, the full scope of what
was thought by many to be a proclamation from a
secretive council driving the vision and purpose of the
affected dioceses and key sponsors in Los Angeles,
Mexico, and Canada, having a global religious impact.

Although extremely dutiful in executing Church
directives with Church guidance, without reservation, in
the administration of the Diocese, Bishop Grielle felt he
excelled brokering many of the meetings, discussions,
and planning sessions in the collaboration between the
Church, Everest, and other associated companies. The

213

liaisons many times covered the governance of clinics and Church-sponsored medical research projects. Yet he heard rumors of numerous reticent dialogues and meetings without his involvement, many allegedly undercutting his previous work. Most of these included Father Gates.

Bishop Grielle couldn't understand why Cardinal Millhouse would exclude him from much of the sensitive, confidential administrative workings and information within the upper echelons of the Diocese. He was well aware that Cardinal Millhouse knew that the chances of upward mobility for either one were restricted. The issuance of an edict helped to provide stability for the congregations after the events more than ten years before. Many of the clergy would remain indefinitely in their posts. Mandatory retirement ages would be waived depending on the extent of vacancies. If anything, the Bishop thought this would remove any suspicions that he would attempt to garner a promotion to Cardinal in another location, if one were to become available.

Cardinal Millhouse did indeed feel threatened. Even though many of the Southern California dioceses felt minimal impact during the mass disappearance, advancements to higher offices in local parishes with a Diocese were curtailed. Yet even after the restrictions on promotions of clergy, Grielle received one of the few during the troubling time being made an official bishop. This elevated him from the honorary position of monsignor. Cardinal Millhouse perceived the career of his subordinate to rise faster than his.

Chapter 20

The Indian summer weather made for a perfect day in the park, although Indian summer for a warm spell in Southern California during early November can sometimes be a misnomer. Alder's 4-year-old daughter, Michelle, was enjoying herself at her friend's birthday party. The main entertainment for the children, a clown, arrived just as parents began herding 4-, 5-, and 6-year-olds to congregate around the birthday girl's picnic table. The clown, with pasty white makeup, wide-bordered red lips, bulbous red nose just off center, eyes encircled with emerald and black eyeliner in an attempted star pattern, curly ruby hair wig, faded white ruffles around his neck, and yellow polka dot jump outfit, was foreign to the children. Seeing him made most of the younger children anxious; many began to cry. Several of the parents didn't want to admit to themselves that the clown was unsettling to them as well, so coming to the rescue of their crying children gave them the heroic excuse of embracing someone for their own comfort. The older children bravely ignored the pancake makeup of the entertainer and enjoyed the plethora of balloon animals and figures he created.

Alder saw that Michelle was engrossed in the show. He searched for Maria and found her encamped nearby with some of the other mothers, each holding an infant, firing off insincere compliments to one another and sneaking in a jibe on the supremacy of their own child. One would brag, "My child is already rolling over." Another would counter, "Mine is sitting up on his own, quick for his age." Maria relegated herself to listening to the women banter, not wanting to get involved in the competition.

The clown moved into performing magic and started to make the children feel more at ease, many of them relaxing into watching the show. After the magic demonstration, partygoer guests consumed hot dogs, hamburgers, and veggie burgers, followed by the birthday cake. The children broke away to play several party games that a couple of parents organized before the opening of the gifts. Alder glanced over to a nearby thicket of trees and saw several dads who were broke away from the festivities. A cooler was at their feet and they were drinking beer. *Pay dirt.*

Alder navigated over to the men, none of whom he had formally met earlier. He'd seen them interacting with what he assumed were their wives and children at the party. Alder must have shown the look of desire for a cold one. The shortest and stockiest of the four standing by the clump of trees opened the ice chest, pulled out a Michelob, and tossed it his way. Thanking the muscular, older-middle-aged black man for the beer, Alder introduced himself. They continued with trivial conversation about the city's two baseball teams, a recent small earthquake that geologists could not associate with a specific fault-line and the state of the local economy, three of the five not faring well jobwise. Then the conversation migrated to current events, including the Crestview and Thomson and Thomson alleged visitations. Once Alder revealed he had been a winner of the company's raffle to the fatal event, and was late because of traffic along with his coworker-friend, who was the lone survivor, the other men bombarded him with questions: "What did the angel look like?" "Do you know how all those people died?" "Did you know anyone who died?" "Why do you think it happened?" A couple of the men began to recall seeing Alder on a couple of the local news channels, interviewed on television as the coworker of the survivor of the headlined "Death Angel Visitation".

Alder answered the questions the best he could and wished he was back with the other partygoers. When he tried to change the subject, the men returned to the funeral homes theme. A group of teenagers playing softball yelled at the men to watch out. A white sphere approached in a downward arc. All five men ducked, the ball sailing over their heads by a couple of feet. Alder saw this as his chance to escape the barrage of questions and chased the ball into large hedges near the trees. Traversing the foliage to where he thought the ball had come to rest, the drifting funky and odorous smell of urine, dirt, and musk his assailed his nostrils. If he didn't know better, there might be a hint of sweet clove, or roses, he couldn't tell which, but more persistent than the stomach-turning odors. Traversing through the hedges, he tripped over the small frame of a woman wearing tattered and stained layers of clothing including a sweater resembling Swiss cheese, a dirt-splotched overcoat out of place for the warm weather, and a scarf that covered her unwashed silver-streaked jet-black hair. She was not happy.

"Hey, what's wrong with you?" she screamed with a thick Spanish accent, "Are you blind?"

In shock from the unexpected encounter, Alder scrambled for words: "I'm just looking for a ball that came over this way."

"There's no ball over here. You blind or somethin', like your friend who saw the angel?" the woman said, her accent almost making her words incomprehensible.

"Look, a ball came ove... what did you say?" he asked the woman, who was grabbing her blankets, a plastic bag of cans, and another bag filled with junk. Alder could hear the approach of either the men he had been drinking with or the teens who had hit the ball into the area. He ignored the onrush of activity and pressed on with his questions.

"What do you mean my blind friend who saw the angel? Who are you talking about?" Alder asked, his stomach turning from her sweet and foul body odor, wondering if she was going to answer with the name he was anticipating.

The stranger stopped picking up her belongings and stared directly at Alder. "Your blind friend who sees angels, who'd you think I'm talkin' about? How many times do I have to say it? Are you dumb or somethin? " she said in a disdainful voice.

"Hey, who do you think you're talking to that way?"

"Who do you think, smart aleck?"

Feeling the blood rush to his face as a burst of anger built up inside, Alder's attention turned to a couple of teens coming through the hedges asking if he had their ball. Alder hadn't noticed the ball sitting next to the thick trunks of the shrubs next to him. The woman picked it up and tossed it to an acne-laden teen. Thanking her, both boys glanced at the surroundings, thought that whatever was happening could be strange, and decided to return to their game. By the look on their faces, Alder felt the same; the situation was somewhat strange.

"Look, I'm just gonna leave you alone," Alder said. He thought maybe she'd caught a picture of him in the newspaper or on the news being interviewed.

"You do watcha you gotta do," the unkempt lady commented, her accent fading. "Just make sure your friend talks to his three visitors."

"What the hell are you talking about?" he asked, extremely puzzled.

She ignored him and finished gathering her possessions, straggling toward another set of hedges. Alder knew he didn't want to stay any longer; she was making him uncomfortable just with her presence. Turning to head back, he saw the other fathers working their way over to him. All of them were curious about the delay after seeing the two teens come out with the ball. Alder found they didn't wait in bombarding him with more questions after he rejoined them, with no concern for the impoverished lady. He didn't feel like continuing with the conversation, especially now that they were asking the same questions in different ways expecting the answers to be different or for the story to be told a bit more dramatically. Grabbing one more beer from the cooler, Alder politely excused himself under the auspices of wanting to check out how his wife and kids were doing, which wasn't too far from the truth.

Returning to the party, Alder's daughter was still enjoying herself, playing a game of tag with several other kids. Maria was engaged in conversation with the other mothers and in the middle of changing Matthew. Alder never knew a baby could expel so much waste. Matthew must have eaten recently and he was holding true to how Alder thought of him, eating, sleeping, and crapping.

"As usual, perfect timing," Maria snickered. Alder reached to pick up his son while Maria secured the final piece of tape on his disposable diaper, "As soon as I finish changing his diaper, here you come to play with Matthew."

Alder could hear the other mothers chuckle. He ignored them. "Hey, since we brought both cars, I was thinking about going to visit Stephen?"

Alder saw that his subtle request garnered approval from his wife, especially because she hadn't had to prod him to go. "That's a good idea," she responded.

"I wanna head over before it gets too late."

"Would you mind picking up some things from the store on your way back. For one, Matthew needs more diapers."

"What? Didn't we just get some? Hell, does food just go straight through him? I swear your son is nothing more than a crapping machine," Alder replied, forgetting his surroundings. He glanced toward Maria, who was giving him a harsh look of disapproval. The multitude of wives sitting around on the blankets had become statuesque; only two of them continued rocking or swinging the child in their arms. He knew there was no real way to recover and decided to retreat and pretend nothing happened.

"What else do you want me to pick up... hon?" Alder said, attempting to sound conciliatory. It didn't work.

"Never mind, just go and see how Stephen is doing. I'll pick up the stuff on the way home," Maria snapped, taking Matthew back into possession.

"Seriously, I don't mi..."

Maria's stare told Alder the conversation was over. Withdrawing from the assembly of mothers, he knew that tonight, once he returned home, the cold treatment would commence. This would be the milder form of retribution for his lapse of judgment and her embarrassment in front of her friends. Maybe on the way back, one drink would help prepare for the inevitable confrontation. Alder knew that if he stopped by for just one, others would follow. Maria was getting thoroughly upset with what she took to be his increasing consumption. But Alder saw it as an effective counterbalance to challenging days at work.

Chapter 21

After overcoming his anger at losing his sight, and fighting temporary bouts of depression, Stephen was still frustrated with the progress of his rehabilitation training. His sister and rehab specialist attempted to educate him on the floor plan, location of furniture, and essentials for day-to-day living. They coached him on the location of cookware, refrigerator, and the appliances and utensils he could safely use. He would need to reeducate himself on using the bathroom, shaving, and showering. Stephen wasn't successful with many of the tasks and was becoming discouraged. His new routine proved troublesome. Finding simple items such as his comb and razor blades did not turn out to be as easy as anticipated.

After living in his house for more than five years, he still had to learn to navigate around the furniture. Things he had taken for granted, location of the couch, coffee table, entertainment system, lamps, and other accoutrements in the living room, were now obstacles. The bedroom wasn't as hard with only a few items to work around. In addition, he was familiar with the orientation of the bed and dresser. The kitchen was the most troublesome in the retraining process. Stephen had to relearn how to work with utensils, many having been removed to prevent from hurting himself; the trainer and his sister rearranged the items in the pantry and cabinets with Stephen having to learn the new order.

With so much to learn since becoming visually impaired, each of the last several days had made more evident how powerless and fallible he felt within his own home. It was as if he were a little child. His sister, Brenda, could sense his helplessness, especially during the times he reacted with angry outbursts. The rehab specialist knew Stephen was trying to cram in too much too soon to try to show his independence, especially with his big sister helping in almost all matters. Brenda's aid added to his sense of inadequacy. It didn't make a difference how hard the specialist tried to nudge Brenda to minimize her assistance; she only became more emboldened to be involved. To change tactics, the trainer used the direct approach of telling her she was more of a hindrance than a help. Offended, Brenda lashed back.

An argument followed. The two agreed to disengage temporarily from their disagreement when Stephen withdrew to the living room couch to sulk. Approaching the end of her four-hour shift, the trainer decided to grab her sweater and purse and dismiss herself for the day. She had learned over the years to maintain patience when training those who were recently blinded. The family, however, was generally not as imposing to the extent of Brenda. Often, in fact, family members were afraid to engage and receded into the background, offering minimal to no assistance. Cordially excusing herself and opening the door to leave, she found Alder on the landing getting ready to push the doorbell.

"May I help you?" the trainer asked, unsettled yet poised.

Alder was startled to see the door swing open without having to ring the doorbell. He suspected that he'd been watched as he approached the doorway. "Uh, yeah, is Stephen here?"

The trainer withdrew, and within a couple of minutes returned to leave the house with Brenda in her wake. "May I help you?" she asked.

"I'm here to see Stephen."

"And you are?" Brenda demanded, attempting to compose herself while still not calmed down from her quarrel with the trainer.

Alder speculated that this was Stephen's sister. Even though he had visited him a couple of times since he had been in the rehabilitation center, and Stephen mentioned she had come down to assist with his acclamation training, he had yet to meet her. "I'm Alder Dennison. I work with Stephen."

"I'm so sorry. So you're Alder? Stephen mentions you all the time, come on in," Brenda said, a huge grin forming on her face and reaching out giving Alder a hug as if he were a welcomed member of the family. "It seems that the times you've been over to the rehab center I've been out running errands for him. You'll have to forgive me for just a minute ago. We still have reporters and religious nutcases coming by here."

Brenda guided Alder into the home. He realized that this was the first time he had ever visited his coworker's house. They'd gone out for drinks and attended parties and events together, a couple of times with Maria tagging along, but he'd never been to his home. Alder saw the interior was immaculate. The minimal amount of furniture appeared perfectly squared with the walls; a nominal amount of accoutrements adorned above. Alder had anticipated the home would be in a similar slovenly condition as when he had been single. As they passed through the kitchen to the back patio, the countertops were austere and bare. Alder wondered why a man would want to live this way. *Oh yeah, a blind man probably needs to.*

Brenda stayed behind in the house when Alder went outside.

"So they're still not leaving you alone huh?" Alder asked Stephen, who was staring into the backyard as if eyeing the rear fence.

"Hey Alder, what brings you by today? How're things at work," Stephen asked, thinking today's visit would be similar to previous visits or calls when Alder would vent or scout for help to assist him through his new position. Several times the requests yielded no useful information, especially since Stephen had had only limited access to many of the projects Alder was currently working on.

"One of Michelle's playmates had a birthday party in McForrester Park not too far from here, so I thought I'd stop by and say hey. Things are about the same at work. Still trying to get my head wrapped around a lot of the crap going on there."

"It's not that bad, is it?" Stephen noted in a reassuring tone.

"You know, sometimes I wonder if Jeffrey was trying to cover up shit more than being just stupid. Hell, maybe both."

"Well, you don't think they're fixing your stuff in the bull pen do you?"

"I doubt it. Remember how they used to be somewhat secretive about projects hitting the bullpen, and would get upset if something accidentally got processed incorrectly and ended up there? Now they've gotten so tight lipped about projects, barely anything makes it out."

"Do they still have you signing shit without knowing what you're signing?

"Yeah, they do. I swear it's gonna bite me in the ass one day, watch."

Brenda decided to break into the conversation and stepped outside onto the patio. "Did you both want something to drink, lemonade, iced tea, water?"

What Alder wanted was a beer or a shot of whiskey or gin. He decided on lemonade. So did Stephen.

"How long is your sister staying here with you?" Alder asked.

"I don't know. She was only down to help get me situated with my rehab trainer but, man, she's getting into some serious rows with her," Stephen responded. "You should have heard the cat fighting before you got here."

"Was that the trainer who left when I got here?"

Stephen was unable to mask being a bit unhappy about the situation between his sister and his trainer. "Yeah."

"So how's it going? Are you getting situated with, well, you know?" Alder queried, finding himself empathetic for his coworker but not quite sure how to complete his thought.

"I don't know. Sometimes I think if my sister didn't get in the way, it could be going better."

"She's just watching out for you," Alder commented, attempting to be supportive.

"She still thinks I'm five years old and needs to watch out for me..."

"Here's your lemonade," Brenda interrupted, bringing out a platter with two tall glasses filled with ice and a pitcher of pink lemonade. Resting the platter on the patio table, she filled both glasses, placing one directly in her brother's hand. "And I'm going keep watching out for you as long as I need to so I know that you're gonna be all right," she said, sounding as if she were addressing an adolescent.

Both men were caught off guard by Brenda's patronizing of her younger brother. They surmised she must have heard part of their conversation. She went back inside after serving their refreshments.

Alder was almost afraid to continue their conversation. "You think she's upset?" he asked.

"Probably. I think she's just being nice because you're here though," Stephen snarked.

"That's not true." Brenda's voice yelled out from inside the house through the patio door.

"Like I said," Stephen continued, "she's just being nice since you're here."

"How much older is she than you?" Alder asked.

"Don't you dare answer that," Brenda yelled out again. "You may be blind, but I hope you're not stupid."

Stephen revealed a small smile. Alder felt the tension ease for both men the first time since the incident. This was the most lighthearted Stephen had been.

The doorbell rang and caught the attention of all three. Brenda called out she would answer the door. Both Stephen and Alder kept quiet until she returned to announce the visitors.

"Stephen, there's a priest, a nun, and some college professor guy at the door wanting to talk to you. They said they talked to you once already when you were in the hospital and have a few more questions they'd like to ask you."

Alder saw Stephen's warm expression go stoic. He sensed Stephen didn't want to be bothered.

"I don't feel like any guests right now sis. Tell them maybe later, but not today," Stephen said.

Brenda went to turn away the unexpected guests. Alder suddenly thought that he should tell Stephen to receive the visitors. Was it the incident in the park? He wasn't sure.

"Stephen, I don't know why, but I think you should talk to them."

Stephen turned his head in the direction of Alder's voice. "What do you mean? They're just a pain anyway. What good would it do?" Stephen asked. "I already told them everything I knew."

Brenda returned and broke into their conversation. "They really want to talk to you Stephen, they say it's extremely important."

Stephen imagined the look on Alder's face as one of petitioning and disappointment. Although Alder thought Stephen should talk to the three, he wouldn't feel dejected if Stephen refused. Stephen surrendered to Alder's request.

"Go ahead and let them in," Stephen said. When it sounded like his sister left, he decided to ask his friend a question. "Why do you think I should talk to them?"

Alder paused for quite a while, not sure how to answer. He finally decided. "Just a bit ago, back in the park, there was this strange homeless woman and she... well, she said some weird things."

"Weird things like what?" Michael asked from inside the house as he approached the patio door, bypassing any formal introductions.

"Sorry about that Mr. Williams," Father Hernandez apologized, also entering the patio. Then Sister Justine continued. "The first gentleman talking was Michael Saunders, I'm Sister Justine and also here is Father Hernandez from Our Lady of the Light Catholic Church. I don't know if you remember us. We're researching the angelic visit incident where you lost your sight. We met you before at the hospital."

Stephen focused on the voices and reached out his hand to shake and greet his visitors. They reciprocated. Stephen noted two of the handshakes were from hands with smooth, supple skin, somewhat weak and limber in their grasp. "I do remember you. What can I do for you?" he asked.

"Your friend here can tell us about that lady in the park," Michael responded in a cocky tone.

"Really nothing to say, just a homeless lady with a bunch of junk and a weird smell. She said some weird stuff like most crazies who live in a park," Alder responded.

"We came out here to talk to you Mr. Williams," Sister Justine said, jumping in on the questioning of

229

Alder to refocus to their original intent, knowing Michael was the one who wanted to come and talk to Stephen again.

Father Hernandez walked over and stood in front of Stephen, then dropped to one knee to meet him at face level. Stephen sensed a slight movement of air and could hear someone breathing directly in front of him, which made him feel rather apprehensive.

"Mr. Williams."

"Call me Stephen," he noted, sitting further back in his patio chair.

"All right Stephen," Father Hernandez continued. "How much of the incident at the funeral home do you remember?"

"Like I told you before when I was in the hospital," Stephen started, and then went through a synopsis of all the events he could remember. He detailed the sight of the angel, the unique smells, the name of the angel, the beautiful tonal voice that essentially sounded like the creature singing, and ultimately the sense of foreboding and feeling that he should leave the chapel area immediately.

The three unannounced visitors continued to ask probing questions. Soon they were asking the same questions in different ways to see if they could garner anything granular he may have forgotten. After a while, they recognized they were only successful in extracting the same information they already gathered and irritating Stephen.

"So, is there anything else interesting you could remember that could help us?" Father Hernandez asked compassionately while attempting to conceal being flustered.

"The whole event was interesting. But you know what was the most interesting of all?" Stephen answered, irked after being asked an incessant number of questions.

"What's that?"

"The fact that I'm blind," Stephen jabbed.

The boy toy walked into that one, Michael thought. Also, after nearly 15 minutes of questioning by all three, Michael speculated that it might not have been a good idea to stop by. He had hoped the visit would've resulted in a revelation that could somehow tie in the fragments of information previously discovered.

"Well Stephen, we thank you for your time," Father Hernandez said standing up, his legs cramped from kneeling the entire time they had interrogated Stephen. "We were hoping you could have told us more about the angel since you were the only one to see it," Father Hernandez continued, getting ready to leave. Michael and Sister Justine were ready to follow the Father, who was heading to the patio door.

"Just like at the TV station. No one else saw the angel there either," Stephen said.

"Excuse me?" Michael exclaimed, all three amazed by the disclosure.

"Yeah, I could have sworn I saw the same angel at the television studio at the same time I understood an angel showed up at another funeral the Sunday I was on the talk show."

Alder saw this new information was of great interest to the visitors by their expressions. They were aware of the event at Crestview Funeral Home. Michael had been

231

pondering the incident since it fueled his insistence in wanting to talk to Stephen again. He didn't know they would find out that Abriel had made another appearance apart from a funeral.

"I thought I was going crazy 'cause no one else said they saw it. But a couple of stagehands and a cameraman said they had this really weird feeling, as if someone was standing there with them, but no one was there. I swear, though, it was right there in front of me. It looked it was the very same angel I saw when I went blind. Everybody thought I was crazy."

"Mr. Williams?" Father Hernandez asked, returning to formality, "We thought you were blind all this time." Everyone sensed the skepticism in the Father's question.

"Is that why you jumped out of your chair when you were on the show?" Sister Justine asked.

"You saw that?" Michael asked, "I thought at least you'd be in mass."

"I had permission to miss that one so that I could watch and see if anything would be revealed during his interview. So Stephen, you said you were able to see the angel even though you're blind?" Sister Justine inquired.

"Look, I can't explain it; I just know that while I was sitting there, an angel shows up scaring the hell ou... sorry Father, Sister, scaring the crap out of me."

"So what exactly happened?" Father Hernandez asked.

"The angel showed up, stood off in the background, and stared me down for what I thought was a helluva long time. Then all of a sudden, it charged at me, stopped, stood face to face, and then disappeared. It scared the hell out of me."

"And what happened after that? Anything else? It could be important," Sister Justine queried.

"Nothing I can remember right now."

"The angel didn't do anything else?" Michael asked.

"No, like I mentioned before, I don't recall anything else."

Brenda stepped out onto the patio and up to the group. "Stevie, remember in the car on the way back, you said you thought it did say something?"

"I'd definitely call that a yes in the anything else category," Michael quipped, of course earning an irate look from Sister Justine.

Stephen's face had an astonished look of recall. "Oh yeah. Thanks sis. It did say something. I think it said Aurora."

The three identified the name hearing it during their recent trip. Brenda could see this was interesting to the three visitors. The long silence made Stephen think maybe his interrogators might have been confused by the response. Michael glanced over to Alder, who'd gone completely pale.

"Excuse me, but does that name mean anything to you?" Michael asked Alder. "You know, I don't think we've been introduced," Michael continued. Father Hernandez and Sister Justine turned toward Alder and saw his pale skin.

"Alder Dennison. I work with Stephen."

"Well, it seems like that name means something to you."

"Not really."

"Not really or not at all?" Michael pressed.

The color returned to Alder's face as he became infuriated. "No, not at all." Alder thought about the name Aurora. It had come across their desks several times before as a secretive project title that shouldn't have been released to their department. Thanks to Jeffrey Bradfield, it had been exposed. Alder had also seen the name several times on his boss's desk. If it weren't for the nondisclosure agreement associated with his new position, Alder felt he could have freely revealed some of this information but decided to protect it. The problem was that Stephen did not have to sign an agreement. Not being at the junior executive level, he did not have to deal with the same concerns of sensitive information.

"Well it seems odd, we heard the name while we were down in Aguascalientes," Father Hernandez exclaimed.

"For some reason the name sounds familiar, I just don't know why," Stephen commented.

Alder knew the reason and was thankful Stephen didn't remember. Even though Stephen was the one unyieldingly blinded, Alder now felt more involved in the shadows of everything currently happening.

"Mr. Williams, please try to remember where you heard the name before," Father Hernandez pleaded. "Did the angel mention it to you the first time you went blind?"

Michael sneaked long peeks over at Alder, still visibly troubled by the conversation and the name Aurora. "Excuse me, what was your name again? I forgot that fast," Michael probed, directing his question to Alder. Michael hadn't forgotten, he wanted to try to keep Alder off guard and get candid responses for the questions he began to formulate in his head.

"Alder, Alder Dennison," Alder responded, a bit perturbed that he had to announce his name again so quickly.

"Alden, are you sure the…"

"Alder."

"Sorry, Alder. Are you sure the name doesn't ring a bell in any way? Maybe at church, work, with friends maybe?"

"Now I remember," Stephen blurted out. "I remember where I saw the name before. It was at work."

"Are you sure Stephen?" Alder asked, stepping in on the conversation.

Stephen recognized the voice asking the question. "Remember Alder, the name showed up on some of the misappropriations by Jeffrey Bradfield before he died. Those were some of the ones he got irate about."

"Wait a minute, Aurora isn't the name of an angel?" Sister Justine asked.

"What Stephen doesn't realize is that our company happens to work on some extremely sensitive projects. Everyone isn't allowed to know all that we do so that our trade secrets aren't revealed," Alder said, making sure he got the information in.

"Trade secrets? Doesn't that sound a little strange Alder?" Everybody noted the ostentatious sarcasm in Michael's voice. "How could something in your company be associated with what we're trying to find out?"

"Maybe the name Aurora is just a coincidence. They do happen you know," Stephen reacted, trying to give a plausible explanation and hoping to close out the subject.

No one believed him. Regardless, Michael, Father Hernandez, and Sister Justine were intrigued by the correlation of the name Aurora from the witness in Mexico, to the visitation at the television station, to a project in a company where many of the employees had died. None of the three could immediately deduce anything to tie the fragments of data together, except perhaps the unique involvement of angels.

"Where do you both work again?" Father Hernandez asked.

Before Alder could answer and divert the attention of the three church visitors, Stephen answered the question. "Everest International Bio-Medical Group."

Father Hernandez remembered the company name because they had asked Stephen shortly after he was admitted to the hospital. He also knew most of those who died were associated with that corporation, but the name didn't seem as important at the time.

"Mr. Dennison, we just got back a short while ago from the city of Aguascalientes in Mexico and an area outside of the town called El Refugio," Father Hernandez commented. "Does that ring a bell at all? And please try to remember. We're working just as hard as the police to try and determine why just over a hundred poor souls were killed and to find out if an angel was the cause."

Father Hernandez hoped the unconscious reflexes in his face wouldn't reveal to anyone acutely aware of body language that he lied. He knew that the police officially closed the homicide portion of the case; they weren't actively pursuing it anymore at the request of the Archdiocese.

"Look, I have no idea about anything in Mexico, and because you're not the police, we don't need to answer any more of these questions. Anything about Aurora is considered proprietary to my employer."

Sister Justine tried to plead for more information. "Alder, Stephen, understand we're trying to find out..."

Alder interrupted, "I'm sorry, but I'm going to have to leave, and Stephen, please don't answer any more questions about the company and respect that we're bound by confidentiality to keep our company information protected."

Father Hernandez considered an attempt for a final appeal, but capitulated. "Mr. Dennison, if you have a change of heart and would like to discuss more of this with us, you can contact me at Our Lady of the Light Church."

Alder didn't respond. Feeling uncomfortable with the discussion, and hearing the three church representatives discussing the name Aurora, he didn't want to stay and risk revealing any more information. He lied about Mexico. There were general ledger charges and capital expenditures for projects associated with a research lab and clinics in the Aguascalientes area. Without even saying goodbye to Stephen, he dashed to the patio exit. He felt he had already been too forthcoming. Stephen would be fine by himself with his three guests since, as far as Alder knew, the name Aurora had only come up a couple of times as part of misrouted accounting paperwork. As for himself, Alder knew more than he let on because he had gleaned some peripheral information working the projects in his new position.

As soon as Alder left the patio, Brenda sensed the three guests were ready to pounce on Stephen with more questions, but she intervened.

"You know, I think it may be a good idea if the three of you would leave please. My brother needs his rest. It's been a long day for him."

"We'd really like to stay and just ask a few more questions," Father Hernandez urged.

Stephen wearied discussing anything else. Alder's hasty exit caused concern. Working with Alder for a number of years, he could sense in his voice that he was upset. "I agree with my sister, please leave now. Maybe later."

Father Hernandez was getting ready to make one final plea. Sister Justine grabbed his forearm and squeezed with gentle pressure, which Michael observed. Father Hernandez caught the hint. "Thanks for your time Mr. Williams," Father Hernandez said.

Brenda escorted the guests to the door and out of the house, her demeanor icy. They weren't worried about her as much as trying to embrace, and comprehend, everything that had transpired in their discussion. With this visit, the entire trip had yielded unique distinct fragments of information to their investigative research. The three had to admit to themselves that their key questions had yet to be answered: Why the visitations, why the two events where so many were killed, and how were they linked by the Everest Corporation?

The three researchers stood in silence by the car, each silently deliberating their next course of action.

Michael knew he didn't want to see Bishop Grielle. Sister Justine could sense this but she knew they couldn't continue to avoid returning to see him. Father Hernandez, who had not felt overwhelmed earlier, now felt overcome by the plethora of unconnected data they'd discovered during the last week. It would be best to amass all their notes and consolidate the information into a single presentation as soon as possible. Bishop Grielle would be anxious, possibly impatient, to be briefed on what they'd found. Michael hoped he could remember all that he had just learned to be able to record it into his personal notes, independent of their official journal.

Sister Justine knew they would need to consider the divergent information before they continued doing anything else. "So, do you think it was a coincidence to hear the name Aurora here and down in Mexico?" she asked of her two companions.

"I don't know if we can really say. But I do think we need to reconcile everything we found out up to this point before reporting back to his Excellency," Father Hernandez responded. "He can probably wait until Monday or Tuesday and we can brief him then. Besides, I want to get ready and oversee all the services for mass tomorrow now that I'm back in town."

Michael was taken aback, more so than Sister Justine, that Father Hernandez wanted to defer presenting any information to Bishop Grielle. She had been the one pressing the case to go and visit the bishop.

"We need to at least need to give him the courtesy of stopping by to debrief him about our trip," she directed. "He is paying you a research fee Michael."

"And what exactly are we going to tell him? I mean, when you get right down to it, we still haven't found any physical proof of what happened. A secondhand witness to our original witness in Mexico, and a blind man here who saw the same angel, that's it." Michael commented excitedly, gesturing with his hand to punctuate his statement. He pointed to Stephen's house and turned his head to emphasize. Father Hernandez and Sister Justine both reciprocated, turning their heads to the house as Michael's eyes widened in amazement. All three saw Brenda standing dead center of the oversized living room window, bordered by blue ruffled curtains, her arms crossed and an expression of contempt on her face.

"OK, that's weird," Michael whispered loud enough for the other two to hear. "Let's get the hell out of here."

They agreed to get in the car and drive off, still unsettled about what to do next, mystified by Brenda's angry demeanor in the window.

As for Brenda, she was extremely hostile toward the Church. Both she and Stephen were raised as Catholics. Their parents felt they both should make their own decision relating to religion and follow their own paths toward belief on their own once they became adults. Both siblings had decided not to partake in any of the Holy Sacraments or pursue other religions or beliefs. Stephen, not wanting to upset his older sister, at times wanted to quench his curiosity about the Church and its doctrines. He would sneak off to talk to their local priest but never fully committed to accepting membership, though he'd come close a couple of times. Their parents, nonetheless, remained active in the Church. Over time, they enthusiastically described how their local parish had veered in a new evangelical direction in its teachings. Both parents abandoned their earlier idea of letting their children decide for themselves and began encouraging Brenda and Stephen to reconsider joining the Church. Both children believed their parents had become extremely religious, reading the Bible more frequently and praying every night. Shortly after, their mother and father, along with many in the congregation of their parish, disappeared, with countless others. Brenda blamed the Church for the loss. Stephen had wondered since then if something religious happened and had always wanted to research more of what the local priest had espoused.

Chapter 22

Alder faced his choice when he dropped by the Goat's Beard tavern before heading home and diving into the anticipated argument; should he grab either a couple of sodas or a couple of shots to help numb his emotions. Going home after drinking alcohol might not be such a good idea. No matter what he did to mask the smell emanating from his breath or through his sweat, she knew he'd been drinking. He was well aware Maria knew about his beers earlier at the park. Somehow, she would be able to gauge if he had had any additional alcohol. Alder didn't know that she had learned that his eyes lost a bit of their brightness, as they became more blood shot the more he drank.

Thinking through his choices, stopping by the tavern at all wouldn't be a good option. No matter how much he wouldn't want to transition from soda to a harder beverage, he knew his willpower was nil. It was best just to head straight home. Alder wasn't sure why; the drinks normally won out, but not this time. Traffic was again surprisingly heavy for a Saturday evening with the main highway home shut down for more than an hour.

Arriving at the house, pulling into the driveway, the urge caught up with him to back the Nissan up, head down the street, and drive the two miles back to the tavern. He knew that if Maria happened to see him pull up or pulling away, that would be three infractions to contend with. He shut the engine off. Walking up to the front door, Alder took two deep breaths before inserting the key and opening. Only a single living room lamp was turned on; all the other lights were off. The early evening twilight through the living room window provided subtle, soft, illumination. Maria sat on the couch, but she didn't look furious or have her standard demeanor of trying to hold back a torrent of rage. Instead, she appeared distressed; her bronze Latina skin clammy. Alder knew something was wrong. He risked heading over to the couch to sit next to her.

"Honey, what's wrong?" he asked in a tone of genuine concern, successfully communicated to his wife.

"I don't know," Maria responded, the shakiness of fear in her voice.

"Everything all right?" Alder asked, "Where are the kids?"

"They're upstairs taking a late nap."

"Then what's wrong? You look upset."

She paused before answering, "It's Michelle."

"Is she all right? What happened?" Alder asked in near panic. Maria was comforted by Alder's concern.

"She was upstairs playing earlier and I caught her climbing on the tall dresser trying to get to my makeup and perfume to play grown-up make-believe. Her friend is a year older, so Michelle wanted to be older. Well, I told her not to do that again. I heard the buzzer on the dryer letting me know a load was done. I started to go downstairs when I heard her scream and a crash; I thought there was a flash of bright white light behind me."

"She didn't hurt herself, did she?"

"It sounded like she did, and when I ran back into the bedroom, a bunch of my makeup and perfume was all over the floor. But Michelle was sitting on the floor laughing."

"Laughing?" Alder asked, confused at first. Maybe with no one around to see the fall and make a fuss over her, Michelle had taken it in stride. "Kids are tough."

"That's not the problem. Michelle claimed that when she fell, a pretty man with wings caught her."

"A pretty what?"

Maria just stared into Alder's eyes. She knew he'd heard her. Alder just wanted to make sure he had heard Maria correctly.

"Did you say pretty man with wings, like an angel?" he asked.

"Yeah, and that's not all."

"Wha' do you mean?"

"She said it was the same angel who was with the lady who talked to you in the park."

"What lady and angel talked to me in the park?" Alder asked, forgetting about the encounter in the bushes chasing the ball.

"I don't know. I just know our daughter is scaring me right now," Maria noted.

"I'm trying to figure out what Michelle is talking about at the park," Alder said. He stayed quiet thinking through the events during the birthday party. Then it hit him. "Wait a minute. The only weird thing was when a softball went into the bushes. I went in after it and came across a homeless woman. She definitely didn't seem like an angel. Oh God, you should've smelled her."

"That reminds me. Go upstairs to the bedroom," Maria gently demanded.

"Why do I wanna go upstairs?"

Maria responded with an intimidating gaze. Alder took the hint and worked his way through avoiding the toys spewed across the stairs. Arriving at the landing and walking toward the master bedroom, a pungent sweet smell hit him, a mixture of what he thought was cinnamon, citrus blossoms, and Rose petals. Inside the bedroom, he saw the king-sized bed exceedingly wrinkled on top, probably the result of Michelle jumping up and down. Alder glanced at the dark cherry wood dresser where Maria kept some of her perfumes and make-up paraphernalia. He reflected on how she kept most of her items on top of most of the room's furniture with little space left for him. Numerous disagreements had occurred. *Now is not the time to start another one*, he thought.

Looking at the drawers, he saw where Michelle had pulled out each one just enough to create an improvised stepladder. On the hardwood floor, some combs, a brush, a couple of mascara containers, and several bottles of perfumes were scattered at the base of the dresser. Alder expected the disrupted items to already having being placed back on top of the dresser, especially since Maria worked diligently to ensure the bedroom was meticulous. She was more relaxed with the rest of the house, not wanting to constrict the children's natural expression and freedom of youth. However, the master bedroom was to remain an adult sanctuary.

The closer Alder got to the dresser, the more pronounce the sweet smell. Each bottle on the floor was intact, their tops securely fastened. Picking up each of the fallen ornate flasks, Alder sniffed each one, opening a couple for a quick whiff. None matched the scent assailing his nose.

"That's odd," he mumbled.

"What's odd?" Maria said from the doorway, startling Alder, her arms folded and what appeared to be two sheets of paper in one hand that he hadn't noticed earlier.

"It smells real perfumy in here. Did Michelle break one of your bottles?"

"I thought so too, but I don't have anything like what you smell now. I even asked her if she broke one of my bottles and tried to hide it and clean it up. Then I realized she didn't even have time for that."

"So where's that smell coming from then?" Alder quizzed.

"I don't know, but your daughter drew this," Maria replied, passing Alder the two sheets of paper she held. The off-white parchment had colored crayon drawings of rudimentary figures having wings and, if Alder didn't know better, each brandished a simplistic image of a sword.

"Michelle drew this?" he asked, thinking they were above par for a 4-year-old yet still consistent with a preschool child's attempt at drawing. "What are they? They look like men with wings."

"She drew these after the dresser mess. She said they were pictures of the angel that helped her from hurting herself when she fell."

"She said what?" he responded, his eyes widening.

"You heard me, angel."

"OK, this is crazy."

"Alder, what's going on? I mean with you, Stephen, and his imaginary angel, the park?

"You're asking the wrong person hon. I'm just as much in the dark as you. I'm not sure what's going on here."

After a minute contemplating drawings, Alder left to go check on Michelle. Maria was right behind him. Gradually opening the door, the umber light from the setting sun accented the nightlight illuminating his daughter's room. Michelle lay napping on the bed, toys and play blocks strewn across the floor. Alder grabbed Maria's hand, and they stealthily moved to her bedside. Alder's heart melted seeing his daughter sleeping peacefully. Turning around to exit, and not wanting to step on any of the toys, Alder glanced at several alphabet blocks on the floor laid next to one another. They formed the word *Aurora*.

"What the hell?" he bellowed, almost loud enough to wake Michelle.

"What?" Maria whispered, pulling her hand from her husband's, jolted by his outburst.

"Were you playing in here earlier with Michelle?" Alder asked, turning to his wife.

"No. Why? It was just her and Matthew."

"Did you do that?" he whispered, reaching a level loud enough to cause Michelle to stir in her bed as he pointed to the blocks on the floor.

"No," she firmly responded, looking at the blocks and noticing the name, thinking that Michelle coincidentally placed them next to each other. "Who's name is that? As a matter of fact, who is she?"

"Have I ever mentioned that name before?"

"No, so who is she?"

"It's not a she; it's something to do with a project at my company."

Staring at the blocks for a couple more minutes, Alder withdrew and Maria followed him after glancing at the blocks for several more seconds.

Chapter 23

"So it's set. Bishop Grielle reluctantly agreed that we can meet first thing Monday morning to collect our notes and prepare our information to be presented to him Tuesday or Wednesday," Father Hernandez confirmed with his two associates as they drove to Michael's house after visiting Stephen Dennison.

"Yeah well, as long as I don't have to deal with that serpent," Michael commented.

"We get it Michael, you don't like the Bishop," Sister Justine said.

"What time do you want us to pick you up tomorrow morning?" Father Hernandez asked.

"Ten o'clock'll be fine. With all this traveling, it'll give me a chance to sleep in and then take a morning run."

"Good, because when I talked to the Bishop earlier, he said he'd like to get an update on what we found out as soon as possible."

"What we found out?" Michael snickered. "We found out this is crazier than I think any of us thought. And we still don't know why any of it happened."

The other two reluctantly agreed with him. Through the flurry of activity, the material they gathered resembled peripheral coincidences and circumstances more than facts around the cause of the deaths they were investigating, and whether in fact, angels were involved.

Michael extracted his luggage and while he was walking up to his house, the front door slung open. Alicia ran out, hugged Michael, and gave him a long, passionate kiss as he stepped onto the front porch.

"I missed you," Alicia whispered.

"I hate to admit I missed you too," Michael replied as they both entered into the house.

Father Hernandez speechless by what he saw, never suspected Michael and Alicia were involved with one another. Sister Justine scoffed and dismissed the event.

"Sister, so you were involved with him before deciding to become a nun?" Father Hernandez asked as they drove away.

"That's history now Father, you know that."

"But he seems so … so …"

"So much of a pain in the ass," she quipped, forgetting formalities.

"I was gonna say he seems so crass," Father Hernandez noted, not expecting such a rough comment from the Sister. "Your colorful explanation I think even God would forgive. How could you have been with someone like him?"

"Believe it or not, he wasn't always like this."

"Stop joking," the Father responded, wanting to laugh.

"I'm not joking. He was a very nice guy," the Sister said.

"So what happened?"

Sister Justine felt comfortable being more open with Father Hernandez. During their excursion, he'd proven himself dedicated to finding the truth. Father Hernandez didn't seem politically motivated like many of the priests she'd worked with through the years on inner-city missions, feigning interest to build up their resumes. "Coping with what happened the first time in Mexico; I mean you have what's thought to be an angel killing those poor souls in in the Church, then his mother, father, brother, and two sisters ending up missing, all the while we lived together for a short while before all of that. I decided to become a nun instead of just a missionary, so our relationship having changed with us drifting apart because of the church, marriage was out of the question. I think he even thought there might be a possibility of marriage in the priesthood, especially since over the years, married Anglicans and Episcopalians were allowed in the Church on a varying basis. With the Roman Catholic priest population severely shrinking, even before the disappearance, he thought the same hope existed for us, especially where I thought I wa…"

Sister Justine caught herself and paused before continuing, deciding not to go into too much more detail with the preceding comment. "But because so much happened that made me consider my dedication to serve God in a greater way, he questioned his faith. Remember what I mentioned before? His faith was never that strong to begin with."

"You know, I'm not sure you or the Bishop mentioned why you thought there had to be an angel involved. I mean, this was before the mass disappearances around the world. Why then?"

Sister Justine remained quiet for a few minutes. Father Hernandez knew she was formulating an answer.

With her hesitation, he didn't know if he could accept its genuineness.

She finally answered. "Bishop Grielle approached Michael and me to investigate the first event down in El Refugio. At first, we were both intrigued. As you've learned, Michael was extremely interested in angels, but he found what we'd been told to be totally preposterous. We were filled with skepticism and debated if we even wanted to go down."

"Why did you?"

"Because the request for someone to go down came from the higher stations in the Vatican, not the Holy Father mind you. We received a communiqué stating they believed there was every reason that this could have been a supernatural incident warranting a visit due to a divine inspiration. That's all they told us."

"Divine inspiration? Rome? Really?"

"Yes."

Speechless, Father Hernandez couldn't decide on other questions to ask. He focused on his driving. Arriving at the address given for Sister Justine's convent house, he was astonished to see a single dwelling.

"Sister, you don't reside with the other Sisters of your order?"

The inflection in Father Hernandez's voice inferred his disapproval. Sister Justine felt a burning sensation, similar to the emotions she'd experienced during the discussion concerning the oversight of the orders of nuns, the first night they were in Mexico. "The Sisters in my order are pretty much allowed to reside alone or in the house if they like. They're more lenient as long as we remain faithful to our supported parishes."

This was partially true. For Sister Justine's continued freedom to serve, she was beholden to Bishop Grielle and Cardinal Millhouse. More important, she was directed to clandestinely report directly to the Cardinal on extraordinary matters. When her liberal sexual past had been revealed during her studies, Cardinal Millhouse, who was then Bishop Millhouse, and Monsignor Grielle threatened to not allow her to join. Her allegiance had already been purchased years before while she was still studying and preparing to take her vows, knowing she wished nothing more than to become a nun. She would inform on those Sisters who might be straying from the rigid doctrinal precepts of their order and responsibilities. By doing this, it would prevent an "apostolic visitation" from the Mother Superior in Rome sanctioned by the Vatican office that deals with religious orders of nuns. She didn't have the impulse to tell Father Hernandez she was subtly coerced to informally provide information relating to their investigation as well. It was a necessary compromise to ensure her order's continued freedom. Sometimes thought to be cavalier, the convent in her order occasionally pursued neighborhood help programs without the full endorsement of their hierarchy or worked with local community groups advocating birth control. The Sisters considered it a means of outreach, feeling that it is best to minister to someone suffering though emotional turmoil and represent the Church as accepting all regardless of their actions.

"I don't mean to be judgmental about this Sister," the Father pressed, "but is the Bishop aware of your circumstances? It seems so out of the ordinary."

Sister Justine's expression communicated to the Father that she was annoyed. "We'll see you tomorrow Father." She grabbed her belongings and luggage from the car, refusing any assistance from him.

Chapter 24

Sunday was uneventful. Alder's attempt to question his daughter more thoroughly about why she decided to draw angels on the previous day yielded only simple "I don't know" and "I don't remember" responses. Michelle was more interested in playing with her dolls and toys than wanting to answer her daddy's questions. On Monday, the only thing Alder could think of while driving into work was whether he should attempt to pursue additional information about Aurora. The name had become prominent over the weekend, and it was something he couldn't ignore.

Alder mulled over ways to just discount his curiosity. The more he tried to dismiss the name, the more it came to the forefront of his thoughts. Branson came to mind first as someone who could possibly yield some insight, or maybe someone in his department. Alder knew if he framed the question correctly, his attempts to bring up Aurora during the normal course of business wouldn't seem out of place but merely be seen as trying to locate information to carry out the duties of his job. Alder and his staff had meetings and discussions with different sections in the division to discuss expenditures, cost overruns, and budget issues. After some consideration, however, there wasn't a reason to communicate with the marketing department on the specifics of projects. Most of his work centered on the production and operations processes within R & D. Another peer would normally deal with operations affecting the marketing section, so there was no real way to try and directly inquire for information.

Normally, getting to work half an hour early paid off, a large number of empty parking spaces would be available near the front door. The morning rush wouldn't have arrived and many of the midnight shift employees would be herding out to head home. Alder observed the stream of cars leaving the company campus while he drove onto the expansive parking lot. Today it dawned on him that after being promoted to his new position, he was still relegated to hunting for a parking spot. He hadn't been assigned a director-level parking space in the executive lot. Then he remembered Sheila was the one responsible for assigning executive parking spaces. Alder felt slighted, another battle to look forward to with her.

Pulling into a parking slot only four rows back from the main entrance to the administrative building, Alder couldn't believe his luck in seeing Branson getting out of his car only a couple of spaces over. The lingering smells of sterile equipment manufacturing from the production facilities on the campus breezed through the vents of the car after he shut off the engine.

"Hey Branson," Alder called out, while exiting his car and greeting his coworker with a sincere smile. "How was your weekend?"

Branson returned the smile. "Pretty good. Yours?"

"If you don't count weird, not bad," Alder responded, heading over to shake Branson's hand while they both strolled toward the entrance to the main building.

"Whadaya mean weird?"

"Remember I planned to go and visit Stephen over the weekend?"

"Yeah, you go?"

"I did."

"How's he doing?"

"He's doing fine but still having a bit of a hard time trying to adjust. While I was there, three Church representatives were questioning Stephen about what happened, and you know what, they knew something about one of our projects, Aurora, and something about Mexico."

Branson stopped walking, his eyes widened. "Alder, you do realize Aurora had its genesis in Mexico when an older subsidiary held by the group was active about ten years ago? Remember what we talked a bit about Friday? And from what I understand, something major is brewing with the project."

"So what the hell is this Aurora project? And why would those three from the Church be interested in it?"

"That project is extremely sensitive. No one here on our side of corporate knows too much about it. The only one I could think of who'd know more would be your boss. And to hear someone from outside the company is interested in it, I'm thinking maybe you should tell someone."

"You're probably right, I should tell Gary. He'd be interested in hearing about this," Alder lied. He was already uncomfortable signing paperwork without being able to scrutinize it with a lawyer. He didn't even want to bring up the coincidental circumstances of his daughter spelling out the project name and complicate the situation. Why would Gary believe him? Now Alder was even more curious about the project. He wanted to put an actual project against the paperwork and satisfy his curiosity, a project with enigmatic underpinnings.

Alder and Branson veered off to their respective offices, with Alder settling in and deciding to head down to the cafeteria for a cup of coffee. He didn't find his marketing counterpart. When he arrived at his office, he could instantly see the effects of Sheila being at work. Several new folders arrived on his desk during the short time he was gone. Grabbing a couple of the smaller packets, he scanned through the paperwork, initialed it, and then headed down to Gary's office hoping to collect some information, albeit it would need to be clandestine.

Sheila was amazed to see Alder returning completed folders. Usually he found ways to procrastinate or hold off heading to her desk, especially with the project folders. The custom had been for her to come to his office, coax him to initial or sign the paperwork where identified, then retrieve the folders from him, barely leaving time for an adequate review. Although she was Gary's administrative assistant, she sometimes exerted herself as if she were the executive vice-president incessantly passing off paperwork to Alder.

Contending with her ego, being swamped in a tsunami of paperwork added to his frustrations. Typically, Alder couldn't dedicate the time he would like to work with his managers. They all considered him to be an extremely laissez-faire director.

"Is Gary in?" Alder asked, thinking it might be best after all to bring up the information about the three visitors to Stephen's house if he wanted to try and find out more about Aurora.

"No, he's gonna be gone for most mornings this week, following up on one of our major projects. What did you want?"

"Nothing much, just wanted to discuss a couple of things with him. What time do you expect him back?"

"Probably after lun …," she said, interrupted by her ringing phone. Sheila answered the without excusing herself or showing any respect to her visitor. "Everest International. Gary Applethorpe's office… Shit, is she all right?" she cried out into the handset.

Slamming the handset down, Sheila grabbed the two folders presented by Alder, put them on her desk, and scurried around the large L-shaped oak-veneered desk.

"Everything all right?" Alder asked.

"Desiree just burned herself badly on a pot of hot coffee."

Alder knew Desiree was Sheila's trusted friend and confidant, the one who helped to provide her with inside information on gossip throughout the building. Sheila paid no attention to Alder still standing in front of her desk as she left in distress, not even initiating the screen saver to lock her computer. He was ecstatic and felt as if he'd been left alone in a bank vault full of money and no one around to watch. Here was a chance to go in and search for documents about the project of interest. Alder could move throughout the office with liberty. He strolled around the desk to see the operating system desktop icons fully visible. She was logged on and had been active on the computer prior to the log-on-activity time-out kicking in to fire off the automatic screen saver. Moving the mouse cursor, he scanned the icons to analyze and determine the possible file structure, navigating to find some information. He knew his time might be short, and that being caught on her computer was a reason for immediate dismissal. After a couple of attempts through a couple of folders, he found the semblance of information he was looking for only on the local hard drive. Checking a couple of project plan timelines, he saw the history of Aurora dating back more than ten years. Nothing else of importance was found. Even Sheila seemed to be restricted from many of the more detailed project files. He was aware that his time for review was getting short. He closed out the documents he had opened and returned the mouse to its original position the best he could remember. Hearing the elevator chime down the hall, he hurriedly retreated to his original position. As soon as he got to the front of her desk, Sheila stepped off the lift and rushed back into the office, distraught. She still managed to give Alder her familiar harsh glare.

"What are you still doing here?" she asked abrasively, returning to the keyboard of her computer to log off and grab her purse to leave again.

"We didn't get a chance to finish talking before you left and …"

"Look, I don't have time for you right now. I'm gonna take Desiree to urgent care. I'll talk to you when I get back." She darted out of the office, going into the stairwell instead of waiting for the elevator. Alder debated exploring for more information in Gary's office since Sheila would be gone for some time. It only took a minute for him to decide to look through the open files in his boss's office.

After less than ten minutes, Alder found the information he was looking for, a project file for Aurora. From what he could extrapolate from the paperwork, the project consisted of two phases. A majority of the information in Gary's office related only to one phase of work finishing up in the Los Angeles area, and the best he could determine, the second phase was predominantly in Mexico. Reviewing portions of the budgetary documents, Alder was stunned finding out one of the major sponsors. *"What the hell? They're paying for a lot of this project,"* Alder thought to himself. He put everything back in the original location and headed out to track down three people who could possibly answer a couple of questions that came to mind based on the new information revealed.

* * * *

Alder walked into the small meeting room of the church. Father Hernandez, Sister Justine, and Michael sat around a table with papers and handwritten notes sprawled around. They remembered Alder from the visit to Stephen's house a couple of days earlier. All three, appearing tense and frazzled, were trying to agree on the information to present to Bishop Grielle.

"Excuse me," Alder interjected, "I finally tracked you down, but I don't know if you remember me or not?"

Father Hernandez answered first. "We do, forgive us if we don't remember your name."

"Alder Dennison," Alder offered.

"What can we do for you Mr. Dennison?" Father Hernandez queried.

"Look, with what happened to my coworker, truthfully, I didn't think too much of it. I mean, yeah, I thought some weird stuff was going on, but when my family is involved, I start to get worried."

Father Hernandez jumped up to grab a chair by the wall and bring it to the table. "Please take a seat and join us," he said.

"Mr. Dennison, it sounds like something is troubling you," Sister Justine remarked.

"I don't know where to begin."

"Well, you mentioned something about your family," Father Hernandez said.

Alder took a couple of deep breaths before beginning with his narrative. Describing the encounter at the park and the odd comments made by the stranger, he then recounted the meeting at Stephen's home. Lastly, he shared the unusual incidences involving his wife and daughter. Ensuring his listeners knew every detail, he worked to be meticulous. Alder's goal was to ensure that they give their best help to him in clarifying everything that happened. He purposefully left off the information regarding his daughter's toy building blocks so as not to reveal too much and he hoped not have to delve into what he had learned at his company earlier that morning.

"Mr. Dennison?" Michael asked, "What did this lady in the park look like?"

"Call me Alder, and it's hard to say." Alder tried his best to describe the alleged homeless nomad but wasn't sure if he'd been successful based on the long silence that followed.

"Do you think it could be her?" Father Hernandez asked, directing his question to Michael and Sister Justine.

"I'd place that bet; sounds like she's a ringer," Michael answered.

"Could be who?" Alder inquired. "You know who I'm talking about?"

"We had a similar situation while down in Mexico. She called herself Ashere. Did this woman mention her name?"

"No, but does any of this stuff mean anything to you?" Alder asked.

"To be truthful, what you've describe here is quite interesting and is in line with the fact that all we seem to be doing is chasing the shadow of angels, nothing concrete," Father Michael lamented.

"Yes, and we thank you for this information, but what exactly is it we can do for you Alder?" Sister Justine asked, recalling his reluctance to provide information earlier.

"Well, there's one more thing I didn't mention, what happened over the weekend that involves my daughter."

The three remained quiet, waiting for Alder to continue. Michael rudely gave Alder hand gestures of pointing his finger to the side and rolling it in a circle meaning, "get to it already."

"Me and my wife went in to check on her while she was taking a nap. When I looked down at some of the alphabet blocks, some of the ones she put together spelled out a name."

"What name?" Father Hernandez asked with heightened anticipation.

"Aurora."

"What?" Michael asked rhetorically. Alder took it to be an actual query.

"The blocks spelled *Aurora*."

Sister Justine was the first to remember how the name had disturbed Alder when it was brought up at Stephen's house. She leaned in to ask her question: "Mr. Dennison, you seem to know something more about Aurora. Is it something your daughter may have heard before from yourself or someone else?

"No, I rarely discuss work at home. Plus, my daughter just turned four. For her to know how to spell that word would be …"

"Mr. Dennison, what is it? Aurora?" she continued. The other two researchers knew he would need to be pressed for more information and were impressed with her skill in presenting a compassionate bearing during the questioning.

Alder was becoming nervous, rubbing his hands together, awkwardly glancing at the religion-based pictures hanging on the walls, fidgeting in his chair; it was obvious he didn't want to broach the topic. He was considering revealing to the three the same restricted company information he warned Stephen not to reveal. Stephen had limited access to Aurora, only knowing the project's name. But Alder had probed much deeper into the project, now knowing more details than he should. Gary purposefully attempted to restrict the information on the true scope of the project. Alder knew the three Church investigators were seriously interested in finding out what he'd discovered. Thinking about his daughter's alphabet play blocks had kept him from having a restful sleep the previous evening. He was curious and knew something had happened for his daughter to come up with the name but didn't want to believe a mysterious, pretty, winged man was involved.

Alder finally decided to answer. "Look, the information I'm about to tell you, you can't tell anyone, especially anyone from my company. Let's just say I happened to accidentally review some files I probably shouldn't have."

"Trust us, this will be kept strictly confidential," Father Hernandez reassured. Sister Justine took a quick glance at Michael, who gave a quick scowl at Father Hernandez but regained his composure. He didn't want to make their guest uncomfortable about revealing any additional information.

"Good, because whatever is happening, it's affecting my family and I don't want anything to happen to them. My wife is pretty much scared shitless, and to be truthful, I'm afraid myself." Alder took a deep breath and continued: "Aurora is a project that started in Mexico. It has two tracks, one in our genetic engineering side of R & D; the other's on the biomedical research side. I didn't get a chance to see a lot of the details for both, but whatever happened down in Mexico severely delayed the project by years. And …"

"Wait a minute," Michael interrupted. "Your company was involved with Aurora in Mexico. I thought a company called ..." he began while rummaging through several sheets of paper on the table before finding his intended target. "I thought a company called Aversol was involved with Aurora ten years ago in Mexico?"

Alder bore a look of skepticism. He had anticipated that the three would be more intimate with the details of the Aurora given that they'd already introduced the subject at Stephen's. Then at least he could justify to himself that someone else knew more about the project and wouldn't feel as guilty revealing confidential company information. "Aversol was one of our subsidiaries. It was renamed when we thought bad press would hurt the project, even more so when a possible virus outbreak might have been blamed on them. They changed the name because some of the research work that was being done wasn't allowed in the states. Same thing for Mexico and a couple of other countries they were working in. They weren't supposed to be working on certain types of genetic research. The rumor is, with the right payoffs, the research rules were made quite a bit more lax. Then there were some employees, researchers and technicians and all, who were killed in the little small town outside Aguascalientes, I believe it's called El ..."

"El Refugio?" All three listeners responded almost in unison, interrupting Alder's explanation.

"Yeah, El Refugio," Alder replied, realizing they were more knowledgeable than he'd given them credit for earlier, forgetting they'd discussed the village earlier at Stephen's home. "Anyway, they renamed the division Waterfall and relocated to another site just outside

Aguascalientes. Internally in the company, they felt there could be a cloud of negativity associated with the original name. They got back on track, and things were progressing well. They hit another major milestone recently; then that was nearly jeopardized when the angel visits recently killed key researchers and some of their family and friends here in Los Angeles. One of the recent notes to the Church, routed through my boss, basically questioned whether angels are attempting to disrupt the progress of the project, as previously predicted."

"Why would he be interested if angels were involved? And predicted by whom? I mean, let's see, the first event here in L.A. pretty much killed everybody in attendance, and the second, only one person died," Father Hernandez commented.

"Yeah, he was one of the key research doctors at Waterfall, a virologist if I read the paperwork right. The company got lucky; they were able to recover a lot of his work," Alder said.

"How'd you come to know about all this?" Sister Justine asked.

"I'd rather not say, but circumstances allowed for me to …" Alder cleared his throat, "somewhat thoroughly review this information."

"Wait a minute," Michael said excitedly, as he jumped up out of his chair and started to walk in a small circle, pointing his index fingers straight up in the air. "Let me just wrap my head around this. It just hit me. You say that Aversol was an old subsidiary of Everest that was closed in Mexico …"

"Companies renamed," Alder injected.

"OK, renamed ten years ago. And the only incidents known to date where an angel decides to go rogue, it seems now, involve the same company's employees working on the same project where many already had been killed," Michael continued.

"Well, let's see, the first witness worked at an Aversol research lab in Mexico," Sister Justine jumped in.

"Then there's the Crestview episode, where the only death is a researcher who worked at Everest, and the angel making the visitation there mentions the name 'Aurora,'" Father Hernandez added to the exchange.

"Could it be that those associated with the project in Mexico, and in L.A., were at a funeral of someone who worked at the labs at both places, then associates, friends, and families attending the funeral all died in visitations from fallen angels?" Sister Justine summarized.

"Let's see, something happens to someone in the company, they die; there's a funeral, as if to gather all those people together, then there's two angels we know who are named Abriel and Gishmael ..." Father Hernandez paused, eyebrows furled, mouth open, his expression suggesting an impending epiphany. "Wait a minute, Gish ... ma ... el ..." Father Hernandez commented, trailing off while pronouncing the angel's name. Both Michael and Sister Justine were oblivious to the change in his expression.

"Then the key question is," Michael noted rhetorically, "why would the angels we know as Abriel and Gishmael kill those associated with the project, along with their friends and family? Could they be considered seraphs in opposition to God, the Church, and this project?"

"They must be fallen angels then if they're against the Church?" Sister Justine responded.

Father Hernandez jumped in excitedly, "Who's to say they're fallen angels? I've been thinking about this for a minute … their names, would it be that simple?"

Michael was stimulated by Father Hernandez's burst of excitement. "You intrigue me boy toy. Go on."

"They may not be as we suspect," the Father answered.

"What do you mean?"

"Look at their names. Remember how, in many Judeo-Christian beliefs, the etymology of a name can have great significance? Well, in Hebrew, 'el' is God, the suffix '-el' means 'of God' or 'like God'; some texts even say 'son of God.' Your name Michael means 'who is like God,'" Father Hernandez commented.

"Yeah, and remember, even though I'm named Michael, I'm an agnostic. Names don't necessarily mean a thing."

"True, we definitely know you're no angel," Father Hernandez jibed.

"Did you just zing me?"

Father Hernandez gave Michael a quaint, wry smile.

Michael returned the smile.

"Father, Michael, can we continue please?" Sister Justine insisted.

"Anyway, none of this applies to us, fallen humans, but what about angels?" Father Hernandez continued. "They directly serve Him or are against Him. All angels at one time or another directly served and worshiped

God. In the Bible, Apocrypha, and other non-canonical texts, those who do are still suffixed with '-el' and those who don't are named or referred to differently. Lucifer, Legion, Moroni from Mormonism …"

"But you have Uriel, keeper of the gates of hell, and many others in apocryphal books and literature who still have the '-el' suffixed to their name," Michael added.

"Then can we say, with accuracy, if they're of God anymore, or serve him? In the canon, only two angel who were associated with God and named were Gabriel and Michael, archangels. And remember in the Bible regarding the Book of Life, if there's one for angels, wouldn't their names be smitten?"

"If these are angels of God, then why pursue the course of action they're taking?" Michael pondered.

"And don't forget what happened the first time Abriel showed up in Mexico," Sister Justine added, "the second one showing up impelling or coercing the first one to leave."

"Crap, that's right. Our first witness said he thought Abriel said to the first angel, 'the Lord rebuke you.' All this time we're all thinking that as angels presented eulogies, not one has ever revealed their name. Come to think of it, none of them revealed their names in the reports I read when I used to research these events a few years ago. Could it be the angels presenting the eulogies want to remain inconspicuous?" Michael questioned.

"Inconspicuous how?" Father Hernandez responded.

"Maybe because they're fallen and not of God anymore?"

"Just because they never revealed their names doesn't necessarily mean they can't be of God." Sister Justine responded.

"After the censure of the very first angel, the best I can remember, most times God reveals the name of his appointed messengers in major ways," Michael answered.

"Most times is key," Father Hernandez responded. "We're just speculating now. And why would the fallen angels be involved in all of this? Too bad we don't have references that present the overall history of angels. I recall coming across an interesting concept during my research though. Someone wrote that if mankind has a Holy Bible, wouldn't God have a Holy Bible for angels full of sacred writings concerning their history?"

"What do you mean 'someone' padre?" Michael barked, "That was me from one of my treatises on angels when I was a seminary student."

"That was you? It was referenced as being from someone who was excommunicated from the Church whose writings should be discredited."

"I can't believe they wouldn't even give me credit for my own work. That's a bunch of bull …"

The Father interrupted, "Mr. Saunders, we really need to get back on track."

"The influence of human history," Sister Justine whispered. Both men were barely able to hear or comprehend her.

"What?" they both said.

"Michael, something else you wrote in one of your treatises years ago, the influence of human history. Angels have been the instruments of God acting as messengers for his word and helping to manifest his provident influence on human history. What if our two primary angels are attempting to impede, or halt, Aurora? Look at who were killed both times. These two angels could be in conflict with the other angels.

"So what are you saying? These angels are now in some sort of war?" Sister Justine questioned.

"Angels have always been at conflict with one another. The battles now, depending on the reference sources, are ongoing between the fallen angels and the elect angels. They struggle now not to determine winners and losers in each contest but for the souls of men," Father Hernandez said.

"Very good boy toy, you're right. They operate in the shadows to make an impact on the affairs of man. Now why would they become so overt?"

"Isn't all of this just conjecture anyway?" Father Hernandez forcefully qualified. "We shouldn't let ourselves be fooled that this is the actual state of affairs for what we're facing."

Alder felt the conversation was getting way too religious for him. He needed to make sure he provided everything that he knew, especially seeing the exchange ignited by the information just provided.

Alder joined in. "There's more. It has more to do with my company's client who's spearheading the project. I was able to correlate some of the information I approved over the last couple of weeks to shadow accounts and budget codings when I got back to my office. The Church, behind the front of our medical clinics and laboratories, is funding Aurora's research and development. The research was to make heartier genetically engineered crops for poor and starving countries."

"We already know that the Church is involved with Everest. What exactly are you saying?" Michael asked.

"I may not know too much about the science stuff, but one portion of the project I read discussed a lot about cloning, and who's paying for it."

The room became silent except for the sound of air circulating through the vents. All three investigators stared impatiently at Alder, perturbed he hadn't finished his train of thought.

"Well?" Michael blurted out, tired of waiting.

"Is the Church funding a cloning project?" Alder queried.

All three were confused. Sister Justine rose up out of her seat after a couple of minutes of silence. "I have to excuse myself; nature is calling. Please wait before you continue with anything else. I do want to find out more."

Out of respect for the Sister, the men waited patiently, thinking she appeared to be taking a considerable amount of time but attributing it to the idiosyncrasies of being a female. After several minutes, she returned, and all three expected Alder to continue. Alder, himself, was still waiting for an answer to his question but, by their extended silence, they may have not thought it was an actual query.

"No seriously, is the Church funding a cloning project?" Alder questioned again.

"What you're saying is that you've seen information that the Church is paying for a cloning project? Doesn't that sound a little strange?" Father Hernandez asked.

"A little strange, yes. But I do know that, from what I've seen, the Church is definitely paying for a major portion of the project. There are other contributing sources of funding, just not as much as the Church. There was more to what I found; I just didn't get a chance to go through everything. I could only take a look at paperwork for a couple of the project folders. But there are other parts to Aurora."

"How did you come across all this information?" Sister Justine asked.

"I'd prefer not to say, and let's leave it at that."

No one challenged him.

"Please don't tell anyone I provided you with this stuff either," Alder pleaded.

"So, Mr. Dennison, what does this have to do with your family?" the Sister continued questioning.

"Because of all these weird things happening," Alder paused, not wanting to continue. But he did. "Hell, all that's been goin' on, a short while back with everyone dying, my friend Stephen going blind, it all started to get to me. Then there was the strange event with my daughter that worried me and my wife, especially with all this supposed angel stuff going on at my house."

"You mean like with the blocks?" Michael asked.

"Yeah, I mean, come on, my daughter claims a glowing pretty man catches her after she falls while climbing on the dresser in our master bedroom. Then some letter blocks in her room spelled out *Aurora*. She claims she didn't do it but, again, the glowing pretty man who was playing with her. What's going on? I've heard of imaginary friends, but nothing like this."

Alder hoped one of the three would be able to provide him with some sort of insight. They remained quiet.

"Well, is there anything you can tell me?" Alder asked.

"Look Mr. Dennison," Father Hernandez replied. "I'm not sure what we can tell you that you already don't know, or what we could do to help. We do appreciate you coming down here. We just don't have any answers for you."

Alder became visibly irritated. "I don't know why I wasted my time coming down here." He stormed out.

Father Hernandez followed and caught up with Alder in the hallway. "Mr. Dennison, we really do appreciate you coming down here to talk to us, but you have to realize, in many ways, we're just as lost as you."

"You'd think you'd know more about all that your Church is involved with Father?" Alder quipped.

"Is that really fair? Just like you know everything about what your company is involved with, including Aurora?"

Alder refused to comment and left.

After nearly a minute standing in the hallway with the accompanying hum of fluorescent lights in the drop-down ceiling, Father Hernandez returned to the room with his companions. "Now it's my turn, I have to go relieve myself. I'll be right back."

As soon as the Father left again, Sister Justine quizzed Michael on a comment he'd made earlier. "Michael, you said you were agnostic. I thought you gave up on God and became an atheist?"

"I never said that at any time, did I? It's kinda why I still teach religious studies. I'm still searching and helping those who are to. Truthfully, I think I've been more agnostic than anything else, questioning but never fully accepting."

"Even during seminary?"

"Yep, I guess you can say even during seminary."

"And all these years I always thought you were a believer in the Father, Blessed Mother, and Son. Why go through seminary if you neve ..."

Michael jumped out of his seat, startling the Sister. "You know what; I have to go take a leak too." He left because he didn't want to try and make up a story to keep from telling her the real reason for going to seminary. Sister Justine suspected. It was to follow her and hopefully serve with her, even if they couldn't be together the way they once had. He had to admit to himself that this was why he agreed to continue to work on this investigation; now his feelings for her were threatening to reveal themselves.

Once both men returned, they were able to finalize their collaboration and complete a rough outline for the final report. Work would still be needed to research references to corroborate facts and minimize theological speculations. One thing was certain; they knew the Church hierarchy would find some of the viewpoints in the material unpalatable. Nonetheless, their goal was to make sure they presented the truth of what they discovered, minus the discussion with Alder Dennison.

Chapter 25

Gregorian chants acoustically pirouetted throughout the Cardinal's chamber, the echoing enhanced by the rustic, handcrafted, wooden wall covering. Led by a seminary intern, Gary saw not only Cardinal Millhouse, whom he'd come to visit, but another clergyman in the Cardinal's private office. When the Cardinal called and requested that he stop by to discuss a serious matter, he had the impression no one else would be involved in the conversation. The Cardinal directed the intern to turn down the music by pointing to the stereo system inset into the custom-built wall-shelving unit.

"Ah, Gary, thank you for coming," the Cardinal noted after waiting for the background music to recede. He stood up and moved from behind his desk to greet his visitor, hand extended.

"Your Eminence, your request sounded urgent," Gary responded, kissing the Cardinal's ring.

"It is, and this is Bishop Grielle. Bishop, this is Gary Applethorpe, a prominent deacon in service to the Church," the Cardinal said, gesturing to the other clergyman sitting in one of the two chairs opposite the Cardinal's desk. "Bishop Grielle is the one overseeing the investigation into the cause of the angelic visitations at the funeral homes and, more important, at Thomson and Thomson."

Gary's eyes widened when he heard the task of the unknown clergyman. He shook the Bishop's hand, gripping extra firmly. "Really? How's the investigation coming along?" Gary asked, taking a seat next to the Bishop.

"So when do we expect to hear from your charges about what they've found?" the Cardinal inquired, directing his question to Bishop Grielle.

"Within a couple of days, I decided to give them more time to collect and compose their notes. You know, I'm sorry once again your Eminence, and not to be disrespectful, what's the purpose of Deacon Applethorpe in this discussion?" Bishop Grielle asked mentally confused as to the purpose of the short-notice meeting.

"Gary Applethorpe is a senior vice president at Everest Bio-Medical Group."

"Everest Bio-Medical? I understand they're a major patron of the Church. They support many of the clinics and free medical aid stations that we provide for the indigent of the fold in parishes here in the States and in Mexico. But I'm not sure what this has to do with the first fatal event here in Los Angeles?"

"You realize that a large number of those who died were from Everest, Andrew?" the Cardinal asked.

"Well yes, and from what you've mentioned your Eminence," Bishop Grielle answered, hiding his annoyance at being called by his first name in front of Gary. Even though he was a deacon, Gary was still considered laity and not official clergy, regardless of being in the privacy of the Cardinal's office. "Some of

278

the departed were associated with advanced genetic engineering techniques to create foods capable of growing in harsh environments as well as distinct and low-cost immunizations and vaccines for our clinics."

"Well, they're working on something important with their vaccine research. What I am about to tell you is in strictest confidence. Only a select few in Rome and a small number in Everest know what I am about to tell you."

"Of course I won't reveal what you're about to tell me," Bishop Grielle replied, bewildered the Cardinal was about to provide more than the cursory information he had in the past.

The Cardinal continued. "If successful, they'll minimize, if not eliminate, a heretical and unbelieving scourge sourced in the Middle East that has plagued the Church for centuries. A most amazing opportunity exists."

"I don't quite understand what you're trying to say. What exactly does vaccine research and Church doctrine have to do with each other that could be considered heretical?" the Bishop inquired.

The Cardinal remained quiet and glanced toward Gary, who, after a short pause, waved his head back and forth to signal his disapproval of the direction of the conversation.

"OK Andrew, here's what I'll tell you concerning the Holy Father," the Cardinal began after taking another quick glance at Gary, who now gave a reaffirming nod. "I've kept this from you long enough. In the other recent event at Crestview, the single loss there was from Waterfall Medical Research."

"And?" the Bishop continued.

"Waterfall is one of the primary subsidiaries working with the Aurora project. The poor soul who passed was one of the lead research doctors," the Cardinal responded.

"With the loss of one of our top genetic researchers, many thought the project would be set back again; yet a miracle happened," Gary interjected. "He managed to record progress for one of the phases of the project he'd been overseeing."

"You see Andrew, you've known this work has been going on for years, with part of it going on in Mexico because certain parts of the research weren't allowed in the United States," the Cardinal remarked.

Bishop Grielle grimaced at the idea that more information was forthcoming because it was information he hadn't been privy to previously yet laity such as Gary had been.

The Cardinal continued, "You know Andrew, I don't believe I ever told you how the project came about. That may explain some of the issues at hand."

"What have I been missing through all of this?" the Bishop asked.

"The work at Everest has been divinely inspired."

"Divinely inspired?" Both men could hear the skepticism in Bishop Grielle's voice.

"Yes," the Cardinal said while getting up to prepare a cup of tea, offering it to his guests as well though both politely declined. "I'm going to tell you something many in the Church are not aware of. You see Andrew, years ago, during special canonical prayers by several members of the College of Cardinals with the Bishop of Rome in the Vatican, they reported being visited by an angelic messenger, a most magnificent creature, its brilliance rivaled only by the sun. The name of this angel was not revealed to the Cardinals. But as its brightness was said to be equivalent to the coming dawn, they named it Aurora. The visit of this messenger was in direct response to the prayers of our brethren. With the turmoil in the world just before the mass disappearance, they were enlightened with the hope that a new world leader would arise. Stumbling blocks to ecumenical progress would be removed and the Church's influence in the world would increase over time. Since the College of Cardinals and I know that we are not to be involved in secular endeavors, or those of politics, economics, and the like, we may only use those instruments sanctioned by God to carry out the Holy Father's and God's will. The angel thus named Aurora commissioned the Cardinals to seek an appointed company to do the work necessary to assist in this endeavor."

"An angel? An appointed company? I would imagine that's Everest?" the Bishop asked, somewhat confounded by the verbal dissertation of his superior.

"Yes, Everest was sanctioned to accomplish the magnificent work as commissioned."

"Are you inferring there's more to Aurora than just simple medical research?"

Both men grew quiet. Bishop Grielle remained patient.

After several sips of tea, Cardinal Millhouse continued, "Yes, there are various parts to the project, but a warning was presented as well. The work we attempt to accomplish would meet with resistance from those against Aurora."

Cardinal Millhouse deliberately paused to ensure this comment was received and comprehended by the Bishop.

Bishop Grielle seized the opportunity to ask another question. "What do you mean by meet with resistance? Who'd be against the angel Aurora?"

"The genesis of the project in Mexico was just more than ten years ago. A research laboratory was established in conjunction with the church-sponsored clinics throughout the Aguascalientes area. It was there that the deaths occurred, in El Refugio; some were medical and genetic researchers."

"That's why you had me dispatch the seminarian Michael and Sister Justine. You were confident it must have been a supernatural event."

"Yes. And again in Los Angeles. Remember what was revealed covertly by Sister Justine during this most recent trip to Mexico concerning the very first visitation. The witness reported an angel showing up to begin a eulogy followed by another one who arrives and intimidates the first away. It then kills all those in attendance, minus the one survivor."

"Then why did you have me pull Michael and Sister Justine the first time they went down?"

"If they were to find out too much about the project that early on in the game, it might have been exposed, which might have seriously impeded its progress. We're fortunate that, now, excellent strides have been made by Everest."

"And what are these strides?" Bishop Grielle asked, directing his question to Gary.

"You've heard of genetic engineering and cloning?" Gary responded.

"Yes, I have."

"Well, at the research lab in Mexico, we genetically engineered a nearly perfect cloned embryo of the Holy Father."

"What?" the Bishop responded, being both apprehensive and excited.

"We removed many of the negative attributes associated with the frailty of us all, and closed in on presenting the first of a new breed of man. We improved upon the genetic makeup for the prototype. We even genetically designed him with two hearts; he's extremely strong and has an extremely high intelligence capacity. He will be the second incarnation of the perfect man and will be established as the ruler and deliverer capable of marrying the Church and all of society."

Bishop Grielle blanched. "What do you mean he will be? You were successful?"

"We were. However, only one of the progeny survived. No matter what our researchers did to allow many of the successful modifications in the other zygotes and blastocysts, they eventually died. Oddly enough, so did many of those involved with the project. And when they died, it was as if their work died with them. We couldn't replicate much of their research, even with what was recorded. Many joked that the doctors and researchers were possessed, or divinely inspired in some unique way, accomplishing what they felt to be a calling. It's as if this one success story is a true miracle."

"This is too fantastical for me to grasp," the Bishop exclaimed, his breathing labored with the shock of hearing the revelation. He never anticipated hearing about cloning being sponsored by the Church and, even more, inspired by an angel.

"What's amazing is that the progeny is brilliant, even at his current young age," Gary added.

"Andrew," Cardinal Millhouse interposed, "no one must know of what we have told you, no one. Only us in this room, and a very few in Rome, know of this. That's why I've been concerned about the latitude you've been giving your team."

"Of course. Now I think it's more important than ever to find out the cause of these events," Bishop Grielle countered.

"Based on this Andrew, I believe it is quite evident why the events occurred, to prevent the Holy Church from presenting the future ruler of the new Church to come."

"Then how do we know this is of true divine origin?"

"I'm surprised Andrew, because of where and to whom the inspiration was bestowed, and the direction given; it must be of divine origin. For the Bishop of Rome himself did receive the angelic visitor that did enlighten the destiny of the Church. Only those angels fallen from grace must be against the Church and the course she is set upon. God would not set up his holy institution only to have it polluted by conjecture contrary to her doctrines, traditions, and miracles. Anything else would be heresy."

"Then whatever they find out won't change what you already know."

"We want to make sure that we can prevent the adversary from impeding the advancement of the Church's greater good."

Bishop Grielle attempted to fully comprehend what he had just heard. But Gary wanted the Cardinal to get straight to the point. He decided to chime in. "Your Eminence, was there a reason you'd called me here?"

"Yes, I'd just like to say that Sister Justine has been extremely faithful in her duties, wouldn't you say Andrew?"

Puzzled, Bishop Grielle answered. "Yes, she has been. Why do you ask?"

"Because she sent word earlier regarding the foundation of what we've been discussing here. It seems, Gary, that one of your employees revealed more of Aurora than what our three already knew. She also noted that doctrinal deductions by Father Hernandez and Michael Saunders are, dare I say, somewhat heretical."

"What do you mean one of my employees?" Gary barked in response to the revelation. "We made sure to put those we could trust as replacements into many of the company's key positions. Who's this leak?"

"The Sister mentioned she didn't have time to say, but I believe she didn't want to say. This is disconcerting nonetheless."

"Damn right it's disconcerting, and what do you mean she didn't want to say? She does work for you, doesn't she? We need to find out who talked," Gary noted harshly.

"I believe we need to maintain her right of confidentiality to see if this leak of yours reveals additional malefactors who may be involved with the release of information," the Cardinal retorted to Gary's aggressive tone.

"We're not ready for any of this information to be released yet, your Eminence. You know that some of our work in Mexico is highly ille … you know we can't let this information get out."

"I know about all the different components of the project, and we're not ready to reveal the child to the Church or the world. We were waiting until he approached adulthood or maybe even full maturity after attending college and seminary," the Cardinal said.

"How is it that you found out about this information from Sister Justine?" Bishop Grielle queried rhetorically. He was somewhat irked, afraid he already knew the answer. He was under the impression that Sister Justine was to provide progress of the investigation directly to himself.

"I know you may feel undermined Andrew, but she was told to deliver information only to myself in case they came across anything exceptional, and I think this qualifies."

"I'm not going to question your motives your Eminence, but I think I should …"

"I think Andrew," the Cardinal interrupted, "that we should be thankful we are all able to serve Rome and the Holy Father in this situation."

Bishop Grielle yielded to Cardinal Millhouse's authority as he had many times before without even attempting to challenge. "What would you like for me to do?" He asked submissively.

"There are many options, and I believe both you and Gary need to just let events unfold, and let the three present their findings. We then may be able to find out who revealed the full involvement of Everest and the extent of the breach."

After some hesitation, both of the Cardinal's visitors agreed.

"Andrew, please leave us. We have additional business we need to discuss."

Bishop Grielle, annoyed that his superior had been calling him by his first name in front of Gary, now felt snubbed and, in defiance, wanted to stay firmly planted in his seat. The unyielding look of Cardinal Millhouse conveyed that he should not even try to attempt to remain. The Bishop reluctantly eased himself out of his seat and departed.

Once the Cardinal saw the Bishop was safely out of the office, he continued his conversation with his remaining visitor. "Gary, you have an odd look about you."

"I can't believe you told him as much as you did. And you almost told him about some of our work in Mexico that is considered highly illeg ..."

"Ahh, ahh, ahh, ahhh. I know the Church has sanctioned work some governments would consider prohibited, especially for the purposes the Church has planned. If anything were to happen due to an accidental release, let's just say the Church will claim full deniability. For now though, we may have to be prepared to announce portions of your work concerning the child pretty soon."

* * * *

287

It wasn't until Gary began to drive away from the Cardinal's office that any restraint on his anger was loosened. *That son of a bitch Cardinal may not reveal who passed on the info about Aurora, but it doesn't mean I won't be able to try and find out the source on my own,* Gary thought. The drive in heavy traffic broke his concentration. Just as Gary attempted to zero in on an approach to finding possible names, a car would cut in front without using a turn signal or prematurely brake trying to adjust to the irregular traffic. Once he arrived at the R & D campus parking lot, Gary eyed several of the director-level and manager assigned parking slots and saw they were already empty, even though it was only 4:30, still half an hour before the scheduled quitting time for the executive and supervisory day shift personnel. Parking his car and briskly heading into the building, those watching him could tell by his gait that he was quite upset. Two employees who happened to be riding up in the elevator felt uneasy by his territorial stance and stern expression. They decided to get off a floor earlier and walk up the stairs instead of remaining in the elevator car.

Gary was pleased to see Sheila at her desk working. He had mentioned that he would be gone for the rest of the day when he talked to her earlier by phone as he accomplished one of his follow-up visits to the main Waterfall research center off campus. This time she hadn't taken off early, as she was accustomed to.

"Sheila. Office. Now," Gary barked as he walked straight past her without his customary request for messages or updates. The abruptness of his request made Sheila shudder with anxiety. She snatched her microtablet

PC and didn't hesitate in following him into his office. Sheila hurried to prep the dictation software on her tablet. These were the times she found working for Gary to be stressful.

Sitting down in his chair, Gary started to blare out his requests. "Get a list of everyone we recently promoted. And get a synopsis of each of their background checks. Then get me a list of anyone who could have had access to any information on our projects that have the highest confidentiality. And get the IT director in here right away," Gary commanded.

"I think Preston may have left early just a short while ago."

"Then get his ass back here. We may need to lock down network access to several of our projects and check security files on recent access."

"Can I ask what's going on?" Sheila asked

"You can, and maybe I'll let you know in a short bit. Now hurry up and take care of those tasks," Gary responded tersely, his demeanor more subdued than when he arrived.

He waited until Sheila left the office before getting on the phone to make the first of several calls. "Hey, this is Gary. Execute the protocols for a breach. Restrict access for all development arms of Aurora."

Resistance met his next call. "We need to do a temporary lockdown on the lab, development center, and on all the files. Then make sure to secure all samples ... I don't care where you're at in testing, just do it."

After only a few minutes, Sheila returned with two items, the first, a list of open positions in the division, and the other, a list of names of those recently promoted to new positions in the company. Gary was impressed with her expediency. In reviewing the first list, the CFO position was still open. Regardless of what he found today, he knew the position would soon need to be filled. Scanning through the names at the top of the alphabetical list, two stood out.

"Are Lucard and Branson still here?" He asked Sheila, who was standing by his desk awaiting further instructions, knowing they would be forthcoming.

"I believe Lucard already left, but Branson may still be here working late again."

"Well let's get them both in here if they're still on site."

Sheila remained and Gary knew she wanted to inquire as to the reason for his serious-mindedness. She knew something must have transpired but couldn't commit to ask.

After a tense moment of silence, Gary posed his question. "Was there something you wanted to know Sheila?"

"Would you mind if I ask what all this is about?" she asked.

Gary sat back in his beige leather executive chair and tried to determine if he would answer. With all the activity buzzing in his mind concerning the leak, he wasn't sure he could trust her. Given that she had direct physical access to many of his files, he knew she might eventually be sitting in the chair across from him answering questions.

"I don't feel comfortable talking about it yet. Go ahead and get Lucard and Branson in here."

Sheila was about to leave the office when the thought occurred to Gary that maybe she could be helpful in one way.

"Sheila, I do have a question for you."

She paused in the doorway with her back turned toward Gary to hide her ire. She had thought Gary trusted her implicitly and without question. "Yes Gary?"

"You're pretty much plugged in around here. Would you happen to know ..." He tried to formulate the exact context of his question but decided not to finish. "Never mind."

Scooping up the project folders from his meeting area, Gary made an effort to spend several minutes securing everything into his credenza and fastening the lock to the cabinet. Lucard knocked on the doorsill of the open door. It appeared he hadn't headed home for the evening. Inviting him in, Gary subtly interrogated him for nearly 15 minutes and then decided he didn't seem to be the one who'd revealed the sensitive information to the Church investigation team, if there were only one. As soon as Lucard left the office, Sheila sent in Branson. Gary offered the seat opposite his desk. Branson knew that if you sat on the couch, the meeting would tend to be more informal and pleasant than at his desk.

Gary wasn't sure but he thought Branson's short Afro had more gray around the temples than when he first started in his new position. Gary decided to use the same approach with Branson as with Lucard. He wouldn't directly ask him but would focus the questions to help him gauge the loyalty and trustworthiness of his junior director. Then he would then zero in on the project of interest.

"Branson, everything we're about to discuss is completely confidential. You mustn't mention anything to any of your peers or your staff. Understand?

"Not a problem," Branson nervously responded, crossing one leg over the other in an attempt to present himself as calm.

"Does your marketing team have all the information they need to accomplish their objectives? I know there were some issues you had brought up before."

Branson hesitated with his answer. "We're doing very well I think."

"Well, has any of your staff had to try to gather additional information, possibly researching or collecting information they may not need? You'd let me know if they did wouldn't you?"

Branson wasn't sure how he should answer. He had recently mentioned to several of his peers his frustration with his team continuing to have problems with gathering company historical data to help on some of their campaigns. Now he was curious if one of them might be trying to subvert him in some way. He decided to become defensive.

"Gary, what exactly are you saying?" Branson asked. Gary noted the tone of his voice changing.

Gary decided to go straight to the issue at hand. "Look, have any of your folks been requesting any information about the Aurora project?"

"No reason for us to. We never had to deal with rolling up information for that project." The project name ignited a memory though. "Although I do remember Alder asking quite a few questions; even as recent as this morning in the parking lot when I arrived at work."

The panorama of events came into focus for Gary. If he hadn't been so incensed over the leak of sensitive corporate information, and had focused on the situation as a whole, he could have come up with Alder as being the possible tipster. Although he didn't have direct access to the files or information, or a need for direct access in his duties, especially as he wasn't assigned any oversight responsibility for the project, he may have found additional information on his own by some other means. And considering his friend and coworker was a survivor of the angelic visitation, his paths could have crossed with the Church's team as it attempted to find out what happened.

"What type of questions was he asking?" Gary queried, softening his tone.

Branson forced himself to try and recall the earlier conversation with Alder. "Pretty much the only thing we discussed was the strange weekend he had, and the fact that some outsiders were asking about one of the company's projects."

Bingo, Gary thought. "Did he specifically discuss Aurora?"

"You know what, I don't remember now that I think about it. I do remember something about Stephen being involved in there somehow. I kinda dismissed the conversation because he mentioned he was gonna bring it up to you."

"He did, did he?"

Branson could hear the skepticism in Gary's voice then remembered that Gary was out of the office. "He may have tried to let you know. I mean you were gone most of the day."

Gary agreed with his comment. He wasn't sure if Branson was attempting to defend Alder or wanted to bring up a cogent point. "And you said he talked to Stephen over the weekend?"

"Yeah, he did."

"Did he mention how Stephen was doing?" Gary asked, attempting to redirect the conversation away from Alder being seen as committing a major indiscretion in the company. Branson knew that Gary was probing for specific information, and he may have just given him some major pieces.

"He said he's doing fine, just that he's not coping well if I recall correctly."

"Hmmm. Did he mention whether Stephen needed anything, or what the long-term prognosis was going to be?" Gary asked with sincerity.

"You know what; he didn't mention anything like that at all."

"Did you both discuss anything else?"

"Nope, went straight to work after that."

"So that's pretty much all you two talked about?"

"Yeah, that's it."

Gary dismissed Branson.

* * * *

Leaving for the day, Alder overheard employees from some of the administrative offices discussing whether they would be able to access their information in the morning when they returned to work. Rumors circulated like fire to dry kindling; Gary was on the warpath. He'd begun a lockdown of all information for high-profile projects because of the alleged release of trade secrets. Alder wondered if Gary could possibly have known someone released information in relation to Aurora. He had talked to the three at the church earlier in the day but dismissed the idea that they could be culpable because they were clergy and promised they wouldn't tell anyone about his visit. Did anybody observe him going through the files in Gary's office when Sheila left her desk and workstation unsecured? The other possibility was that one of the three he visited earlier in the day might have contacted the company to confirm the truthfulness of the information he provided. Maybe there were no mention of names; however, the fact that specifics for the project were exposed could be enough to warrant the lockdown. After all, Alder thought, Gary hadn't approached him. Even though the company was getting comfortable putting large amounts of information back into the data systems again after the loss of its IT personnel, he himself hadn't tried accessing any unauthorized files, so an electronic audit shouldn't direct anyone toward him.

Chapter 26

Getting off the phone with Stephen, Gary was uncertain if he should accept what he heard as gospel truth. Stephen confirmed that Alder was present when the three church representatives were there to interview him and wanted to know more about Aurora. He then stated that Alder was defensive of the company's trade secrets and directed Stephen not to mention anything more. So Gary was faced with the question, if Alder wasn't the source of the information on the more detailed portions of the project, who was? Just by the circumstantial nature of the encounter at Stephen's home, Alder was still the most likely suspect. Gary knew that, regardless of the leak, the bleeding of information needed to stop right away. He would need to direct the IT department to retrieve the audit logs to determine who did access any of the directories and files relating to the project and not having authorization. Gary's biggest fear was that someone working directly on the project had released the information intentionally having authorized file or data access. He would need to call the company's contracted investigative team.

Pulling out the paperwork files he previously locked in his credenza, Gary scrutinized the file folders to determine if any of the paperwork was missing. Then he realized it would have been easy to photograph the information with a smartphone. Although many of the facilities on the campus and all of the remote labs had restricted any type of personal electronic devices, a lawsuit allowed them into the headquarters administration building. Only certain areas such as information technology and accounting could ban any devices. For the next several hours, Gary focused most of his attention on keeping personnel working late to lock out accounts, initiate access audits on electronic files, secure paperwork, and increase security at the laboratories and research sites. Sheila threw out hints that he might be overreacting. She was acting in her own self-interests because it was close to 10:00 p.m., she was getting tired, and wanted to head home Gary continued to ignore her requests, considering them weak pleas. The questioning would need to continue the next day. The first would be Alder.

Coming into the office the next morning, Sheila greeted Gary with blood-shot eyes and her makeup barely up to her normal standards of acceptable. Her natural curly hair was slap dashed up into a frizzy bun. The director of IT was already waiting on the couch across from Sheila's desk. Gesturing the director into his office, Gary stayed behind, standing at Sheila's desk.

"After we're done, get Alder in here. I want to talk to him first thing. Cancel the staff meeting for later this morning and hold all calls," he kindly directed to Sheila.

In his office, Gary found the IT director already made himself comfortable on the couch. Gary went directly to his desk and motioned for his visitor to take a seat in one of the two chairs opposite his desk. The IT director, sensing the obvious power play, capitulated.

"So what did you find out about the files?" Gary asked.

"For all intents and purposes, the audit logs for the files you requested show no one out of the ordinary having access. We checked with other dates and times, access was consistent across the board."

"And what about the access for Alder Dennison, more so yesterday and the last couple of days?"

"Nothing out of the ordinary there either. He logged in first thing in the morning yesterday, stayed logged in only for a short while, logged off, and just before lunch, logged back in until the end of the day when he logged out again. The only files he accessed were the ones he historically would pull up. Nothing flagged as out of the ordinary."

"He was logged out for most of the morning?"

"Yeah, maybe he had a couple of meetings with his managers or was doing a walk around through his department offices," the director answered, subtly attempting to defend Alder, sensing a witch-hunt. The IT director found he could barely tolerate Gary, greatly preferring his previous superior during his employment a year ago in the agro-engineering production division. Gary perceived the IT department as an undesirable but necessary cost center, and the two locked antlers over many of the data systems projects.

Dismissing the director's comments, Gary pondered why he would attempt to defend Alder. The phone rang, upsetting Gary, who was a little miffed Sheila sent a call through against his orders, until he saw the caller ID. He decided to answer.

"Yeah, this is Gary."

After several minutes of silence, Gary's expression changed and his mood elevated. An extremely large grin erupted on his face.

"Are you serious?" Gary continued, waving for the director to leave the office. "Even with the all the international and in-country research restrictions you have to deal with? ... Damn, that is good news. How soon do you think you'll be able to accomplish live testing?"

Gary again waved for the IT director to leave, realizing he was still in his office, having not understood his previous hand gesture.

V. The Anthem of Angels: Requiem

Chapter 27

Bishop Grielle tried to control the flurry of his thoughts, wondering how he would approach talking to Father Hernandez about giving him a private report prior to information going to Cardinal Millhouse. A call might have sufficed, but driving over first thing in the morning to discuss the situation with the Father face-to-face would show how emphatic he was with his petition. Getting closer to the parish, Bishop Grielle now wasn't sure if his mentor had already received the information the three collected. Reflecting back ten years, thinking how he had directed the unknowing acquirement of Michael's and Sister Justine's research data during the first investigative trip to Mexico, the Bishop now considered why Michael held such animosity toward him. The Bishop had been in his new post for only a few months before being placed in charge of the two and their trip to Mexico. His leadership directed the confiscation any and all information they may have uncovered during their initial investigation.

In the church, the Bishop found Father Hernandez already working hard sorting through notes, papers, and several open books, some, the Bishop noted, covering church doctrines on Angelology. Father Hernandez was shocked to see Bishop Grielle coming through the doorway of the catechism meeting room reconfigured as a mini-conference room.

"Your Excellency? What're you doing here?"

"I see you're hard at work compiling the information on what you found out during your trip."

"Yes, but what're you doing here? We're attempting to finish this today so we can discuss this with you and the Cardinal tomorrow, worst case Thursday morning."

"That's why I'm here," the Bishop commented as he took a chair next to the table while trying to sneak a quick glance at some of the notes and papers before continuing. "I understand you've found out some pretty interesting pieces of information during your probing for answers."

"We have a couple of ideas, but couldn't all of this have waited until we came to present our findings?" Father Hernandez asked, extremely curious. He must've driven out here for a reason beyond just trying to get an early glimpse of their research.

"Your Excellency, I'd have to think there's some other reason you're here," Father Hernandez continued.

The Bishop decided not to answer; a silent void formed between the two. During this period of silence, Sister Justine walked in. Expecting only to see Father Hernandez and finding the Bishop in the room, she surmised the reason for his visit. Feigning interest, she presented the Bishop with a pleasant smile, not wanting to show her hand in case she was wrong.

"Bishop Grielle, what a nice surprise to see you. What brings you here this morning?" Sister Justine asked in flowery tone. Both men consciously noted the plastic emotions wrapped in her comments.

The Bishop accepted the pseudo sincerity and warmth of the Sister while standing to greet her. "It's nice to see you as well Sister. I was getting a little impatient and wanted to see how things were coming

302

along in regard to the information you're putting together." Father Hernandez was upset, feeling the reverence was misplaced.

"We'd be delighted to do that," she answered, hoping to disarm any planned surreptitious objectives.

Nearly 20 minutes elapsed as both Father Hernandez and Sister Justine presented the Bishop with a synopsis of most all the data they collected and possible explanations. Bishop Grielle's face flushed as the two provided their primary conjecture for the possible tie-in of the angels and the Everest cloning project. The speculation by the research team was something the Bishop did not expect; the angels of God were the ones attempting to disrupt or cease the work of the Church's patron, and the work in progress possibly considered an abomination. The Bishop asked himself the question of the true intentions and impact of the unique visitor upon the Bishop of Rome. The Bishop's original purpose for driving out to the church became vaporous.

"These are some serious conjectures you're making," the Bishop commented, overwhelmed by the revelations.

Father Hernandez interjected, "Understand, it's just conjecture at this point. This is just us pulling some weak correlations that may have nothing to do with one another."

"But if true, the cause of what happened all those years ago could be related to the event here in the city," Sister Justine added.

"Do you both understand what you're saying?" Bishop Grielle asked, beginning to massage aggressively his left shoulder and upper left arm.

303

"I'm not sure you understand what we're saying your Excellency," Father Hernandez responded.

Bishop Grielle, sweat forming on his forehead, gasping for air in short, arduous breaths, put one hand on his chest and the other on the tabletop. "May I so much as ask for a glass of water? I'm not feeling too well; I think I may have indigestion," he labored.

Both Father Hernandez and Sister Justine understood what was happening.

Chapter 28

Michael was relieved not to be working with Father Hernandez anymore, or Sister Justine, and anxious to get back to teaching. His reorientation to his syllabus was almost complete. His final activity was to review the lectures with the associate professor who had filled in for him. Michael also felt comforted by his usual jogging dominion by the beach. His favorite portion of the jog was the reserved bicycle and jogging road running parallel to the beach between the multicolored and multileveled houses. The weaving through Rollerbladers, bicyclists, walkers, and other joggers added variety to each run. Michael was accustomed to Tuesdays being less crowded, with just enough activity to keep the jog interesting but not bothersome in trying to avoid someone every other minute. This day was not a typical Tuesday's.

A bicyclist, 50 to 70 yards ahead of him, was more interested in talking into his Bluetooth headset than in paying attention to the other exercisers. The biker periodically steered left into the lane of opposing traffic. A couple of joggers would weave out of his way to prevent from him colliding with them. Even when they yelled out for the cyclist to stay in his lane, Michael could tell the cyclist feigned an apology but continued on his way indifferent. Michael moved as far right as possible and dedicated all his attention to the one distracted bicyclist. He didn't notice a more skilled bicyclist, wearing a black-and-gold spandex outfit with matching helmet, speedily arriving on the left of the distracted cyclist. In a blur, they both were almost upon Michael, the faster cyclist passing the slower cyclist and attempting to call out he was passing on the left. The slower cyclist, startled by someone instantly showing up at his side, flinched and disrupted the grace and agility of the faster bicycler, which sent him straight into Michael, who tried to jump out of the way but couldn't. His leg sustained the majority of the impact.

After he returned to his house with the assistance of a couple of joggers, Alicia attended to his severely scraped calf and ankle and worked to dress the injury. Each time she touched close to the distressed ankle, Michael grimaced. She knew it was more serious than he claimed. Already seeing swelling, she hurried to retrieve a cold pack. When she returned, tinges of discoloration developed under his tanned skin. She decided he should head to the emergency room. No matter how much Michael tried to rationalize that there wasn't any reason to go to urgent care or the hospital, by the end of the brief disagreement Alicia overruled him.

Chapter 29

Waking up, Stephen hoped today would be better than yesterday. His sister Brenda had been successful in igniting another argument with the new rehab trainer and hindering his progress in his adjusting to his handicap. Today was the trainer's second day, and if the situation continued to trend, she would either be let go or become frustrated and not want to return after day three. Stephen began to feel that Brenda was becoming overly protective. He would have to talk to her about her aggressiveness. He didn't remember her being this protective of him while they were growing up. He did remember how they fought like the typical brother and sister – possession of the bathroom, access to the computer, taunting of one another at the dinner table. Stephen felt maybe she was overcompensating for the disappearance of their parents ten years earlier and her being closer to both than he'd been.

Lying in bed for several more minutes, Stephen concentrated on listening to determine if Brenda was already awake and moving about the house. He sensed the quietness of the home and couldn't hear the radio or television that she was accustomed to turn on when she first woke up in the morning. He determined she was either asleep or out running some quick errands. Of course, the time would determine her possible location. Reaching over to the other side of his queen-size bed, he probed the top of the nightstand with his hand searching for the clock. Clicking the large button on top, the audible clock blared nine-thirty. She must be out. Removing the covers and navigating to the end of the bed, he tried to ensure he went in the right direction to retrieve his bathrobe. The next objective would be underwear. After retrieving the garments, he maneuvered through his room to the bathroom. Stephen found it a little easier today getting ready for his shower than on previous days. Having forced himself to memorize the location of the items he needed, some activities were now more natural.

Stephen eagerly anticipated a relaxing shower. He didn't concentrate on pulling the shower curtain fully closed and didn't notice the bath rug was situated in a different place on the floor after Brenda had washed it. The warm water melted his imbued tension from the anticipation of the afternoon's bickering. The shower was so relaxing that Stephen didn't focus on the amount of shower gel he used to lather his body or the amount of shampoo he used in his hair. The excess splattered onto the side walls of the shower and over the side onto the floor next to the bathtub. When he finished, Stephen stepped out onto a tile floor lubricated by the spatter of gel and shampoo suds. He lost his footing. Brenda came home to find her brother knocked out and naked on the bathroom floor.

Chapter 30

Michelle tossed and turned all night. She was hot and nauseous, even throwing up a couple of times. After Maria and Alder alternated checking on their daughter during the night, Alder didn't have his normal morning grogginess and got ready for work more speedily. But shaving was more challenging for him as he tried to apply the proper pressure on his razor to his morning stubble. The five toilet-paper-dotted nicks showed he failed. After he was finished getting ready, Alder stepped into Michelle's room. Maria sat on the bed next to their daughter, her hand on Michelle's forehead. He could see his daughter was still in distress.

"Is she doing any better?" he asked.

"She's still pretty warm," Maria gently responded, looking up at her husband. "Shouldn't you be getting ready for work?"

Alder wanted an excuse for not going in to work today, but not at the expense of his daughter. Even though Maria had made it easy for him to head out, he could easily tell she preferred that he stay home. While Alder felt he and Maria might not have much in common, he was extremely devoted to his children and knew Michelle was in the care of a mother who loved her and Matthew as much as he did.

"I think I'll stay and help out and watch Matthew today. I got plenty of sick leave to burn through."

Maria smiled. She observed ever since the funeral home incident where his friend went blind, Alder slowly became more involved with the children.

Leaving his wife and daughter, Alder went into Matthew's room, where his son was contentedly playing with toys in his playpen. Seeing Alder come in, Matthew smiled, dropped the large plastic teething ring of multicolored keys, and elevated his arms for his father to pick him up. Reaching down to lift up his son, Alder could easily tell his diaper was extremely wet and couldn't believe how easily Matthew accommodated the discomfort of his diaper when other toddlers tended to cry incessantly. After replacing Matthew's soiled undergarment and playing with him for a few minutes, the pangs in Alder's stomach made him realize just how hungry he was. Normally a quick stop by the cafeteria at work would help, but he was still at home. The thought of the cafeteria made him realize he needed to call Gary and let him know he'd be taking a sick day. He decided to address his hunger first.

After putting Matthew in his kitchen high chair, Alder scanned the refrigerator to decide what to make for breakfast. Since he would be staying home, he thought about making omelets stuffed with onions, bacon, and cheddar cheese. He pulled out a steel skillet from one of the lower cabinets, then gathered the seasonings he thought he would use--salt, pepper, basil, tarragon, and garlic powder. At the refrigerator, Alder pulled out bacon, onions, and cheddar cheese. Sorting the ingredients and prepping his work area, he thought

310

himself an idiot for not gathering everything he need the first time he searched the cabinets and refrigerator. Back to the refrigerator, he pulled out several eggs, the most important component for omelets, and put them on the countertop. Maria called from upstairs.

"Alder, please hurry and get up here," she yelled. Alder heard panic in her voice.

Darting upstairs and straight to Michelle's room, Maria was holding a small trash-bag-lined wicker basket by the side of the bed where Michelle was resting her head. Maria turned to see her husband enter and Alder saw the alarm and fear on her face.

"Alder, she's throwing up, and it looks like there's blood in there," Maria wept.

"We're taking her to the emergency room," he responded.

Chapter 31

Alder hadn't reported to Gary, who was irritated that he hadn't heard anything from his junior director. For this meeting, Gary had postponed his trip out to the research lab to view firsthand the progress of all the final phases of his pet project. He was unhappy not to be on site during the implementation of key components after numerous years of research. The culmination of so many recent successes helped to anchor some positive introspection. Even with several key researchers and scientists killed at the recent alleged angelic visits, almost putting the overall projects at risk, the success didn't counterbalance the intense emotions stirring due to the recent breach of security. Stepping out into the reception area, he saw that Sheila was just hanging up the phone; Gary's face was constraining an angry flare-up.

"Where the hell is Alder Dennison?" Gary barked but limited his volume to prevent other offices down the hall from hearing his outburst.

"That was him on the phone," Sheila answered. "He had to take his daughter to the emergency room this morning. I guess she had a fever and was throwing up blood."

Gary smirked, a look of disbelief flashing across his face. His immediate thought was that Alder had gotten word about the inquiries and was now finding ways to avoid him. After the thought dashed through his mind, Gary reconsidered and wondered whether Alder's daughter being sick was just an inopportune coincidence.

"Find out what hospital and send him my regards and wishes for his daughter," Gary commented.

Sheila smiled. Although she held Alder in disdain, believing he had gotten lucky in getting his position as he wasn't of the same caliber as the other directors, she was sympathetic hearing about his daughter.

"As a matter of fact, he mentioned he's heading over to Mercy Memorial. I'll order some flowers and say they're from the company," Sheila said.

Gary considered sending flowers to the ER, thought it kind of strange, and disregarded the gesture as he returned to his desk. He didn't know that Sheila was overcompensating for her negative attitude and behavior toward Alder by feeling empathy for his daughter. Gary, activating the videoconferencing software on his desktop computer, clicked the name he was searching for on the contacts list, Dr. Anton Petroyev. An image of an older gentlemen, unkempt thinning gray hair, cracked skin, wrinkled plaid shirt, and crisp, clean, white lab smock, answered. Even though he appeared senior in age, he was only 51 years old.

"Gary. What can I do for you?" the image asked.

"Doc, looks like I may be able to make it over a little earlier than I thought. How's our little patient?" Gary responded.

"Talked to the site this morning. He's doing quite well and I just got an email from Dr. Solandar concerning the other phase of Aurora. The second set of tests went well. Looks like we got a winner. We just need to finish up some more testing in a controlled environment and begin planning for a field test."

"Good, the investors will be extremely happy. That's why I want to come down and see what the test parameters are and the projected impact. I'm scheduled to head out to the site here in town later and hoping to fly down to Mexico by the end of the week. "

"Well, we're more than happy to have you go down. Hell, I may just go with you. Oh, and by the way, thanks again for the heads up on those three going down from the Church. Apart from the research staff, we made sure the entire team pretty much stayed on lockdown at the lab. Rumor has it, though, that they were able to talk to a former cleaning crew member from ten years ago," the videoconference image stated.

"Yeah, the Cardinal up here passed that on. We're getting it all sorted out," Gary responded, intentionally not revealing the recent leak of information.

"Oh, one other thing," the doctor noted.

"Yeah? What?"

"Just thought I'd let you know that one of the researchers down in Mexico seems to be having an ethical change of heart."

"I thought your staff understood what was going on and that we wouldn't have these types of problems," Gary responded. Dr. Petroyev sensed Gary was troubled by what he had told him, not realizing Gary was beginning to fume hearing about an additional possible personnel issue.

"They did, but from what I was told from the site lead in Aguascalientes, hearing about that angel stuff happening up there, and those rumors about what happened years ago, I guess it was getting to him."

"What do you mean, 'I guess'?" Gary inquired, the doctor noticing the ire in his voice.

"Some former close colleagues who initially worked with him on the project moved up here to the States to help stabilize our half of the work, and they were killed at Thomson and Thomson. The biggest hit was when he found out that his mentor, who'd recruited him to work on the genetic engineering and virology project, died at Crestview."

"Should we look at having him transferred or replaced?" Gary asked with serious resolve, "especially with the stressors you mentioned?"

"Don't think that'll be a problem quite yet. Moving him won't be necessary. Plus he's one of the key developers on this project."

"So if he wasn't part of your team down in Mexico anymore?"

"It could be catastrophic to our success depending on our testing, but we'd get by."

"Then look, I expect you to handle the situation Doc. We can't risk the leak of any more information."

"What information was leaked? Did some news already get out?" The image asked excitedly.

"Well, let me know what you need from us, and keep me posted on your progress," Gary replied and then disconnected the videoconferencing software, upset he'd inadvertently made a comment about the leak. The doctor's image disappeared from the 26" OLED monitor.

Gary now mentally prepared himself to question the final two personnel on his staff regarding the breech of information. Alder would wait. But it occurred to Gary that he still hadn't talked to Sheila. She knew something serious had transpired but he hadn't fully explained the exact details. Nor had he considered, until just this moment, talking to Sheila to see if she had any ideas or heard of anyone who may have been acting suspiciously at the executive level in the company. On the contrary, he trusted her unreservedly, especially as by proxy she shared full access to his email accounts and many of the same electronic and hard copy files. He did limit access to the most sensitive projects, but if she found a way to procure the information, this could make her one of the most likely suspects to have contacted the unsanctioned outside recipients. Nevertheless, Gary couldn't draw any direct correlations between her and the Church's investigation team.

Heading out to the reception area, he saw Sheila typing on her computer keyboard, working on what appeared to be the interoffice memos he requested that she complete.

"Sheila?" Gary asked, interrupting her typing, "With what's going on around here, we've had to be more careful with the security of the information for some of our projects."

"Yeah, I kinda noticed," she responded. "Especially with the lockdown of all the files and accounts. What's going on? How can I help?"

Gary sensed the sincerity of her question. "Someone may have revealed some sensitive information about one of our R & D projects to unauthorized recipients. I don't want to tell you which project, but it's pretty serious. I almost think it could be one of the directors."

Sheila visualized the list of junior executives and managers under Gary; the R & D production VP, marketing VP, marketing manager, accounting director, and the CFO position, which was still vacant. Gary was still handling many of the key duties he could legally become involved with, having the CFO of the manufacturing division accomplish the remainder. Running through who occupied each of the positions, the one who came to mind was Alder, the accounting director. Contemplating her ideas and getting ready to answer, both she and Gary were interrupted by ringing on personal phone line. The caller ID displayed a direct outward-dial number from the offices of the Archdiocese. After minimal communication over the years to prevent any type of connection between the R & D division of Everest and the Church, beyond the work of and provisions for the sponsored free clinics handled by operations division, Gary thought it strange for the Cardinal to be calling so close to their last discussion identifying the release of information. He decided he wanted to take the call. He returned to his desk and answered.

"Hello Gary," the voice on the other end responded. "This is Cardinal Millhouse."

"Your Eminence, what can I do for you?"

"I just received word that Bishop Grielle was taken to the emergency room at Mercy Memorial Hospital due to a possible heart attack. We're not sure how serious it is yet, it's just that I wanted to let you know that I'm going to see how he's doing, considering what we discussed with him the other day."

Gary had to orient himself to recall Bishop Grielle, and then the discussion in the Cardinal's office.

"I'm sorry to hear that your Eminence, but I'm not sure what I can do?"

"He was visiting Father Hernandez and Sister Justine at the time of the heart attack. He may have been trying to gather more information as well as attempting to find out where they both may have found out about our pet project."

"OK, that is a bit interesting ... wait a minute ... did you say Mercy Memorial?" Gary asked excitedly.

"Yes. Why?" the Cardinal asked in return intrigued by Gary's curiosity.

"One of my directors is taking a day off. His daughter was just taken there. She wasn't feeling too well."

"How does that involve what we're discussing?" the Cardinal reacted. Gary detected a bit of sarcasm in his voice.

"The director is Alder Dennison, the one who missed attending the Thomson funeral home incident and friend of the only survivor, Stephen Williams."

The Cardinal remained quiet.

"Your Eminence?" Gary asked, making sure the Cardinal was still on the line.

"I'm still here. I'm just trying to figure out if this could be a strange coincidence," the Cardinal responded.

"At this point, I'm beginning to doubt that."

"I'm going to head down to the hospital just in case I have to administer last rites."

"Love your confidence that he's going to get better," Gary quipped.

"Prefer to be ready. We never fully know God's entire plan. I'll keep you informed." With that final comment, Cardinal Millhouse hung up the phone.

Gary didn't appreciate the abrupt end to the conversation and was a little perturbed. Yet the information from the Cardinal strengthened his theory that Alder appeared to be the leak of information. He would postpone talking to anyone else until he could rule out his prime suspect. Sheila now came in, looking puzzled.

"What is it Sheila?" Gary asked.

"I was talking to one of my friends down in accounting and they got word that Stephen Williams fell in the bathroom while taking a shower and was taken to the hospital."

"And your point is?"

"I just thought it odd that he was taken to Mercy Memorial, the same one where Alder took his sick daughter."

* * * *

Another individual was heading in a direct beeline toward the research compound; but this one approached from the north. Of the other three, one was from the south, one from the east, and one from the west. One straggler out this far from the nearest town, maybe an accident, but four, it was no longer a coincidence or someone simply lost. The sleek Sikorsky helicopter made another pass high above the tall male figure clothed in a burlap toga-like wrap and weather-worn sandals walking through the sparse desert brush. It wasn't a mirage. The aircrew thought the attire was severely inappropriate for the intense heat of the southern Mexican desert outback. Through the binoculars, the security officer sitting behind the pilot discerned the intruder was either of Asian or Latino descent. He suspected as much since of the other three, one was Caucasian, one black, the third assumed to be Semitic in appearance. Because of the distance, it was hard to tell. The pilot radioed in the coordinates of this final trespasser. His response from Dr. Petroyev was similar to the one from the other three sightings: a ground security unit from the gendarmerie paid to respond and secure their compound would intercept the potential intruder and handle accordingly. Continuing the reconnaissance of the surrounding area, the pilot thought it safe to travel to other patrol zones to make sure no one else was approaching.

After several minutes flying over the outer perimeter, a radio message came in from the ground unit: "Wolf Two confirm position of sighting. There seems to be no one out here either."

The pilot's observer reviewed his notes and transmitted the location. The ground unit response was the same; nobody was at the coordinates or along the projected walking route. The control center also asked for confirmation by reviewing the ground sensors and motion detector logs. With no human activities recorded, the compound didn't sound an alarm.

The aircrew emphatically confirmed there were four different individuals. Dr. Petroyev was uneasy someone might be trying to probe the security of the research compound and decided to put the site on high alert. Also considering how his earlier conversation progressed with Gary, and since no one was found, he'd hold off calling back to and report this; he'll just submit it with his security log entries and discuss it with him later.

Chapter 32

A young couple out for a night's walk embraced each other under a bright, umber-tinted moon near a decaying cathedral with major walls crumbling from years of silent erosion and weathering. Standing remnants of gray brick stood amongst the remainder of the wall. Disparate-sized pieces lay scattered along the ground, some the size of tiny boulders, many adorned with graffiti. A set of layered, Romanesque archways of successive heights, walled off at the smallest one that rose 15 feet nonetheless, stood erect as the only remaining full-height portion of the edifice, the remains of the crossing to a transept of the old church. Dandelions, tall strand grass, thistles, and other weeds grew between most of the seams and cracks in the once-pristine stone flooring, no longer resembling anything hewn by skilled craftsmen or artisans. On one side of the structure, down a small incline of plush grass, a still lake reflected the muted glow of the moon.

The couple's walk took them toward the lake; both ready to retreat home and settle in for the evening. Nocturnal sounds whispered in the evening air, crickets, owls, bats fluttering, and the rustling of scavenger animals in the nearby hedges. Ready to dismiss any other sounds as they strolled away from the wasted ruins and focused only on the rest of the night before them, several vocal melodic and polyphonic tones wafted through the air to form a somber harmony. The two at first assumed the sounds were coming from the radio or other device of someone in the vicinity. They then comprehended the source to be the standing ruins of the old cathedral. As suddenly as the vocalized harmony started, it stopped. All other nocturnal sounds ceased. The couple was now feeling uncomfortable, both standing firm by the lake, the smell of sweet spices and flowers perfuming the silent, still air. After several minutes, even though none of the normal evening sounds returned to their ears, they decided to continue walking, the young woman of the couple tightening her grip on her new husband's hand. Within a few steps, the somber harmony returned, the two now quite sure it originated from the ruins, echoing from inside the walled portion of the transept.

In Chicago, on the south side of the city, was an abandoned church with windows boarded, parkway in patches of grass and dirt, and parking lot fenced with posts topped by a loop threaded with a rusting chain and dandelions and grass working their way through its split and cracked asphalt. Several of the neighborhood kids played touch football with one boy's girlfriend sitting off to the side, all enjoying the school holiday until they were interrupted by what sounded like orchestrated vocalizations originating in the empty edifice. The five young teens, no longer interested in the game, were disturbed at hearing anything from the church. They knew that most of the items that were capable of making the sounds they were hearing had been either removed or destroyed. A couple of them had caused much of the damage inside shortly after the church closed two years before. As they approached the structure, a police car on patrol pulled to the curb and gave one quick burst of the siren indicating that the five should step away from the building. Initially startled by the noise emanating from the patrol car, they refocused their attention to the source of the unique sounds. Angry at being ignored, the patrolman stepped out of the car, his ears now assaulted with the haunting melody that was growing in intensity. He debated whether to call for backup, especially if one or more trespassers had entered into the church. Assistance would be needed to expel them. Walking up to the building, fear and trepidation enveloped him; the singing voices didn't sound human.

Outside the city of Aquascalientes, in a region called El Refugio, after an unexpected deluge of rain, activity steadily returned to the streets. An abandoned church no longer stood quiet. The dulcet sounds of a choir with perfect harmony, perfect pitch, without a single voice out of tune wafted onto the town streets. The few scattered wanderers in the town, walking through the park across the street, and the children playing in the street at first thought nothing of the melancholy euphony. They dismissed it as simple background noise. Minutes later, the realization manifested in the same fear among all those in hearing distance; the church was now alive with spirits, the spirits of the ones who passed ten years earlier. No one could come up with another explanation.

One of the townspeople gathered outside Our Lady of Hope made the comment: *"Los espíritus malignos han llegado"* ("The evil spirits have arrived").

Across the nation and throughout numerous countries, in abandoned churches, cathedral ruins, old store fronts, closed schools, or vacated office spaces all once used for religious services, ethereal and supernatural singing arose. The sound of what could be only one or two vocalizations emanated from many of the locations; in others, perfectly harmonized choirs. In many of the places, no one felt brave enough to enter to determine the source of the sounds. At sites where those were bold enough to enter, nothing could be seen, only heard. They weren't able to remain long as a sense of dread built up exponentially the longer they stayed.

Chapter 33

Father Hernandez and Sister Justine sat on the cold, plastic red and blue chairs of the emergency room without saying anything to each other. They felt the location was not the place to discuss their current investigation, especially with Bishop Grielle being examined by an ER doctor. After nearly an hour, Father Hernandez was allowed to go visit the Bishop, who was resting in one of the roomettes, to provide the sacrament of the anointing of the sick over his mentor. In the waiting area, Sister Justine, bored, passed time observing the activity of those entering and leaving. One man walked up to the receiving nurse pressing a wet, ruby-colored rag on the palm of his left hand. Crashing through the ambulance entrance, paramedics and nurses rushed a young man on a gurney hooked to tubes, wires, and IV drip pouches, one paramedic frantically on top administering chest compressions. Realizing she hadn't prayed for the Bishop, she decided to recite a litany in her thoughts when Father Hernandez came through the ER doorway. The Father was thankful he wouldn't have to provide the last rites. Becoming hungry, he perused the set of vending machines opposite the open doorway of the waiting area. The variety of potato chips, corn chips, blue corn chips, cheese puffs, cupcakes, Danishes, and beef jerky didn't ignite any desire for a snack. The other machine displayed gum, trail mix, granola bars, peanuts, and several varieties of candy bars. The urge hit Father Hernandez for a candy bar. He was unsure if he wanted a Three Musketeers bar or the Almond Joy. He stood in front of the machine for a couple of minutes before deciding on a Milky Way. He noticed as a set of double doors at one end of the waiting area swung open and saw an orderly pushing Stephen, who was wearing a bandage and dressing on his head, in a wheelchair, his sister walking next to the two, all three moving through the waiting area back to the noncritical exam area of the emergency room.

Father Hernandez called out to him. "Excuse me, Stephen I believe. I don't know if you remember me or not?"

Brenda turned to see Father Hernandez and recalled who he was right away. The voice was somewhat familiar to Stephen but he couldn't remember where he'd heard it before.

"Who is that?" Stephen inquired, the conversation distracting Sister Justine's attention from reading a *Ladies Home Journal* magazine.

"It's Father Hernandez. I'm here with Sister Justine. We came to visit you at the hospital and later at your home a short while ago about what you witnessed at the funeral home."

"Really, you guys again. I don't think there's anything else I could tell you. Besides, I don't want to talk anymore about ..."

"Father, could you please leave my brother alone. He'd prefer not to have to discuss any more about that horrible situation," Brenda interjected.

"Look, I believe you may have misunderstood. I just came over to see how you're doing. What happened?"

A skeptical retort came to Brenda's mind, but she decided to politely respond in case the Father was genuine. "Well thank you, he's doing fine."

"Uh...the bandage on his head would say otherwise?" Father Hernandez retorted. Brenda could feel her cheeks becoming ruddy from a quick flash of anger and she was especially now wishing she hadn't made the terse remark. The orderly chuckled, which further infuriated Brenda. The look on her face made Father Hernandez regret his sarcastic comment. He remembered, through the years, the way some of his peers were considerate or sympathetic. And then there were his counterparts who were more abrasive just to strengthen the impact of their sarcasm, which sometimes upset the parishioners further.

"Look, my brother just had a nasty accident and I'd like to take him home to rest," Brenda retorted.

"What's that weird music?" Stephen asked, disrupting the strained engagement between the Father and Brenda, who both surveyed him with confusion. Keeping quiet and concentrating to hear over the audio of the television, they distinctly heard a cappella singing. Thinking this was the music Stephen referenced, due to the way it floated and echoed in the air, they both dismissed it as piped in over the public address system.

"It's nothing Stephen," Brenda responded.

"Look," Father Hernandez said, "I didn't mean to offend you; my only intentions were just to say hello.

We're only here because we brought our Bishop, who may be suffering a heart attack."

Brenda was a bit remorseful, realizing she had been somewhat rude, but was still agitated at seeing Father Hernandez. "Well, I'm sorry to hear about whoever it was you said was here with the heart attack, but we'd like to be left alone," she responded in a discourteous tone, her dislike of the Church leaking through.

Sister Justine, who'd witnessed the exchange, walked over to try to pacify Brenda. As she came upon the group, Sister Justine saw, through the glass of the double doors, someone looking like Michael in the same hallway as Stephen and Brenda. Alicia accompanied Michael, supporting himself with crutches, his ankle wrapped in a compression bandage. Right away, Michael identified Father Hernandez and Sister Justine, paying no immediate attention to Stephen in the wheelchair, escorted by his sister and an orderly.

"I'll be damned," Michael blared, those in the waiting area turning toward him. "What the hell are you guys doing here?"

The look on Sister Justine's face told Michael she didn't appreciate his expletive.

"We're here because we believe Bishop Grielle was having a heart attack. They're getting ready to take him upstairs to run some more tests," Father Hernandez responded.

"You mean that snake actually has a heart?"

"Do you hear that?" Stephen asked, forcefully interrupting the conversation. He heard something that didn't sound normal and wanted to make sure everyone was listening.

"It's just the television or music someone's playing Stephen," his sister responded.

As everyone paid attention to the muffled music because of Stephen's strong reaction, they thought it sounded inappropriate as the melody was extremely melancholy, which made for a somber atmosphere in the emergency room. They noticed the singing didn't emanate from the PA system because the otherworldly sounds didn't cut out when an urgent page broadcasted to request that the senior maintenance supervisor report to the first-floor chapel. Michael now became aware of Stephen and his sister.

"Someone just has their radio or MP3 player turned up loud, that's all Mr. Williams," Sister Justine noted.

"No, it's more than that," Stephen replied. The more he heard, the more disturbed he became and then he recognized one of the voices within the saintly choir. His face became flushed and he began to get out of the wheelchair.

"You gotta take me to that music sis," Stephen demanded.

The orderly was visibly angry. "Sir, you need to sit back down so that we can finish discharging you."

"Stephen, you're going to stay here like the orderly said," Brenda repeated.

Stephen ignored both of them. "Damn it sis, help me or get out of the way." He pulled his retractable cane from its holder, extended it, and started probing his way toward the double doors in the direction he believed the sounds to originate.

Father Hernandez and Sister Justine observed several other people in the waiting area themselves rubbernecking, also curious about the source of the music. A spry elderly woman requested that the receptionist turn down the volume on the television. The only background noise now was the distinct singing, its audio levels increasing, and several people murmuring while trying to guess the source. The emergency room door that led outside, boomed open and interrupted the concentration of patients and visitors in the waiting area. A young maintenance tech was moving speedily while fumbling with a ring of keys to the set of double doors at the end of a hallway that led deeper into the bowels of the hospital. The distracted janitor almost knocked Stephen down. Stephen sensed someone had brushed past him but continued working his way through the doorway with Brenda catching up. Father Hernandez and Sister Justine both followed Stephen. Michael decided to finish processing his discharge from the ER. He and Alicia worked their way over to the reception area.

The murmuring in the waiting area intensified, with one woman garnering a husky feminine voice blaring out for someone to turn up the television volume. The admissions receptionist complied with the request. Several other people in the waiting area had their eyes locked on their smartphones to absorb streaming media presented by their news apps. Regardless of how they watched or read, there were special reports about strange happenings around the world. Haunting vocalizations and singing had begun spontaneously at abandoned or closed churches and other religious sites. No one could explain their source. With the exception of Michael and Alicia, individuals were extremely focused on the news reports and didn't take notice to the distinctive audible harmonies drifting into the waiting area from an unknown source.

Michael watched as a man carrying a little girl rushed into the emergency room from outside followed by a panicked young Hispanic female carrying a young toddler. He recalled it was the same fellow they'd met when they went to interview Stephen Williams. As soon as the thought of Stephen Williams came to mind, while looking at the hallway double door, Michael's eyes widened as Stephen Williams was passing through into the hallway. Turning back toward Alder and his wife, he saw they were anxiously attempting to garner medical attention for their daughter. Snapping his head back and forth between the hallway double door and Alder several more times, he decided it might be more interesting to follow Stephen, Father Hernandez, and Sister Justine. Being here with those involved with the previous tragic events, even those on the periphery, seemed out of the ordinary, maybe even extremely coincidental, especially as Michael had thought, for all intents and purposes, he wouldn't be bothered with the Father or Sister Justine again.

"Where're you going?" Alicia asked as she saw Michael crutch away from the gaggle of patients and their companions in the waiting area hypnotized by the televised and streaming news reports.

"Just wait here," he responded.

Michael expected to see his earlier traveling associates passing through the swinging double doors. Entering the hallway, he saw it was empty audibly flooded. Following the sound, the crutches impeding his speed, he ignored his temporary handicap. Michael hurriedly traveled to the end of the corridor, turning right to where a small band of curious spectators gathered around a set of closed double doors. Above the doors, a small hanging sign displayed "Chapel 2." The maintenance tech Michael had seen earlier in the waiting area was fumbling through the collection of keys on the silver hoop, trying each one in the door lock. He nervously appeared to retry the same key multiple times, distracted by the noise of the small throng of those anxiously waiting to enter. The singing originated from inside the chapel. Several hospital employees in the mini crowd that had formed around the entrance knew the chapel was locked and had been unused for several years, the primary one in another wing of the facility being used for services. The small mob anxiously anticipated the doors being opened, excited from hearing the recent news of similar events across the country. Father Hernandez and Sister Justine stood patiently along the edge of the small group. Stephen and Brenda stood just in front of the two clergy members. Michael perceived Stephen to be visibly agitated. Brenda reassuringly held her brother's hand and attempted to calm him. A small-framed, bronze-skinned, middle-aged Latina with a mole over her right eye, dark hair streaked with silver, wearing a disheveled, tattered outfit with many layers walked into the foyer area and stood off to the side unseen.

Sister Justine caught sight of Michael approaching out of the corner of her eye and gave him a chiding smirk. "No girl toy with you?" she asked, not sure why she decided to make the quip.

Michael ignored her and suppressed the many witticisms that flooded his stream of consciousness, some of them not so nice. Father Hernandez heard her comment and resisted chuckling.

Stephen whispered several words; they were incomprehensible with the activity around him. Brenda leaned in closer to her brother. Father Hernandez and Sister Justine attempted to understand Stephen's remark. Michael stayed focused on the activity at the door.

"What'd you say Stephen?" Brenda asked.

"It can't be," Stephen responded, slightly louder.

"It can't be what?"

"A voice in there singing sounds familiar."

Father Hernandez couldn't resist injecting a question due to Stephen's odd comment. "What sounds familiar?"

"I've heard it twice before, once at Thomson and Thomson, then again at the television station."

Michael became interested in Stephen's observation, and it was then that the service tech found and inserted the correct key. The lock on the door clicked and the doors swung open. The singing stopped. Several members of the small crowd stood in place disappointed. Some of the others followed the service tech into the chapel. When he turned on the lights, the only items to be seen were mundane, ten dust-covered rows of marginally warped bench pews, and an altar with cracked and stained varnish standing erect upon a small dais, raised up one-step, opposite the entrance. A crumpled maroon velveteen curtain covered the entire back wall ceiling to floor. A large crucifix hung suspended by a single support wire fastened to the ceiling, cocked at an angle just in front of the curtain and spotlighted by a recessed light in the drop-ceiling panel. A set of six fluorescent light fixtures with soft, natural light bulbs illuminated the chamber, one of the fixtures randomly flickering. Faded white paint on the walls was transformed to a muddy shade of ivory. Four large wood-framed faux-stained-glass windows lined each of the side walls, a light recessed behind each to simulate side lighting as if coming from outside and through the window to evoke a religious experience.

Most of the spectators were unsatisfied to find only an abandoned chapel and left to return to their previous activities; many wanted the singing to return. Father Hernandez took a quick scan and requested that the doors remain open after seeing Stephen guided to the doorway clenching his sister's hand tightly, his face flushed. Knowing him to be blind, Father Hernandez thought Stephen's eyes widened as if something he was staring at troubled him. The service technician himself dismissed anything enigmatic and was ready to shut down everything.

"I'd like to close up everything, so could you all go ahead and please leave?" the janitor said to those remaining.

The last of the stragglers became disinterested, leaving Father Hernandez, Sister Justine, Michael, Stephen, and Brenda alone in the chapel with the service tech.

"We'd like to stay for a few minutes please?" Father Hernandez asked. The technician gave a disapproving response. Father Hernandez pointed to his priest's collar. "Don't worry, you can trust us."

Discounting Stephen and Brenda still standing in the doorway, the janitor reluctantly showed Father

Hernandez how to lock the door and darted off to answer another page.

"Stephen, are you all right?" Father Hernandez asked, observing Stephen's strange body language and perusing the room to determine if he could find anything that might be causing his uneasiness.

Stephen wasn't sure how to answer. His surroundings appeared hazily visible to him, illuminated by the radiance of a figure standing in front of the altar. Stephen wanted to faint.

"Does anyone else see that?" Stephen uttered in a shaky voice.

"You can see?" Brenda answered excitedly.

"The same angel that I saw earlier," he responded, his voice quivering even more.

Everyone froze. Father Hernandez glanced back toward Stephen from halfway down the aisle. Stephen was now trembling. The wafting scent of cinnamon, roses, and a blend of other flowers assaulting their noses was apparent to everyone. With a sense of foreboding, at the same time, a foundation of awe and excitement began to build.

"What's that sweet smell?" Brenda asked the group.

Sister Justine approached Stephen. "Stephen, what are you saying? Abriel is here now?"

"That's exactly what he's saying," a feminine voice, with a refined Spanish accent, said as she came through the doorway. Michael, Father Hernandez, and Sister Justine recognized her. It was Ashere. She stopped next to Brenda and smiled gingerly, touching her on the side of her upper arm. "Be a dear and go and grab me a bottled water?"

Brenda found herself wanting to refuse the request. Looking into Ashere's eyes, Brenda beheld a sincerity she never experienced before. The urge to comply nearly overcame her impulse to ignore the unknown woman. Brenda stood fast.

"Don't worry; your brother will be fine," Ashere tenderly added.

As much as Brenda wanted to stay with her brother, when she looked into the compassionate eyes of Ashere, her resistance melted, she found the desire to go and retrieve the water for this stranger to be more powerful. She gently released her grip on her brother's hand and kissed him on the cheek. "I'll be back in a few minutes Stephen."

Hearing the voice of a female he had never met increased Stephen's anxiety while still looking at the angel standing magnanimously in front of the altar. He didn't feel the sense of apprehension he anticipated from his sister leaving. In some ways, the voice of Ashere pacified him, muting the swelling uneasy emotions washing over him.

Michael, Father Hernandez, and Sister Justine couldn't think of anything to say. They were hesitant to ask any questions of Ashere as she sat down in the third pew from the rear without wiping away any of the undisturbed lingering dust. Alder came running up to the doorway not expecting to see anyone he personally knew in the chapel.

"Stephen? Father? Sister?" Alder had forgotten Michael's name and ignored the courtesy of reintroducing himself. He focused on the middle-aged Hispanic female sitting on the bench pew looking straight ahead. "And you, you were in the park the day I met everyone here."

"Alder, is that you?" Stephen asked, focusing his question in the direction from which he heard the voice.

"Yeah, and what are all of you doing here?" Alder answered.

"What do you mean she was in the park the day you met us?" Sister Justine asked, bypassing Alder's question.

Stephen minutely adjusted to the image of the angel. "What're you doing here Alder?" Stephen inquired.

"Michelle was sick so we brought her here. When we came into the emergency room, I briefly saw him," Alder replied as he pointed to Michael, "over by the television. Several minutes later, I saw her," Alder pointed to Ashere, "and I thought this was all too weird, so I followed her here. And what is that damn smell? It smells familiar." Alder inhaled the same aromas as those in his and Maria's bedroom from Michelle's mysterious guest.

"Well I see we're all here now," Ashere interjected, capturing the attention of the room's occupants.

"And why are we here?" Father Hernandez asked, watching Sister Justine attempting to assist Stephen safely between the pews.

"Because you all have become distracted in finding out all that you need to know."

Father Hernandez was becoming a bit irritated. "What do you mean, as if we've given up? We found what we were looking for."

"Have you found all the answers you were looking for? Then why do the angels sing?"

"How the hell are we to know why the angels sing?" Michael retorted. "And just who in the hell are you?"

"I told you before in Mexico, my name is Ashere."

Michael rolled his eyes, annoyed with her answer. "Then how in the hell are you able to seem to just pop up out of nowhere?" he asked.

"When no one is looking for you, you're not seen," Ashere responded.

"What the hell are you talk ..." Michael tried to continue but was interrupted by Sister Justine, who felt she needed to step in.

"Please tell us, first off, are you an angel?" she asked compassionately.

Ashere chuckled. "Why would you think that? I'm no angel. I'm nothing more than a simple servant, much like your friend Stephen there."

They had all temporarily forgotten Stephen, who was himself so consumed with the image of Abriel standing before him that he was completely oblivious to the conversation until he heard his name.

"Why are you here? I imagine it's no coincidence all of us being here either," Michael questioned.

Ashere smiled. "How astute. I see you still understand the providence of the Father."

"What does providence have to do with all of this?"

"So much seems like it has been coincidence; so much before you will seem like it is coincidence; all things work together as the paths cross before you."

"So why the sad-sounding singing?" Sister Justine quizzed.

"They lament what is to come," Ashere answered.

"And what is to come?"

339

"It is those who are the source of Aurora that you should be troubled by."

No one observed Stephen's skin turning pale as he watched the angel's luminosity intensify with each pronouncement of the name Aurora.

"Wait a minute," Father Hernandez injected. "We thought Aurora had to do with a cloning project?"

"That's all you've been able to learn? It was thought you may have known more than that by now," Ashere responded.

"What are you saying? Then who should we be worried about in Everest regarding Aurora?" Alder asked, considering the possible employees involved with the project.

"Who said anything about anyone from Everest?" Ashere countered.

"You said we should be worried concerning the source of Aurora," Michael probed.

Ashere launched out of the pew into the aisle and stood glaring at Michael. "Do you understand what is going on?"

Michael was irritated again. "I understand that for about three weeks now, hell, I don't remember, these two come standing on my doorstep, tell me an angel who I attempted to chase down over ten years ago returned killing everyone at a funeral; then we end up in Mexico. Then we find out there seems to be a connection between those who died; somehow, they're all associated with the same company. Now we come to find out this same company is somehow involved with a cloning project, which is the reason the angels are pissed, killing people willy nilly. End of story."

Alder peeked out into the hall through the doorway. No one paid any attention to the elevated voices of those in the chapel. Hospital staff members, future patients, and visitors were passing by the opened doors to the chapel oblivious to any noise emanating outward. When what appeared to be a thin Indian man walked by with a little girl holding his hand, Alder remembered his daughter.

"Look, I gotta go. I brought my daughter here and my wife is probably mad as hell I'm not there with them in the emergency room. I told her I was only gonna be gone for a couple of minutes," Alder commented, deliberately stepping backwards. Brenda returned with a half-liter bottle of water.

Stephen witnessed the majestic creature radiate intensely and wondered why no one else in the area couldn't see such a spectacle. He sensed this was in response to Alder's desire to leave. "Alder, you need to stay," Stephen requested, awestruck, still staring in the direction of the altar.

"No disrespect Stephen, my family is more important right now than some silly mystical fantasy stuff that everyone here is talking about. If these angels are around, then …"

"Your daughter will be fine Alder Dennison," Ashere commented, "compared with the chosen."

"What the hell do you know about my daughter? Just because you say she's gonna be fine doesn't mean that she is gonna be fine."

"Don't worry; all things are under the Father's control. Just like the way traffic was heavy on the day of the funeral you were to attend when your friend went blind, what has happened then has led up to what is happening now."

Alder became uneasy.

The glowing and shimmering angel locked its gaze with Stephen. He responded subconsciously by becoming rigid and tense. Even though this was the third time encountering Abriel, the repeat of the television station routine made him queasy. He sensed the entity was going to charge toward him again. The angel stood still.

Brenda attempted to nudge her brother to turn around, wanting to guide him out of the room. He remained steadfast, uneasiness settling over his sister. "Stephen, we should leave. This is all worrying me," she pleaded.

"That's not a bad idea," Alder remarked, as if answering for Stephen.

"There are more important things than your daughter," Ashere said in Alder's direction.

Alder felt the rush of blood filling the vessels in his face; hearing the comment from Ashere infuriated him. "You know what, the hell with you!" Alder erupted, no longer willing to remain in the chapel. He darted out, not wanting to communicate with anyone, now thinking they were all just chasing fanciful events.

"Ashere, you may have crossed the line. He's a father who cares a great deal about his daughter," Father Hernandez noted, trying to sympathize with Alder.

"His child is not as important as Aurora's child," Ashere said with her face hardened in her response to the Father, conveying the staunch impact of her comment,

"Especially as the child has been spiritually taught to have an enmity against the chosen of God."

Michael and Father Hernandez were both extremely curious about her statement. "What do you mean Aurora's child? And against the chosen?" they both asked.

"The clone, the child, Aurora's child; you both should have heard of *neph' shamah*."

Michael smirked, the word not awakening any memories. Father Hernandez's expression showed he did recall a sliver of information. The linguistics of the word sounded familiar. "Isn't that Hebrew?" he asked. "I remember a little from seminary."

"Yes. It is Hebrew for the 'breath,' 'the breath of life.' You see gentlemen," Ashere responded, noticing a quick scowl on Sister Justine's, face, and knowing she was irked at not being included with the men. Ashere continued to ignore her. "It is said that whenever a child is born of a mother from the union of a man, the two shall become one, and in a distinct way, the one being a distinct offspring genetically unique and derived based upon natural workings of God's creation. As a result, you see, God is said to give unto each child *neph'shamah*, the breath or spark of life, yielding a human spirit. That's the miracle of life. Otherwise, you just have a stillborn--a human biological mass."

"So is Aurora the mother who gave birth to the clone?" Sister Justine asked, making sure her voice was heard.

Ashere's stern expression softened. "No my dear, you do not understand. The child is the lone success to date worthy of a bastardized human spirit. At each birth of a potential enhanced clone, even though advances were made for years in the area of cloning for numerous animals, for some unknown reason, the human attempts resulted in nonviable fetuses and stillborns; that is, it was said, until an angel was witness unto the birth. It breathed life into the fetus that lived. It is an angel understood to be in league against the defender of the chosen. You see, the child is the miracle of the fallen cherub."

"An angel?" Father Hernandez asked. "An angel breathing the breath of life into this purported clone? And a miracle of the fallen? What you're implying is that the Church is sponsoring the ..."

Ashere interrupted, "I know what I'm implying. The angel is called Aurora, a principality under the order of the Prince of Persia."

"How do you know so much about all of this?" Michael asked, curious about the way she came to know such intricate detail. He found a lot of the information she presented to be somewhat fanciful. Parts of it contradicted all he'd learned while in seminary, from what he could recall, and was counterintuitive to the religious studies courses he taught.

Father Hernandez himself thought what Ashere presented was preposterous. It sliced through countless underpinning of his existing beliefs, especially to hear the Church was being influenced by a fallen angel. Her disclosure disrupted his notion of the infallibility of the Church, the prominence of the Holy Mother, and the preeminence of the Holy Father.

Ashere stared long at Father Hernandez before continuing her comments. "I can say Stephen and I are

344

kindred pawns by means of circumstance. I've been instructed not to reveal any more than I have. And just remember that our heavenly friends cannot become fully involved with the affairs of men to the extent as Aurora. To do so would be a severe transgression. We are now dealing with a much different church than the one before the disappearance of so many. There is nothing much more for me to say. I must go now."

"What do you mean there's nothing more for you to say? I don't think you said enough." Michael furiously challenged.

Ashere simply walked up to Stephen, who, feeling her presence, was distracted from the angelic visitor. She gently stroked his cheek with her extremely smooth, petite hand, smiled, and walked toward the double doors unchallenged, no one finding a reason to attempt to coerce her to stay and answer more questions.

"And do remember this, there are no such things as coincidences, as you will find the city of the cross will be upon you three"

Ashere walked out, and no one wanted to admit their having uneasy emotions. They all thought their anxiety would subside once she was no longer present.

Stephen, not aware of Ashere's departure, stayed focused on the angel. It decided to move after standing erect during the duration of the conversation. The personage, appearing waiflike, walked as if it glided up to Stephen. A powerful urge to kneel overcame him; his unexplained motions mesmerized the occupants of the room. As Stephen was ready to put one knee down, the angel spoke. "Do not bow before me," the angel commanded to him. All anyone else could hear was the

345

sound of a muffled trumpet. Everyone in the room became apprehensive unsure for the origination of the noise. For many, the accompaniment of a strong floral aroma assaulted their nostrils; a sense of unexplained fear flooded their emotions. "Your part is done," the angel continued.

"I don't understand--my part?" Stephen asked, the chapel occupants bewildered by his question, thinking it was directed to them. Once again, the subdued sound of a trumpet echoed in the room; Stephen himself heard, "You were the vessel to bring all these together over these critical days so together they could learn of Aurora. Upon waking, seek the truth of whom I serve."

"Who do you serve?" Stephen queried, with everybody else now even more curious at the apparent one-sided conversation.

"That not of whom Aurora serves," the angel Abriel responded, with the occupants in the chapel extremely agitated by the trumpet sound after listening to Stephen's question.

"That not of whom Aurora serves?" Stephen repeated. "I don't understand."

"Stephen, who are you talking to?" Sister Justin inquired, the others pondering the same question.

The lights went dark. For an instant, the full radiance of an angelic creature materialized saturating the room in ethereal light, then disappeared. The ceiling lights returned to full luminosity.

"Son of a ... did you see that?" Michael blurted out.

Sister Justine kneeled down, made the sign of the cross, and began to pray. Father Hernandez followed his companion. Michael, himself feeling the urge to join the two, resisted.

Stephen's vision went dark. He collapsed into a coma.

Chapter 34

Alder returned to the emergency room waiting area. Many of those waiting for the medical staff were still gathered around television sets or focused on their smart phones. They tried to glean information from news reports on the mysterious singing across the globe that by then subsided. A nurse repeatedly called the name of a patient waiting to be seen, and everyone was oblivious to any other activity in the area. Alder himself wasn't sure how to comprehend the situation or even if it could be considered in the same category as one of the bizarre angelic events witnessed through the years. He hadn't seen an angel, but his friend and coworker, who was now blind, said he did.

Alder found his wife still sitting in the same spot on one of the bright red plastic chairs. Matthew lay sleeping in her arms with his head supported on her shoulder. Michelle was resting her head in her mother's lap, sitting in the next chair; her fair complexion pale. Maria saw her husband return and greeted him with furled eyebrows and a grimace.

"Where were you?" she whispered angrily.

"I came across Stephen and his sister down the hallway," Alder responded, hoping this would mitigate some of her anger, especially as she'd made a concerted effort during the last couple of weeks to make sure he kept up contact with his handicapped friend.

"So you think your friend is more important than your daughter?" Maria queried.

Alder miscalculated. "Of course not. How many times do I have to tell you? You know that you and the kids are the most important things in my life."

Maria was unaffected by her husband's attempt to placate her and relieved when the attending nurse called their name for Michelle to be seen by the ER doctor.

After several hours of questioning, examining, and testing, the doctor was convinced he couldn't find anything wrong with Michelle. Ordering a couple of additional tests just to rule out other possibilities for the cause of her symptoms, he was confident he would discharge her after reviewing the results.

"So how is Stephen?" Maria asked, sitting on the opposite side of the ER bed from her husband. Alder was thankful that she usually didn't stay quiet and angry for long.

"Fine. Just sorting through some weird stuff going on."

The doctor walked into the curtained area reading the papers on his clipboard. "Mr. and Mrs. Dennison, we can't seem to find anything wrong with your daughter. I think we should be safe in discharging her."

"But doctor, she was throwing up blood," Alder pointed out.

"Well, she seems to be doing much better now, and you mentioned the vomitus contained blood. It might have been something as simple as viral gastroenteritis." The puzzled look on both Alder's and Maria's faces

349

made him realize he would need to clarify. "Stomach flu, she'll be fine."

"Stomach flu?" both parents asked in unison, both with disbelief.

"Yes, we'll go ahead and work on the discharge paperwork."

Chapter 35

Michael plopped down on the futon in his makeshift office and stared off toward the opposite wall. Alicia was worried about how muted and motionless he'd been since they returned from the hospital. Normally engaged into some sort of activity, whether passing off papers for her to help in grading, modifying elements of the syllabuses for his current classes, or working on one of his research projects, he would be occupied with some form of intellectual endeavor. Many of his peers would have some level of trepidation in working on Religious Studies Department-mandated dissertations or essays for the college journal. Michael enjoyed it. There was still a demand for information about what had happened to the millions who'd disappeared ten years earlier.

Even though many theologians and he himself didn't have any direct answers, Michael felt the answers could be revealed somewhere in the background of the various world religions. Many contained distinct dogmas stating that there would be a great evacuation of unbelievers in their respective beliefs. They had all fallen into disfavor, however, since the prophesized chronological events purported to follow immediately never materialized. There was no worldwide tribulation, no great peace awakening, and no great return of a foretold desert prophet. After three years of cleanup, successive rioting, and stabilization for the world's governments, the remaining of the world's population wanted things to go back to normal. Quickly, the world returned to status quo. The only supernatural events were nearly ten years of unsubstantiated angels appearing at funerals and presenting eulogies. Numerous people still doubted these events because most of the population hadn't witnessed any alleged spiritual beings. Now Michael had seen one, or so he thought.

"Hon', is everything OK?" Alicia whispered as she sat down next Michael. He remained silent.

She'd never experienced him like this before. He just sat there contemplating whatever was running through his mind.

"I'm going to get ready to head out and catch up with my study group. Did you want anything before I go?" Alicia offered. Michael remained silent.

Sitting for only a couple more minutes, Alicia kissed him on the cheek and got up, not sure what else to say to him. She wasn't even sure why he'd become so withdrawn. Something happened. When Michael followed the Father and Sister Justine from the waiting area of the emergency room at the hospital and then returned nearly 15 minutes later, he'd changed. Alicia recalled that an unconscious man was brought out on a gurney attended by a medical team. A woman in her early thirties, crying hysterically, was holding onto the man's hand. Michael, Father Hernandez and Sister Justine followed, all three appearing to have a mild catatonic expression. The Father's fawn complexion was disturbingly bloodless while the Sister's face was rosy as if she was emotionally overwhelmed. Michael's honey-toned complexion, one of the attributes she thought made him extremely handsome, was flushed and discolored.

Twenty minutes later, after taking a shower, Alicia had changed into jeans with holes ripped at the knees and a vibrant, lightweight red-and-blue-patterned blouse. She grabbed her book bag and then glanced into Michael's office one final time before leaving. He was still sitting on the futon unresponsive. She decided to leave without saying good-bye or letting him know what time to expect her back. Early in their relationship of four months, when she'd mention an approximate time for her return, he'd act like he didn't care. Lately, though, he'd signal a sigh of relief when she returned safely.

Michael's focused contemplation shattered when he heard the front door being shut, and the locking latch click, as Alicia departed. He snapped back to the environment of the house. Usually Alicia played music in the background or tried to find a way to start up a conversation. It was uncomfortably quiet. He'd lost track of time in the last hour or so. He barely remembered Alicia mentioning she was leaving to study. All that kept coming to mind was that for a flash, maybe less than a second, his eyes pierced beyond the natural realm. He beheld an angel. With each passing minute, he was reminded of its countenance. He pondered whether it actually existed or whether he witnessed some sort of strange lighting effect. If this was true, Michael thought it funny that if Father Hernandez and Sister Justine saw the same peculiar illuminated optical illusion, they prayed to a mere shadow.

Michael wanted to add these new events to his current collection of notes. He got his notepad but words couldn't come to him. Maybe he could type something on the computer to help collect his thoughts. Turning on the workstation, waiting for it boot up, it became harder to recollect the hospital events. Sitting at the keyboard for almost half an hour, he forced himself to spew indiscriminate thoughts of what happened into his word processor knowing he'd return to edit his work later.

"You're back," Michael heard from the doorway as he was inputting the last of his contemplations. He saw Alicia drop her book bag onto the floor, flash him a large grin, and approach with her arms out to give him a hug.

"I didn't go anywhere. I've been here all along," he consoled when he returned her embrace, confused by her comment, taking her comment literally.

"You know that's not what I meant," she said and gave him a reaffirming squeeze. "So what happened?" she asked Michael. "Why were you tripping out like that?"

"What do you mean?" Michael still had no idea he had exhibited the symptoms of mild shock.

"You seemed like you were out of it really bad. I was really worried about you."

Michael pondered Alicia's being troubled about him thinking it was misplaced. "Just thought I saw something that kinda bothered me, that's all."

"What'd you think you saw?

Michael didn't know how to explain it. "You wouldn't believe me. Anyway, I don't think it's important."

"Whatever. What was all that back at the hospital with your friends looking all freaked out too? And who was that guy on the gurney you followed into the emergency room?"

"While we were talking to that guy, he fell into coma. That's all." Michael decided not to elaborate any further.

"OK, weird."

The longer Alicia talked to Michael, the more he became his normal self. And the more Michael considered what happened earlier, the more he thought what he perceived to be a supernatural creature was just an insignificant shadow, caused by the reflection of failing lights in the unkempt hospital chapel. Scanning what he just typed into his computer, he read incomprehensible sentence fragments with words that made no sense without context. He saw "breath of life," "clone child," "fetus," "neph' shamah," "Rome," "angelic visit." *This crap won't help me with my classes,* he thought and deleted the document.

Chapter 36

With the Cardinal resting his thin, frail, aged body in Bishop Grielle's favorite chair, the Bishop received the Cardinal's loutish imposition with cool acceptance and sat down on the chair reserved for guests. Having known the Bishop for so many years, the Cardinal could easily see through his calm façade. But the Cardinal dismissed his colleague's feelings with the thought that Bishop Grielle must be feeling better since returning from the hospital if he was concerned with something so trite.

"I'm glad you're doing well Andrew," the Cardinal commented. "Bit of a scare there I would say."

"Yes, I'd like to think it was due in part to Father Hernandez's Anointing of the Sick and calling upon his patron saint to petition for my health that it turned out to be just an extremely bad case of heartburn."

"Hmm, I guess that's why I'm here. It's regarding Father Hernandez."

"I'm sorry, I don't quite understand," Bishop Grielle said in response to the hint of discontent he'd heard in his superior's voice. He assumed the Cardinal had stopped by to check on how well he was doing since being discharged from the hospital but his intuition ignited that there was another motive.

"Yes, you see ..." the Cardinal began to comment with a subtle sharpness then dropped off into an uneasy quiet.

"Your Eminence, is everything all right?" Bishop Grielle asked, sensing hesitancy and subdued hostility. He gauged his superior's body language and knew he was formulating a rebuke in his thoughts. The Bishop patiently awaited an answer.

After a couple of minutes, the Cardinal broke his silence. "Do you have any tea?"

Bishop Grielle was a bit dumbfounded. "Tea?"

"Yes. Tea. I feel like a cup of tea."

The Bishop knew the Cardinal was being diversionary and thought it might be that he wanted to find a way of changing his approach, not wanting to begin the formal portion of the conversation in an adversarial tone and possibly shutting out a genuine response. He capitulated by going into the kitchen and preparing a cup of Earl Grey. He returned several minutes later to find the Cardinal had gotten up out of the chair and strolled around the office. He was fingering and making quick glancing probes into Diocese-administration paperwork on the Bishop's desk and the news articles and editorials attempting to explain the mysterious singing reportedly heard around the world. Observing Bishop Grielle return to the room, the Cardinal returned to sit in the Bishop's favorite study chair.

Irked, Bishop Grielle skin complexion flushed and decided to readdress his question while handing the Cardinal his tea. "So Your Eminence, you started to mention something about Father Hernandez?"

Cardinal Millhouse's frail hand quivered while he took a drink of tea. For the first time in a while, Bishop Grielle thought about the age of his mentor and church elder and remembered that he could be facing mandatory retirement within a year.

"This is very good tea Andrew. Thank you," the Cardinal said, returning to drink his beverage and noting Bishop Grielle's stoic, patient look. "So, have you had a chance to review the information Father Hernandez and Sister Justine drafted regarding their investigation?"

"They were ruminating about some ideas and speculations the morning I was taken to the hospital. Some of it I would say is controversial."

"Heretical I would say," the Cardinal sharply responded, nearly slamming the tea cup onto the table next to the chair. "You never told me Father Hernandez would be so idealistic. I've reviewed their notes and commentary, and they contain some damnable blasphemies. I can only imagine they were influenced by their godless associate during this little investigation."

"You know your Eminence, you have me at a disadvantage. I haven't had a chance to vet the full scope of what they must have presented to you."

The Cardinal cut off the Bishop before he could continue. "Nor do I think you should or anyone else. It's absolute heresy! I can't believe I let you talk me into letting those three research the incident. For that matter, I should've ceased everything the moment we found out they were interested in going to Mexico."

"I would think if the Church is interested in finding out about what happened, we should be open to all interpretations presented. They were the most qualified in this situation. I'm sure they would've presented multiple theological possibilities if this were supernatural."

"What they've espoused is somewhat disturbing. It flies against everything the Church is currently working on."

Bishop Grielle desperately felt he needed to interrupt with the previous thought that the Cardinal ignored. While he waited for an answer, he found himself becoming irritated again. "Once again your Eminence, I have to say that I don't understand the source of your concern. Since you were able to review the information they presented, I feel as if I'm blind to what has you so distraught. What exactly did they present to you?"

Expelling a breath of exasperation, the Cardinal sank in his seat and gave the Bishop a strong and steady stare. "At one point they speculated that the fatal events could be the angels attempting to prevent the culmination of the work being accomplished by our patron benefactor in our unique endeavor," the Cardinal explained after a couple of minutes.

"What're you saying? That they speculated what's being backed by the Church could be malevolent?"

"What they speculate flies in the face of the divine guidance given by the miraculous visitation upon Rome."

"You'll have to forgive me if I seem a little offended, but I do remember when Father Hernandez and Sister Justine started mentioning this, I was taken a bit by surprise. Before they took me to the hospital, they did note that they were also considering other possibilities as to what happened as well. No offense Eminence, to learn that Sister Justine in effect undermined my guidance during their research by your bidding, through all of this, I feel as if you are telling me something you already know."

"Let me just say their primary hypothesis is severely unwarranted and unfounded," the Cardinal responded, ignoring the portion of the response relating to Sister Justine.

"Then why agree to have me pair the two up if it caused so much discontent with the Church?"

The Cardinal was offended by the obstinacy of the Bishop.

"Based on the writings of Michael Saunders, it was thought the two would balance each other out to try and find out what happened," the Cardinal answered. "It's their final hypothesis as to what most likely happened that is the cause of the most consternation. They were pretty firm in leaning toward the heretical view of accepting the evil of those who were killed, including many of the researchers and pioneers with their families. They assumed that the work with Aurora was not being accomplished for some greater good. The Church's direction is clear, anything against the Church's greater plan is to be condemned and will not be tolerated," the Cardinal declared.

"With so much in the shadows concerning Aurora, their suppositions are probably based in ignorance. The Church is taking an extremely stern position ..."

"The Church is taking the correct position on this," the Cardinal interrupted. "Nothing more needs to be said. All of the research information is being collected as we speak. No one is to mention any of this or our previous conversations. And just so you'll hear it from me first, we're looking to have you reassign Father Hernandez and Sister Justine. He will become chaplain for the Dawles treatment facility. Sister Justine will be assigned to a new order, one not as lenient in serving the Church."

"Are you kidding?" Bishop Grielle blurted out, ignoring protocol. "Father Hernandez has been one of our most faithful vicars. He's one willing to assist other parishes in need, extremely good at mentoring the junior seminary students, excellent in administration, and impeccable with the way he manages his parish."

"I understand you have an affinity for him, but the decision has been made."

"Damn it, I'm in charge of this Diocese. I wasn't even consulted."

"Well I'm consulting you now. And to think of the arrogance those two displayed to think they actually saw an angel. What makes them think that they're actually worthy to witness such a divine marvel?"

Bishop Grielle looked like he'd been hit in the stomach with a bat. The Cardinal ignored the Bishop's physical response to his comment.

"What do you mean the two of them saw an angel?" the Bishop asked.

"You're telling me you don't know about the alleged visit in the hospital chapel?"

"No. Remember I was somewhat incapacitated?" the Bishop quipped, still a bit angry because the Cardinal called to say he would come to visit him in the hospital but he never showed up.

"Well, even when there was visits all around the world, and Father Hernandez and Sister Justine say they witnessed one with the same man who claimed to have seen one at other times, no one is able to produce any evidence."

"Didn't you say the Holy Father had received an angelic visitor? How're we to take his word for truth and not theirs?"

Cardinal Millhouse's nostrils flared. "You dare question the infallibility of the Holy Father? He is one worthy of such a visit. I will tolerate your insolence for only so long Andrew. Nothing more needs to be said."

Chapter 37

The call that Gary made to him at home the prior evening to see how his daughter was doing, Alder knew, was a guise. Gary's message was emphatic: Report first thing to his office; they need to talk. As Alder sat in the reception area outside of Gary's office waiting, a twinge of nausea made the anticipation worse. Sheila worked on updating file folders and barely acknowledged the waiting junior executive. She made no pretense of attempting conversation with Alder, nor did he have an interest in starting one with her. Several minutes passed until Gary finally walked in carrying his attaché in one hand and supporting a file folder jacket under his other arm and holding a cup of Starbucks coffee.

"Morning Sheila," Gary said, presenting a small grin while passing through the reception area to his office. Then he saw Alder waiting on the couch. "Alder," he said, his grin vanishing. Alder's nausea increased. He wasn't sure what to expect.

"Give me a couple of minutes to get settled, then head on in," Gary continued, ready to step into his office. Then he stopped and turned back toward Alder. "You know what, just come on in. We need to discuss this issue right away."

Springing off the leather couch, Alder promptly followed his boss, who took a seat at his desk in the chair known to be used by Gary for rebuking or firing personnel. Placing the paperwork and attaché on the credenza behind him, Gary inserted his access control card into the card reader and logged onto the company's network.

"OK Alder, how's Stephen doing?" Gary asked after he finished typing on his keyboard.

"He's doing fine I guess, if you call being in a coma fine."

"He's in a coma?" Gary questioned, attempting to feign sympathy.

"Yeah, they're not sure how lo ..."

"Well look, I'm not gonna skirt around the issue here," Gary continued as he didn't know Stephen personally. "I don't know if you heard that some sensitive R&D information was somehow released. We're fortunate it was somewhat contained, but the implications are still significant. Are you aware of anything like that?" Gary asked.

"I'm sorry, I'm not quite sure what you're talking about," Alder replied, knowing there was a good chance Gary was referencing the information he communicated to the three church investigators.

Narrowing his eyes, Gary watched for any ticks in his interviewee's body language, hoping to discover the veracity of Alder's response. Noting a couple possible nervous movements with his indirect question, he continued to press.

"Look Alder, I'm going to be truthful with you. I'm not very happy right now. I've been trying to find out something over the last couple days. There seems to have been a serious breach of information. Did you or did you not tell anyone outside of Everest sensitive information about any of our projects?"

Alder could sense his voice would crack while attempting to formulate an account for releasing the information and explaining why. For the first time since all of these strange events, he found himself praying for something, anything, to occur for him not to have to answer the question. If there was a God, he hoped he would manifest himself in some way.

"So Alder, do you know something?"

Alder swallowed, ready to present an answer, when Sheila rushed into the office unannounced. "Gary, you need to catch the vid call right now!" she said excitedly.

Every time I've been trying to have important conversations, there've been these damn interruptions, Gary thought.

"Sheila, not now," he responded, visibly agitated.

"No, you need to pick up now."

"I'm busy. Just tell whoever is trying to get through that I'm busy right now."

"It's Dr. Petroyev from the facility across town. He really needs to talk to you."

Acquiescing to Sheila's persistence, Gary turned to his computer and focused on the video software icon to see a small dialog bubble: "1 Inbound Call – Dr. P." He moved his finger over the touch screen to expand the icon; a windowed image of Dr. Petroyev appeared in the middle of his OLED monitor.

"Doc, I need to call you back, I'm in the middle of an important di …"

The computer image interrupted, "Gary, I think there's a serious problem with the Aurora team and facility down in Mexico."

"You know Doc, can you hold on?" Gary turned to Alder, "Can you leave us please? I'll call you back down when we're ready to finish our conversation."

Alder got up from his seat and returned to his office thinking that perhaps his prayers had been answered. Gary turned his attention back to the video call once the office was clear and glanced at an indicator in the status bar of the application window; the icon of a padlock was illuminated, which ensured that encryption was turned on.

"So what the hell are you talking about doctor? What do you mean there's a problem?" Gary inquired.

"There hasn't been any contact with my team in Mexico for two days now. And just when we were ready to start testing."

"What do you mean you haven't heard from them? You must have heard from them. This is unacceptable. What was the last thing going on that you know of?"

"Remember a bit ago it looked like there were four intruders who may have been trying to probe the Mexican facility and approach the compound?"

"Yeah? So? You told me the security team reported to you that they couldn't find anybody."

"Well, it looks like they showed up again, and, well, hold on. I'm sending you a file of an e-mail fragment they sent four days ago."

A few seconds later, an icon image of a sheet of paper appeared in a pop-up window titled "Current Call:

Anton P. -- Shared File(s)." Tapping the icon on the monitor, the image exploded to scale for easier reading.

The four previously reported intruders by Wolf Two appear to have returned. This time the security detail was able to retrieve and return them to the compound. Upon their arrival, we separated them with an attempt to ascertain their identity, with each one being questioned independently. They all remained quiet. Nobody could get them to talk until later when one did. When asked why they arrived there, he said, "They were sent forth in response to supplications to intervene in hindering the inspired work of Aurora by Doctor Ezekiel Frost". This started a firestorm amongst the team here as to how these four strangers knew of the primary project name and its primary research doctor. Some suspect Doctor Cochrane leaked the information.

Gary read the extraction a couple more times just to see if anything apart from the question of the trespassers could clarify the overall concerns of the doctor.

"So why's it the first I'm hearing about this?"

"It's not. Remember, it wasn't that important before when we discussed the previous logs and updates and the compound went on alert when there was the suspicion of four possible intruders. The risk was later reduced since no evidence of them could be found then," Dr. Petroyev snapped back angry he just mentioned something similar to his superior.

"Have you tried calling down there?" Gary could tell by the doctor's expression he was peeved by the question.

The doctor decided to answer anyway. "We tried calling, faxing, initiating videoconferencing, texting; no

367

one from up here can get in touch with anyone down there. It's like the place just disappeared. I even contacted one of my local police contacts outside the gendarmerie from El Refugio to head out and take a quick look. We warned him not to go too close. A security team should come out to meet him. He said the place is like a ghost town; nobody met him at the boundary of the compound."

"Well, I hope you're gonna tell me that you started executing a recovery plan of some sort. The damn sites associated with this project are your responsibility."

"You don't have to remind me about that Gary. A specialized response team is already en route to investigate. They should be on site in about six to twelve hours."

"Nothing better have happened down there. You know how important their work is to the overall plan. When are you going down to join them?"

"What?"

"When ... are ... you ... going ... down? I don't have a good feeling about this, especially with what's been going on up here. Hell, in a lot of ways, this sounds like what happened ten years ago with the director you replaced. Dr. Ashere Valdez was one of the best geneticists and virologists on the planet, better than you, and she ended up becoming disloyal before disappearing. I think this is too important for you not to see this through directly and make sure everything is all right. We may have a level one incident on our hands."

"Gary, I have too much to do up here."

"Know what, I'll work over at your facility to see your side of the project through. I need high-level management on this one, just in case--you know--special precautions are needed. Plus the kid seems to be stable; we should be fine up here."

Dr. Petroyev's reluctance was evident on his facial expression. Gary wasn't pleased by his lead doctor's excuses. "We're not going to have a problem are we doctor?"

Dr. Petroyev paused before answering, "No."

VI. The Shadow of Angels: Las Cruces

Chapter 38

Father Hernandez appreciated that he never had been on an extended train excursion. Even though he could walk from car to car, being confined in the silver passenger tubes was exhausting. The undersized pillows barely provided comfort for him to rest his head. The oversized seats were flat, firm, and without ergonomic consideration. The longest of any of his previous rail jaunts was on the Metrolink commuter line when he made short trips around the Los Angeles and Inland Empire areas. The trips were for extended vicar backfill duties or supporting special events at sister-diocese parishes. Now the Father found himself on an Amtrak heading to New Mexico knowing this assignment equated to a demotion. His final stop would be El Paso, Texas; a vehicle from the treatment center in Las Cruces would pick him up. Taking a glimpse at his watch, he estimated another two or three hours before arriving at his station. Although the reclining coach seats were oversized and allowed for a pseudo-sleeping assemblage, Father Hernandez found he could only sleep for a couple of hours in the makeshift bed. The loud snoring from the overweight college student who'd boarded in the middle of the night didn't help. There was more than enough time to head down to the lounge car and grab something to eat if it was open this early.

No one was in line to be served. Grabbing a breakfast sausage sandwich from the small shelf refrigerator, a bag of salt-and-vinegar flavored chips just below, and a large cranberry juice, he walked around to the lounge car cashier station and handed the attendant his entrée selection. The attendant put the sausage sandwich in the aged silver microwave with only seven large white buttons down the front side, closed the door, and selected the third button from the top; 45 seconds showed on the dim LED display. Waiting for the time to elapse, the Father paid for his food, collected several napkins, and accepted the heated sandwich.

He chose an empty table near the end of the car and, glancing out the large window, saw the morning sun's corona peeking off in the distance just above the desert floor. Looking across the aisle out the opposite side of the train, the pitch of night was still framed in the window; flickering stars resisted the coming morning and made their last stand of glory before the full revelation of the sun. Off in the distance, the shadow of hills and mountains draped the awakening view. Father Hernandez watched a young lady, blond hair uncombed and matted, wearing several layers of worn, wrinkled clothing, walking back and forth down the aisle holding a book that she appeared to be reading aloud. The more she spoke, the more fragmented and unintelligible her sentences sounded. He thought maybe she wore a Bluetooth earpiece and was engaged in a unique conversation. During her next pass, he noticed she put special emphasis on each proper noun and he saw no electronic device or ear buds. She continued through into the coach car. The Father dismissed her until she returned several minutes later, still reading what sounded like the same pages she had when she'd passed through the first time. She moved ahead to the dining car.

Father Hernandez finished his meal and returned to his seat through half-empty cars. Passengers tossed and tussled in their seats as the morning sun penetrated the windows with open curtains. In one pair of seats, a middle-aged father fed his baby son a bottle while the mother still slept. Several rows later, an elderly woman the Father remembered as being spritely when they boarded in Los Angeles was lying across two seats yawning and stretching her arms. Behind her, a young child played with his portable game machine while his mother frantically dug through one of their three backpacks, relieved to find a prescription medicine container.

Arriving at his seat, the college student sitting across the aisle was still snoring. Looking out the window at the rustic environment, he decided now would be a good time to catch up with some more reading. He pulled from his briefcase the profile information forwarded on the mission, background, staffing, and patient makeup at his new assignment, the Dawles Psychological Hospital and Treatment Center, which had recently been built just down the road from the minimum security federal corrections facility where many of the patients originated. The treatment center provided support for those suffering through addictions and minor mental disorders. It was billed as one of the largest in the West for rehab, treatment, and psychological research away from the influence of large cities or universities. The center sponsored several desert retreat centers nearby to provide isolation for those with severe addictions to minimize accessibility. Before heading out to New Mexico and talking to several staff members to get an idea of what to expect, they all pretty much said the same thing, it tended to be extremely busy.

According to his assignment paperwork, he would play the perfunctory role of chaplain for both staff members and patients. Father Hernandez wasn't sure why he'd previously overlooked a section stating, "He would be working in a pluralistic environment and must be sensitive to the religious needs and beliefs of the other religious denominations and faith groups." Father Hernandez thought his assignment was to a facility owned or sponsored by the Catholic Church; it now appeared it was more ecumenical in its staffing and operation. Demotion now cemented in his consciousness.

He thought of acclimating to his new environment once arriving at Las Cruces with the same reluctance he'd had when accepting the assignment of finding out what happened in what would now be called the Los Angeles Angel Incident. Content and not wanting anything to change, he just wanted to be left alone to work diligently to serve the Church by ministering to his congregation. Having previously succumbed to Bishop Grielle's subtle strong-arming, Father Hernandez found himself being unwillingly reassigned as a punishment for attempting to present what he considered the truth of what he'd discovered.

After reading the paperwork on the facility, and then reading his daily devotionals for nearly an hour to counteract the emerging feelings of being spurned by the Church, the Father was bored and weary of the trip. He decided to head back down to the lounge car, now brimming with more activity, and the line for food possessed more passengers than when he'd come down earlier. Finding an open table, he took a seat by a large window and looked at the vista of the Painted Desert-like landscape flitting by. Glancing at his watch, he saw he'd be arriving at his stop soon.

Chapter 39

"Tell me you got some good news Petroyev? It's been a couple days since you last reported," Gary asked the image in the video chat software of his computer.

"Eyes rotted out, tongues blackened, looks like ..."

"Don't go any further. What type of containment protocols did you initiate?"

"That's the odd part, it's not hot. None of the live specimens appears to have been released. As a matter of fact, it looks like most all of the specimens, samples, cultures, everything, were destroyed. Nothing survived. Hell, even most of the cockroaches, rats, you name it, within a kilometer of the site were dead. Know what though? I don't think it was due to our work."

"What the hell do you mean? It sounds like there was a breech."

"The team on site tested everything. From what you've mentioned from your source in the Church, the bodies here appear to have gone through the same postmortem effects as those at Thomson and Thomson. Everything else that's been found seems to have just ... kaput."

"Were you able to collect any of the data or research information?" Gary asked.

"That's the other thing. All of the records seem to have been purged, no matter what the media--gone, everything. Hell, even handwritten notes seem to have disappeared."

"Wait a minute, aren't there protocols to encrypt and distribute backup fragments of the research and testing data to prevent a catastrophic data loss? Our sites in Canada, yours here where I'm at with the kid, France, Saudi Arabia, all should have portions of the data so that we can recombine and move forward."

"You won't believe this. They all reported having terabytes of data but all of it unintelligible. The CRCs, hashes, other algorithms, all failed. None of the data decrypts with the standard key information. Cleared Research Group IT staff at each of the sites are working it, but nothing's been retrieved. Even hard copies of the data seem to have disappeared."

"Bullshit. You mean to tell me there's nothing that can be salvaged?" Gary queried. "This smacks of organized sabotage."

"Not sure about that yet, but I think we may've caught a couple of breaks."

"What do you mean?"

"Well, first, there seems to be a hermetically sealed stage one sample or culture that was found. Looks like it could be the precursor to the final product. It was in a testing chamber. I think they were getting ready to release it to test, but then whatever happened prevented that from happening."

"Well, keep me posted. And let me know if we do have a viable strain. What's the other break?"

"With hard copies of data missing, we're thinking someone pinched or destroyed them. Or maybe they did both. We already did a body count; it appears Dr. Cochrane is missing."

Gary sat back in his chair, frustrated, attempting to contain an eruption of anger. "Damn it, was it sabotage? Didn't you mention earlier there were some reservations about him?"

"Yeah, but still not quite sure if it was sabotage yet. We sent a security team into town and they said the locals mentioned something about a weird crazy man that showed up talking all types of crazy stuff about angels and viruses. They claimed this loco man was trying to make his way to the States. Looks like he made it. Somehow he got across the border."

"What the hell are you talking about? You found him?"

"The security team was able to track him all the way through Mexico. We found out he went back into the States in New Mexico. Our contacts in the Border Patrol rounded him up near a bunch of illegals scurrying across the border. He didn't try to run and they found out by his fingerprints he was an American, so he was handed off to the state police when they thought he was a danger to himself. He reportedly was acting very erratic and strange, so they admitted him to a mental hospital. He's at the Dawles Hospital in Las Cruces, New Mexico."

"Doctor, you need to make sure they keep him isolated, goddamn it. I'm heading down there and retrieving his ass," Gary barked. As he reached to terminate the videoconference call, an idea came to mind. "Know what, I'll send you the company plane to pick you up with the sample. Then fly up to New Mexico to meet me. We don't have time for normal Customs with something so hot. Use our special contacts in the Justice Department and Customs to find a way to either expedite or bypass the normal roadblocks. Get in touch with the same persons who helped us with the Church to shut down the Fed investigation at Thomson and Thomson. Then we'll take Dr. Cochrane and escort him with the sample up to our facility in Canada."

Chapter 40

"One, two, three, four, five, six, seven, eight, nine, ten, eleven, twelve, thirteen, fourteen, fifteen, sixteen, seventeen, eighteen, nineteen, twenty, twenty-one, twenty-two, twenty-three, twenty-four, twenty-five, twenty-six, twenty-seven, twenty-eight, twenty-nine, thirty, thirty-one, thirty-two, thirty-three, thirty-four, thirty-five, thirty-six, thirty-seven, thirty-eight , thirty-nine, forty, forty-one, forty-two, forty-three, forty-four, forty-five, forty-six, forty-seven, forty-eight, forty-nine, fifty, fifty-one, fifty-two, fifty-three, fifty-four, fifty-five, fifty-six, fifty-seven, fifty-eight, fifty-nine, sixty, sixty-one, sixty-two, sixty-three, sixty-four, sixty-five, sixty-six, sixty-seven, sixty-eight, sixty-nine, seventy, seventy-one, seventy-two, seventy-three, seventy-four, seventy-five, seventy-six, seventy-seven, seventy-eight, seventy-nine, eighty, eighty-one, eighty-two, eighty-three, eighty-four, eighty-five, eighty-six, eighty-seven, eighty-eight, eighty-nine, ninety, ninety-one, ninety-two, ninety-three, ninety-four, ninety-five, ninety-six, ninety-seven, ninety-eight, ninety-nine, one hundred, one hundred and one."

The orderly observed the disheveled patient in the corner lying on his side curled into a fetal position, taking a break from counting. Then the senior orderly just as muscular as his partner, walked over to stand next to his junior peer from the doorway of the large dayroom fascinated with the odd behavior of their charge. No other patients allowed in during this time; this one was their responsibility. This was interesting to both men because he didn't seem to be a threat.

The patient sneaked a glance up at the ceiling at the aged light-tinted tiles and continued counting, rocking incessantly on the floor. "One, two, three, four, five, six…ninety-five, ninety-six, ninety-seven, ninety-eight, ninety-nine, one hundred, one hundred and one."

He paused again but the rocking continued. The patient's upward glance made the orderlies think he might have been counting the ceiling tiles. When the younger of the two orderlies took a long look at the grid of ceiling tiles and did a quick count, the 20 by 30 segments didn't add up to one hundred and one. So he dismissed the idea of some sort of autistic or psychotic episode. This was the first time he considered the patient to act distinctly peculiar. He typically performed in a way they didn't understand, standing erect, hands to his side, and looking down at the ground. After standing still for several minutes, he would then raise his arms from the side, look straight ahead, then cower on the ground.

"Is that all he's been doing?" the older orderly asked. "Just counting like that?"

"Yeah, he was quiet when I brought him up from his room. As soon as he got in here and I closed the security gate, he started counting. He's been doin' that for the last five minutes."

"He hasn't said anything else?"

"Nope."

"So why in the hell are they so interested in keeping this 51-50 isolated from the other head cases?"

"It's nothing you two need to be concerned about," an alto voice with Hindi accent remarked from behind them. They both snapped their heads around to see a tall, thin Indian doctor with a metal clipboard. "It's my job to worry about why we do things in here, not yours." The doctor himself didn't know why the patient was to be kept segregated from the general patient population, just that the order had been given.

Walking up to the cross-patterned white gate separating the dayroom from the hallway with its flaking paint, and observing the man on the floor, the doctor glanced through several sheets of notes and charts as he walked away from the orderlies.

"Uhh, Doc, whaddya want to do with our patient?" the younger of the two asked.

"Don't do anything, just keep an eye on him," the doctor responded, still reviewing the paperwork on the clipboard to make sure there weren't any changes to the patient's medical orders. Stopping midstep, one of the forms caught his attention. "When did they bring him in?" he asked.

"A few day ago."

"Well, looking here," the doctor commented, puzzled, "I don't see anything on his chart about him acting this way since he was admitted. He was disoriented and catatonic, maybe mumbling something every so often. Anything interesting happened that you're aware of?"

"Nope, we weren't briefed on anything this morning. He just seems to go from quiet crazy to number-counting crazy," the older of the two orderlies answered.

"Welllllllll," the younger orderly interjected, "down in the locker room during shift change, Bull told me that last night this wing lost power and that a weird light could be seen down the hallway from the security observation pen. That's when our friend in there really started to flip out. Of course, no one could explain the light in his …"

"How come this wasn't recorded in the shift log? What time did this happen?" the doctor interrupted.

"Around 9:30 last night."

Flipping aggressively through the sheets of paper on the clipboard, nearly ripping several in the process, he glowered at the orderly. "There's nothing noting any change with our patient here."

"Kinda quiet up here, isn't it?" Father Hernandez said as he walked up to the three men, unnerving the two orderlies unaware of his presence walking up to them. The Father, astonished by the silence on the floor, expected a considerable amount of activity from patients who were normally allowed to spend time in the dayroom. The only activity he could hear apart from the conversation of the doctor and two orderlies was that of the patient in the background counting.

"Hello Padre," the doctor returned. "I'd thought you'd be in a counseling group, in the south wing with the druggies and alchies."

The Father disregarded the doctor's insensitivity, having already been warned about his character by other staff members. "My counseling sessions aren't till this afternoon. I'm still trying to get a lay of the land. Anyway, I'm here for these souls, to aid those here who are suffering from the enemy's vices that hold them."

"Whatever," the doctor said as he rolled his eyes, thinking no one would notice. The other men did. The doctor focused his attention on the younger orderly. "The only thing here is the order to isolate our patient during his dayroom time. What happened?"

"The evening security staff and Bull went down to take a look at why our friend in there had a weird, glowing, goldenish, dancing light coming from his room. At first they thought it was a fire, but the closer they got, Bull said all three of them started to notice a strong sweet smell. I don't know, he said they couldn't quite describe it, just smelled real flowery and..."

"Smelled like what?" Father Hernandez asked, somewhat excitedly interrupting the orderly and considerably upsetting the doctor.

"Padre, please," the doctor responded, unsuccessfully holding back a display of irritation at the priest.

"Go ahead and finish," Father Hernandez continued.

"Well, they ran down and when they got there, he said they couldn't see through the window because the light was so bright coming from inside. When they tried to open the door, everyone swore they got a big static electricity shock. A few minutes later, power came back on, and the weird light was gone, and they were able to open the door again.

"Didn't the generator kick on or the battery-powered emergency lights?

384

"Bull did say that was odd. Nothin' else but the patient's floor of the wing went dark. The rest of the facility didn't experience any problems whatsoever."

"So what else happened at the patient's room?" Father Hernandez asked.

The orderly, himself irritated at being interrupted again, continued. "After getting into the patient's room when the power came back on, and they could unlock the door without getting zapped, our boy over there was on the floor balled up, counting to himself. He didn't say much of anything. When he did say something, they think it was like Gishal, Gishmal, or something like that."

"Gishmael?" the Father asked.

"Yeah, that could've been it."

"He didn't say anything else? Where did he come from?"

The doctor knew he needed to interject before allowing the orderly to answer. "Whoaaa buckaroo. You're not entitled to that information."

"Look, I just want to find out ..."

"Padre, he's my patient as of the start of this shift and these two couldn't release the information even if they wanted to."

"Well, can I at least talk to him to assess his spiritual state? It's not against your rules to know his name, is it?" Father Hernandez inquired. He was pleased with himself for coming up with this option in attempting to maneuver around the doctor, who responded by curling his lips and grimacing.

After a tense minute of quiet, the doctor finally commented. "We don't know his name. He was brought to us by the police for evaluation. Go ahead and talk to him about your spiritual bullshit. Just make sure one of these guys is with you."

With that, the doctor left and Father Hernandez made his way to the gate that secured the dayroom entrance. The older of the two orderlies searched his set of keys and isolated the one needed. The gate was opened and all three men walked up to the patient still lying on the floor counting to one hundred one. Father Hernandez was about to kneel to attempt and ask a question when the younger orderly motioned for him to remain still.

"You have a visitor," the younger orderly commented, kneeling next to the patient and keeping a close distance to make sure the patient didn't try to unbalance him.

Looking up toward the orderly, the patient displayed a temporary semblance of lucidity while trying to have a long look at the person talking to him. Looking at the other two men, seeing the countenance of Father Hernandez and observing the collar around his neck, the patient's face became pale. He tried scurrying along the tile floor away from the three men.

"Whoa, whoa, whoa, whoa, whoa," the orderly said, reaching out attempting to arrest the movement of the patient, who skidded himself on the floor over to the windowed wall of the dayroom. "The good Father just wants to talk to you."

"Well I don't want to talk to him," the patient blurted out coherently, leaving the younger orderly astounded by the patient's snap to mental clarity.

"And why not?" Father Hernandez asked.

"I know I should confess, but he told me not to worry about confessing to any man, penance has already been made and I have so much to conf… I didn't know he would … all of them … one, two, three, four, five, six, seven, eight …"

"Hey there buddy," the older orderly barked. "The Father is still talking to you."

"Who told you not to confess?" the Father said, rocketing toward the patient.

"We thought we were serving the greater good of man. I began to question if what we … deceived … the four who came … all one hundred and one …" A tear seeped out from the patient's right eye as he looked up into the soft turquoise sky through the crossbar-covered window.

The two orderlies moved in closer, interested in the patient's comments. Father Hernandez concluded their presence would prevent him from finding out anything substantive.

"You know what, could you two please give me some time alone with the patient?" he asked the orderlies.

"Sorry Father, can't do that," the older and slightly stockier of the two responded.

"I'm asking because there's something spiritually distressing our friend here, and many times one is more than likely to open up without others around. And he mentioned confessing. That must be done one on one and in privacy. Please offer us that? Is either of you Catholic?"

The younger one sheepishly raised his hand. After a couple of minutes presenting the two ward aides an impassioned expression to petition their empathy, they capitulated.

"We'll be back by the dayroom entrance if you need us."

"Thank you both."

Making sure both men fully departed from his vicinity, Father Hernandez continued. "My son," he said in a soothing tone, kneeling down next to the patient, "I'm afraid you're not making any sense. Please allow me to help you. What exactly are you trying to say?"

The patient stared directly into the Father's eyes. "They say I can be forgiven, but with what I helped to create, could there really be any forgiveness? That's why they are all dead, because of me."

"Who's dead?"

"All one hundred and one."

"What are you saying? All one hundred and one in Los Angeles?" Father Hernandez asked, remembering the number of those who died in the incident.

The patient returned a look of disbelief. "No, they were the reflection of what was to come. He came to visit me you know. He told me one and his friends who seek why the angels have come. Are you him? If you are, he said what you do, can defend the chosen."

"Who, who are you talking about? Defend who?" Father Hernandez queried, becoming frustrated with the change in focus in the context of what the patient said.

"Did you know the four who came to the lab already knew of Aurora, of its intent? Our helicopter patrol saw them walking in the desert to the lab. They brought them in, we interrogated them, our investigators couldn't find any information on who they were. We were gonna test a prototype bug on them since they each were representative of one of the major races. I was the one to release it on them. I definitely had my hesitations realizing what I was about to do. They somehow knew and told me directly, my repentance will be rewarded and to leave right away and not to look back. Somehow I was able to leave without being caught. The four had said the other's mind would be clouded."

"What four? What are you talking about? And what do you know about Aurora?" Father Hernandez needed to ask. Maybe the name was just a coincidence with no correlation to his earlier explorations.

"Four in league with Abriel and Gishmael? It was Gishmael who came to visit me the other night." The patient's eyes glistened with the formation of tears. "He said all who remained were killed."

The Father's eyes widened, his body shuddered from the revelation. Enthralled by the Father's reaction, the patient grabbed the priest's shirt to pull him closer to his own face knowing what he said was important. "Do you know of Aurora Father, know of its evil?"

Father Hernandez raised his hand for the two orderlies to stop and not come over to provide assistance knowing they thought the patient was attempting to attack him. They both complied.

"You're talking of the clone child?" the Father whispered, thankful still to have isolated time with the patient.

The patient's facial expression showed he thought the Father should have been the one in the institution based on his question. "What are you talking about? I was talking about a virus. The child, that abomination, he was only half of what we were working on."

The conversation caused Father Hernandez to question why this patient was committed to the psych ward based on his apparent rational intercourse. Father Hernandez forgot the psychotic episodes he'd witnessed just prior to their discussion.

"Wait a minute, what are you talking about?" Father Hernandez asked, continuing to whisper.

"I'm talking about the work on Aurora I did down in Aguascalientes."

Father Hernandez felt an icy apprehension fill his veins. The name Aurora had made him extremely curious. Now for the stranger to mention the city of the first recorded deaths related to angels, a city he'd recently visited, was chilling. "What do you mean down in Aguascalientes?" he asked. "What happened in Aguascalientes?"

The patient once again glared at the priest in disbelief. "I thought you knew Aurora? Our work was done on the outskirts of the city."

"You mentioned a virus. What were you working on?"

"Something so ... the intent ... it was engineered to attempt to kill as many racially pure Jews as possible, and those remaining would accept the child as the Messiah for their belief in him. Then all men would follow him; the miracle child finally able to bring all religions together."

"Do you know how fantastical this sounds?"

"I'm not the one chasing angels. I'm surprised I've stayed alive this long," the patient noted, upset. "They'll find me. God may forgive; men do not."

The patient's eyes glazed, he began his litany of counting from one to one hundred one continuously no matter how many times Father Hernandez attempted to interrupt him to probe for more answers. The orderlies, observing from the opposite side of the dayroom by the entrance, witnessed the conversation between the priest and the patient deteriorate to being one sided. They escorted Father Hernandez away from the patient for his own safety. The doctor returned from a couple of quick assessments on other patients down the hall as part of his rounds, checked on the status of the consultation between the priest and the dayroom patient, and noted it appeared to be complete. Hearing a simple bell sound from his smartphone, the doctor realized he had received a text message.

"Well padre, it looks like our friend in there has a name. It's Dr. Justin Cochrane. I guess he works for some company called Waterfall Medical Research. I guess some staff from E.B.G., Waterfall's parent company, will be coming to pick him up."

Reflecting on everything said, Father Hernandez felt a yearning to tell someone about the conversation he'd just experienced. Aurora, Waterfall, Everest, Aguascalientes had all reemerged after he'd thought they weren't of concern to him anymore. These were also the reasons he'd been sent to the desert of New Mexico. The problem was who he would discuss these new revelations with. He no longer wanted to mention the situation with his former mentor, Bishop Grielle. The Bishop had shown himself to be unreliable and untrustworthy. Without telling him why, the Bishop issued orders for him to report to New Mexico after squaring away all of his personal and Church matters.   Father Hernandez didn't trust his new administering Principal Bishop in charge of his newly assigned diocese and counseling center-support ministries.   The Father considered him more of a poster boy for Machiavellian politics. After several minutes of contemplation, his two former associates came to mind: Sister Justine and Michael Saunders.   He would attempt to call both, hoping he could get in touch with at least one of them.

Chapter 41

Sister Justine still had a couple of free days before having to fly to Chicago for her new assignment. Getting her personal affairs in order to relocate from her order had taken less time than anticipated. Like the other Sisters in her order, she didn't understand the need for the hasty transfer. The official word of her move came through an email sent to her Mother Superior from Cardinal Millhouse, "Sister Justine Dawson of the Benedictine Order of Sisters in Los Angeles is to report within two weeks to the Benedictine Sisters of Chicago. She is to develop and focus on the monastic aspects of her future spiritual growth, her relationship with the Church, the Blessed Mother, and God." She understood through the language the intent of the Cardinal's message: report to Chicago and keep quiet. Sister Justine thought this was a bit ironic. For years she'd been informing on those sisters whom the leadership might've been interested in as not following Church orthodoxy; now she was being sent away as a result of doing what she'd been directed to do. She wouldn't protest the decision; sorrow crept in and took root. As in the past, she would manage to repress and confess her emotions of guilt.

In the process of attempting to establish teaching continuity for the Woodlawn neighborhood education and school mission programs she had been in charge of, Sister Justine would need to say good-bye. She didn't know how to tell the impoverished women in her adult education classes, or the sisters of her order, the true reason she had to leave. Making her final rounds in the neighborhood center with tearful departures, many of those whom she'd helped over the years felt she was abandoning them. Her simple excuse was that it was part of God's plan for her to pursue her gifts in Chicago. Many of the women asked the same question, why couldn't God just let her stay and do her work in Los Angeles? She was becoming prominent throughout the city among the parishes as the Sister of education and hope. Many of those Sister Justine had taught and ministered to over the years seemed to be more blessed than others when searching for jobs, raising families, or attempting to straighten out their lives.

Reflecting on all that was happening, Sister Justine now felt compelled to see Michael for one final time and say good-bye. Not speaking to him in years, then recently brought together by extraordinary circumstances, she felt she would need to tell Michael the truth regarding his notes and research material from the first time they investigated the events in Aguascalientes. She didn't understand why. Even though she confessed her sins to her priest about what had happened years ago, she would need to tell Michael she took them before he had the chance to transcribe them into the electronic journals of the Church. The grudge he held against Bishop Grielle was misplaced. Sister Justine was feeling guilty.

When Sister Justine stopped by Michael's house, Alicia had accidently disclosed that in the last couple of days he had been in the process of cataloging the information they'd recently gathered. Alicia thought the Sister was fully aware of Michael's possession of the notes. Realizing the misstep of informing Sister Justine about Michael's stash of notes, she stood resolute in not letting her into the house. Alicia courteously communicated that Michael was currently teaching a class, and if she wanted to take or even review any of the information, she would need to get Michael's permission. Sister Justine accepted the challenge. By the time she arrived on campus, Sister Justine's remorse transformed to fury ruminating that Michael hadn't turned in all of his notes from their investigation in the prior weeks.

Finding the building, then classroom, Sister Justine walked in and to the top row of the lecture hall. Plenty of seats were available as the classroom was only half-full with 22 students. She'd learned the start time of the class from the department's administration office down the corridor; the class would end in almost half an hour. Sitting in the rear of the lecture hall for the entire remaining 30 minutes, Sister Justine threw Michael a piercing stare every time he took a glimpse in her direction, derailing his train of thought while presenting his lecture. He recovered but not because he could see she was angry; he didn't care about that. He was more interested in what could have caused her to transform from her typical calm demeanor to being openly incensed.

Watching each lagging second to the scheduled end of class time on their watch or time display on their cell phone, many of the students expressed their disinterest in the lecture, closing books, putting away pens, nervously tapping their feet, waiting for the second they could to dart from the lecture hall to whatever affairs of the day awaited next. The clanging bell indicating the end of the class hour signaled the start of the human race toward the door. Only a handful of students remained to discuss questions on what they just learned or to clarify future assignments. Sister Justine walked down the aisle stairs between the desks to give those students assaulting Michael a chance to ask their questions and leave. Plus, out of courtesy, she didn't want to confront him with anyone else around. After the final student departed, Sister Justine glared at Michael, who was putting his notepad, several papers, and a textbook into his attaché case.

"What can I do for you Sister?" Michael asked nonchalantly as he finished gathering his belongings and ignored her scowl.

Sister Justine sensed her body tensing and her face flushing; she wanted to tongue-thrash Michael. Nevertheless, she remembered her duty and calling, recalled verses to contain her anger, and serenely replied. "Michael, I'm strongly encouraging you to turn over all your notes that you have on our recent work."

She seized Michael's full attention. "I don't know what you're talking about?"

"Michael, Alicia already told me that you've been working on notes you took while we were working together."

Michael stood in place for a minute mystified at how she got Alicia to reveal his private notes. "You know

396

what, I'm not gonna let that slimebag steal my notes again. Anyway, there's some pretty cool stuff that I could probably add to my new classes with the research I've been working on."

"Michael, you were paid by the Church. That information rightfully belongs to Rome," Sister Justine noted emphatically.

"No, I'm just counting this as restitution from what was mine the first time. You and Father Boy Toy should already have more than enough to continue to work on whatever crusade you're on," Michael chided but observed a change in the Sister's expression after his comment, almost as if she were about to tear up.

"Michael, there's something, well, a couple of things, I need to tell you," Sister Justine said with a softened demeanor. "Our investigation was officially terminated by the Church; Father Hernandez was reassigned. I'm being reassigned to a monastic convent just outside of Chicago. It's a convent of isolation Michael. "

"Tough shit. Sorry to hear that."

"Doesn't it seem strange that when we began to formulate what they considered dubious alternatives as to what could have happened, they separate us and seize all of our notes and journals?"

"And yet you still want me to turn mine over even after what they did the first time?"

"Michael, they didn't steal your notes and information the first time."

"Bullshi…"

"I did," Sister Justine interrupted. "I took your notes and turned them over."

The sensation of having walked into a wall overcame Michael. His legs felt gelatinous. Michael retreated to the seat behind the instructor's desk. "What do you mean you did? Why?"

Sister Justine could hear the disbelief in the tremor he attempted to conceal in his voice.

"I'm sorry Michael. It was the only way I was allowed to take my vows in the order I had my heart set on. Archbishop Millhouse at the time held that over me. My order even then was considered extremely liberal in the Church's eyes. They wanted to make sure I could be trusted to follow Church doctrine and the hierarchy rather than the extreme views of my order." Hearing herself say this to Michael made her consider the legitimacy of her past actions.

"And you still want me to turn over everything to you? I don't think so."

"I still serve God and the Church, first and foremost, Michael," she responded, more doubt creeping into her thoughts, which cemented her need for penance.

Like a dog given an order he didn't understand, Michael slanted his head sideways, flabbergasted as to why she would be complicit without questioning or resisting her church's leadership.

"And the lemming of the year award goes to ...," Michael ridiculed, regaining his usual demeanor. "You're not getting my notes. Sorry about you and the boy toy, but your crusade is none of my business, especially now."

"Excuse me professor," a female voice said just inside the entrance of the lecture hall, surprising both Michael and Sister Justine. They didn't notice the fiftyish woman, both being engrossed in their quarrel.

Michael knew her to be a student from an earlier class, a recently divorced mother returning to school. She challenged Michael on varying viewpoints in his Introduction to Religious Studies course.

"Sandra? What can I do for you?" Michael asked.

"Sorry to interrupt your discussion professor." Michael and Sister Justine knew she was being courteous in not acknowledging their argument. "Yesterday while at the coffee house, I was debating if I should follow through with withdrawing from your class, and this weird Hispanic lady came up to me, almost knowing what I was thinking. She said if I were to come down to talk to one of the department heads about my final decision, I would come across you and a lady arguing."

"I'm sorry Sandra, I don't follow," Michael commented. "What lady and what the hell are you talking about?" Michael continued, still unfocused after being thrown off-kilter by Sister Justine's admission.

"Just some Latina with a small mole over her right eye and black-and-silver-streaked hair who told me I would probably be speaking to you today."

"Where did you speak to this lady?" Sister Justine asked with trepidation.

"At the coffee house just off campus."

"Did she say anything else?"

With a quick pause, Sandra recollected her thoughts before continuing. "You know, she said something about a cross, or a crossroads, in New Mexico."

"Did she say what she meant by that?" Michael asked, noticing Sister Justine's sudden pasty complexion.

Sandra shrugged her shoulders. Sister Justine focused her attention on Michael, who was already focused on her.

"Michael, do you understand what she just said?"

"Uhh, no," he responded. "And frankly I don't give a damn."

"Was there anything else? Anything else about New Mexico maybe?" Sister Justine asked Sandra, ignoring Michael's rude response.

"No, there wasn't anything else. She left right after that." Not wanting to spend any more time in the lecture hall, Sandra left to go and finish her task of withdrawing from Michael's class, especially sensing the tense relationship between her soon-to-be-former instructor and the Sister.

"I don't get why New Mexico is so important Justine," Michael noted.

"Michael, Father Hernandez was transferred to Las Cruces, New Mexico."

"Wah, wah. My heart is broken."

Sandra timidly returned to make one final comment. "You know, she did say something else. She said, 'There's no such thing as coincidences; all things happen for a purpose.'" Sandra departed again.

"Michael," Sister Justine began, "it's no coincidence. What if that lady was Ashere, and she's involved and ..."

"And the fact that Father Hernandez is in New Mexico and one of my students says that a strange lady tells her to tell us about something crossing ..."

"Cross or crosses," Sister Justine corrected.

"Whatever."

"Michael, the city name of Las Cruces means ..."

After Sister Justine's statement, Michael recalled his Spanish and the translation of las cruces. "Just a coincide..." Michael then interrupted himself. "You sure you didn't set this up?"

"Michael, I came here to apologize for taking your notes and information ten years ago, and to petition for you to release what you have now. I didn't set this up."

"Like hell. I find out you stole my notes when all along I've been blaming Grielle. And now you come here where it almost seems contrived with weird circumstances for me to turn over what I have now. I'm sorry Justine, I just can't do it."

"You can't escape everything that's happened. I mean, look what happened at the hospital chapel. You saw the same thing I did."

"So, I saw something, the hysteria of a man who ended up in a coma. And do you know that after we submit our findings, I'm called in by the head of my department threatening me with dismissal, even though I have tenure? The Church called and said I've been submitting fallacious and inflammatory research work. Did you know that? You may have stolen my earlier notes, but Grielle and Millhouse are still f'in snakes trying to steal my career."

"Michael, you and I know the truth. We must be onto something. Why else separate us?" Sister Justine countered. "And look at everything, Aguascalientes, hot waters, two words implied from the deaths at the funeral home. Some of the victims tied together through one company; we run into the survivor and the one man who helped tie in to the same company at the hospital. Then there's Las Cruces somehow connected. Divine providence must be at work."

Michael's cell phone rang. Pulling it out from his pocket, the caller ID showed a number with the area code of 575. He didn't recognize the number and considered letting it go to voice mail, but then decided to answer it anyway. "Yeah, this is Michael."

Sister Justine witnessed a look of disbelief flash onto Michael's face. After a minute of silence, he finally made a comment, "Oddly enough, she just happens to be standing right here."

Sister Justine was confused. Who would've known she was here to visit Michael?

"Hold on boy toy. Here she is," Michael said, handing Sister Justine the phone. Now she knew.

"Father? How did you know I would be here with Michael?" she inquired.

Michael watched Sister Justine listening on the phone, the look of apprehension growing the longer the conversation continued, until she finally made a comment apart from a periodic gasp. "Father, there's no way I would be able to come out there. They're expecting me in Chicago in a couple of days. Plus, what could we do?" the Sister said, pausing to listen before continuing. "Can you tell me that? Isn't what's said between the two of you confidential?"

After another short pause, she continued, "I could say that due to the abruptness of the transfer, I need to take a retreat before heading out to meditate, reflect, and accomplish some private devotions."

With another pause following her comment, she responded with a remark she hoped would evoke a reaction from Michael. "How do you know he would want to help?" she asked, her eyes becoming glassy from the stream of tears she held back, upset from the information the Father told her. To hear the Church was involved with a modern-day inquisition, and sanctioning the potential destruction of an entire race, threw her into turmoil. She suspected the Cardinal's anti-Semitic tendencies in many of the inferences he'd made reviewing the notes, minutes, and statutes developed and published from the conference of Bishops. Many of the Orders of Nuns represented by the Leadership Conference of Women Religious in the United States were under fire from the Bishops, with Cardinal Millhouse subtly implying that the views of nuns equated to the heresy of the Jewish nation. Now she felt the true remorse of being a quisling, betraying many of her companions in her order whom she thought might have become too liberal in their views. She passed the phone to Michael.

"This is Michael," he said, speaking into his phone and realizing that his impulse to taunt Father Hernandez, who had been the symbol of his rage with the Church, had diminished. Father Hernandez reprised what he'd learned with a heartfelt fervor. Michael did not recall experiencing such an enormous amount of passion during their time working together. The Father conveyed almost all of the fragmented comments broadcast by the unknown and mysterious patient, emphatically stressing the strange incidents having the semblance of angelic appearances.

"Come on, do you know how crazy that sounds? I mean, something like that seems very illegal, a biological virus capable of killing millions. You know, this sounds like something you should be telling the Feds or someone, especially if whoever told you all that stuff is telling the truth," Michael said into the phone, glancing toward Sister Justine, whom he sensed, by her penitent and contrite expression, was genuinely affected.

"I've considered whether he's truly crazy," Father Hernandez entreated.

"You're not helping your cause padre. Especially if he is crazy, you still want me to come out there with Sister Justine. I don't think so."

"We're not through with this yet. Consider the odds of him being here in New Mexico, where I'm sent to keep me quiet. The angels aren't quiet. We need to try and see what they're truly saying to us." The exhortation by Father Hernandez caught Michael off guard. He couldn't see the correlation the Father had attempted to brick together. Yet Michael felt incomplete in his views, even though observing the angel in the hospital chapel, or what he thought to be an angel, was forcing him to consider the veracity his religious beliefs. And what if angels did make an appearance in New Mexico where the Father was located?

Maybe they aren't being quiet, Michael thought.

Observing Michael's countenance, Sister Justine felt she needed to contribute to attempting to persuade him. "Michael, something is happening, something bigger than both of us, and we need your help."

"Why would I want to help?" Michael asked, reminiscent of his normal brashness.

"We need you to help us sort this out. For Father Hernandez to be sent to New Mexico and still somehow be involved with Aurora, this can't be a coincidence. Have you even thought that all of this could be a part of God's providence?"

"Father, we'll call you back," Michael said, ending his call.

Sister Justine waited for a reaction from Michael, unsure what to expect. He himself wasn't sure why he hadn't just shooed her out of the classroom. Hearing her plea and the information from Father Hernandez, he knew it was of importance to both but felt no vested interest in the current events. Yet Michael couldn't believe that, as Sister Justine continued to press the case, he felt his inhibitions to support her and the Father diminish. Deep down if this occurred a couple of weeks ago, he knew it would have been because he wanted to spend more time with Sister Justine, especially as up to a short time ago he was considering breaking off his relationship with Alicia. Michael had wanted to manipulate his college-aged girlfriend to end their relationship by subtly becoming more aloof and adversarial than normal. In the end, he admitted to himself that he was starting to care for Alicia more deeply and was becoming comfortable having her around. There'd been other women before her, but she had stuck it out the longest and said she was really beginning to care for him. One of her friends even implied she had ended the relationship with her current boyfriend.

Then there came the revelation that Sister Justine had stolen his notes. A fresh burst of outrage washed over him. How could he even consider wanting to spend more time with her? After all the time they'd just spent researching the recent events, she could have at least told him. He'd even begun to tolerate Father Hernandez and had warmed up to the Church. That was until Cardinal Millhouse and Bishop Grielle tried to derail his career as a professor. They sent correspondence with harsh accusations Michael's research and works should be considered trite, pedestrian, but most significantly, inflammatory, divisive, and fabricated, with consideration to remove him from the department. Michael was thankful the dean of his department personally knew of his work. The dean dismissed anything presented by the Cardinal, especially knowing two of Michael's works were up for prestigious awards. However, hearing that Father Hernandez was relocated out to the desert in New Mexico, and Sister Justine being reassigned to a traditional convent in Chicago, he suspected the Church hierarchy was disturbed by their findings.

"Damn, I have to think about this. You just don't know how angry I am," Michael said.

Chapter 42

After a couple of hours, the drive through the desert could be boring and taxing for those not accustomed to the endless landscapes of mineral-laced painted rocks structures and gray-green sagebrush blanketing the desert floor. Gary would have preferred to have taken the company plane out to Las Cruces. It was down for major maintenance and wouldn't be available for nearly another eighteen hours. There were no aircraft immediately available either through the company's contracted charter service.

Although the flight from Los Angeles to Tucson was under two hours, after working part of the morning before going to the airport and then driving over four hours from the Tucson airport, twice Gary found himself drifting lanes and his eyelids felt like two bags of cement. Gary was exhausted as the high-ridged mountains in the distance walled off the fading blue sky invaded by night. Las Cruces was only a few miles away and, knowing the excellent work of Sheila whenever she scheduled his business excursions, his comfortable business-class hotel room would be awaiting him.

Gary was confident the lawyers were working hard to secure guardianship so his assigned escort team would not have any problems with legally extracting Dr.

Cochrane from the institution. His major concern was not having heard from Dr. Petroyev in more than 24 hours. Before heading to the hotel, his first stop in the town would be the airport. He wanted to check with the operations office to find out the scheduled arrival time of the company jet en route from Mexico. If luck was on his side, they would already have arrived with the special package and called it an early evening. He'd been calling Sheila frequently, just in case the team had tried to call his office directly, but she hadn't heard anything either. No text messages or emails on his smartphone meant chances were they were either still finishing investigating what happened at the site or were airborne on their way to Las Cruces. It wasn't until he checked into his hotel room that he received the call.

"Where the hell have you been?" Gary barked when he answered the phone.

"We had an in-flight emergency. We diverted to Durango. I didn't have a signal till just a couple of minutes ago. We've got the repairs completed and now we're refueling," Dr. Petroyev answered.

"When're you scheduled to arrive here in town?"

"We should be there tomorrow sometime in the morning; remember, working around being found co..." The call dropped. Static flooded the earpiece of Gary's phone, then a fast warbling tone. No matter how many times he tried calling back, he couldn't get through. After nearly 15 minutes of attempting to reconnect, he decided to wait until the doctor's arrival the next morning.

Chapter 43

Michael and Sister Justine were able to find Father Hernandez despite the robust morning activity at the Dawles facility. After asking at the information center at the main entrance where they might find him, they luckily found him talking to a doctor in the main hallway of the administration building prior to their traipsing toward the rehabilitation wing. Michael's first thought was breakfast since he was hungry from his morning run.

Michael reached out his hand to shake the Father's hand extended to greet him. "Padre, I'm starved. Is there someplace in this facility where it's good to eat?"

"Glad to see you too," Father Hernandez, replied smiling.

"I'm a bit hungry myself. I'd like to get something to eat before we get started," Sister Justine added.

Father Hernandez directed them to a diner about a mile away from the hospital. The drive over to the eatery was pretty much like the entire trip to New Mexico, quiet and tense. Entering the sandstone-colored strip mall, they found the Mex-Tex-style diner comprising several storefronts. The interior was country-style tables made with a light blonde wood surrounded with chairs having tightly weaved straw seats and high backs. Large squared beige and brown floor tiles lay at a 45-degree angle to the wall. A rustic adobe brick façade ran halfway up the wall with desert murals on the upper half and wagon wheels and various articles of horse paraphernalia hung throughout the restaurant. It made sense since the name of the restaurant was Caballos. Seated at a table near a window with a view of the strip mall parking lot, they were handed a trifold menu inset with a breakfast special handout. Perusing the selections, Sister Justine selected a traditional eggs, bacon, toast, and hash browns. Michael felt more adventurous and ordered the house specialty of a spicy egg and chorizo burrito covered with both red and green sauces.

"Are you sure?" the weighty waitress with Native American features asked.

Thinking he possessed the palate endurance to attempt the New Mexico red and green chili sauce made from ancho, pequin, and other regional peppers, touted by the waitress as having a velvety texture with heat that would blister the sun; he insisted on trying it. The waitress smiled. She returned in a few minutes with several more glasses of water.

"Do you think we'll find out anything more while we're here?" Sister Justine asked, passively attempting to avoid an uncomfortable silence coming up again.

"We've found out so much yet I'm not sure if we really know out anything at all. I mean I tried to go over my notes about what happened and nothing is congealing right now." Michael didn't intend for his comment to be sarcastic or full of guile, and he hoped Sister Justine didn't take it that way. He was also upset with himself for deleting his earlier notes about their hospital chapel experience.

"Look Michael, I know we've never really had a chance to talk about it yet, but I'm sorry for lying to you all those years about the notes. You know how important it was for me to become a nun."

Michael realized he still bottled simmering bitterness at being deceived, but wanted to attempt being conciliatory. "Truthfully, I guess I could never accept everything that happened. I mean, us no longer being together, then so many of our family members missing with all the others. Then you show up after ten years, and everything that's going on now, it's been hard."

"I know. It's been tough for all of us."

"I mean, come on," Michael retorted, becoming a bit riled but succeeding in keeping his composure. "Couldn't you have just told me? Especially after all we've been through. I mean since we were freshmen in high school. You were my first and only girlfriend. I would've never thought you could betray me like that, especially to the Church."

"Michael, were you really gonna become a priest? I mean really, or did you just tag along because of a little bit of puppy love?"

"It wasn't puppy love. I did love you, at least what I thought was love at the time."

"I did care for you Michael, but my calling to God was greater, much greater."

"Here are your meals," said a skinny Latino teen, breaking into the conversation placing the meals on the table in front of Michael and Sister Justine. "Would you like more water senòr?"

"No thanks. What I have here is fine."

While Sister Justine took time to pray, Michael started in on the meal. After a couple of bites enjoying the flavors of the sauces, the heat on his tongue ramped up. Tears blurred his eyes as his taste buds endured intense searing by the oils from the spices. Michael quickly downed one of the glasses of water.

"I think milk might be better for you Michael, you look like you're sweating," Sister Justine noted with friendly compassion.

He was sweating. "Naw, it'll dull the flavor," Michael gurgled while downing another glass of water. He continued the meal, not wanting to appear gastronomically fragile, but called for more water making several of the locals chuckle. Taste buds going numb, Michael gave up on the burrito. After he gulped down a final glass of water and paying their bill, they departed.

Driving back, Sister Justine said, "Michael, about what we were talking about earlier."

"Don't worry about that, I just want to get back. My mouth is starting to burn again," Michael responded, accelerating. He hoped the remaining lights would be green and that he wouldn't get pulled over for speeding. He actually didn't want to discuss their earlier exchange.

Chapter 44

Gary tried to arrive at the hospital earlier than he actually did at 10:30. The paperwork assigning guardianship with original signatures wasn't delivered to his hotel until just after 10:00. He was a little perturbed when the lawyers found out the institute would only accept electronic forms temporarily and only to start the process to allow Dr. Cochrane to be discharged into their custody. Having received most of the final paperwork and presenting it to the institute's legal department, Gary requested the primary care doctor for Dr. Cochrane to be paged. The staff informed Gary that many of the patient wards, counseling rooms, and rehab areas did not contain public address speakers so as not to disturb counseling sessions or startle and frighten any of the patients. It was very possible the doctor wouldn't hear a page.

Why not just send an orderly? Gary thought, wanting to take charge of retrieving the doctor himself. Within minutes, the doctor had arrived, and Gary was pleased he wouldn't have to insist the staff have someone find him. After an hour with all the signatures garnered onto the documents, the doctor finalized the discharge orders.

"Well, thank you for working this," Gary remarked. "We should have a couple of our company's employees arriving from the airport in a short while to pick him up if the institute isn't able to transport him."

"Very good," the doctor replied, placing the paperwork into proper order.

"By the way, though, just wanted to know if there were any visitors who came to see Dr. Cochrane after he was brought here?" Gary asked wanting to make sure there was no exposure to sensitive information.

"None that I'm aware of. The only one to talk him was the chaplain."

"What kind of chaplain?"

"A Catholic chaplain, Father Hernandez I believe is his name."

Gary was troubled. "What do you mean 'chaplain'? The Father talked to Dr. Cochrane? No one was supposed to talk to him."

"I mean that the priest, Father, holy man, named Father Hernandez, talked to your blue-papered patient, Dr. Cochrane. The order just said keep him isolated. And even if the order did say for no one to talk him, chaplains don't count. They're part of the staff authorized to talk to patients and can maintain confidentiality."

"Well, can you at least tell me what they talked about?" Gary asked.

"Hell, I don't know. Some spiritual bullshit according to the orderlies."

"They heard everything as well?"

"No, when I got there, they were by the ward's dayroom entrance for priest confidentiality rights. Why're you so worried about it?"

"Where's Father Hernandez now?" Gary asked, ignoring the doctor's question.

"I don't know. I talked to him a short while ago. He mentioned he was going to try and spend some time with a couple of friends who came out from L.A. You should be able to find him at his office in the main admin building."

"What do you mean friends from Los Angeles?"

"Yeah, some nun and some professor."

"And you said they were friends of his?"

"His friends, his life, I only need to keep close tabs on the patients," the doctor retorted, placing the papers in a folder and turning toward the other wards to continue his rounds, dismissing Gary. The priest's name didn't arouse any suspicions until Gary heard about the two visitors from Los Angeles. He pondered whether the Father Hernandez mentioned by the doctor was the same one that Cardinal Millhouse mentioned was researching the angel events, or was just another priest with the same name assigned to the institution. Gary called the Cardinal to resolve his question.

* * * *

Gary entered the Father's small office and looked visibly disgusted at the size and ascetic nature of the furniture. "Kinda small isn't it Father? Needs a little pizzazz?" he chided.

"Humility. I'm not one for excess. If I were, I wouldn't be doing this job. The less I have of this world to encumber me, the closer to God I feel. May I help

415

you?" Father Hernandez responded to the tall, thin, moderately gray-haired visitor wearing an Italian double-breasted suit.

Gary closed the office door and sat down before being offered a seat. Father Hernandez ignored the actions of his impolite visitor. "Father, I'm Gary Applethorpe. I work for Everest Bio-Medical Group, vice president in charge of R&D operations."

"Yes, I believe I'm aware of who you are."

"I understand you talked to a patient named Dr. Justin Cochrane a couple of days ago."

"Yes, there was quite a bit on his soul to confess. Plus he didn't seem to be mentally astute and cogent enough to focus on the stresses he'd undergone."

Gary responded with a little chuckle, somewhat insincere, liking the euphemism Father Hernandez selected in describing the doctor's mental state. "I like that, loss of focus, no longer mentally astute and cogent. Most wouldn't be so politically correct and would just say he snapped or went crazy. Sometimes we need to call things as they are."

Father Hernandez didn't want to mention to Gary that the catalyst for the departure from sanity for Dr. Cochrane might have been the experience of a possible angelic visit in Mexico. Nor did he want to bring up the possible event during one of earlier evenings as reported by the orderlies. Not sure if Gary was aware of this information, the Father decided not to tell him.

"So Father, are you going to tell me what Dr. Cochrane told you during your private time together?" Gary queried, jumping straight to the point.

Father Hernandez flashed a scowl at Gary, who was unaffected by the gesture. "You know I can't reveal what he discussed with me in private. What's said between a priest and parishioner cannot be told to anyone else. The doctor has full confidentiality for what he confessed." The Father knew this was a lie since Dr. Cochrane didn't reveal the information during an official confession.

"Look Father, I'm not gonna play around here. We both know why you're here in this shithole of an assignment. You know a little too much about what's going on with our company. Somehow, that information was revealed to you. I know because Cardinal Millhouse told me as much."

"Believe it or not, I'm still in the dark as to why your company is doing what it's doing and why the angels seem to be against you."

Staring at the father for a moment to garner his body language as to if he was disingenuous, Gary laughed. "You don't know do you?"

"Know what?"

"It's because of an angel we're doing what we're doing. We're working under divine inspiration, serving a higher calling of the Church that reinforces our beliefs."

Father Hernandez was extremely confused. Not because Gary didn't fully understand, there could be more than one perspective based on the unique events but because Gary was overly zealous in his purpose of serving the Church. The dialogue with Ashere along with the events in the hospital chapel, the dialogue of Dr. Cochrane in the dayroom, coupled with his recent studies and interpretations from verses in the Bible led the Father to believe that their angelic revealer Aurora could have

417

deceived the Church. *I wonder if this is how Martin Luther felt?* Father Hernandez thought. "What do you mean?" Father Hernandez asked.

"Let's make a deal. I tell you what I know, and you tell me what our friend said."

Father Hernandez felt alarmed knowing that Dr. Cochrane could be viewed as inconsequential or worse yet; a major threat by Gary and Everest if damaging information concerning the project had been released. That wouldn't bode well for his survival. "Well let's be real, you'll probably find a way of, dare I say, liberating Dr. Cochrane from being a burden to you."

"Still being politically correct Father? We haven't decided what's going to happen at this point. Now what about that deal?"

"I don't see the benefit of any deal."

Gary sat and stared at the Father for a couple of minutes. "Don't let it be said that what I'm about to tell you won't whet your curiosity to know more about what's going on," Gary commented.

"How do you know I won't tell the authorities what you've planned, especially if it's malevolent?" Father Hernandez asked, knowing the information was already gathered and, when aggregated, sounded disturbing.

"Really? Who'd believe you? What're you gonna tell them? We both loyally serve the same Church. It was the Church that was the primary sponsor for the research and work we've accomplished over the years. Other governments, private entities, and religious organizations provided portions of the resources; however, the Church provided a majority of the funding and inspiration. In the end, you'd just be implicating your Church and its leadership."

"What are you talking about?

"Look, I already know you're aware of our cloning project. The work we do is to cement the bridge between all religions and beliefs. The events ten years ago shattered many beliefs, left many governments on the brink of collapse. The world had been simmering in chaos even before the mass disappearance. It was then that Rome received its divine inspiration from Aurora."

"What do you mean from Aurora? We thought Aurora was just the name of your project." Father Hernandez lied, not wanting to reveal that he knew more than Gary anticipated.

Gary presented Father Hernandez with a sardonic smile. "You really don't know, do you? Aurora is the name given to the angel that visited the High Holy Bishop of Rome and several members of the College of Cardinals at the Vatican. From that inspiration, we used the name as the fountainhead of our inspired core projects."

Father Hernandez forgot this part of the information that Gary had just provided. "So, is this why the Church is so involved with sponsoring patronage toward Everest?"

"Remember, it's part of the Church's doctrine that the laity is to be her direct influence in secular society. They're to take what Catholics are supposed to believe and apply it to everyday life. The Church may only influence society; however, it's through the laity that the Church may affect society directly. The Church doesn't become involved in the politics, but the laity does. As a

419

result, through our humble efforts, a perfect child will grow and become the perfect man born of the Church, to lead the society backed by the Church. You can truly say you'll have an infallible New World leader."

"How would that bridge the Church and society? Man by his very nature is rebellious; he'll rebel against the Church and this man. Man is flaky to say the least."

"This one man will be able to attract all religions and all nations to follow. Most important, he genetically has no propensities for doing anything wrong. Remember that over the years we've found, with genetic mapping, the locations of the impulse to steal, lie--you name it. We corrected this in his genetic code. He's super intelligent, already more intelligent than any of us imagined. Like the meaning of Aurora, we are seeing the dawn of a bright future for the Church and mankind, and we're a part of it. Hell, he's already charismatic. For all intents and purposes, he appears to be the perfect child, who will become the perfect man--the masses so awed, they would be willing to worship and serve the one who'd stand side by side with the Holy Father. I must say, this project has been very close to my heart," Gary boasted. "It's an honor for Everest to be appointed for such a historic purpose."

Father Hernandez disdained the self-importance and arrogance Gary exuded and didn't want to continue a theological discussion on misplaced veneration toward a man instead of toward the Holy Mother, the Holy Father, and the Holy Spirit. He decided to change the direction of the conversation. When Gary mentioned the project being close to his heart, the Father realized something he had learned early on. "Is there something about him having two hearts? And I'm not going to say where I heard this information, but why would this grand plan of yours with Aurora and the child with two hearts? And why the need for viruses?"

Astonished, Gary gazed at Father Hernandez for a couple of minutes before answering but guessed the source of the question was Dr. Cochrane. "So you know about that do you?"

"Not necessarily. We can never be sure of anything we learn," Father Hernandez responded with a small smile. "We are talking about a crazy man."

Gary reciprocated with a small smile of his own. "There are those who may be against the Church and all that we seek to accomplish. The inspiration of Aurora has been quite … unique … our purpose is truly divine."

"Divine? Really? To create something that could be considered evil?"

"And how do you know its evil?"

"Why would you think that what you're doing is not evil?" Father Hernandez inquired; intrigued by the fact that Gary exhibited true dedication and religious fervor.

Gary raised an eyebrow. "What evil are you talking about?" he asked.

"What's to say that you and the Church aren't being inspired by evil?

"Why would you say that against your own Church? According to Church leadership, Aurora said we would be successful in creating all that was prophesized. We would see setbacks and attempts to subvert our grand plan. And we do know in our own hearts that, in the end, those against Aurora will experience defeat. Those fatalistic angels along the way were just bumps in the road."

"Well, Mr. Applethorpe, in studying angels and other Church doctrine, I'd be remiss if I didn't look at everything from every angle. In doing so, I'd like to think I'd be validating my own beliefs and faith. I don't know if you realize, one possibility is that the angels you called road bumps have names as well, and they may reveal more than you realize," Father Hernandez said.

"So what does that have to do with this?"

"The names of the primary angels we know of are Abriel and Gishmael. And the interesting thing about their names is the last part, the 'el.' Do you know what it means?"

"No, why don't you tell me?" Gary answered incensed that Father Hernandez projected theological superiority. The names held no significance to him.

"Well, what myself and my companions found is that names ending in '-el' mean 'of God.' These are the ones having a higher purpose in service to God. So why those 'of God' would be interested in …"

"I don't see how this is important," Gary interrupted.

"Well, also understand, I just happened to come across this the other night during my studies that even Satan disguises himself as an angel of light and …"

"So you're saying then that the Church is sponsoring Satan? Do you know how silly that sounds?"

"I understand that he may misguide those who think they're following a divine revelation when they actually aren't. Many false religions and movements within the Church started under false premises, many because of an angel considered to be fal..."

"So, I understand a couple of your friends from Los Angeles are out here visiting?" Gary inquired, interrupting Father Hernandez yet again to sway the conversation from theology. Father Hernandez became perturbed and also worried about how Gary knew Michael and Sister Justine were in New Mexico.

"I think our conversation is done," Father Hernandez said austerely, emphasizing that Gary shouldn't try to ask any other questions or attempt to garner any additional information. Father Hernandez's biggest concern was not to further expose Sister Justine or Michael if Gary wasn't actually discussing the two. Gary didn't mind terminating the conversation and didn't want to carry on too much longer, apprehensive he could accidently reveal the possibility that the live virus was sitting in a secure storage container under guard at the local airport.

"I agree Father, this conversation is done," Gary commented. "Maybe one day you'll see the benefit of what we're trying to do for the Church and human history."

Just as Gary raised himself from the chair and was ready to leave, Father Hernandez assailed one final question. "Why tell me so much of what you just said?"

"With the successes we've made, I've come to realize you're not threat to our progress."

With that, Gary left the Father's office. Father Hernandez was fascinated by Gary's surplus confidence and proud boasting during their conversation on the work his company was accomplishing as if it were the greatest invention since the wheel, even implying the clone could be equal to the life of Jesus. After a few more minutes of reflection, he decided to check his schedule. With no counseling sessions or confessions scheduled for the morning, Father Hernandez left to see if Michael and Sister Justine had returned from breakfast. He found his two companions several minutes later just as they were entering the hospital. Michael bore a sweaty face and a small smile showing he must have been satiated from his morning meal. Nonetheless, the heat from his spicy breakfast continued to inflame his mouth. Michael desperately wanted to find the cool relief of something to drink to help soothe the irritation that, although lessening, was still agonizing.

"Padre, where can I find some water?" Michael asked.

"Breakfast must have been good?" the Father responded, enjoying seeing Michael suffer and not directly answering his question.

"It was damn good, but spicy as hell."

"There's a break room nearby, just down the hall next to one of the waiting areas. You should be able to find something in there," he said pointing down the hallway through the admin building.

In the sparsely populated vending machine room, Michael passed by Gary and Dr. Petroyev, who were sitting at a table talking near the water fountain. Consumed with their conversation, they weren't interested in the few passersby milling around. Slurping water from the fountain, Michael determined he now wanted a bottle of flavored water, so he started scanning the vending machine for a flavor-infused drink. He narrowed the decision to lemon flavored or vitamin-infused Apple Pear flavor, but had a hard time deciding.

"What about the cleanup down in Mexico?" Gary asked the doctor.

"Everything at the El Refugio site is pretty much done. And we cleaned up the loose ends with the local authorities there and in Aguascalientes," Dr. Petroyev replied.

Michael's curiosity embraced him as he listened to the two men sitting chatting, especially hearing the names of cities he was familiar with. He prevented himself from showing any interest in the two strangers' conversation.

"So any problems with the surviving specimen?" Gary continued with his questioning.

"Nope, the package is secured on board the plane now. Things went smoothly and should be the same up through Canada."

"Good. And the passport for our passenger pickup today?"

"Found it at the lab site. We're good to go."

Gary glanced at his watch. "Good, I just got word a short while ago that the release paperwork should be ready about now."

The two men got up and left the break room, which left Michael unable to capture any more of the conversation. Forgetting about buying flavored water from the vending machine, he hastily drank enough water to make the burning sensation in his mouth subside and went to meet up with Father Hernandez and Sister Justine. It was odd he found himself following the same path as the two men whose conversation he'd overheard. Both men stopped to discuss some paperwork they were carrying when a man wearing a casual outfit joined them. Michael passed them and continued toward Father

Hernandez and Sister Justine, who were both waiting further down the corridor suddenly frenzied with activity. Father Hernandez waited until Michael came up to him and the Sister then directed his companion's attention toward Gary talking to Dr. Petroyev.

"You see the two men down the hallway, tall thin one with the nice suit?" Father Hernandez asked his companions. They both acknowledged they did.

"That's Gary Applethorpe, he works for Everest. Extremely arrogant. He stopped by my office earlier and had the gall to pretty much tell me his entire plan knowing there's nothing I could do to stop him. He probably knew no one would believe me because it sounds so preposterous. He told me about the cloning project and implied quite a bit about the virus. He even came out and said that the Church and other backers were behind much of the project."

"You know those two?" Michael whispered and both Father Hernandez and Sister Justine heard fear in his voice. Understanding who at least one of the two was, the context of their discussion in the break room was illuminated.

"He was the one talking about the virus?" Michael continued with his questioning.

"Yeah. Why?" Father Hernandez answered.

"I could be crazy, but I overheard a bit of what those two were talking about in the break room, and I think a sample of the virus may be here in town on a plane at the airport," Michael said with intensity as he watched the two men in the hall.

"You're not crazy; that's why they were working in Mexico, not to have to deal with U.S. laws."

"They mentioned something about the site in Mexico having to be cleaned. Then they started talking about moving their work to Canada. What if something happened down there, something bad? Especially with what your irrational friend said?" Michael whispered apprehensively, thinking Gary and his associates would be able to hear him from down the busy hallway.

"Why would you think something bad must have happened?" Sister Justine asked.

"Duhhhh, remember you have a nut ball doctor who you mentioned spouts on sporadically about a virus and other weird stuff. He mentions Mexico, and those two mention they found a passport and it's for a pickup they're doing today, and who is being released today I bet?" Michael answered, and while he was expressing his opinion, the three saw Gary take a quick nonchalant glimpse in their direction while talking to Dr. Petroyev. Gary observed the three church investigators. At first considering them background noise, part of the crowd of doctors, orderlies, janitorial crew, and counselees going to and from the counseling rooms in the hallway, he recognized Michael as a bystander in the break room a few moments ago talking to the man he recognized as Father Hernandez. Even though there were nuns working in the institute, the woman next to the two men in casual street clothes was wearing a modified simple coif and veil covering her hair; Gary surmised she was the nun initially charged with investigating the angelic events as reported to him by Cardinal Millhouse. Noticing Gary's eyes widen staring down the hallway, Dr. Petroyev was now interested in the three who were the objects of Gary's attention.

427

"What is it Gary? You look worried about something. You know them?" Dr. Petroyev asked.

Gary regained his composure. "Damn. That priest is Father Hernandez. I just met him. And those two with him may be a problem. I bet they're the ones who're with him investigating for the Church. We may have to change our plans and expedite everything. Let's go see." Gary raised his hand and waved to Father Hernandez. Father Hernandez reciprocated the wave.

"So who are they?" Dr. Petroyev asked.

"Sshhh. Just keep quiet," Gary whispered as he approached the three. "Father Hernandez, good to see you again," Gary roared confidently and reached out to shake Father Hernandez's hand. Everybody noticed the mild insincerity in his forced greeting. "Thank you for your time earlier today. I hope you found the conversation enlightening. By the way, who are your friends here?" Gary queried, presenting the three with a forced counterfeit smile.

Father Hernandez reluctantly introduced Michael and Sister Justine, then realized he should have given fictitious names. Gary purposefully didn't introduce Dr. Petroyev.

A stocky, comb-over-balding man wearing a sports jacket approached the group and interjecting into the conversation by passing Gary an 8x11 manila envelope. "Mr. Applethorpe, Dr. Cochrane's release paperwork is almost finalized, we forgot a couple of pieces. You and Dr. Petroyev can retrieve him after we get some final signatures. We'll have one of our vehicles transport him to the airport for you in a couple of hours."

The look on Gary's face acknowledged the bad timing on the lawyer's part. "Thanks Mr. Lawrence. We appreciate you working with us so expeditiously."

"Well, when we get word from the ..."

"Uh thanks Mr. Lawrence," Gary interrupted, "We've got it from here."

The lawyer became aware of the others around him and, taking the hint from Gary, departed.

"Well as you can tell, my time here is done. Nice meeting all of you," Gary said, prodding Dr. Petroyev. Gary, now sure of the two companions with Father Hernandez, knew he needed to accelerate his plans. He made a mental note to call Cardinal Millhouse to express his anger at him for not being able to keep a leash on his troops.

With Gary and Dr. Petroyev walking away, all three stood speechless for a minute attempting to comprehend the preceding event.

"What just happened?" Michael asked, flabbergasted by Gary's unexpected maneuver.

"I think he wanted to find out who we were, and now he knows."

"And from my discussion with Dr. Cochrane, Dr. Petroyev is probably a researcher on the virus portion of the project."

"You think he has the virus with him then?" Sister Justine asked.

"If he does, we need to do something," Michael responded.

Father Hernandez became disappointed with himself for not putting together what Michael deduced.

"What can we do?" Sister Justine questioned. "Would the police or anyone else believe us? A private plane has a deadly virus sponsored by the Church as part of a grand plan to control the world? Sometimes the truth is the best disguise."

"Do we think there's a virus? What if he's just bs'ing us?" Michael wondered aloud.

"It could be why there was distress when we first went to Mexico, Michael. They could have been working on a virus all these years," Sister Justine added.

"And he seemed serious enough when I talked to him. Combine that with everything else, the man has an air of being a megalomaniac of sorts," Father Hernandez said.

"Now you're being dramatic Father," Michael responded.

"Am I? I don't know why, but I worry for the safety of whomever the virus is intended for."

"You seem to think there's a specific purpose for its creation Father," Sister Justine said with anxiety.

"Why else create something so … I don't know, he just made it sound like there was some sort of inappropriate use for the virus."

"Aren't all viruses bad?" Michael asked.

"I don't know, is there such a thing as a good virus?" Father Hernandez replied. "What if they're creating something beneficial for mankind?" Father Hernandez asked actually considering the possibility himself, directing the question to his two associates.

Neither one could answer.

"We need to find out. Let's hurry and see if someone in the medical wing could answer that for us," Sister Justine said.

"I got one better. You two go wait in my office. I might know how to find out exactly what was going on in Mexico and the specific nature of the virus," Father Hernandez said with animation, then went down the hallway toward the asylum wing, leaving Michael and Sister Justine dumbfounded.. They followed his directions and went to his office to wait.

Almost ten minutes passed when Father Hernandez returned to his office to find both Sister Justine and Michael sitting patiently in his guest chairs. His natural golden-brown complexion had turned colorless, his skin clammy.

"Father, everything all right?"Sister Justine inquired.

"We need to get to the airport and stop Gary Applethorpe from leaving."

"What's wrong boy toy? You seem worried about something."

Father Hernandez could hear genuine thoughtfulness hidden in Michael's voice. He didn't call him by his nickname as a jibe. "We need to go now. Do you have a car here at the institution?"

"Yeah, we're parked on the other side of the treatment center," Michael answered.

"Good, let's go. We can't waste any time here, especially if we want to save the lives of thousands, or millions," Father Hernandez said and grabbed his Bible, a stole embroidered with two crosses that was hanging in a small wardrobe cabinet in the corner, and something resembling a flask, embossed with a cross on each side.

Michael and Sister Justine followed him out to the parking lot until Father Hernandez realized he didn't know what type of car his two companions were driving.

"Where're you parked?" Father Hernandez asked.

"We're over there padre," Michael responded, pointing to the west in the direction of a remote parking lot.

The Father darted off toward the car with his two companions trailing a couple of paces behind.

"Father, why the rush?" Sister Justine asked.

"They're transferring Dr. Cochrane and we need to get to the airport right away."

"Is this wise padre?" Michael asked.

"Yes, this is wise. If you both had learned what I have over the last couple of days, you might think I'm not acting fast enough. Which car are we going to take?"

Sister Justine took the lead in directing the three to the rental vehicle. Having the keys, she jumped into the driver's seat, with Michael in the passenger seat and Father Hernandez in the rear. Driving out of the parking lot, Sister Justine pressed with another question. "So, do you mind telling us what's going on Father?"

"Do you know where we're going Sister?"

"The airport? I remember seeing it on the outskirts of town along I-10 when we drove out here."

In the rearview mirror, Sister Justine saw Father Hernandez present a little smile. "So Father, please tell us why the big rush."

"Well, when I left you two in the office, I went to go visit Dr. Cochrane. They were just getting ready to sedate him for the trip. I convinced the staff to let me talk to him one final time in the guise of him wanting to give a confession and receive blessings in case something happened during the trip and not having a chance for final rites. Michael, it appears you were correct about what you heard in the break room."

"What do you mean?"

"Many of those in Everest believed the alleged divine inspiration, which led to the recruitment of many devout in the company. Over time, while working on the project, Dr. Cochrane started to question everything he was working on. Just when they were ready to confront him, four trespassers arrived at a highly secure site just outside of Aguascalientes. No one there knew who they were, where they came from, or why there were there. According to the doctor, they talked to him and knew about the project. Seeing him talk to the four, many thought the doctor was involved with their arrival. Then after that the entire staff at the site was killed by the virus."

"How'd he survive?"

"Dr. Cochrane believes they were going to test the virus on him because they felt he was a risk. He mentioned they pretended they wanted to ask some questions regarding his loyalty to the project. They had isolated him in a hermetically sealed testing room as a temporary detainment location. That's when everyone apparently died. The four visitors were unaffected by what happened and let him go. Seeing the dead bodies, he asked what happened. One of the four told him they were judged and for him to continue on his path of repentance. Traveling further away from the site, he thought more about what happened and began to feel extreme remorse for all those who'd died. He continued to reflect on everything they were working on, and began to consider it extremely evil. He said he started feeling like he lost it but all the while was working his way up back to the States and ended up here in New Mexico."

"Ok, that's just too weird. Do you believe any of that?"

"That's not all he said. It's more the target of the virus," Father Hernandez's noted in a somber voice.

"What did he tell you?" Sister Justine asked.

"The virus wasn't necessarily to kill those against the Church's progeny but to be genetically engineered, modified, and target as many racially pure Jews as possible, with the perfect child to be the deliverer for those who remained. Thus the survivors would see the Church as their salvation. He would bind all religions and races together, minus the one. The Church believes the deliverer would not be able to establish the Church universal and new kingdom on earth until the Jews were removed. For years, Jewish orthodoxy stiffened where they were focused only on the coming deliver, not wanting to join religiously with the Church."

Michael raised an eyebrow. "So your crazy man was lucid enough to tell you all this?" Michael asked skeptically. "That's too fantastic to believe. And now you think they're going to try and spirit him …"

"And the virus."

"And the virus out of the country, and you're gonna stop them?"

Father Hernandez felt the old Michael returned. "Look, I can't explain it, but we need to stop them."

"How do you think you're gonna get out to the plane? Do you think they're just gonna let you get on board? How would you know if they have the presumed virus on board? And how would you keep the plane from taking off if it was?" Michael continued with his cynical questioning.

Father Hernandez hesitated in providing an answer. He hadn't thought that far ahead and wasn't sure how to respond to Michael's questions. "Look, all I can say is that through all that we've experienced and learned thus far Michael, I believe we are in the middle of something serious. You have to believe me. Sometimes truth is stranger than fiction."

"We're getting closer. Do we know what we're looking for?" Sister Justine asked.

"When we get to the airport, just look out for the center's van. It'll probably be at Gary Applethorpe's plane," Father Hernandez responded. "Knowing we know more than he would like, Gary is probably hurrying to get the doctor and virus out of town."

"Look, so what are you gonna do if we find it?"

"Don't know, I'll have to play it by ear."

"Well they're not going to let you near that plane."

"If we're lucky, I may be able to. Part of what I was doing when I left you both in the office was to talk to the team transporting the doctor. I told them he wanted to have the plane blessed for his trip. Because of religious confidentiality I asked them not to tell anyone."

"I can't get over the fact that they believed you," Sister Justine commented.

"I was surprised myself, but they seemed to be buying it. Besides, over the years, you'd be surprised by what people have requested be blessed. I've blessed dogs, shoes, houses, jewelry, a swimming pool, ca..."

Michael felt he needed to interrupt after hearing one of the objects in the liturgy of items the Father blessed. Never finishing seminary, he hadn't fully trained to accommodate potential congregational blessing requests, so this was somewhat foreign to him. "You blessed somebody's shoes? You gotta be kidding me!"

"No, I'm not," the Father replied. "I've blessed the shoes of those who were going out to do God's work, for them to be successful in their undertakings."

Exiting the freeway and driving up to the airport, the three observed the collection of hangars, ramp access ways, and structures. Aircraft parking spaces were interspersed between the flight line buildings that acted as a barrier from the parallel main roadway. With nothing more than a five-foot chain-link fence bordering the open ramp areas, getting onto the ramp if needed would be easier than anticipated. Scouting while driving along the roadway, the three saw a petite Beechcraft Lear-type jet near the small airport terminus with a fuel truck and connected fuel hose. During the next several minutes they observed a white van with Dawles Center painted on the door drive up near the building, so they felt confident the aircraft must be the anticipated transport for the virus and Dr. Cochrane.

"OK, we're here and we think we found the plane. Now what hot shots?" Michael asked.

"Well let's wait a minute. Gary could pull up any second. We need to figure on how to get around him," Father Hernandez responded.

Minutes passed, and even with the scattered number of vehicles scurrying on the airport road, none appeared to be transporting Gary. Apart from the driver of the van entering the terminal building, no one had exited the van to enter or carry anything into an aircraft. Then the driver returned to the van from the terminal with someone else carrying two laptop bags and something resembling a mail pouch. Getting into the van, the three in the car watched the two unknown men drive away from the airport.

"Were those the men you talked to at the hospital who were supposed to bring the doctor here?" Sister Justine asked.

"No, that's not them. They must not have gotten here yet," he answered.

They waited patiently.

"I got an idea," Father Hernandez commented, breaking the silence after nearly twenty minutes in the vehicle since watching the activity with the van. "Sister, call the police and tell them there's a bomb on board one of the planes out here at the airport. We can't let them leave the airport."

"What? I don't feel comfortable doing that Father," Sister Justine reacted, her voice an octave higher in apprehension.

"Well fine," Father Hernandez retorted with a grunted sigh. "Hold on then until I get back. I'm gonna head over and see what I can find out."

The Father ignored Sister Justine's look of disapproval. Putting on his stole and grabbing his ceremonial blessings book, he walked across the road from where the car was parked. He reconnoitered and found a simple swing gate opening in the fence next to the terminal. He purposefully strode across the pitch-colored ramp up to the aircraft the three deduced was for use by Everest. Michael and Sister Justine watched the Father confidently approach a young man wearing a well-pressed pilot's uniform. After a couple of minutes, he walked around the airplane holding his book of blessings open and sprinkling water from his flask of holy water. After making an orbit around the jet, the two observed Father Hernandez converse with the pilot for several more minutes. The pilot bowed his head; the Father then rested his hand on the top of the pilot's head and bowed his head as well. After witnessing what appeared to be Father Hernandez speaking several words, Michael and Sister Justine observed that both men made the sign of the cross and embraced in a swift hug. After a few more minutes of discussion between the two, they both entered the plane.

"I'll be damned. Boy toy managed to get on the plane," Michael said, impressed.

Both Michael and Sister Justine could sense their heart rates increasing with the possibility that Gary could drive up and find Father Hernandez on the plane. They knew he wouldn't accept the blessing of the aircraft as an explanation for the Father being at the airport. They relaxed when the Father deplaned, shook the hand of the pilot at the base of the boarding stairs, and returned to the car.

"Well, that's definitely the Everest plane," Father Hernandez said, jumping back into the rear seat of the car. "The pilot was kind enough to give me a quick tour of the plane when I told him I've never been in a private jet before. He showed me all the elaborate, cool amenities like the leather seating with inset entertainment system, refrigerator with ice, mini-bar, and microwave. It so cool," the Father commented with giddiness."

"Boy toy, concentrate," Michael interjected.

"Sorry. Anyway, nothing that seems like it could contain the virus appears to be on board right now."

"I'm impressed boy toy," Michael said. "You think our passengers and package are already dropped off and in the building? If they are, what if they saw you?"

"He mentioned he was still waiting for his passengers and didn't seem to know his scheduled destination. He's going to file his flight plan when they get here."

"Odd. Shouldn't the van or delivery vehicle with the doctor from the treatment center be here already?"

No one could answer. Still waiting, nearly 20 minutes more passed. The three observed a Bombardier Learjet-styled plane, similar in size to the one they were watching, taxi down the ramp, then marshal and park near the first aircraft. None of the three noticed it had landed several minutes prior. At first they dismissed it as superfluous until a taxi pulled up on the street side of the terminus with Gary in the rear seat. He paid the driver, grabbed his luggage, and entered the building. After another quick minute, he exited directly onto the ramp way and walked up to the newly arrived jet that was opening up its door and locking the boarding stairs down in place. Gary boarded the aircraft after communicating with the pilot, who then stowed his luggage. The three observed Gary's pilot walk over to the first aircraft, communicate with its pilot, and then return to his original aircraft to secure the boarding stairs door assembly, perform the engine start, and taxi toward the runway.

Seeing the first pilot sprint into the building, Father Hernandez jumped out of the car and walked smartly toward the terminal.

"What was that, and what the hell's he doing?" Michael noted excitedly.

"I don't know, but something strange is going on. Where's the van?" Sister Justine responded.

As the Father got to the fence, he felt his heart racing with doubt that the pilot would again believe the premise of being there to bless to plane. Maybe he'd been warned by Gary or his staff not to communicate with anyone asking questions concerning the flights. The pilot exited the building as both of Father Hernandez's companions observed him call out and talk with the pilot for a couple of minutes. Both nodded their heads and appeared to be praying; the Father made the sign of the cross, then each ran to his respective mode of transportation. As soon as Father Hernandez returned to the car, the three observed the remaining aircraft being secured by the ground crew, perform its engine start and begin taxiing toward the primary runway.

"What the hell was that padre?" Michael asked.

"Could one of you get on your phone's GPS and find out how far El Paso is from here?"

"What's going on Father?" Sister Justine asked.

"I told the pilot I'd try to stick around to bless his trip once he knew of his destination. Well he was just told he was being diverted to El Paso to pick up his passengers."

Michael and Sister Justine realized what had happened and gazed at one another knowing Father Hernandez thought the same.

"They wouldn't have done that would they?" Michael commented, the first to respond to the situation.

Sister Justine pulled out her phone and searched on the map application for the distance from Las Cruces to El Paso. "From airport to airport, it's about 55 to 60 miles."

"So if we left now, we should be there in a little less than an hour if we push it," Father Hernandez said.

"I don't think so Father. If the van we saw did pick up the virus from here and head straight down to the El Paso airport, they'd already have probably a 30- or 40-minute head start. And chances are they took Dr. Cochrane straight down from the treatment center and not risk us seeing him here. So even if we sped, it would take us about 35 to 40 minutes to get there. Depending on the speed limit, they would be there in only another 15 or 20 minutes with all the time we wasted here. And we're definitely not going to beat that airplane taking off now if that's where it's headed. So even if we sped at 100 miles an hour, they could already be airborne. We're fucking screwed."

"Michael!" Sister Justine snapped.

"Sister, he's right, even though I wouldn't put it that way. There's nothing more we can do. It's in God's hands."

The sound of the jet taking off in the background signaled to the three that they'd been outsmarted.

Chapter 45

Gary was feeling extremely confident. Even though he was flying back toward Los Angeles, he was elated at receiving word the second plane had taken off with all its cargo without observation or hindrance from the three Church investigators. Years of research and development were saved, despite the destruction of the research compound outside of Aguascalientes. With millions of dollars expended, the hard work and dedication of virologists, genetic engineers, biologists, and doctors, a single sample of their sought-after prize survived and was now on its way to their facility outside of Montreal, Canada. Only one of the sponsors for the project knew of the recent incidents threatening the success of the project. He could now report to all the sponsors, clients, and patrons that the company was capable of meeting the projected time lines. His only hesitancy was in becoming overconfident, considering the strange coincidence of Father Hernandez and his companions serendipitously showing up at the same institution where one of the key researchers was admitted. Their actions were more troublesome than he anticipated and could still disrupt in some way the entire project. Gary knew it was necessary to minimize any more chance encounters, thus his plan to have the precious cargo and only witness who knew what happened in Mexico embark from El Paso instead of directly out of Las Cruces. If any one of the three happened to try to go to the airport, which they did, the hospital vehicle and temporary diversion of the aircraft would have confounded them. This allowed Dr. Petroyev's assistant to transport the hermitically sealed package at the airport right in front of the three Church investigators. They would be focusing on the doctor to arrive from the hospital under guard. It appeared the deception worked. The only action to accomplish once returning to the office would be to terminate the employment of Alder Dennison.

With just over 30 minutes before landing at the Van Nuys Airport, Gary decided to attempt a quick nap. As he reclined in the leather seat and closed his eyes, the phone inset into the armrest chimed.

"This is Gary," he answered after flipping the tan-leather cover from over the armrest and pulling out the handset.

"Oh thank God you're alive," the voice on the other end of the telephone blurted.

Gary recognized it was Sheila's voice. "Of course I'm alive, you're talking to me aren't you?" he snapped back.

"We thought the worst after what happened with the company plane. We thought you were on it."

Gary raised his chair to the inclined position. "What do you mean what happened with the company plane? I decided to take the chartered plane back to L.A. since the company paid for it to help with our diversion trick. Petroyev went with the packages to Montreal."

443

"You didn't hear then," Sheila responded, Gary hearing the angst in her voice.

"Sheila, just tell me."

"A sudden storm came up and the plane attempted to divert around it and somehow ended up losing control. It went down outside an incorporated area called Angel Fire in New Mexico. Everyone on board was lost."

VII. Debrief

Chapter 46

Walking into his office, the thin, aged cleric was startled to see Bishop Grielle sitting in one of the visitor chairs across from his desk. "Andrew? Didn't expect to see you here," he said, somewhat annoyed at his new intern for not telling him about the visitor. "What can I do for you?"

"I'm here to petition for Father Hernandez to be able to return to his parish here in the city. I'm sure he wouldn't be a threat to your pet project considering what I heard when I talked to him. He's heard about what's happened to part of the work on Aurora, although he wouldn't reveal all the details of all he's found. He felt that his role to keep the confessions confidential shouldn't end even though the one who confessed most everything to him passed away."

"Well, I appreciate his dedication to his spiritual mandates, but I feel the Church's destiny will keep its course regardless of these recent events," the Cardinal responded as he sat down at his desk.

"You realize it seems this would call into question everything about Aurora don't you?" Bishop Grielle noted.

"I would disagree with you," Cardinal Millhouse replied. "I've already talked to Gary Applethorpe and he's confident they should be able to make progress, regardless of whatever events may have transpired."

"It just seems with all the impediments, the Church should reconsider these worldly pursuits."

Cardinal Millhouse's face depicted a veneer of rage Bishop Grielle wasn't accustomed to.

"Andrew, this is not some whim the Church is following!" the Cardinal harshly declared. "I know I mentioned this to you before; there is a divine purpose to our endeavors."

"Think about some of the unique insights Father Hernandez, Sister Justine, and Michael Saunders extrapolated from their research and investigation."

"We're not going down this heresy road again for them to think the named angels are of God just because of something as simple as the ending of their names or simple hearsay comments by a missing alleged witness. I don't care how much research they've committed to this thesis. Remember, we embrace the miracles, the traditions, the supernatural when confirmed, and they have been. For those of us able to read the notes and writings of those who witnessed the divine revelation and to be able to understand experiencing the majestic, the beautiful, light-emblazoned cherub—what a truly inspiring experience to know a new age is upon us."

"I don't know why, but a verse just came to mind, 'Even the enemy can appear as an Angel of Light' from 2nd Corinthians if I recall correctly. Are we truly to know those that are fallen versus those that are elect?"

Cardinal Millhouse was not happy being lectured to on the verse and follow on rhetorical question. He wanted to ignore both as if they were inconsequential. "The angels presenting their gift of death to those, their friends, and their families who served the Church in their unique ministry through science, science we've come to accept after so many centuries, those angels deceive and attempt to present darkness upon the Church's path? No Andrew, those spirits only confirmed what Aurora predicted. They would attempt to impede the overall plan of one church, one religion, being diametrically opposed to what we strive to achieve, the Church universal. God would not be against his own church."

Without a knock or mannered process for interruption, the assigned intern rushed through the door into the office, surprising both men.

"Rome is on the line," the intern exclaimed, and both clergymen in the office noted the excited jitters in his voice.

"Thank you Antonio. Andrew, we're done, and your request for Father Hernandez to return is denied, especially since he and his companions attempted to prevent Everest from moving forward, with their little escapade in Las Cruces."

"Well, is it true you're thinking of relocating him again?"

"Like I said Andrew, we're done."

No emotion breached the Cardinal's concrete expression. Stubbornness painted his countenance. Bishop Grielle knew it would be of no benefit to attempt and press for a harder sale and decided to leave. Patiently waiting for both Antonio and Bishop Grielle to depart his office before picking up the phone handset, he answered. "This is Cardinal Millhouse."

After a short pause, listening to the caller on the other end, he continued. "I'm thankful to be talking to you again. And yes, I do have an update. You can pass on that I've talked to the primary representative from Everest earlier today and although his package did go down in the aircraft, he was lucky his lead doctor transporting it had ensured it was in an extremely secure and ruggedized container. It was found intact with no apparent rupture, so the area wasn't declared dangerous; but he was able to work with a contact in the CDC just in case things did go awry. They were going to use the Hanta virus as a cover if the unfortunate did happen. The only problem, however, was the heat. They weren't sure if the fireball destroyed the protein bonds or some such. Anyway, more to come when they're able to start up work at their Canadian facility."

"Yes, if it did survive, the Holy Church will be ready to initiate the purge of the Middle East nuisance nation as declared from the secret Council of Rome."

After listening for a few minutes to the speaker on the other end of the phone conversation, Cardinal Millhouse continued. "I agree, we should at least be thankful for a child so perfect."

Epilogue – The Unrecorded First Eulogy

The first eulogy incident occurred without warning or premonition. In the funeral, as in any many other funerals, a simple planked-wood casket lay up front. For this culture, it laid closed, contrasted as opposed to America, where the body is presented in the glory of its decaying and rotting mass. The decedent's family occupied the first two rows of pews. Friends, coworkers, associates, others who knew the deceased and were there only for the semblance of support, sat scattered throughout the chapel. The weighted emotional pressure of grief suffocated the chapel.

Something sweet, flowery, too evanescent to explain wafted in the air. Everyone breathed in a smell unfamiliar to the accustomed acrid, dusty, and desiccated summertime air of the Mexican village. The torrent of a thousand spring times flooded the memories of most in the aromatic environ.

How could something so beautiful just appear? Its eyes were black within what appeared to be another shade of black. Some were at first shocked, unsure they even saw the radiant seraph. Others were fully aware of the vision before them, which was not the aura of some ghostly apparition but an actual physical creature. Their bladders emptied. The warm, soft, compassionate expression upon the angel's face eased the apprehension of those in the sanctuary. As unexpected as its arrival, the being charmingly and benevolently began the eulogy of the funeral of the deceased. First, a summary of his birth, the synopsis of his childhood, the recapitulation of his youth, a memorialized voyage of his teenage years, college, and medical school leading into a dissertation of the wonderful research work by the decedent prior to his passing. Throughout the eulogy, many began to recite rosaries; some prayed; others so affected by the beauty before them cried.

A second angel appeared. The expression on its face, some would say, was anger and fury, a radiant sword held across its chest. With a thunderous voice, it interrupted the first and made one boisterous statement, "The Lord rebuke thee and depart!" The first angel flashed a scowl toward the second and then disappeared. The new arrival perused the small sanctuary with a disapproving look; the growing intensity of the lustrous sword increased the feeling of impending malfeasance. Some fainted, some began weeping in fear this was the angel of death. Those whose bladders had emptied earlier were surprised to have involuntarily relieved themselves again.

Terror, fright, and fluctuating ranges of horror flooded the attendees' emotions since the second seraph-like creature appeared. The officiating priest was one of several falling unconscious onto the floor. Many no longer wanted to stay. The stampede of mourners who were conscious flooded toward the exits. Children were dragged like little rag dolls; an old man falling was snapped up, only the love and consideration of his adult grandson reaching down in the panic, grabbing him by his old cracked leather belt, and almost fracturing the bones of the elderly man's frail body. The doors of the church now mysteriously locked prevented anyone from departing. Many looked back toward the main sanctuary. They wondered what would happen next and then witnessed their final sight.

The chapel evinced silence; most were now dead, except for two, one male on the floor, alive but unconscious. The other, a middle-aged Latina, a mole over her right eye, emotionally frozen in place, paralyzed with fear throughout the entire incident, which altered her hair to have silver streaks interwoven with the black. Her name was Ashere. The angel, Abriel, spoke to her, "Do not reveal what was witnessed, nor what is to come, yet you shall be guided."

Acknowledgements

I have to thank Pamela and Emily K. G. for their wonderful help in moving me forward to finish this project and very much appreciate their insights for the story. This is also so very true for Cesar, Cynthia, Monika, Shirley, and William, without a doubt, your support in helping to keep it real and truly providing substantive input is appreciated very much.

I also have to thank the crew at the now-closed Coffee Depot in Riverside, CA, for listening to my ramblings of this story and providing the feedback to keep it plausible and interesting, which I hope comes through.

Most important of all, I would like to thank you the reader for travelling along with the story. I thoroughly hoped you enjoyed it.

Discover Other Works by Jerry J. K. Rogers

Novella and Novels
Legend of the Salad Traveler
The Fallen and the Elect
North of Elysium

Short Stories
Rebel Marriage
Light in the Eyes of Father

About the Author

Jerry Rogers is a career airman working both in the United States Air Force and in the California Air National Guard, with over 26 years' experience working in technology supporting legacy and state-of-the-art telecommunication and data-communication systems. He also worked for nearly seven years at two post-production film companies working in Information Technology. He's traveled extensively across the county to each of the contiguous 48 states and across the world to both Asia and Europe.

Ever since he was a teenager, Jerry's always had a fascination with Religion and Science Fiction and has always enjoyed writing, starting with writing short stories over the years. He took the next step and wrote a humorous novella called "The Legend of the Salad Traveler." He later began working on his first novel, the Fallen and the Elect in 2011 developing the concept after months of research, building notes, and jotting down ideas into developing a full story outline and plot.

See what else is brewing at his website at http://www.jjkr-writings.info.

Connect with Me:

Follow me on Twitter: http://twitter.com/jjkrogers

My Site (with blog): http://www.jjkr-writings.info

Smashwords:
https://www.smashwords.com/profile/view/jjkrwritings

Made in the USA
San Bernardino, CA
03 August 2016